P9-DMO-722

By Harold Robbins

Tycoon
The Stallion
The Raiders
The Piranhas
The Storyteller
Descent from Xanadu
Spellbinder
Good-bye, Janette
Memories of Another Day
Dreams Die First
The Lonely Lady
The Pirate
The Betsy
The Inheritors
The Adventurers
Where Love Has Gone
The Carpetbaggers
Stiletto
79 Park Avenue
Never Leave Me
A Stone for Danny Fisher
The Dream Merchants
Never Love a Stranger

Harold Robbins

TYCOON

A NOVEL

SIMON & SCHUSTER

SIMON & SCHUSTER
Rockefeller Center
1230 Avenue of the Americas
New York, NY 10020

This book is a work of fiction. Names, characters, places, and incidents either are products of the author's imagination or are used fictitiously. Any resemblance to actual events or locales or persons, living or dead, is entirely coincidental.

Nearly every conceivable combination of letters has been used as the call letters of a radio or television station somewhere. The call letters used for stations mentioned in this work of fiction, as well as television network initials, are emphatically not meant to be the letters of any real station or network anywhere. Every station or network mentioned in this story is fictional or is used fictionally, even if by coincidence its letters are those of a real station or network.

Manufactured in the United States of America

10 9 8 7 6 5 4 3 2 1

Library of Congress Cataloging-in-Publication Data

Robbins, Harold, date.
Tycoon : a novel / Harold Robbins.
p. cm.
I. Title.
PS3568.0224T93 1997
813'.54—dc21 96-48523 CIP
ISBN 0-684-81068-9

To my wife JANN*,*
with all my love
and happiness.

ONE

One 1931

THE CENTRAL and defining facts of Jack Lear's life were that he was a grandson of Johann Lehrer and a son of Erich Lear and that he was married to the most beautiful woman in America.

His wife's name was Kimberly—Kimberly Bayard Wolcott Lear. Late in the evening of Wednesday, August 19, she sat at a dressing table in their room at the Ambassador Hotel, brushing out her dark-brown hair. For the dinner earlier that evening with the Lears—Jack's grandfather, father, brother, and sister-in-law—she'd had it styled curling behind her ears, exposing her diamond earrings; but now she was brushing it out, making it smooth and glossy, the way Jack preferred it. She had not yet wiped off her makeup. Her eyebrows, plucked into two delicate arches, were dark and well defined, but she had accentuated them even more with pencil. Her lashes were sharply delineated by mascara, her cheekbones were highlighted by rouge, and her carefully applied lipstick made her lips look lusciously dramatic. Brushing with her right hand, she held in her left a Herbert Tareyton cigarette in an amber holder.

She was wearing a pink silk crepe de chine teddy.

"Was it as bad as I warned you it would be?" Jack asked.

Kimberly chuckled and shrugged.

They had been married for two months. Although they had sent invitations to his family, none of them had come to

Boston for the wedding. Jack and Kimberly had made this trip to Los Angeles to meet—or rather, to *confront*—the Lears.

"I told you my grandfather would like you. I can tell he thinks that it's odd, and maybe amusing, that I married a *shiksa.*"

"You said your father wouldn't like me, and obviously he doesn't."

"If my mother were alive, she'd make him like you. Actually, he doesn't dislike you. It's just that he sees you as disrupting his plans for me. My father is accustomed to having his own way."

"It's also obvious there's no love lost between him and your brother," said Kimberly.

"He thinks Robert has gone into a silly business, one that may be a fad and may not last. Motion-picture production. *Leichtgewicht* he calls him. Lightweight. He talks that way, but I happen to know he's put money into Bob's business."

"Wait till he finds out what business *you're* going into!"

"That will produce a frothing fit."

Jack picked up a bottle of Black Label—real stuff, "off the boat," as they said—and replenished her glass and his. He used silver tongs to lift ice cubes from the silver bucket.

Jack Lear was not one of America's handsomest young men. He was characterized by a straightforward open face, with eyes that looked directly at you, and a heavy-lipped mouth that smiled readily and ingenuously. Already, when he was only twenty-five years old, his black hair was making a slow retreat, and he was at pains to comb it forward and try to cover the widow's peaks that were developing. He had not bothered to shove his Camel into a holder and held it between two fingers as he pulled smoke deep into his lungs.

"I really don't think I could live in California," Kimberly murmured. "It's sparse. It's barren. With a gaudy palace stuck up here and there to house the moguls."

"You don't have to live in California," said Jack. "We're not even talking about living in California. We don't belong here."

"You grew up here."

"Yeah, but *nobody* belongs here."

"Nobody *we* would want to know," she said with a grin.

Jack stared at his wife with unalloyed pleasure. He had never known anyone else whose mind ran so closely in the same channel as his. He could have anticipated her comment.

She shrugged out of the teddy, pulling it down and stepping out of it. That left her nude except for her stockings and the garters that held them up, plus her shoes. He drew her down on the bed beside him and began to fondle her breasts. He loved her breasts. They were small and firm, with deep-pink nipples. He bent over her and sucked her left nipple between his lips.

"Fuck soon, but talk first," she said. "Your father still thinks we're going to live in Los Angeles. Even when he talked about houses you could buy, you didn't tell him we are not going to live here. You didn't tell him you're not going into his business."

"Can you imagine me in his business? He's called a ship breaker, but what he is is a glorified *junkman*—as my grandfather occasionally reminds him. I can't even think of it, Kimberly."

"Well, we did talk it out, didn't we? It's not just the business that's wrong for you. It's the idea of living under him! You warned me that your father is crude and . . . and—"

"Ruthless."

"All right. He *is* your father, and I wasn't going to use a word like that. But you *can't* work for him, Jack. You're too good a man. He means to dominate you. Besides, you're too *intellectual* to go into—all right, *your* words—to go into the junk business. An intellectual needs a career that offers a chance to be creative."

Her words didn't surprise or trouble Jack. He considered himself an intellectual. His father and his brother were intelligent—one might even say aggressively intelligent—but they were not deep thinkers who were given to study, reflection, and speculation. Maybe he had inherited his intellectuality from his grandfather, Johann Lehrer, who had been a professor before he left Germany.

Kimberly had also inherited an intellectual bent. There was a Yale professor of rhetoric on the maternal side of her family. And on her father's side, her great-great-grandfather had been an inspired Yankee tinkerer who had invented the simple device that extracted and expelled spent cartridges from firearms when they were opened after firing, thereby sparing the shooter the task of pulling each hot empty casing out with his fingernails. On this invention the Wolcott family fortune had been established. It was the foundation of Kettering Arms, Incorporated, of which Kimberly's father was president.

"You are headed for a bitter confrontation," Kimberly warned. "When are you going to tell him?"

"Tomorrow."

"For sure?"

"For sure."

"He's not going to take it kindly. He's not going to take it temperately."

Jack shrugged. "He can take it any way he wants, Kimberly. Our decision is made."

Two

THEY FLUFFED UP the pillows. Jack tuned the radio to a station that was playing music and set the volume low. They lay back against the pillows and snuggled.

"I've told you a little but not enough about my grandfather," Jack said. "I told you the family name is not Lear but Lehrer, and I told you *Lehrer* is the German word for 'teacher.' Well, my grandfather was a professor of revealed and rational religion. He was an intellectual by anyone's definition: a brilliant man.

"What I didn't tell you is that he was also an eminent rabbi. Even though he was young, men came to him with questions of Judaic law and abided by his decisions. He was a learned man, Kimberly. In 1888 he fled Germany because he was subject to Prussian universal military conscription and lived in fear of being called into the army. Can you imagine a Jewish professor and rabbi, wearing earlocks, as a private in a Prussian regiment? He couldn't. He left his home and country rather than risk it. And in America he wound up being what he called a 'junkman.' "

"A scrap collector," she suggested.

"A junkman. He couldn't find work as a professor in this country. He didn't speak English. So he became a junkman, at first with a pushcart. But he made a hell of a lot of money. My father runs the business now."

"As a ship breaker," said Kimberly. "*My* father checked to find out who Erich Lear is."

Jack nodded. "Being a ship breaker only means he sells scrap metal in thousand-ton lots. When my grandfather retired, the last suggestion of ethics went out of the business. Among other things, my father is a union-buster. Like Henry Ford, he hires thugs."

"I— Dammit, Jack! You're distracting me. How can we talk about anything serious when your cock's standing up like a sailboat mast?"

Jack grinned as Kimberly reached for his penis and closed her hand around it. She bent forward and gave it a quick, affectionate kiss. "You have to promise to do it at least twice," she said with a wicked gleam in her eye. "The first time you're going to come before you get it all the way in."

"Premature ejaculation."

"Well? But you won't 'premature' the second time. Or the third. You've got to keep at it till *I* come."

He grinned. "Deal. I'll work on it."

They had stopped using condoms because they had decided they wanted a baby. Just the other day, Kimberly's doctor had told her she was in the early stage of her first pregnancy. Although Kimberly was petite and Jack's cock was imposing, they knew by now that she could accommodate all of him, though she did need for him to enter slowly at first, to give her time to stretch. He pushed in a little and then a little more. She grunted, then nodded. He began slow strokes, and she opened gradually, until shortly all of him was in her. Their bellies slapped together as he thrust down and lifted her hips to meet him.

It was as she'd predicted, though. He reached his orgasm very quickly and ejaculated a great flood, part of which ran out of her and glistened on her legs.

"I'll refresh our drinks before we start again," he murmured.

Three

WHILE JACK WAS UP pouring more Scotch, they heard a knock at the door.

He went to the door and asked, "Who is it?"

"Grossvater!"

Kimberly heard. She tossed Jack his navy-blue robe. She jumped out of bed, snatched up an orange silk wrapper and put it on.

Jack opened the door. *"Willkommen,* Herr Professor," he said. He had addressed his grandfather that way for years, knowing how much the old man liked it.

Johann Lehrer glanced around the hotel room. He smiled, more with his eyes than with his mouth. "I fear I am interrupting . . . what I am interrupting," he said.

Kimberly clutched her wrapper closer around her. Pulled tight, it revealed much more than it had when it was loose.

"Ah, so . . ." said Johann Lehrer. "Well, you will have other times. May you have many, many times when you are not interrupted, even by an intruding thought."

"A drink of Scotch, Herr Professor?"

"A small one."

While Jack poured the drink, Kimberly fled into the bathroom and returned wearing a terry robe. Johann Lehrer did not pretend he didn't know why she'd changed. His smile widened.

Jack could not cease being surprised, and distressed, by the way the old man had deteriorated physically in recent years. Every year he seemed to wear his trousers higher, until by now his suspenders drew them almost up to his armpits. He was still wearing the light-gray suit with black pinstripes that he had worn at dinner. In the past he had never entirely uncovered his head. Now, when he put his hat aside, he revealed a bald, liver-spotted pate and no yarmulke. His eyes watered, and his lips trembled.

At Kimberly's insistence, Johann Lehrer sat down in the hotel room's best chair. "I interrupt for good reason," he said. "My eldest grandson has married a fine goyish girl. I have had your family history researched. Did you know that one of your Yankee ancestors was a peddler, going up and down the roads in a wagon, selling pots and pans, Bibles and almanacs, hats and shoes? Subsequently your family became manufacturers, making guns. Also, later, in your mother's family, a Yale professor. Has Jack told you *I* was a professor?"

Kimberly nodded. "Yes. He told me."

"My story he has heard many times, until it bores him. Maybe you it does not yet bore. When I come to America, I was a ragpicker at first. Der Herr Professor Lehrer pushing a handcart! Then scrap metal in a cart pulled by horse. *Junk!* But you know . . . When you collect a little junk, it's junk. When you collect a lot, it's *salvage!* Lehrer Salvage Company! When you tear apart old ships for the scrap metal, then you are a ship breaker. But it's the same thing. We are still in the junk business. But some of us want to move into other things. The movies! Jack's brother has gone into *this* business. Once I thought the younger grandson might become a rabbi or a teacher. But . . ." The old man shook his head.

"Grossvater . . ."

"*Ja, ja, ja.* Kimberly . . . *Shiksa* . . . Marrying you, my grandson has done well. But not so well if he does not escape from my son. Erich is a good man. But he thinks he has made all Jack's decisions for him. He has laid out his life for him. He cares little what Robert does. It is Jack that he cares about. He wants you to become a *junkman.* It is the family business. You don't like that, huh, *shiksa?* Well, why should you? The daughter of Boston Common does not want her husband to be a junkman."

"I don't scorn your business, Herr Professor," said Kimberly. Her German accent was perfect, her vocabulary small. "*Ich bin in Boston geboren. Das ist richtig. Aber—*"

"We have nothing for which to apologize to each other, Kimberly. I like you."

"*Danke schön,* Herr Professor."

"I decided so this evening. My son Erich means to compel both of you to accept his idea as to what you should be. He was willing to let Robert go into the film business without interfering, even lending him some support. But Robert is the younger son. You, Jack, are the elder. He expects you to—"

"I won't do it, Grossvater!"

"—to become his successor, to serve an apprenticeship, then to succeed him eventually."

"Eventually," Jack muttered wryly.

The old man shook his head sorrowfully. "You should live so long."

"I don't want to live under his domination," said Jack.

"No," said Johann Lehrer. "So I make for you an option, Jack. I trust you to choose well." He withdrew an envelope from his jacket pocket and handed it to Jack. "This will make a choice possible. Add it to what your grandmother left you. Deposit it before your father learns of it. He may claim I've lost my mind."

Jack glanced at the check inside the envelope. *"Grossvater!"*

Johann Lehrer rose from his chair. He stepped toward Kimberly and embraced her. "Take good care of him, Kimberly. A man needs a good woman. I judge you are a good woman, pretty little *shiksa.*"

The old man moved to the door. Jack kissed his hand before Johann Lehrer stepped into the hall and pulled the door shut behind him.

Kimberly rushed to Jack. "My God, Jack! How much?"

"He matched what my grandmother left me. Half a million dollars."

Kimberly shrieked. "Oh, my God! We're *rich!* We can live the rest of our lives on it. That and what your grandmother left you makes a *million!* You don't have to go into *any* business!"

Jack tipped his head to one side. "Oh, yes, I do. We'll do great things. We'll go into the business your father is offering me. I'm not willing to die of boredom, Kimberly. And, if you think about it, neither are you."

Kimberly reached inside his robe and seized his cock. "A man with this is never going to be bored," she said. "Neither is his woman. And he's going to do great things, for sure."

Jack laughed. "Let's get back to it. We should have more such interruptions!"

Four

IN 1931 ERICH LEAR was forty-six years old. Twenty years before he could have been the model for the strong-jawed, cleft-chin, wavy-haired male who courted the handsome girl in drawings by Charles Dana Gibson. He was a Gibson male no more. The Lear men developed receding hairlines early in life, and in Erich's case the retreat had been abrupt and complete. Where wavy black hair had once flourished, a bulbous dome now gleamed. The strong cleft chin had been softened by added flesh. His dark eyes remained penetrating and still had the ability to switch instantaneously from a warm, caressing gaze to a glowering stare. His mouth still had a sensual look about it, and he continued to smoke Marsh Wheeling stogies: strong, thin, cheap black cigars that emitted a formidable stench.

On the morning after the dinner party at which he had gotten better acquainted with his new daughter-in-law, he received Jack in his office. He waved him toward the couch. He himself sat down behind his desk, in the huge high-back judge's chair that was meant to intimidate. He lit a stogie. His black double-breasted suit was already streaked with ash from the last one he'd smoked.

Jack sat down.

"I meant to take you aside last night and say a word to you about your new wife. The opportunity did not present itself. So now—I need hardly tell you that I was not pleased when you announced your intention to marry a *shiksa.* From Boston, too. What was wrong with all the nubile girls of our own kind? I had in mind one or two I wanted you to consider —fleshy, heavy-titted girls taught by their mothers to be good wives. This one you chose . . . Well, she is *sleek.* She is smart —maybe *too* smart. She contradicted you twice last night."

"Kimberly is intelligent. I respect her opinions. I don't always agree with them, and I don't always accept them but I respect them."

Erich Lear flipped his right hand in front of him. "This is immaterial. But what kind of wife is she going to make? I wanted for you a wife who would be appropriately deferential, as your mother was to me. This goyish girl from Boston will defer to no one—not to you, not to me, not to anyone. Is she good on her back? Does she suck you off? A woman has got to learn to suck cock—and like it."

"I'd be grateful if you would speak of my wife with a degree of respect," Jack said solemnly.

"Respect . . . You get *that* started, and you'll be *respecting* her for the rest of your life. Well, it's done. I suppose Kim is all right. She can be *made* all right."

"Please don't call her Kim, as you did last night. Her name is Kimberly, and she doesn't like to be called Kim."

"Already she has taught you what she likes and doesn't like! How well does she know *your* likes and dislikes?"

Jack decided to try to lighten the conversation. He smiled at his father. "I've got something she likes," he said.

"Yes, I imagine. Your mother and I were astonished by it. Aside from that, what about you does she respect?"

Jack blew a loud sigh. "What's the point? What are you driving at?"

Erich blew a blast of heavy blue smoke from his stogie. "You ever hear of a ship called *Kaiserin Luise,* later called *Erie?* I will recover approximately forty-five thousand tons of steel from her, plus miles of lead and copper pipe, and . . . But that's not the half of it. She is fitted out with gorgeous woodwork, tons of oak flooring, crystal chandeliers, bath fixtures plated with gold, elevators, staircases, and so on. In years past, assets like that got away from us because we didn't know how to appraise them and so let subcontractors remove them. I'm not taking bids from subcontractors on this job. This becomes your role in the business. I want you to go through the ship and make an inventory and appraisal. With your fine Harvard education and the elevated tastes you acquired in Boston, you'll know what's valuable and what's not; you'll be able to distinguish the good stuff from the schlock and dreck. That's your assignment: to strip these old liners of their treasures, find a market, and sell them. If you think being a junk dealer is beneath your dignity, you can be an antique dealer."

"Father—"

"I'll make you an executive vice president, at a thousand dollars a week. I'll get you a secretary who fucks and sucks. You need a little time to find a home and settle in. Then I want you to go aboard that ship and—"

"*Father!* I am not going into the business. I will not accept a vice presidency. I am going into an entirely different line of business."

"*Oh?* And what line of business is this?"

"I am buying a radio station."

Erich stared at his stogie for a moment, then flung it across the room, where sparks set the rug smoldering in two places. Jack did not stand up and stamp on the fire; he just sat calmly and watched as his father poured a carafe of water on it.

"You haven't got the money to buy a radio station," he grumbled. "If you came here to ask me for a loan—"

"I *have* the money."

"What your grandmother left you. You mean to sink all you've got into—"

"I don't have to do that. Mr. Wolcott is forming a corporation that will buy the station. He's giving Kimberly and me a block of the stock and an option to buy more."

"You're going to work for your *father-in-law?* What kind of a man does that make you?"

"What kind of man would I be working for *you?*" Jack asked.

"You'd be the son of the *founder of the business,* getting ready to take over when the time comes!"

"Well, I'm going to take over the station right now. And maybe other stations if I can make this one work."

"*Radio!* Like your brother a—"

"I know. A *Luftmensch.* Well, Bob is a fool, but even Bob understands there are better things than the junk business."

"The junk business was not beneath the dignity of Der Herr Professor Lehrer. But— Oh, I understand. It is beneath the dignity of the Wolcotts of Boston, beneath the dignity of the outstanding debutante of 1929. Oh, yes, I understand these things. The cunt, I imagine, doubts that a kike junk dealer could even know the definition of a Boston debutante."

"You've called my wife a cunt for the last time."

"I will call her anything I wish!"

Jack stood. "Good-bye, Father."

Erich raised his chin high. "My son . . . *Fuck* the *shiksa!*"

"I already have. She's pregnant."

His father glowered at him. "You walk out of here, you will never see me again!"

"Good-bye, Father."

TWO

One 1931

THEIR HOUSE was not grand, but it was old and graceful. Jack and Kimberly were proud of it. It was located on Chestnut Street, not far from the Quaker Meeting House, and was one of six red-brick houses that stood in a row, sharing walls. These houses had been built in 1832 as homes for two intermarried families, the Hallowells and the Lowells, so that the elder generations could live in close proximity to the younger and conveniently supervise their lives. A century of rain and wind—plus the aggressive tendrils of the ivy that had to be torn off from time to time—had softened the severe lines of the old brick. And at night, the greenish glow from the mantles in the gas lamps on either side of each front door made them look quaint and inviting.

Inside, the rooms were of modest size but sumptuously furnished, almost entirely in antiques. Kimberly's mother had found the house and had proposed to buy it with its contents intact. While Kimberly and Jack were in California, Mrs. Wolcott had overseen the sorting and hauling away of a truckload of the clothing and other very personal possessions of the late owner, retaining only the furniture, curtains, and rugs, all of which she had subjected to professional cleaning. She had bought new mattresses and new bedding. For two autumn days the house had stood with every window wide open, to air before the young couple returned to occupy it.

In California, Jack had known all this activity was

going on in Boston. His father had never had a chance of talking him into staying in Los Angeles.

Jack had invested $60,000 of the money from his grandmother in the purchase and renovation of the house. It was an investment. A house like this, in this part of Boston, would always be marketable, Depression or no Depression.

"You agree to the Christmas party, then?" Kimberly asked, as she sat on the bed and watched him dress for the evening.

"Yes. Of course."

She was inviting more guests than could be squeezed into the house at one time: her parents, her brother and his wife, her sister and her husband, and a score of couples, some of whom were her friends, some only acquaintances. He knew what she was doing. She was testing the waters, to see who would accept and who would not accept an invitation from her now that she was married to Jack Lear.

She knew that a few of the people she had invited would not come. They refused to accept or understand the fact that Kimberly Bayard Wolcott had married a Jew—and not only that but a Jew from California, the son of a salvage baron. The party was to be a challenge flung in the face of Boston society.

Kimberly went into the bathroom, which in this house was not adjacent to the bedroom but was down the hall. Jack knew why. She was washing out her mouth with Lavoris. A few minutes ago she had knelt before him and given him a vigorous blow job. She sucked all right. But Erich didn't need to know that.

"How long do you think you'll be with Daddy?" she asked when she returned.

"Let's say an hour."

She was wearing a powder-blue dressing gown. She stood in front of him and helped him with his shirt studs. He was dressing for a drink with her father at the club bar, then for the dinner they would have later.

This was one of the reasons he had married Kimberly, and it was one of the reasons she had married him. She was making a *gentleman* of him. When he'd proposed marriage he had frankly told her he hoped she would consent to make of him the kind of man she would want for a husband, which he certainly wasn't already. The idea of being invited to make a man over had intrigued her, she had confessed. It was one of the reasons she'd finally consented to become his wife.

The other reasons, he had deduced. He'd then had half a million dollars of his own and was an up-and-coming man. He had impressed her as limitlessly ambitious. He had impressed her also as independent, willing to break away from his awful family. Once she got her hands on it, she had been fascinated by his cock, which was the term she had elected to use for it. She insisted still that it was the only one she had ever seen, but Jack figured she must have had some basis for comparison (statues in the Museum of Fine Arts?), since she understood it was extraordinary.

He only vaguely understood another reason why he had appealed to this exquisite girl. Jack Lear sensed but did not really know that he was singularly charismatic. He had seen the quality work sometimes but had not yet fully learned to appreciate and use it. The truth was that people were inclined to *like* him. He was now pondering ways to exploit this asset.

Anyway, Kimberly had exuberantly accepted his invitation to make him over into a proper gentleman. Sometimes he felt he paid a price. Tonight he would not only venture onto the street in white tie but would wear a cape and a silk hat and carry a stick as well. He knew that was how her father and the other men at the club would be dressed. Even so, Jack found it difficult to feel comfortable in such rigging.

He had been accepted into the Common Club as Harrison Wolcott's son-in-law, not as a Jew from California. He suspected that his father-in-law had called in a few IOUs to get him into the club. It was by no means the most distinguished gentlemen's club in Boston, but it was a gentlemen's club, and acceptance there clearly implied acceptance in Boston society.

As he walked to the club, along streets paved with brick as old and worn as those of his house, some of them green and slippery with decades' accumulation of algae, lichens, and moss, he noticed he was not the only man on the street dressed in formal evening attire.

At the club he checked his hat, cape, and stick and mounted the broad carpeted stairway to the second floor.

With the coming of Prohibition, the bar had been moved to the second floor. In the event of a visit by Prohibition agents, someone downstairs would step on a button and sound an alarm in the bar. By the time the agents climbed the stairs, all of the drinks on the bar would have been poured into buckets and the buckets emptied into a sink. The agents would face the hostile glares of gentlemen sipping ginger ale or lemonade.

It had never happened. Prohibition might have altered the drinking habits of the common folk in the Midwest, but it had required only minor adjustments among the Boston Brahmins and the Boston Irish.

Harrison Wolcott was at the bar, an Old-Fashioned before him.

"Ah, Jack! Scotch?"

Jack nodded. The bartender saw the nod and took a bottle from the cabinet behind the bar.

"How's the little mother-to-be?"

"She's doing fine," Jack said.

"When is it due, exactly?"

"The middle of April, we think."

"She's not very big yet," Harrison Wolcott observed.

"She's petite. She may not get very big. The doctor doesn't want her to gain any more weight than necessary."

"Well, then . . ."

Harrison Wolcott was a comfortable and self-confident man—whose self-confidence had been reinforced when the Depression had hardly touched him. His company, Kettering Arms, Incorporated, had worked to capacity between 1914 and 1919 and had made huge profits. He had been prescient enough to retrench drastically in 1919 and 1920, and the company remained only big enough to supply its specialized market for high-quality hunting and target rifles. That market had diminished only slightly when the Depression came. Moguls and magnates still prized Kettering rifles and bought about as many of them in 1930 as they had bought in 1928.

What was more, Harrison Wolcott had invested conservatively and diversely. His book value was no more than half of what it had been in 1929, but he was satisfied his investments were sound, and he kept them.

He was just fifty years old, but his hair had turned white. It lay thick and smooth across his head. His complexion was ruddy, his eyes pale blue, his mouth wide, his chin square. He was, in short, a handsome man.

"How are the bridge lessons going? Kimberly tells me you have a real flair for it."

Jack grinned. "I've learned not to trump my partner's ace."

"Kimberly says you're better than that."

"Kimberly has her enthusiasms."

"I won't ask how things are going at WCHS. I'll rely on you to tell me when you want to tell me."

"Actually," said Jack, "things are going quite well, I think. I'm learning the business, but strangely enough the principles I learned studying business administration at Harvard seem to apply."

"Adding that little girl has made your *Wheaterina Show* more popular."

"Yes. Betty's an asset. She's a natural comic. It was her own idea to use malaprops."

"I really broke down laughing when she said, 'Oh, no! Alice couldn't be in the family way. She hasn't even got a *husband!*' "

"We got a dozen letters and half a dozen calls complaining that was too risqué," said Jack.

"I'm interested in your claim that WCHS has more loyal listeners than any other station in Boston. To get Langdon and Lebenthal to put their name on the survey that says so was a real coup. Your advertisers—"

"We fudged a little," Jack said with a sly smile. "All we hired Langdon and Lebenthal to do was send out the canvassers. We didn't ask them to tabulate the results. We did that ourselves."

"But you've invited your advertisers to stop in and look at the cards."

"We tabulated the results and came in third. So we took about half the cards that favored other stations and stuffed them in the furnace. What remained favored us—and they're there to be inspected by anyone who wants to see them."

"Langdon and Lebenthal . . . ?"

"Did what they were paid to do. Each canvasser was scrupulously honest and dumped a bag of cards on us at the end of the day. So far no one has thought to ask who tabulated the results."

Wolcott frowned. "You'd better be careful, my boy. That sort of thing can ruin you."

Jack smiled. "What's the old saying: 'faint heart ne'er won fair lady'? Well, faint heart never turned a profit in business, either. And neither did rigid rectitude. I did learn *something* from my father."

"Be sure you keep the secret."

"Only three people know," said Jack. "You're the third."

Harrison Wolcott grinned and signaled the bartender to refill their glasses. "I have a feeling you're going to be a successful businessman, Jack."

"That's what I've got in mind."

Wolcott glanced up and down the bar. "Jack . . . I want to raise a very personal matter with you."

Jack nodded.

"Uh . . . Kimberly is a wonderful girl, I believe. She's also, as you have said, petite. I might say delicate. Her mother and I are concerned about her pregnancy. Petite girls sometimes— Well, you know what I mean. The two of you were married only a short while before she got pregnant. And that is fine. But I hope you realize a husband's marital rights sometimes have to be put in abeyance for a time, lest the girl be harmed."

"I understand."

Wolcott put his hand in his pocket and palmed a business card. He slipped it across the bar to Jack. "That's the telephone number of a girl you can count on to be discreet, should you want to engage her services. She has a very small clientele: a few businessmen. Expect to pay her generously."

Jack put the card in his pocket without looking at it. "I appreciate this," he said. "But I doubt I'll call her."

Two

JACK AND KIMBERLY were home from dinner by half past ten, having eaten rare roast beef in a speakeasy on the north bank of the Charles, where the proprietor had no qualms about serving his guests a genuine and excellent Burgundy. Kimberly had drunk a glass and a half of it, though she had generally given up alcohol until the baby was born. Before he joined her in bed, Jack turned the radio to WCHS, where music being played by the dance band at the Copley was being fed through a telephone line and onto the air.

He tossed his pajamas aside and lay down nude. Kimberly had not taken off her silk tap pants or her garter belt and stockings. They fondled and stimulated each other until she was flushed and her mouth was dry.

"Mmm . . . You want it, don't you?" she whispered, smiling fondly at his pulsing erection.

He took seriously what his father-in-law had said at the bar early in the evening. He hadn't told Harrison so, but for several weeks now he had not mounted Kimberly, had not penetrated her all the way. Her doctor said it was better not to. She was petite, and though it was unlikely they could injure the fetus, it was not impossible, if they were too vigorous. They had experimented with other ways, doggie-style for one, but had found less than complete satisfaction.

Jack nodded. He wanted it. "Baby. Would you be willing to commit the horrible and abominable crime against nature again? I suppose that doesn't do much for you, but it does *everything* for me."

"A second time in one day?" she asked with a faint smile.

"That one was a quickie."

"And tasted like garlic," she said. "If I'm going to suck the juices out of you, you've got to leave off the garlic."

"I swear I'll never touch garlic again. On the other hand, a little variation in flavor might—"

She shook her head petulantly. "Chocolate. Brandy. Beef and Burgundy. But not garlic!"

"It's a deal, then."

"All right."

She lowered her face into his lap and began to lick him. She had learned that taking him into her mouth and working up and down with tight lips would bring him fast. She also knew he didn't always like being brought fast.

"It's going to take all night," she whispered, opening her eyes wide and shaking her head.

Jack arched his back and closed his eyes. "I don't have to go to the station in the morning," he said.

She lowered her head more and began to lick his scrotum. "If somebody had told me two years ago that someday I'd put my face down in a man's crotch and lick his balls, I'd have called them insane."

"If somebody had told me two years ago that the most beautiful Boston debutante of 1929 would be licking my balls in 1931, I'd have called them insanely optimistic."

"Mommy and Daddy didn't bring me up to be a cocksucker."

"I want an honest answer to an honest question, darling," said Jack. "You do kind of like it, don't you? At least a little bit?"

She looked up and smiled. "Well . . . it's an acquired taste. When I first tried it, I thought I might throw up."

"I remember."

He remembered vividly. He had made the suggestion diffidently, apprehensive that he might offend her and even more apprehensive that she would think it was a suggestion that could be made only by a lubricous California Jew and never by the gentleman he was supposed to become.

At first she had kissed him tentatively, well down his shaft, then, more firmly, on his grayish-pink glans. She had looked up and smiled shyly, and he had whispered the suggestion that she lick. She did.

That first time she had clenched her lips tight against his ejaculate, certain its taste had to be nauseating. It had streamed over her mouth and chin and dripped on her breasts. Without his suggesting it, she had taken a drop on her finger and put it on her tongue. Then she had licked it off her lips and laughed.

She hadn't thrown up. She had never thrown up. She had gagged once, when she lowered her head too much and took him too deep down her throat. After that she knew how much she could take and where to stop.

The loveliest debutante of 1929. Her parents had not brought her out at the annual Debutante Cotillion but at a party of her own, for one hundred guests, in the same ballroom where the cotillion was held, at the Copley—an event that fascinated Boston but was, even so, judged as verging on ostentatious. That her escort that evening had been not a Bostonian but an unknown young man from California named Lear had caused much comment, not all of it favorable. It had been mildly scandalous. That he was a Harvard senior and was going to continue to a master's degree had suggested he might be the right sort, though.

That he had already taken Kimberly's virginity would have been conclusive evidence that he was not the right sort.

"Whatever are you thinking, husband?"

"I'm thinking about you," he said. "Remembering when—"

"Well, you had better focus your mind on what I'm doing, or we *will* be at it all night."

THREE

One 1932

THE STUDIOS and transmitter of WCHS were not on the Charles River as its call letters suggested but in Southie. Jack Lear was not willing to commute to Southie every day, so his executive offices were located in a suite of rooms above a theater southeast of the Common.

"Executive offices" was actually too grand a term for the rooms from which the radio station did business. Its executive staff consisted of just two men: Jack himself and Herb Morrill, whose job was to sell advertising. Jack had inherited Herb, who had been employed by WCHS since 1928 and was thus a veteran not only of the station but of radio broadcasting. He sold advertising, but he was also the source of ideas.

It had been Herb's idea in fact, not Jack's, to do the survey. When the results came in and were not favorable, Jack decided to fake them and then tout the faked results so often and for so long that it became gospel that WCHS was Boston's favorite radio station, in spite of other stations' frenzied efforts to set the record straight

One morning in February, Herb brought to the office a singing trio, and Jack reluctantly auditioned them.

Herb Morrill was a man of infectious enthusiasm. The story told of him was that he had been a successful bootlegger but had left that business because he foresaw the repeal of Prohibition. The truth was that, as a boy, he had developed a fascination with radio when he wiggled a wire whisker around on a quartz crystal and strained inside his earphones to hear the signal all the way from Pittsburgh—station KDKA. His father repaired shoes and apprenticed the boy to learn the trade. For a while, Herb re-soled and re-heeled shoes until he could hurry home, bolt down a meal, and don his earphones to hear stations as far west as Kansas City and Chicago. In 1928 he abandoned his trade to go to work for WCHS. He wanted to be an engineer but lacked the education for it. By default, he gravitated into selling advertising.

Herb was only two years older than Jack but had the look of a man ten years older. He shared with Jack the tendency to baldness, but his was far more advanced. He wore round, gold-rimmed eyeglasses and looked pedantic and timid. His appearance was deceiving because he was aggressive and outspoken.

"Wait'll ya hear these guys! Wait'll ya hear these guys!"

Jack was accustomed to Herb's exuberance. He lit a cigarette and regarded the trio—all dressed in identical double-breasted tan suits—with skepticism.

"Listen to this!"

The trio opened by striking a note: "Hmmmmmm."

Jack covered his eyes. "Don't do that. Just sing some thing."

They did:

I'm Geraldo Cigarillo, and men all say,
I'm the finest cigarillo you can buy today.
With the choicest tobacco, I will please you,
You can't find better, and that is true.
For the finest smoke that can't be beat,
Buy a pack of Geraldos and enjoy the treat!

"Jesus *Christ!* Herb! What have I done to you to make you do this to me?"

"You don't like it? I don't like it. The audience that hears it won't like it. *But they'll remember the message!* Geraldo Cigarillos are best! They'll remember the goddamned message. Merchandising by irritation, Jack!"

"Irri— Are you out of your mind? Make your potential customers mad at you?"

Herb grinned. "The Levy brothers like it. *They* see the

point. Your potential customers may be irritated by the message, but they'll goddamn well *remember* it. The Levys will sign a six-month contract to sponsor a *Geraldo Cigarillo Hour.* These guys sing the message, they sing another song or two on each show, and we fill in with a band and somebody like the Wisecrack Guys and Betty."

"Six— Well . . . what do you call this kind of shit? I mean singing the message. What do you call it?"

Herb shrugged. "The musical message, say. Why just have some mellifluous announcer *intone* the message when you can have—"

"All right, all right! Have you signed these guys?"

"Fifty dollars a week."

"Okay."

"Apiece."

"*Apiece?*"

"They sing for us. Messages. Songs. Whatever. Not just on *The Geraldo Cigarillo Show.*"

"What are they called?"

"The Bronson Brothers."

"Jesus *Christ!* Jack exclaimed. From now on they're . . . the Harmonics, the Tone Brothers, the Mellow Fellows. Something. Mellow Fellows. How you like that, guys?"

The Bronson Brothers nodded solemnly.

"Okay. And put the 'hmmmm' back in, at the beginning and the end. If we're going to be memorable, we may as well be *memorable.*"

Two

ABOUT SIX WEEKS before the baby was due, Kimberly's belly grew and she began to look pregnant. Her mother started to spend a lot of time at the house. And they found a nanny, an English girl from Lambeth named Cecily Camden. She moved into a room the Lears prepared for her on the third floor of the house.

The house, unfortunately, had only one bathroom, on the second floor, plus a toilet and a basin in a closet off the kitchen. Cecily would use that closet except when she bathed, which she could do only in the second-floor bathroom. She had been in the house less than a week when Jack accidentally walked into the bathroom and saw her in the tub. She smiled and grabbed a towel to cover herself but didn't shriek, and Jack apologized and backed out in no great hurry.

"I've got to go to New York this week," he told Kimberly over dinner the same evening. "If you weren't so far along, I'd take you with me."

"What's the occasion?"

"Well, you know how Herb's a man of enthusiasms. His latest is for a vaudeville comic who's playing in the *Earl Carroll Vanities*. He thinks we should try to book the guy to come up to Boston and do a weekly radio show, half an hour of his jokes and routines. He doesn't work cheap, and I can't even think of signing him until I see his act."

Kimberly shrugged. "You've got the Wisecrack Guys. How many comics can you use?"

"Bert says they're a pair of amateurs compared to this guy."

"Why would he leave the *Earl Carroll Vanities* to come and work on a Boston radio station?"

"Being in the *Vanities* is great. But it's not permanent. The guy's bread and butter is vaudeville, but the movies and radio have all but killed vaudeville. Like a lot of vaudevillians, he's been casting a nervous eye on radio."

"You think it's really worth your time to go all the way to New York to catch this act?" Kimberly asked skeptically.

"I promised Herb I would."

"What's this comic's name?"

"Jack Benny."

Three

KIMBERLY INSISTED he pack white tie and tails, plus his collapsible top hat, to wear to the theater in New York. There, where she couldn't see him, he went to the *Vanities* in a dark-gray double-breasted suit.

Herb went with him. He'd reserved seats down front.

Benny was the lead comedian. He appeared in a number of sketches, then did a monologue.

"Herb," Jack said quietly as they walked up the aisle to the exit, "that man is not funny."

"I disagree with you, Jack. I think he's the funniest man I've heard in a long time."

"Is there any way to get out of this dinner?"

"I don't see how. That'd be very awkward."

Forty-five minutes later they sat down at a table in the Stork Club with Jack Benny.

Benny had just celebrated his thirty-seventh birthday. Jack saw a certain appeal in his innocent, open face and in the flat, hesitating manner in which he delivered his gags; but he simply could not see that the man was funny.

"Two Jacks," said Herb. "That makes conversation a little awkward, doesn't it?"

"You can call me Ben," said Jack Benny. "My real name is Benjamin Kubelsky."

The Stork Club was a speakeasy. The proprietor, their host, was an ex-convict named Sherman Billingsley, who had served time in an Oklahoma prison before he came to New York and became the bootlegger to café society. He knew Jack Benny and came to the table to welcome him and his friends.

"Pleasure to see you here, Jack," said Billingsley. "And to see you, too, Mr. Lear, Mr. Morrill." He nodded toward the bottle of Johnnie Walker sitting on their table. "That's on the house, gentlemen."

"Thank you, Sherm," said Jack Benny. "Anybody interesting in the joint tonight?"

"You might be interested in the gentleman over there," said Billingsley, nodding discreetly at a table where a tall, distinguished-looking man sat smoking a cigarette and talking earnestly to a diminutive girl.

"Who's he?" Benny asked.

"That's General Douglas MacArthur, Chief of Staff, United States Army. The girl is his mistress. She's a Filipina."

Jack Benny shrugged. Apparently General MacArthur didn't interest him.

"Don't turn around and look, whatever you do," said Billingsley, "but the swarthy fellow two tables back—the one with the eyes of a wolf—is Lucky Luciano."

"Who's Lucky Luciano?" asked Jack Lear.

Billingsley's chin and brows rose, as if he could not believe anyone did not know the name of Lucky Luciano. "He's the head man of all the mobs in the States. He and his guys took over everything not long ago. They just killed off their rivals."

Jack Benny did not turn and look at Luciano. He didn't seem any more interested in the gangster than he was in General MacArthur. His focus was on showbiz people, and nobody else made much difference to him.

"Tell ya what, Jack," said Billingsley. "Look to your left. Lucille LeSueur, lately known as Joan Crawford."

"Aha," said Benny, and he turned and looked, catching her eye.

"Aha is right," said Jack Lear.

"Ask you something, Mr. Lear?" said Jack Benny. "Radio. I got in trouble with the following joke. What would happen if I told it on your radio station? I come onstage carrying a girl in my arms. I say to the man in overalls, 'Mr. McDonald, your daughter fell in the river, but don't worry, I resuscitated her.' And the farmer says, 'By golly, you resuscitate her, you gotta marry her!' "

Jack chuckled. "I'd get shrieks and tears from the Legion of Decency. But off the record I'll tell you how I feel about the Legion of Decency. Fuck 'em."

"Saying 'Fuck 'em' and making it stick are two different things," said Herb. "The Babbitts of this country are really taking over."

"I'm not sure I agree," said Billingsley. "I predict that Prohibition will be repealed within two years."

"What happens to you then, Sherm?" asked Jack Benny.

"Respectability," said Billingsley. "Well, gents, I've got to move. Uh . . . if any of you feel a need for a first-class, clean young girl for the night, just say the word."

As they left the club, Jack shook his head. "Maybe I should've taken Billingsley up on that offer—so the trip to New York wouldn't have been a *total* loss."

Four

IN MID-APRIL Herb came into Jack's office, grinning happily. "Looka this," he said. He handed Jack a copy of *Variety*. A headline read: BENNY TO BE STAR COMIC ON CANADA DRY HOUR ANOTHER VAUDEVILLIAN IN THE LITTLE BOX.

Jack glanced through the story. "I don't care, Herb. The man is not funny. He's simply not funny. The show'll be a bust."

"Whatta ya bet?"

" 'A funny thing happened . . . on the way to the *theater.*' Not funny, Herb. I especially don't like a comic who starts a routine by telling you it's going to be funny. I—"

He was interrupted by a ringing telephone. He picked it up.

"Something . . . ?" Herb asked.

"I'm going to be a daddy. I have to get out of here and over to the hospital."

Kimberly gave birth to a boy. Even though he was named for his father, he was named John, not Jack. John Wolcott Lear.

FOUR

One 1933

Jack and Kimberly loved the house on Chestnut Street, but its modest size imposed too many limitations on them. Their ability to entertain was severely hampered by the bathroom facilities: one bathroom on the second floor and a toilet closet off the kitchen. Cecily, the nanny, occupied all the servant quarters the house afforded. Kimberly had hired a maid and a cook, but neither of them could live in, so she was deprived of maid service after early evening, when she had to let the girl leave for her home in Southie. Also, the house had no garage.

In the fall of 1933 a much larger house, facing Louisburg Square, became available. Jack reviewed their financial situation and decided he could buy it. He sold the Chestnut Street house for $67,500, making a profit of $7,500 on his investment. Refusing to deal with real estate agents, Jack insisted on dealing directly with the seller, and he bought the new house for $135,000.

This house was neither as old nor as elegant as their first house, but it would better suit their needs. From the foyer guests entered a living room or could turn right into a library. There was a formal dining room, and the kitchen was large and fully equipped. There was also a small handsome guest bathroom on the first floor.

Four bedrooms occupied the second floor. The master bedroom opened on a sitting room and on a bathroom. An additional bath served the other bedrooms. On the third floor there were three small bedrooms for servants, a little parlor for them, and their own bathroom.

The bathroom off the master bedroom had an immense claw-footed tub. Jack liked to joke that it was so big he was afraid he might drown in it. The bathroom's most interesting feature, which both Jack and Kimberly showed off to their close friends, was a marble-walled shower room big enough for five people to shower together if they were so inclined. The nickel-plated shower head, as big around as a dinner plate, was so high above that a person standing in the shower couldn't reach it. Three of the walls of the shower room were surrounded by nickel-plated pipes perforated with tiny holes, forming what was called a needle shower. A bather using the needle shower was stung by tiny streams of water under high pressure, which stimulated almost to the point of pain. A bidet on a hinged pipe swung out and would emit a stream upward.

The first night they spent in the new house, Jack and Kimberly showered in the shower room. After that, they decided to forgo tub baths and instead took showers, most of the time together.

Two weeks after they moved in, Jack invited Cecily to join him in the shower. She oohed and aahed to the sting of the needle shower and offered no resistance when he embraced her from behind and entered her. When it was over, he helped her use the bidet to wash herself out and hoped it would prove sufficient.

Cecily looked like a typical English girl. She had a fair complexion with apple cheeks, large blue eyes, and sandy-red hair. She was built like a wet nurse, Kimberly had joked: her breasts were enormous. Her belly was prominent, and she had broad hips with a pelvis like a great bowl.

Having spent a year or so at a red-brick university near London, Cecily was well educated and spoke with an Oxonian, not an East End, accent. Coming to the States represented an opportunity for her, and she said she wanted to stay and become an American citizen. She told the Lears that she was grateful for her job as a nanny but that she hoped in time to find better employment.

After that first time in the shower, Jack took her from time to time, maybe once a week, thereafter always using a rubber. She was casual about it, seeming to accept having sex with her employer, as though it were a part of her job. He could not take her to her bedroom or often have her in his. Typically she came into the library when Kimberly was away, and sometimes she just pulled down her panties, pulled up her skirt and slip, and sat facing him on his lap.

It was simple and good. All that troubled Jack was that she smothered him with great wet kisses while he was inside her, and he wasn't quite sure what that implied.

Two

JACK'S ABILITY to buy the larger house on Louisburg Square said a lot about how his business was performing.

WCHS hadn't lost money after its first year on the air. Jack Lear and Harrison Wolcott had bought a station that was making a modest profit. Shortly after Jack began to run it, it was making more than a modest profit because—although he could be wrong, as he had been about Jack Benny—he created programming and if it didn't work, he destroyed it with never a backward glance. He gained a reputation for being savvy and tough.

Wash Oliver was a piano player who sang a bit as he played. Someone said he sounded like a whorehouse pianist, which was an astute remark because he *was* a whorehouse pianist. He continued to play in a bawdy house in East Boston even after he had made a deal to play half an hour five evenings a week on WCHS. Jack Lear wasn't troubled by this; he liked Oliver and his music, and that was all that mattered.

In the neighborhoods of Southie, Herb Morrill found the personnel for *The Shamrock Hour*—Paddy McClanahan, a comedian who did broad Irish-ethnic jokes; an Irish tenor named Dennis Curran; Colleen, a female singer whose last name was never used; and a quartet that played and sang rollicking Irish ballads.

Jack affiliated WCHS with UBS, the Universal Broadcasting System. It was not a network but a recording company. Affiliated stations subscribed to programs, which were recorded in various cities and the records mailed to the stations. Briefly, before it became an NBC network program, *Amos 'n Andy* was distributed this way, and Jack took a chance and subscribed to it for his Boston station. It was wildly popular, and when it left WCHS to be broadcast on the NBC station, its absence left a gaping hole in the WCHS schedule.

Mostly with actors hired from university drama clubs, Jack initiated a morning drama series he called *Our Little Family.* The show had only two permanent cast members, Mama and Daddy. The real-life Mama was an alcoholic who endured in her private life dramas as real as those written for the show; but listeners, who knew nothing of that, envisioned her as the good-hearted, beleaguered mother of a family that didn't appreciate her. She confronted every situation with the perfect cliché—"A stitch in time saves nine," "A rolling stone gathers no moss," "Marry in haste, repent at leisure," "A cheerful countenance turns away wrath"—and at the end of every adventure she offered a heartfelt "All's well that ends well."

Jack developed the idea of what he called the hypochondriac hour, a daytime show on which a succession of quack doctors dispensed medical advice. Sufferers would write letters describing their symptoms, and an allopath, homeopath, hydropath, naturopath, chiropractor, or some other "specialist" would read the letters on the air and recommend a cure—usually "Just call at my office on Such-and-such Street."

The medical quacks were not sponsored, implying that their valuable advice was broadcast as a public service. The fact was that Jack took a substantial fee from each quack; they were glad to pay for the privilege of touting their quackery and soliciting patients.

Advertisers gravitated toward the station and its popular offerings. By the end of 1932 WCHS was drawing significant revenues from the manufacturers of motorcars, breakfast foods, soaps ("Only Lifebuoy kills Bee-ee-ee-ee-Ohhhh!"), hair dressings, deodorants, and a wide variety of patent medicines.

Jack Lear and Herb Morrill had found the formula for

turning a profit from radio. Although the Wolcotts, father and daughter, deplored it, the station made money by doing what Kimberly scorned as 'downscaling'—that is, by dropping a lot of its classical music programming and broadcasting to a more popular taste. Kimberly liked Jack's success, but she was embarrassed by the way he won it.

Three 1934

HARRISON WOLCOTT spent half his week in Connecticut, in his office at Kettering Arms, and the other half in his Boston office, where he attended to other business. His Boston office was a huge walnut-paneled room with furniture upholstered in black leather.

His desk was made of wood from the hull of the frigate *Constitution*—Old Ironsides—taken from her during one of her several restorations. Wolcott sat behind it proudly, in a black wool suit. He rose when Jack entered the room.

"It's good to see you, young man," he said. "You're so dedicated to your business that I don't see you as often as I'd like."

Jack shook hands with his father-in-law and sat down. "I'd thought of business more in terms of making something work than in terms of overcoming the opposition of people who don't want to see it work."

The older man smiled. "Two sides of the same coin," he said. "Scotch?"

Jack nodded. Wolcott put his cigar aside in an ashtray and took a bottle of Scotch from a drawer. He poured two drinks: straight, without water or ice. They saluted each other with their glasses and drank.

"Has Kimberly told you," Wolcott asked, "that there is a station available for purchase in Hartford? Has she mentioned that she'd like to see WCHS, Incorporated, buy it?"

"It loses money," Jack said bluntly.

Wolcott picked up his cigar. "Does that conclude the discussion?" he asked.

"Not at all. But I'd want to be persuaded that there's

some potential before I agreed to buy a station that loses money."

"She likes its broadcasting."

"I know. She's told me. Classical music and information. She goes so far as to say she's embarrassed to be married to the president of WCHS. She says my tastes are too much like my father's."

"She's said *that*? Well, I wouldn't take that seriously. Women, young women especially—"

"I know. I don't let it bother me. I suppose you know she's pregnant again."

"Congratulations. The two of you are building a fine family."

"Yes. John is quite a boy. He's a pleasure. I, uh . . . I had a purpose in coming by."

"I imagined you did. What can I do for you, Jack?"

Jack reached inside his jacket and took out his billfold. From it he took a certified check for $300,000 and handed it to his father-in-law. It represented all but a little of what was left of the money his grandfather had given him.

"What's this?"

"I want to exercise my option and buy three thousand more shares of WCHS, Incorporated."

Harrison Wolcott stared at the check for a long moment.

He had formed WCHS, Incorporated in 1931 to buy the radio station and had given Jack and Kimberly two thousand of the ten thousand shares as their wedding present. He had given them an option to buy the remaining shares at 1931 book value. In March of 1932 Jack had exercised the option and bought another thousand shares. Now he was buying three thousand more, which would give him 60 percent and clear control. Harrison Wolcott, who had not been told of the money bestowed upon Jack by his grandfather, had supposed it would take Jack a minimum of ten years, maybe even fifteen or twenty, to gain control of the corporation.

"You didn't borrow this?"

"No, sir. My grandfather gave it to me. He wanted me to have a business of my own."

The older man grinned, though not without some irony

in his expression. "Well, you now have a business of your own."

"I hope this in no way offends you," said Jack.

"Not at all. I think I've refrained from interfering in your management of the business."

"Of course you have. I've been aware, though, that you've had a lot of capital tied up in WCHS, and I've felt an obligation to release you from that."

Jack said that before he realized he shouldn't have. It would take Harrison Wolcott less than five minutes to figure out that he'd had the money to exercise the option for a long time and was exercising it now only because he had become satisfied that the business was a success.

He essayed a repair: "Of course, I was reluctant to invest all my grandfather gave me until I could feel reasonably sure I wouldn't lose it."

"Do you want to make changes in the membership of the board of directors?" Wolcott asked.

Jack shook his head. "I want you to remain as chairman of the board, if you will consent."

"Very well. I congratulate you. There is, uh, only one element of this to which I could possibly take exception. I—"

"What is that?" Jack interrupted nervously.

The older man turned the check over and over in his hands. "When you and I do business, Jack, don't give me certified checks and don't expect certified checks from me. I will accept your personal check for any amount, and I expect you to accept mine."

Four

THE HOUSE on Louisburg Square was not ready for any elaborate entertaining until the spring of 1934.

Although Jack had made a liberal budget available to Kimberly for redecorating the house, the money was not enough, and she accepted generous gifts from her mother and father. Mrs. Wolcott accompanied her when she shopped for rugs and furniture and often paid for her purchases.

Kimberly was determined to turn the house into a showplace. She had the floors in all the principal rooms sanded and refinished. Then she bought Oriental carpets and placed them so as to expose and display the rich pegged oak. For the living room she bought a thirty-year-old Bakhtiari Persian rug, woven in a bold geometric pattern of bright colors. In the dining room she laid a Laver Kerman rug of darker colors and more elaborate pattern. In the center of the library she placed a smaller Indian rug. Since this one had not been woven by Muslims, it featured prowling tigers, running elephants, and chariot-borne hunters, all in a stylized landscape of fantastic foliage.

Most of the furniture from the smaller house was moved to Louisburg Square, but some of it was banished to the bedrooms. For the living and dining rooms, Kimberly needed a few extra pieces. She selected Queen Anne chairs and a William and Mary highboy, none of which actually dated from those reigns but were fine antiques made during the long period when those styles were popular.

Kimberly was particularly pleased with a japanned highboy whose drawer fronts were adorned with chinoiserie depicting men and women, camels and birds.

She took down the chandelier and had the entry hall lit with torchères.

On an evening early in April the house was open and lighted for the arrival of fifty guests. Since the dining room could not seat that many, the party was a housewarming, with drinks and hors d'oeuvres.

As before, in the early months of her second pregnancy Kimberly showed no sign of her condition. She was as lithe and slender as she had been as a girl of twenty. For her party she wore her hair behind her ears, showing off her diamond earrings. She had applied all her makeup with care and precision, and she wore a pearl choker and a bracelet of three strands of pearls.

As yet she had not put on her dress. She wanted Jack's help with it. The pink silk brocade dress was tight-fitting and showed cleavage. Because she did not want to risk a strap straying and showing, she was not going to wear a brassiere. She didn't need one. Similarly, because she did not want the outline of a garter belt and its clasps making lines and lumps on her skirt, she was using garters of black silk ribbon to hold up her sleek dark stockings. As she waited for Jack to come out of the bathroom she sat at her dressing table checking her hair and makeup, wearing only silk panties and the stockings.

"You look like a queen tonight," Jack said when he came out of the bathroom.

Kimberly turned and looked at him, then sighed. "Let me fix your necktie. You never will get them straight, will you?"

The party was black tie. He wore a double-breasted tuxedo.

"Remember," she said, "Do not pluck hors d'oeuvres off the tables or trays. They must be served to you on a plate. You must have a plate."

"Yes, ma'am," he said jovially.

"I mean it, Jack. This is not California."

"In other words, don't act like a California Jew."

"All I ask is that you don't embarrass us, for God's sake. Help me with this." She pulled her dress over her head and writhed as she drew it down over her body. He pulled up the zipper in back and fastened the hooks. "Don't mention Betsy Emerson's divorce," Kimberly continued. "If someone mentions it to you, say you hadn't heard of it. She'll be introduced to you as Mrs. Otis Emerson. That's the correct form. Her maiden name was Otis. Her Christian name is Elizabeth, and the second or third time you talk to her she'll invite you to call her Betsy."

"All right. Shall we go down and check everything?"

"Yes. And don't forget that the Horans are Catholics. They'll be the only people here tonight who are. Connie is one of my best friends."

"I never make anti-Catholic jokes," Jack reassured her.

"I know you don't. But there are little ways of saying things. I mean, some things are better said in other ways."

"Jesus Christ, Kimberly! Don't you think I know *any thing?"*

Five

WHEN THE HOUSE was full of people and nobody was particularly noticing who was talking to whom, Jack slipped up beside Mrs. Otis Emerson, who was gathering some crackers smeared with caviar onto her plate, and murmured, "H'lo, Betsy."

Her eyes flashed. "You bastard!" she whispered. "Where have you been?"

"I've been busy as hell."

"Bull. I'm a fallen woman, Jack, and need someone to comfort me. Did you arrange to have me invited tonight?"

He shook his head. "Kimberly invited you."

"I'm off about half the invitation lists in town."

"Really?"

"Absolutely. In Boston society, divorce is still a major scandal."

"Even if the bastard beat you."

"Even if the bastard beat me. Listen. My family tried to talk me out of the divorce. My lawyer tried to talk me out of it. The *judge* tried to talk me out of it. They all said any husband is better than no husband."

Betsy was a comely blond woman of maybe thirty-two or -three, but she was not nearly as beautiful as Kimberly. Her nose was a little too long and sharp, her mouth was a little too wide and toothy. What Jack found most attractive about her was her air of comfortable self-esteem.

"I'm sorry, Betsy," he said earnestly. "I'll make a point of getting together with you as soon as I can."

"Make it soon." She spoke in a very low voice because she had noticed Kimberly approaching. "Any woman who's ever had a feel of the Lear cock wants another feel."

A moment later Kimberly was beside them.

"I see you two have met."

Jack nodded. "And she's already invited me to call her Betsy."

Kimberly pretended not to notice Jack's catty comment. "I know you're something of an expert on chinoiserie,

Betsy," she said. "Have you noticed my new highboy? I'd like your honest opinion."

"Jack . . . ?" Betsy asked.

Kimberly grinned. "My husband wouldn't know chinoiserie from Duncan Phyfe. It's something I've got to teach him. Maybe you can help."

Betsy looked directly into Jack's eyes. "I'll be glad to try," she said.

Dan Horan was an easy man to get to know. A good deal older than his wife, Kimberly's friend Connie, Dan was a big, bluff man, overweight but still hard-muscled and athletic. He had curly dark hair and wore gold-framed eyeglasses. He had no reason to go to any special effort to make friends, yet he seemed to seek them assiduously, like a bibliophile who collected books he did not read.

"I congratulate you on the house," he said to Jack. "To be able to snatch one up here—"

"You watch for opportunities."

"Well, you found one. And Kimberly has done a hell of a job on it!"

"I need a drink," said Jack. "Bar?"

Kimberly had hired two maids for the evening, to wander through the house in short, flared black skirts, with white aprons and caps; but on their trays they carried only glasses of champagne and hors d'oeuvres. The cook, an Irishwoman of formidable proportions, had proved a knowledgeable bartender and was serving in that capacity behind a table set up in the library.

"Connie tells me you're going to buy WHFD in Hartford."

"So Kimberly has told Connie, and so she tells me. I haven't decided yet. Kimberly wants it because it broadcasts only classical music. She's a little embarrassed by WCHS."

"It's the most *interesting* station in Boston," said Dan Horan.

Jack laughed. "Thanks for the careful choice of words. It's also the most profitable, according to the latest numbers."

They walked away from the bar with their drinks, and in the foyer between the library and the living room they came across Kimberly and Connie.

Jack had decided that Constance Horan was the only woman he had ever seen who rivaled Kimberly in grace and beauty. But her style was completely different. She was taller than Kimberly, had long sleek legs, and was blond. Her mouth was softer, but she hardened it with cold-red lipstick. The chief difference between the two women was that Connie carried herself with a defiant dignity that bordered on arrogance.

She was also a superior bridge player. She and Jack were sometimes matched as partners because they made a formidable team.

Tonight she was wearing a white silk-satin dress with a loose V neck, a sleeveless bodice, and a clinging skirt that flaunted her slim hips and long slender legs. Jack was stirred by the sight of her.

"Jack . . . how many Scotches have you had this evening, darling?" Kimberly asked with a pinched little smile.

"I haven't been counting. Have you?"

"No, not really. But I hope that's the last one."

Six

JUST BEFORE MIDNIGHT, in the sitting room adjoining their bedroom, Jack flung his jacket on the floor. *"Goddammit! Enough!* Enough goddamned faultfinding."

Kimberly unhooked and unzipped her dress, and with it hanging loose she went into the bedroom. *"You're* in a foul mood," she called back.

"Why wouldn't I be? You go out of your way to humiliate me."

"How did I humiliate you?" she asked with a calmness that begged for a challenge.

"You said to Betsy that I wouldn't know chinoiserie from Duncan Phyfe—"

"Do you?"

"Yes, I do. I don't suppose I'd always recognize a piece as Duncan Phyfe, but I know what chinoiserie is. I ought to; I paid enough for an item of it."

Kimberly returned, knotting the cord at the waist of

her blue silk dressing gown. "Do you have other complaints?" she asked.

He'd tossed his clothes on the floor as he spoke, and now he stood before her naked, flaunting his cock. "Barbara handed me a canapé from her plate, and I took it and ate it. You didn't have to ask me where my plate was. What was I supposed to do, accept a canapé from her plate and put it down on mine before I picked it up again and ate it? Is that what I was supposed to do?"

"What was more, you didn't have a napkin."

"Well, I had a drink, didn't I? And in front of the Horans you asked me how many I'd had and advised me not to have any more."

"It's well that I did, too, isn't it? Listen to yourself."

"I am not drunk, Kimberly!"

"I'll take your word for it. But I thought you looked to me to make a gentleman of you. That was part of our deal. You asked me to. And you are still a long way from—"

"Not in public, Kimberly! Not in front of other people!"

"Ah. I see the distinction. I put you on show tonight, my husband. I showed off a man who can afford a home on Louisburg Square, decorated as this one is, who knows how to dress and how to receive and converse with guests—as he didn't know three years ago. I showed off a man who may not know exactly who Duncan Phyfe was but who recognizes chinoiserie and the several different kinds of Oriental carpets we have—and has the money to buy them. I *presented* you to Boston tonight. And you came off pretty well, Jack. And frankly, it was among people who doubted you could. The thanks I get is a petulant series of little complaints from a man who is, no, not drunk but is on the verge of it. If I advised you to make that Scotch—your fourth or fifth or whatever it was—your last one, it's a damned good thing I did, because you could have destroyed everything we've worked and spent to achieve. I'm going to bed." She paused, then added, "I have one more suggestion. I suggest you shower and brush your teeth before you join me. If you can't do anything else, at least you can make good use of that circumcised dick."

FIVE

One 1934

ON JUNE 10, Jack received a telegram:

> LA 61034 1000AM
>
> LIFE OF JOHANN LEHRER RAPIDLY COMING TO END STOP DAILY WEAKER STOP IF YOU WISH TO SPEAK WITH HIM WHILE HE IS STILL ALIVE URGE YOU TRAVEL HERE SOONEST STOP
>
> MICKEY

Mickey Sullivan was Erich Lear's factotum and Jack's lifelong friend.

At noon the next day Jack boarded an American Airlines Condor biplane for the flight to Los Angeles. The route was Boston to New York to Washington to Nashville to Dallas to Douglas, Arizona, to Los Angeles, with a stop at each city. Because the flying continued overnight—a recent and daring innovation in air travel—the airplane was equipped with seats that converted into comfortable berths. After the ten passengers had eaten a hearty meal, complete with liquors and wine, they were invited to retire. Somewhere over Virginia or Tennessee the berths were made up, and the passengers donned their pajamas and lay down to sleep. Those who were still asleep were wakened at Dallas and told their flight was more than half complete. They ate breakfast, lunch, and a late-afternoon snack with cocktails aboard the Condor and touched down in Los Angeles in time to have dinner there.

Before he left the airport, Jack dispatched a telegram to Kimberly:

LA 61234 915PM

HAVE ARRIVED HERE SAFELY STOP WILL RETURN BY TRAIN STOP ALL MY LOVE TO YOU AND LITTLE JOHN

JACK

Mickey Sullivan met him at the airport. Only after Jack had sent his telegram did Mickey tell him he had not arrived in time. "The old man died about four hours ago."

"Did he say anything about me?"

"He didn't say anything about anybody. Your father and your brother tried to talk to him the last couple of days. He knew they were talking to him—his eyes followed them—but he ignored them. That's the way death is, Jack. Nothing special. People just retreat inside themselves and spend their last hours with their own private thoughts."

Mickey Sullivan was eight years older than Jack. He had sandy hair and a square, bland, honest face. Many people said that Erich Lear's demands on his time and energy had ruined his marriage, which had ended in divorce.

"Your father is angry," Mickey said as they walked to his car.

"Fancy that. Pissed off or horny. The only two conditions he knows."

"They've looked at your grandfather's will. He left your brother a million dollars and you half a million, saying he gave you a half a million advance on your inheritance in 1931. Your father is very upset that neither of you told him about that."

"My grandfather didn't want him to know."

"Well, he thinks it was a betrayal. The residue of the estate, which is what *he* gets, won't amount to a million."

"He got his. He's the president and chief stockholder of Lear Ship Breaking and Salvage."

"They are going to sit shivah. Will you stay?"

"I can't stay that long. In fact, since the old man is dead I'm tempted to ask you to drive me to the railroad station so I can start back tonight."

"I don't see how you can do that, Jack," Mickey said gravely.

"Well, take me to the Ambassador. I've got a reservation. Stay and have dinner with me, will you? I don't want to face my father and brother before tomorrow."

Over dinner Jack told Mickey a little about the house on Louisburg Square and about his son. Mickey told Jack about what was happening with the California Lears.

"The business is going great. You know your father. He's bidding to break up the *Mauretania*. And I'll bet he gets it. What the man sets out to do, he does. He ought to be happy, too. He's up to his usual tricks."

"Who now?"

"You wouldn't believe it. She's nineteen years old. Luscious. I mean, *luscious!* I'm ashamed to say I set it up for him. My mother didn't raise me to be a procurer." Mickey shook his head.

Jack grinned. "But you're good at it. If I didn't have to catch a train for Boston in a couple of days, I'd ask you to set up one for me."

Mickey glanced at his watch. "Not too late, really. I can probably set you up with—"

"Tomorrow night, maybe."

"Okay. Listen. The man who's unhappy is your brother, Bob. And worse than him, your sister-in-law, Dorothy."

"What? A couple who just inherited a million dollars is unhappy?"

"It's a matter of backbone. You had the backbone to walk out on your old man. Bob doesn't. In spite of the fact that Bob's got a business of his own, Erich sticks his nib in everything. Carlton House was set up with Erich's money, of course. Every time Bob signs a promising starlet, Erich wants to bang her—and after he does, he pushes Bob to give her a part she's not ready for. He even reads scripts and hounds Bob to turn them into pictures. Erich makes Bob's every day hell on earth."

"What does he make *your* every day?"

"You know how it goes."

"What's he paying you?"

"Eighteen thou."

Jack pinched his chin between the thumb and index finger of his right hand. "Would you take twenty-four to move to Boston and come into the radio business?"

"Christ, yes!"

"How much time you need?"

"Well, I ought to give Erich thirty days' notice."

"Fuck him. You don't owe him any more than I do. Get us a roomette on Thursday. You can send him a wire from Chicago."

Two

JOHANN LEHRER would be buried in a wooden coffin with rope handles. It was his express wish. In accordance with another of his wishes, the coffin sat on a simple wooden trestle. But when it came to flowers his wishes were disregarded. After all, he was the grandfather of the head of Carlton House Productions, and Hollywood had sent vans loaded with floral tributes.

The chapel seated only two hundred, so loudspeakers had been set up outside so the eulogy and the Kaddish could be heard by hundreds more who had gathered on the lawn.

"So . . ." said Erich Lear. "My son the proper Bostonian, dressed to the nines. Look at the suit," he said to Bob. "He makes us look cheap."

"Out of respect for"— Jack said. He paused and nodded toward the coffin—"I won't tell you what I think of your judgment of my clothes or anything else."

Erich glanced at the coffin. "Okay. Out of respect." He extended his hand. "Our feelings today ought to be about him."

"Yes. Professor of rational and revealed religion. Ragpicker. Then, to use his own term, 'junkman.' And finally so great a success that he could fund you in your business and me in mine. I'm proud to be his grandson."

Bob scowled. "We hear you have a fine home in Boston.

I don't believe you ever invited our grandfather to see it. Or your father or brother, for that matter."

Bob Lear was as bitter as Mickey Sullivan had said he was. He had a pronounced capacity for petty nastiness, unlike his father, whose nastiness was never petty. Looking nothing like the other Lears, he was blond, plump, and bowlegged. His light-gray, double-breasted suit with white buttons emphasized his ungainliness.

"Kimberly and I will make you welcome . . . if you should choose to come," Jack said frigidly.

A chapel attendant approached. "Yarmulke, sir?" he asked Jack, offering a black satin skullcap.

"Yes. Of course."

The service was brief. When it was over, four men carried the coffin to the open grave a hundred yards away and lowered it into the earth.

As they walked back toward the chapel and the cars, Erich asked Jack how long he would stay in Los Angeles.

"I have to take tomorrow's train. Business. I don't have to tell you it demands a man's time and attention."

"Mr. Lear!" A photographer lugging a big Graflex camera trotted across the lawn toward them. "A picture of the son and two grandsons?" he asked.

"Sure," said Erich. "Why not?"

They posed: Erich in the middle, a son on either side.

"Well, then," Erich said to Jack. "I take it you're not planning to come to the house tonight."

Jack offered his hand to be shaken, and Erich took it. "We've managed to spend an hour together without unpleasantness. I'm glad to have seen you. And you too, Bob. Let's not tempt God to set us against each other during this trip."

"As you want it," said Erich brusquely. "Give me your yarmulke. I'll return it."

"Oh, yes. Right. Here." He saluted his father. "Next year in Jerusalem," he said.

Erich and Bob watched Jack stride toward Mickey Sul livan's car. Erich glanced around and raised his hand to summon the photographer.

"Make sure those pictures get in the mail, airmail, to Boston as fast as possible," he said, handing the man a hundred-dollar bill.

Three

MICKEY DROVE JACK back to the Ambassador. He went with him to his suite and watched him toss back two quick Scotches, then light a Camel. He puffed heavily as he paced the room.

"I know," said Mickey. "It's tough all the way 'round. Look. I offered to set you up with a broad tonight. Maybe I can get somethin' good for right now. Let me make a couple calls."

Jack went to the bathroom and took a hot shower while Mickey made his telephone calls. When he returned to the living room, Mickey showed him a thumbs-up and grinned.

"She'll be here within the hour. Don't turn her away at first look. She's okay. I'll be back later. Let's go out to dinner our last night in L.A."

Jack nodded and poured himself another Scotch.

The girl, who was obviously a teenager, was plump. She was not terribly attractive, though he could see something erotic about her that he might not have noticed if Mickey had not urged him to give her a second look. From her swarthy complexion and her dark brown eyes, he guessed she was of Latin American extraction, probably Mexican. She wore a loose white peasant blouse, an exceptionally full black skirt decorated with green and red stripes just above the hem, dark stockings, and shiny black patent-leather shoes.

"Mr. Lear? You expecting me?"

He nodded, showing her a reluctant smile. "I guess I am. Come in."

She entered the suite and looked around. "This is nice," she said simply.

He heard little clicks as she walked across the parquet floor. He stared at her shoes and realized they were tap shoes. "You are a dancer?" he asked.

"Yes. I dance for you first . . . if you want."

"Do you dance on the stage?"

"Yes. You have never heard of me. But I think you will."

"I hope so," Jack said. "And your name is . . . ?"

"Consetta Lazzara."

"You are very young," he said.

She smiled wryly. "I am old enough for what you require, Mr. Lear."

"What were you told I require?"

"Mr. Sullivan said you are depressed. You went to your grandfather's funeral today."

"Well, Consetta, if you dance for me, will you dance nude?"

She grinned. "Yes. I knew you'd want it that way."

She went to the radio and began to scan the stations for suitable music. She found it. She stripped off her clothes quickly—all but her black garter belt, dark stockings, and shiny black shoes—and began to dance, slowly and sinuously at first, then faster, tapping and whirling.

He was glad she hadn't brought castanets. Maybe she was wise enough to know they would damage the mood she meant to create. Her dancing was sensual; more than that, it was lascivious. Her chubby breasts bounced. So did her belly. She was conscious too of the erotic effect of showing off her round little bottom and from time to time bent forward to wiggle and flaunt it. She had the most generous bush of dark pubic hair he had ever seen. Except when she spread her legs as she danced, it hid her cleft completely.

She danced for maybe five minutes, then threw herself down on the couch, glistening faintly with sweat. "What do you want now, Mr. Lear?" she asked playfully.

"Guess."

He led her into the bedroom, where she lay down on her back on the bed with no embarrassment or hesitation. Totally aroused, he tugged off his clothes with an urgency that made her laugh. She laughed again and offered her nimble little hands to help him when he fumbled at drawing on his rubber. She pulled it on him with a dexterity that indicated she had done it before, more than once. In a moment he was on top of her, unable to delay himself. She grunted when he thrust in, but she did not complain. She closed her eyes and received his fervid strokes complaisantly, even as she shook under the impact of his ardor. He did not deceive himself that she enjoyed it as he did.

When he erupted, she sighed and put her arms around

him to draw him down on her. His weight did not seem to bother her. When he rolled off, she astonished him by pulling off his condom, putting it in a bedside ashtray, then cleaning his shaft with her lips and tongue.

They lay quietly together for a time. She whispered to him that she would be happy to take him again. He said sure, in a little while. He lit a Camel and offered it to her. She took it, and he lit another for himself.

"Do you do this regularly, Consetta?"

"Only with people like you," she said simply.

"Only with people like . . . what?"

"People who can help me."

Jack nodded as if he understood perfectly what she was talking about, but his mind rushed to discern her meaning. He groaned inwardly. Mickey had told this girl—maybe had even told her parents, who might know what she was doing—that Jack's brother was head man at Carlton House.

"You want to make it in the movies?" he asked her. "Is that it?"

"Yes. I think what I need is an opportunity."

"So you . . . And with others besides me."

"Like any girl who wants to make it in Hollywood," she said, as if it were common knowledge.

"Well, I'll see what I can do for you, Consetta. You understand that my chief interest is in radio. Do you sing?"

"I can sing."

"Maybe we'll get you a start that way."

"But it is the movies that I want more than anything. You understand?"

"Understood. Do you mind giving it to me with your mouth?"

"I know how to do that," she said simply.

Jack grinned. "Okay."

She did know how, for sure. Even though he had come only a few minutes before, he came quickly again. She fled to the bathroom to spit in the basin. When she came back, she stared at his cock and smiled and shook her head when she saw it was still erect.

They smoked two more cigarettes.

"How old are you, Consetta?"

"I'm not sure you want to know."

"Tell me."

"I'm sixteen," she said quietly.

"Ahh. Well, I'll do whatever I can for you. Some money, incidentally."

"No. I don't do it for money. I'm not a whore, Mr. Lear."

"Of course not. I didn't mean to suggest you were. But would you accept, say, a hundred dollars just because you've pleased me more than you had to?"

"Well . . ."

"Okay, then."

She dressed. "Mr. Lear," she said, "how much should I consent to?"

"What do you mean, Consetta?"

"Well, somebody wants me to have my eyebrows plucked. They want to kill the hair on the front of my head, to make my forehead higher. They want me to lose weight. And somebody has said that Consetta Lazzara is not the name of a girl who is going to make it big. Somebody says I ought to change my name."

"To what?"

"Well, I've heard several suggestions. One of them is that I should call myself Connie Lane." She said the name as if it were a magical charm.

Four

"CHANGE OF PLANS," Jack said to Mickey over dinner. "You can't come with me on the train to Boston tomorrow."

"Change your mind?"

"No. I offered you a deal, and the deal goes. But you've got to stay around here awhile. A week, two weeks. Whatever it takes you to get Consetta Lazzara a chance in pictures. Uh . . . I know. Turn her over to Mo Morris and tell him I sent her. After that, take the first train to Boston."

"What? Uh-oh. I get it. I guess I screwed up on that one, didn't I?"

"Mickey, I may call on you again sometime to get me

laid. But please understand that my standards are higher than my father's. No more sixteen-year-old girls. A man may get away with that in California, but in Massachusetts it can put him in the slammer."

"Sorry . . ."

"Right. On the other hand, Mick, she's got to be one of the best pieces of ass I ever had."

"I'll set her up with Mo Morris," said Mickey. "He's a hot agent. If anybody can get her into the movies, Mo can."

Five

KIMBERLY MET JACK at the station. Their car waited outside—a chauffeur-driven Duesenberg.

"I suppose I could wait until we get home before showing you this," she said. "But . . . page four."

Page four carried a modest headline:

RADIO EXEC AT GRANDFATHER'S FUNERAL

Below the headline was a three-column photograph, the one taken on the lawn outside the funeral chapel, showing Erich and his two sons. The caption read:

CALIFORNIA SALVAGE TYCOON ERICH LEAR IS FLANKED BY HIS TWO SONS, MOVIE PRODUCER ROBERT LEAR, PRESIDENT OF CARLTON HOUSE PRODUCTIONS, AND JACK LEAR, PRESIDENT OF BOSTON'S WCHS, ON JUNE 13, AT THE FUNERAL OF FAMILY PATRIARCH JOHANN LEHRER, WHO DIED TUESDAY IN LOS ANGELES.

The photograph showed conspicuously that all three men were wearing yarmulkes.

"Oh, shit," Jack muttered.

"My reaction entirely," said Kimberly.

SIX

One 1935

THE TODDLER, JOHN, was a handful for the nanny, who felt so overwhelmed that she told to Kimberly she was not sure she could continue in the job. Her major complaint was that the boy's demands made it all but impossible for her to give much attention to the little girl, Joan Edith.

She had been born two months after Jack returned from his grandfather's funeral, and Jack and Kimberly had wanted to honor Johann Lehrer in naming this child. Johann's wife had been named Shulamith, but Jack did not even suggest that name be given to his daughter. Kimberly pointed out that Johann was the German equivalent of John and that Joan was the feminine form of John, so their baby daughter was named Joan for Johann and Edith for Kimberly's mother.

Kimberly persuaded the nanny to stay with the family by telling her she would personally take more responsibility for Joan.

Jack had moved his offices. He needed more space, especially since Mickey Sullivan had arrived from California and was installed as a vice president of WCHS, Incorporated. Herb Morrill was also a vice president.

Since the corporation now owned WHFD, Hartford, as well as WCHS, Boston, the corporate name was incongruous; and Jack changed it to Lear Broadcasting, Incorporated.

He upset a great many people in Hartford—as well as Kimberly—by changing the programming schedule for

WHFD. Though it remained chiefly a classical-music station, he scheduled the piano playing of Wash Oliver for half an hour five evenings a week, the daytime drama *Our Little Family* five mornings a week, and Hartford's own medical quacks on the same terms he offered the Boston quacks—in other words, they paid for their airtime.

WHFD had lost money for years, which had enabled Jack to pick it up cheap, but within six months it was making a modest profit.

The Catholic Archdiocese of Boston asked for a Sunday morning hour to be filled with lectures and prayers. Jack gave them the hour, from nine till ten. Then the Council of Churches demanded an hour for Protestant services. Jack responded that he would be happy to sell them the hour from ten till eleven—and at a ministerial discount of 25 percent. The council was pleased and began to broadcast services live from various churches. Jack did not tell them the archdiocese got its time free. He did tell the suffragan it would be wise to keep their little secret.

With the settlement of the Johann Lehrer estate, Jack had another half million dollars to invest. He invested in two things. First, he applied for an amendment to the station license for WCHS, to authorize an increase in power that would make it one of the most powerful stations in New England. When he got the authority he bought the new transmitter. Next, he bought radio station WHPL in White Plains, New York.

As he'd done with the Hartford station, he made the White Plains station an outlet for the programming he developed for WCHS. With the two new stations, the piano playing of Wash Oliver was heard throughout New England and now in New York City, where it gained a devoted audience. Jack hired Oliver away from the whorehouse and made him a full-time musician for Lear Broadcasting. They recruited backup men: a guitar and drums, then also a banjo; and the Lear Broadcasting Quartet, starring Wash Oliver, played in roadhouses and dance pavilions all over New England. People came to hear the famous jazz pianist they had heard on the radio.

Similarly, housewives all over the region became addicted to the dramatic doings and soapy optimism of *Our*

Little Family. When the original Mama had to be replaced, the change was made so seamlessly that audiences seemed not to notice that a new actress was reading lines like "A family's love overcomes everything."

Regretting that he had renamed the Bronson Brothers the Mellow Fellows, Jack changed their names again, to the Minstrels. He dropped the Wisecrack Guys and built a new show around Betty, the malaprop comedienne, and the Minstrels. A professional staff supported Betty and fed her straight lines for her malaprops.

Some of Betty's lines—and she was still called simply Betty; no last name was ever suggested for her—became catchwords even beyond the area where she was heard. She pronounced the word breakfast "brake-fast," pronouncing it to reflect what it meant, breaking the overnight fast before starting the day's labors. Shortly, people all over New England, young people especially, were laughing and saying they wanted ham and "aigs" for "brake-fast."

Kimberly couldn't bear to listen. Jack couldn't either, but *The Betty and the Minstrels Show* was a moneymaker. Shortly it became *The Best Beauty Bar Show, Starring Betty and the Minstrels.*

Betty, however, was the subject of a dark secret: she was a Negro. From Huntington, West Virginia, she spoke with the accent of the Ohio Valley, naturally, saying "feesh" for fish and "deesh" for dish. Nothing in her accent suggested her race. Her show was broadcast and recorded from a closed studio. Even the Minstrels had never seen their star. A white actress was employed to slip in and out of the studio, and Betty came and went in the uniform of a maid.

Jack was immensely sympathetic to Betty's situation, but there was nothing he could do. Amos 'n Andy were successful as whites who pretended to be black, but America was not ready to listen to Negro comics.

Kimberly knew. She invited Betty and her husband Charles to dinner at the house on Louisburg Square. Betty's real name was Carolyn Blossom. Both she and her husband were the grandchildren of slaves. In the early 1920s they had come to Boston, thinking that the home of abolitionism could not be racist. They found it was.

Carolyn had made her way into radio by cutting records and submitting them by mail. A dozen times she had met broadcasters who were enthusiastic about her comedic talent—until they saw her. The maid uniforms she wore to slip in and out of WCHS were her own; she had worked in them for years.

Jack took the attitude that the money was more important than the principle. "Let's make a pisspot full of dough, kiddo," he said to Carolyn. "When your bank account's healthy, then's the time to make a point."

Two

IN JUNE, Jack went to White Plains to review the programming and management of WHPL. Since it was summertime, he had his chauffeur drive him there in the Duesenberg. It was something of an adventure, making their way down U.S. 1, the Boston Post Road, through Providence, New Haven, and the shoreline towns of the Connecticut Gold Coast.

Since he would be gone four days, Jack decided to take along a pleasant companion—the comely blond divorcée, Betsy Emerson.

A thick glass separated the driver's compartment from the passenger compartment, and during most of the trip Jack kept the blind lowered, so the chauffeur could neither see nor hear him and Betsy in the rear seat.

This made it possible for Jack to keep Betsy's skirt pulled up to the edge of her panties and to fondle her legs. The privacy made it possible, too, for her to fondle his crotch. They talked about many things, most of them funny, but after their lunch stop Betsy turned thoughtful.

"I thought about saying no to this invitation," she said soberly without lifting her hand from the stiff cock she was stroking through the fabric of his pants.

"I can think of one or two reasons why you might have said no. Which one bothered you?"

She brushed his cheek with a light kiss. "Kimberly. What we're doing to Kimberly."

Jack slipped his fingers inside her panties and ran them over her cunt. She was wet. "I thought seriously about not inviting you," he said. "For the same reason."

"And?"

He pulled his hand out of Betsy's panties. "What am I doing to Kimberly? Doesn't there come a time when I'm entitled to ask what's she doing to *me?*"

"And that's why you—"

"No, that's not why I invited you, not why I arrange to be with you whenever I can. I'm not *using* you, Betsy. I need you. I need to be close to a woman who doesn't think I'm . . . Well, doesn't think I'm . . . You know what I mean."

She ran her hand down his cheek and across his neck. "Is it that bad?"

"What do you think? You've seen . . ."

Betsy nodded emphatically. "I've seen. And heard. And it pisses me off!"

"It's worse when you can't see and hear. It's worse in private. I'm not a Wolcott. I'm not a Bayard. I'm the grandson of Johann Lehrer, who was a rabbi. Harrison Wolcott accepts that and doesn't scorn it. But Kimberly—"

Betsy interrupted. "The other evening she said to Connie and me that she guessed she never would be able to teach you to fold your pocket handkerchief right. 'He's got a certain capacity for the crude,' she said. 'No matter how hard I try, I can't entirely civilize him.' Connie agrees with me that she ought to be proud of you. You ought to fuck Connie, too. If Kimberly found out you were diddling both of us, that'd get to her."

"Why did she marry me, Bets?"

"I can think of two reasons. In the first place, Kimberly was always obsessed with the idea that some guy would marry her for her money—her father's money. When you came along, she knew she didn't have to worry about that, because you had money of your own. She even knew how much, Jack. At least she said she did. She told me you had half a million, all your own, plus more coming."

"She talked about that, huh?"

"But there's another reason, I think, why she married you. I don't know when she first got a look at, a feel of, the

Jack Lear schlong; but I have to suspect it was before the wedding. I mean, Jack, she wasn't a virgin. You didn't think she was, did you?"

He shook his head.

"She used to talk about sex. Girls talk about those things, but she talked about it more frankly than most. She said she wanted a peter that would go all the way up to her belly button."

"Well, she's got it," he said bitterly. "That's the one way I satisfy her."

"Jack. Why don't you get out of it?"

"Same reason as everybody else that's stuck with— I . . . Bets, I thought it was the *perfect* marriage. Kimberly's beautiful. She's smart. She's chic. Maybe a Jew from California did think he would move high in the world if he married Kimberly Bayard Wolcott. And, Christ—you should forgive the expression—I thought I was the cat who swallowed the canary. Trouble is, that's how she thinks of herself, too."

"I'm divorced, Jack."

"Yeah. But I've got two kids. Old, old story, no? People shouldn't have children until they've been married five years."

Three

THEY HAD A ROOM, not a suite, in a hotel in White Plains. It had a radio speaker above the door, and the radio was tuned to the station the hotel management had chosen. The first time Betsy switched it on, it blared in a crackly tone:

Where, oh, where
Has my little dog gone?
Where, oh, where can he be?
With his tail cut short and his ears cut long,
Oh, where, oh, where can he be?

Jack called the front desk and ordered a radio brought up. They said they didn't have one, and he told them to go out and buy a radio and charge it to his bill. Within an hour the radio was in place.

For a while before they went down to dinner, Jack and Betsy listened to WHPL. Then, while he took a bath, she tried some other stations, wanting to hear what might be coming in from New York City. When Jack came out of the bathroom, she was listening to a newscast from New York.

Jack frowned. Then his attention was caught by the measured cadence and mellifluous voice of a newscaster.

"Mr. Anthony Eden . . . British minister for League of Nations Affairs . . . arrived in Rome today for a series of meetings with Signor Mussolini. They are expected to confer at length on the situation in . . . Ethiopia. It is well known that Signor Mussolini hopes to add the Kingdom of Ethiopia to the Italian empire he wishes to build in Africa.

"Meanwhile, in Washington, President Roosevelt renewed his plea to Congress to move more quickly to pass the Social Security Bill. Calling it the most important legislation before Congress in this decade, he—"

"My God, listen to the man!" Jack exclaimed. "Who is he?"

They had to wait through the rest of the broadcast and through its commercials before they finally heard the newscaster say, "This has been Curtis . . . Frederick, reporting from New York. Good . . . night."

"Now, that's the way to read news! My God, Bets, compared to that staccato ass Walter Winchell, this man is . . . Well, he has dignity! God, what I'd give to get him to Boston!"

Four

JACK ASSIGNED Mickey Sullivan to find out all he could about Curtis Frederick. Mickey reported that Frederick had been a print journalist originally, starting at the Cleveland *Plain Dealer,* then had moved to New York, where he became a political writer for the *Herald Tribune.* When the newspaper decided to have its lead stories read on the air, it handed the assignment to Frederick because of his smooth baritone voice. Within six months he switched to the *Times* station, WQXR, because he felt it was more committed to quality newscasting. Mickey told Jack that it looked as if Curtis Frederick could be lured away to Boston.

Jack arranged to meet Frederick over dinner in a suite at the Waldorf. He chose a room-service dinner because he suspected the newscaster would not want to be seen in public with the owner of other radio stations.

For this meeting, Jack took Kimberly with him. Mickey Sullivan came, too, but he would not appear at the dinner.

"I may know something about Curtis Frederick that you don't know," Kimberly said as they were dressing.

"What is that?"

"Wait a minute," she said as she focused all her attention on snapping a strap from her garter belt to her stocking. "He was educated at Yale. Graduated in 1921. My friend Brit Lowery's husband graduated in 1922. I thought he might know this Frederick, so this afternoon I got her to introduce me to her husband, Walter Lowery. He does in fact know Frederick and still sees him occasionally."

"You never cease to amaze me," said Jack dryly.

"Perhaps because that's not terribly difficult to do, my dear. Anyway, Frederick is thirty-eight years old, which means he was exactly the right age to be drafted into the army in 1917—which he was."

"I knew that."

"Okay. The French liked him enough to award him the Croix de Guerre, and the Americans liked him enough to award him a Silver Star. He'd had two years at Yale before he was drafted, so he finished in two years after he was discharged."

"I knew all that."

"Then let me tell you something you don't know," Kimberly said with ice-cold precision. "Mr. Curtis Frederick is a *fairy!*"

"Kimberly—"

"He's kept his secret very well. If half a dozen people know it—"

"It's *despicable* that anyone should—"

"Boys who live in college dorms learn things about each other that no one else ever finds out."

Jack drew deeply from the Camel he was smoking.

"Jesus *Christ!* You say not half a dozen people know. If Lowery told *you*—"

"I explained the circumstances, that you were thinking of hiring Frederick and making him—"

Jack began to pace. "Well, what do I do now?"

"Hire him, if you want him."

He stopped in the center of the room and stared at her. "Five years from now my star newscaster—"

"If somebody finds out what nobody has found out in twenty years . . ."

Jack ground out his cigarette in an ashtray. "I don't even know what they *do,*" he muttered.

Kimberly grinned. "The hell you don't. You're not *that* naive. Anyway, five minutes ago you thought he was the best newscaster you ever heard."

"I can't hire him without mentioning it. And I don't know how to mention it."

"I'll take care of it," she said firmly.

Five

NOTHING ABOUT Curtis Frederick's appearance suggested that he was a homosexual. He was a rugged-looking man, with a long, strong face, great bushy black eyebrows, steady dark eyes, a craggy nose and jaw, and a wide mouth with thin lips.

After saying no to a Scotch and asking instead for a gin, he sat down and lit a Chesterfield from a slender sterling silver case. His superbly tailored black suit was single-breasted, which was unusual for that year, and his necktie was black and narrow. The man had style, and it was not the style of 1935.

"Well, Mr. Frederick," Jack said, "who is going to be elected President of the United States next year?"

"Franklin D. Roosevelt," Frederick said without hesitation, "will be reelected in a landslide."

"No chance it will be otherwise?"

Frederick shook his head. "No chance."

"You've met him?" Kimberly asked.

Frederick nodded. "Oh, yes. In 1921, for the first time. I wouldn't have predicted then that he'd ever be elected anything more than a congressman from the Hudson Valley."

"How well do you know him?" asked Jack.

"No one knows him," said Frederick. "The biggest mistake anyone can make in politics or journalism is to think he knows Franklin D. Roosevelt. His career is based on making certain that no one knows him."

"Then I take it you don't like him," said Kimberly.

"I like him very well—in the context of the men who might replace him. In that context, he's a giant among pygmies."

They had two more drinks before their dinner arrived. Jack had ordered the best the hotel offered: caviar, pheasant . . . He became aware, though, that Curtis Frederick was not impressed with the meal. He ate it and obviously enjoyed it, but it had been wrong to suppose a fine meal with fine wines would have any influence on his judgment.

"My WCHS broadcasts with greater power than WQXR," Jack said midway through the dinner.

"WLW in Cincinnati, 'the nation's station', broadcasts with even greater power," Frederick pointed out with a shrug. "But I wouldn't identify with WLW for a million dollars a year."

"Well, let's put it another way, then. What do you want from broadcasting?"

Frederick smiled at Kimberly, then at Jack. "I want the prestige of WQXR and the power of WLW or KDKA."

"I can't give you that much power," said Jack. "I approach it, but I don't have it yet. On the other hand, I'm syndicating. I have three stations and may have five or six in time. So far as prestige is concerned, a broadcaster *makes* it. You contribute to the prestige of WQXR. You can contribute to the prestige of WCHS and its affiliated stations. Is your broadcasting prestigious? Respected? That's up to you, my friend. If I sent you out on five times the power of WLW and you spieled trash, you'd just be delivering high-powered trash. The world of broadcasting is full of that."

"A *Boston* station?"

"We're not a clear-channel service, so-called. You can't hear us in Chicago or Atlanta. But you can tune in WCHS in Boston, Providence, New Haven, Hartford, Albany . . . We have some listeners in New York City. We'll have more. I plan to lease a telephone line, so some WCHS programming will go out simultaneously on WHPL. I suppose you have a following in New York. Those with good receivers can pick you up from Boston, but those with cheap radios will pick you up from White Plains."

"People are putting radios in their cars, you know," said Frederick. "A lot of businessmen listen to my morning news in their cars on their way to their offices."

"White Plains is twenty-five miles from Manhattan," said Jack. "Even radios in automobiles can pick up stations twenty-five miles away."

Curtis Frederick smiled. "Am I being rushed?" he asked in a tone of mock innocence.

"I am trying to establish a programming schedule that will mix entertainment with information in such a way that the stations will make money and still provide a public service. When I heard you for the first time, I decided you are the man I want to head my news department."

Frederick shook his head. "I'd make a poor department head, Mr. Lear. I'm a reporter and broadcaster. I couldn't administer a candy store. Don't want to."

"As head of my news department you'd do exactly what you're doing now. I'd want you to choose the stories to broadcast, then broadcast them."

"You understand," said Frederick, "that most of the news you hear on radio is taken from the papers or wire services. We don't send out reporters to get news for us—except occasionally."

Jack glanced at Kimberly, then took a sip of wine. "Suppose I hired an assistant for you. Suppose we sent him to Washington. Suppose we sent him to the political conventions next summer. Better yet, suppose we sent *you* to the conventions in Cleveland and Philadelphia and you broadcast directly from there."

"You make it all sound very interesting," Frederick replied.

"This will be a big decision for you," Jack said. "There are details to work out. I want us to get to know each other better. You used the word 'rush.' I am rushing you, in the sense of a fraternity rushing a prospective member. I do not want to rush you in the sense of asking you to hurry up and decide."

"Maybe you should come up to Boston for a weekend, or two or three weekends," Kimberly suggested.

"Yes. Maybe I should."

"And of course bring Mrs. Frederick," she added. "If there is a Mrs. Frederick."

Frederick didn't see Jack frown at Kimberly.

"I'm afraid there is no Mrs. Frederick. I've never been married."

"Uh-oh!" She laughed. "You'll be the cynosure of all eyes in Boston. I'll be able to introduce you to a dozen or more lovely women who'll want to know you—that is, if you don't mind."

Frederick shrugged. "That should be an interesting experience," he said.

SEVEN

One 1936

CURTIS FREDERICK joined Lear Broadcasting in 1936. He immediately brought prestige, but years would pass before he brought in revenue.

He was attracted by the academic community and leased an apartment in Cambridge, half a mile from Harvard Yard. His brother, Willard Frederick, came up from New York with him and rented a smaller apartment in a building across the street. Willard was working on a biography of William Lloyd Garrison, and the Boston libraries would be of immense help to him. Willard was a shy man who was easily flustered. Jack tried in vain not to dislike him.

Curtis Frederick was not at all disturbed by the Lears' unwillingness to include Willard in their circle of friends. "Willard," he said, "is his own sort of man and would not fit in. He has his interests and is very happy pursuing them."

As she had promised she would do, Kimberly found female companions for Frederick. He was gracious to them, seemed in fact to go out of his way to court them, and soon convinced Kimberly that the rumor about his sexual proclivities was probably unfounded.

Betsy sat down across the table from Jack in an Irish pub in Southie. She was angry.

"All right! You *let* this happen! You *let* it happen, goddammit!"

Jack shook his head. "Bets, I swear to you I had nothing to do with it. I didn't even know about it until you told me."

"What's she trying to pull?"

"Bets, I don't think Kimberly is trying to pull anything. When we talked about Curtis moving to Boston, she said she'd introduce him to some women. You're divorced. I think she innocently supposes the two of you might—"

"*She knows about you and me!* That's the point."

"No. She doesn't know about us. If she did, she'd—"

"Do you mean it? She doesn't know?"

"Bets . . . she doesn't guess. I'd know if she did. She's not capable of that much subtlety."

"So what do you want me to do?"

Jack shrugged. "Go out with the guy. Or don't if you don't want to. What harm could it do?"

"What if he tries to put the make on me?"

He glanced around the room, then put his hand on hers. "You can handle that, Bets. And how you handle it depends on your judgment at the time."

"You mean you wouldn't care if I let him?"

"I can't marry you, Bets. You know that. I can't give up John and Joan. I *can't!* If you find something good with somebody . . . Well, Curtis Frederick's a first-class guy."

Betsy lowered her chin and stared down at the table. "Thanks, Jack. . . . Oh, thanks one hell of a lot."

Two

KIMBERLY POURED TEA. She sat with Betsy—Mrs. Otis Emerson—in the living room of the house on Louisburg Square. She wore a beige linen dress embroidered in a floral pattern with green and red thread. In her movements, her clothes, her manner, she was the epitome of Boston elegance—meaning that she was strikingly beautiful, and precisely restrained by practiced dignity.

Betsy, not as beautiful but a handsome woman in everyone's estimation, was wearing black and was visibly uneasy. She was unsure as to why she had been invited to tea with Kimberly Lear.

"How long have we been friends, Betsy?"

"Years," said Betsy.

"Good friends," said Kimberly. "Such good friends that I'm going to ask you to do something I would never ask any other woman to do."

"Kimberly . . .?"

"A confidence."

"Yes . . ."

Kimberly handed Betsy a cup of tea. She offered tongs to use in selecting tiny squares of bread with butter or little cookies. "Curtis Frederick," she said. "I want you to tell me something about Curtis Frederick."

Betsy tried to conceal the relief she felt. "What do you want to know about him?" she asked.

"I am going to take you completely into my confidence," Kimberly explained, "and then ask you to take me completely into yours. And whatever we say will never be repeated. Okay?"

"Okay."

"Well, as you know, my husband has hired Curtis Frederick to be news director of the Lear stations. But there may be a damaging scandal in his background. You remember Brit Taylor? Brit Lowery? She married Walter Lowery."

"I remember her. She lives in New York now, I think."

"Exactly. Her husband was at Yale when Curtis Frederick was there. And her husband says Curtis was . . . well, you know. Queer."

"Queer? Meaning exactly . . . ?"

"A fairy. A homosexual. Since Jack trusts the man a great deal, I'm hoping it's not true. And that's why I'm intruding into your personal life. Ever since I introduced you to him, you've been seeing him. And not just occasionally. I thought you might know by now. Forgive my asking, but it's important to Jack, and it's important to me."

Betsy sipped tea and nibbled at bread and butter to gain a moment to compose herself. "There's only one way I could know, isn't there?"

Kimberly nodded. "Yes. And that's why you have to forgive me for asking."

"How could I tell?" Betsy asked. "Even one of those men can—"

"I think you could tell," said Kimberly firmly.

Betsy put down her teacup. "Okay, kiddo," she said. "If you want a personal confession, get me a gin; I'm not going to talk about my intimate life over a cup of tea."

Kimberly poured gin for Betsy and Scotch for herself. Each of them took a swallow. Then they faced each other.

"What do you want to know?"

Kimberly half grinned and shook her head. "Well, what's obvious. Does he? Do you?"

Betsy nodded. "Yes. Twice."

"And he *does it?* I mean, does he like it?"

Betsy laughed. "Ha! I judge he likes it all right. I mean, can a man fake a hard-on?"

"Is he . . . well equipped?"

"I haven't much basis for comparison, Betsy. Compared to my ex-husband, he . . . compares very well."

"Is he comfortable with things?"

"Yes. He does what a man is supposed to do. With enthusiasm. To put it crudely, once he's in the saddle he's a real cowboy."

"Then you'd judge he's not—"

"That's right. I'd judge he's not. The fourth time we went to dinner together, he asked me if I'd like to stop at his apartment for a nightcap. I knew what that meant, of course. But I thought, well, what the hell? If I was going to . . . resume that sort of thing, why not with Curt Frederick? What's wrong with him? So I went to his apartment with him."

"And he—"

"We had one drink, and then he very straightforwardly asked me if I'd go to bed with him."

"Straightforwardly."

Betsy smiled. "I'd guess he'd been thinking about, probably rehearsed in his mind, how he'd ask me, and then decided to just come out with it, bluntly. If he'd started groping at me, I think I'd have been offended. But he simply asked me. The way he put it was 'Do you think you'd enjoy going to bed with me? Could you possibly enjoy it as much as I would?' "

"And you said yes."

"I said I might. We went into his bedroom. He undressed me, then undressed himself. He suggested we take a shower together. He said that was a wonderful way for two people to get acquainted. And it was. He soaped me, and I soaped him. You can't be shy about each other after you've run your hands all over each other that way. I played with him, and he climaxed. I said, 'Uh-oh,' and he said not to worry, he could do it again. And he could, too. Twice more. Then the next time we were together was at my house. I don't have a shower, but we sat in the tub together." Betsy grinned. "We got so excited we damn near drowned."

"What's developing here?" Kimberly asked, a bit taken aback.

"We'll see, hmm?" Betsy mused before downing the rest of her gin.

Three

CURTIS FREDERICK broadcast live interviews and reports from the Republican National Convention in Cleveland and the Democratic National Convention in Philadelphia. The NBC network offered coverage too, but Frederick concentrated on the New England and New York delegations and offered politicians a chance to be heard on the radio back in their hometowns—an opportunity they eagerly grabbed. To win his attention, some of the politicians brought him useful information. An experienced journalist, he knew when to attribute and when not to attribute—when to say "Mr. So-and-so tells me" and when to say "A reliable source tells me."

His deep voice, his vocabulary, his restrained cadence, and his selection of stories to cover made him a voice of calm authority in contrast to the near-hysterical jabbering of a broadcaster like Walter Winchell. Curtis Frederick was not the most popular broadcaster who reached his region, but he was the broadcaster educated people tuned to when they wanted information.

Betsy accompanied him to Philadelphia. When they returned, they announced that they intended to be married immediately after the election.

The *Literary Digest* took a mail-in poll and announced

that Governor Alfred M. Landon would defeat President Franklin D. Roosevelt in a landslide. Curtis Frederick did not say so on the air, but he told Jack he remained confident that the result would be exactly the opposite of what the poll indicated. Jack respected his judgment and told Kimberly and her father, among others, to expect a second term for the New Deal President.

On the eve of the election, Jack stood at the bar of the Common Club with his father-in-law Harrison Wolcott. They had listened to the evening news broadcast by Curtis Frederick in the radio room, a private room on the third floor where the sounds of the radio would not disturb other members. When Frederick went off the air, they went to the bar. He would join them there as soon as he could.

"I have not entirely lost my optimism," Wolcott said to Jack. "I simply have to believe that a man who has the support of probably seventy-five percent of the nation's newspapers stands a good chance of being elected."

"The problem is," said Jack, "that newspapers are themselves big businesses. The men who own them are capitalists."

Frederick arrived twenty minutes after the end of his broadcast. Jack and his father-in-law still wore white tie in the club, though most members now wore business suits at the bar, as did Frederick.

"This is an interesting bar," he said. "I've been a guest here before—in 1928, I think it was. I wondered if the club wouldn't move the bar downstairs again after the repeal of Prohibition."

"We got used to having it on the second floor," said Wolcott. "And you know how it is in Boston—if you get used to something it becomes a tradition. But tell me, Mr. Frederick, why are you so sure Mr. Roosevelt will be reelected? A lot of respected journalists don't think so."

Frederick asked the bartender for a gin on the rocks. "Well," he said to Wolcott, "I think we would agree that William Allen White is about as respected a journalist as we have. The North American Newspaper Alliance wired him a request to write a story they could run if Landon is elected. White wired back, 'You have a quaint sense of humor.' "

Two days after the election, Curtis Frederick married

Mrs. Otis Emerson, who was happy to escape what she called "that odious appellation." Frederick moved into her house in Boston. His brother Willard took over his apartment in Cambridge.

Four 1937

LEAR BROADCASTING was on the lookout for new stations. One became available in New Haven, as did another in Stamford, Connecticut; but Jack was not interested in them because his stations in Boston, Hartford, and White Plains already covered their broadcast area.

During his visit to Cleveland for the Republican Convention, Curtis Frederick had renewed his friendship with the editors and reporters for the *Plain Dealer,* and one of them told him that Cleveland station WOER might be available if someone offered the right price. Jack hurried to Cleveland, appraised the opportunity and liked it, then returned to Boston and borrowed part of the money he needed to buy the station. He experienced some difficulty leasing the telephone line he needed to introduce the Midwest to the newscasting of Curtis Frederick and to *The Best Beauty Bar Show, Starring Betty and the Minstrels,* but he ultimately succeeded in leasing it and then used it also to introduce the East Coast to the music of the Cleveland Symphony.

From this point on, Curtis Frederick reported no local news stories unless they were of national interest. His broadcasts had to be as interesting to listeners in Cleveland as they were to the audiences in Boston and New York.

Five

KIMBERLY BEGAN to insist that Jack smoke his Camels in holders, the way President Roosevelt did. Holding them between his fingers was staining his fingers yellow, which was boorish, she claimed. She scrubbed his fingers with a brush and Fels

Naptha soap until she took off the yellowed skin, then presented him with a black cigarette holder trimmed with silver bands. He felt effete smoking with it but used it in her presence. When she was not around, he held his cigarette in his left hand or between his thumb and third finger, switching it around to avoid staining his fingers.

Connie Horan laughed at him.

"So she's teaching you how to smoke! How long have you been smoking—fifteen years? I'm surprised she lets you smoke Camels. They are rather blue-collar, you know. I'm surprised she doesn't demand you switch to Tareytons or Pall Malls."

Curt's brother had gone to New York for a week, so Jack and Connie were taking advantage of his absence to meet in his apartment.

Sitting on a red plush couch, dressed this afternoon in a lime-green silk dress that clung to her voluptuous figure, and smoking her own cigarette, Connie looked, as usual, as if she were posing for a photographer.

Jack stood looking out the window. He had brought a bottle of Johnnie Walker Black, and both of them had glasses with two fingers of Scotch in the bottom.

Jack left the window and sat down beside Connie. He crushed his cigarette in the ashtray on the coffee table. "You're just about the only woman I ever really wanted that" —He stopped and shook his head—"that I couldn't—"

"Why, Mr. Lear, you have overcome my virtue already," she said, batting her eyes and mimicking the accent used by the heroine of the novel everyone was reading, *Gone With the Wind*.

He put his arm around her and kissed her on the side of her neck. "Connie . . ."

"Jack . . ."

With his right hand he gently turned her face toward him and kissed her ardently on the mouth. Then he put his hand on her left breast.

"No, Jack. No."

He sighed. "Connie, why do you come here with me if you won't let me touch you?"

"I like you very much. But we can't go as far as— As far

as you want to go. I'm a married woman in love with my husband. I'm the mother of three children and may in fact be pregnant right now."

"That would solve one problem," he suggested quietly.

"What?"

"Well. If you're pregnant already—"

"Jack!"

"Well?"

She lifted her chin high. "I think of myself as having *some* morals. I'm Catholic, you know. There are certain things that— Certain things that I don't do."

"Will it help if I tell you I love you?"

Connie shook her head. "No. That makes it worse. And what about Kimberly?"

"Kimberly makes life more and more difficult for me. You know. The way I smoke, the way I dress, the way I eat, the way I talk—"

"Even so, do you still love her?"

Jack hesitated, then nodded.

"You can't love more than one person at a time," said Connie.

"Who made *that* a rule? I can. And do."

She took her cigarette case from her purse, but Jack reached out and restrained her hand. He kissed her again.

"My husband would kill us both. And God knows what Kimberly would do."

"They don't have to find out. I'll never ask you to take risks."

She sighed heavily. "I'll have to think about it. We can come again Thursday. By then I will have made up my mind."

Six

UNSURE OF WHAT Connie's decision would be, Jack nevertheless stopped by the Cambridge apartment the following Thursday morning and put a magnum of Piper-Heidsieck in the refrigerator. He returned at two that afternoon, not even certain she would come.

She did.

She was superbly beautiful. Today she was wearing an off-white knit dress trimmed with narrow blue and violet stripes at the neckline, the wrists, and the hemline. Her matching tiny hat sat on the back of her head like a yarmulke.

He seized her at the door and kissed her before she was inside. The way she yielded to his kiss told him what her decision was.

"I love you, Connie."

"I love you too, Jack."

She let him undress her before he poured the Piper-Heidsieck. He was surprised. The body beneath the corset that confined and shaped her was fleshier than he had imagined. Her flesh was lush. Her breasts, belly, hips, and tush were generously rounded. She sat on the red plush couch, naked, and drank champagne from a water glass.

They did not speak. They had nothing to say. He saluted her with his glass. He bent forward to kiss her breasts. She winced when his tongue caressed her nipples. He drew as much of one breast into his mouth as he could and sucked on it gently. She gasped.

With his hands he urged her to spread her legs. He wet his fingers on her juices and stroked her clitoris. Connie shrieked.

He discovered to his surprise that Connie was hesitant about touching his penis. When he led her hand to it, she pulled back. This twenty-seven-year-old woman, mother of three, was acting like a virgin. With calm, quiet insistence he brought her hand to his inner thigh and tried to guide it to touch his penis.

She resisted. "That's a circumcised penis, isn't it? Does that make them bigger, Jack? Dan's is nothing like that. His is the only one I've ever seen, and it doesn't look anything like yours. Don't ask me to touch it."

"For God's sake, Connie. You must have—"

"No," she whispered. "Why would I . . . touch it? *He* manipulates *that*."

She was fascinated just the same. Finally she let him guide her hand to his cock, and she ran her fingers over his shaft from root to tip. She lifted his scrotum and discovered his testicles. Her eyes widened. She closed her hand around his penis and tightened her grip gently.

"Connie! Oh, God, Connie!"

He slipped his middle finger up and down inside her wet cleft, stimulating her clitoris.

She began to cry. "We're not supposed to—"

"Connie!"

"Either I'm committing a great sin," she said hoarsely, "or a greater one has been committed against me."

"Are you telling me you've never enjoyed it?"

She shook her head. "I'm not supposed to."

"Bullshit," said Jack. "Feel this!" He ran his finger around her clitoris. *"Feel it!"*

"Oh . . . do it, Jack! Do it! Come inside me!"

He grabbed for a packaged condom and unwrapped it.

"No!" she blurted. "I'll do it, but not with that! Not with that!"

He put the condom aside.

She turned over on her back, spread her legs, and whispered, "Trump my ace, partner."

EIGHT

One 1938

On March 12 the German army marched into Austria, and Hitler proclaimed Austria a new province of the German Reich. On March 14 he was driven on a triumphal progress through the streets of Vienna.

On March 19, Curtis Frederick arrived in Vienna, where he witnessed the persecution of Jews. He saw Jewish businessmen scrubbing sidewalks and sweeping the gutters, and he learned from reliable sources that many Jews had disappeared into what the world had learned to call concentration camps. Curt reported none of this in the wires he sent to Boston. He knew the Germans read every wire that left Vienna, and he kept silent about the atrocities, lest they decide he was an enemy of the Reich. Others were doing that. He had another idea in mind.

He traveled to Berlin. There he contacted Ernst Bauer, a journalist he had known in the past who was now an undersecretary in the Ministry of Propaganda. He suggested to Bauer that Americans were interested in the *Reichskanzler* but knew almost nothing about him. He proposed an interview with the Chancellor, to be broadcast live to the United States.

After a few days Curt got his answer. Because of difficulties in translation and in scheduling, the Führer could not possibly sit down for an interview with Herr Frederick. He would, however, consent to the broadcast to the United States of an interview he had recently given to a German journalist, for which the ministry would supply a translation.

Curt proposed that the interview be sent out over a powerful shortwave station operated by Norddeutsche Rundfunk. It would be picked up by a sophisticated shortwave receiving station on Cape Cod and sent by leased telephone lines to Boston and the other cities served by Lear Broadcasting.

The Ministry of Propaganda accepted that proposal, and Bauer delivered two big disks to the station. The broadcast began at two in the morning with a brief explanation by Curtis Frederick of how the event had been arranged. Then the interview began. At first the dialogue was in German, followed by the translation. After a while the translation became a voice-over, with the interpreter speaking in the foreground and the voice of Hitler in the background.

Curt suspected that the whole performance had been specifically made for this broadcast. The shortwave transmission distorted the voices slightly, but that served only to lend the broadcast unique drama. Hitler spoke in a quiet, persuasive voice.

The German consulate in New York wired Berlin within minutes after the interview was aired, saying that the program had been clearly heard in America and was a complete success. Fifteen newspapers editorialized to the effect that "When Herr Hitler is heard in person, his comments unfiltered by journalistic prejudices, he makes a case in which Americans can generally believe, though we might not be ready to accept every element of his reasoning."

Now Curtis Frederick went to Ernst Bauer with another proposition. Why not do a live broadcast of one of the *Reichskanzler*'s speeches? Most Americans would not be able to understand it until after it had been translated, but many Americans did understand German, and those who didn't would catch the tone of the oratory. To Curt's amazement, the Ministry of Propaganda agreed. Three weeks after the quiet-and-persuasive interview, Americans heard the German Führer haranguing a crowd in the Sportspalast. This was a very different Hitler, screaming into his microphones. Americans also heard thousands of his followers yelling "Heil!"

The Nazis seemed to have no idea they had been gulled.

When Betsy arrived in Berlin to spend two weeks with Curt, Ernst Bauer invited the couple to a candlelight dinner in a private dining room at the Ministry of Propaganda. After the dinner, Bauer presented them with two autographed photographs of Adolf Hitler, one addressed to Curtis Frederick and one to Jack Lear. Apparently no one in Berlin guessed that Jack Lear was a Jew.

Two

In July Jack received word that a Los Angeles radio station was for sale. He made his second flight to the West Coast, this time in a DC-3, and was so comfortable with the experience that he decided to fly back as well.

He could not buy the station because his brother, who had never before expressed any interest in radio, had bought it while Jack was en route. Robert's motive was all too obvious: over lunch with Jack and their father, Bob offered to sell him the station. Jack told him he'd paid far too much for it. For that reason as well as because he knew nothing about running a radio station, he would lose a lot of money on it.

Erich just shook his head as he watched Jack eat a shrimp cocktail and said he obviously didn't care *what* he ate.

Dinner that evening was far more pleasant. Jack had arranged a room-service dinner in his suite and had invited Mo Morris and his client Connie Lane—the Consetta Lazzara who had danced nude for him four years before. She was twenty now and was modestly successful in pictures. After dinner she told Jack she'd stay if he wanted her. He did.

On the return flight the airliner made an unscheduled landing at Omaha. The pilot explained that just to the east a line of thunderstorms extending hundreds of miles north and south had stalled instead of continuing to move east as expected. As the passengers waited uncomfortably in the airport terminal building, from time to time the pilot visited them and explained what the storms were doing.

Jack was fascinated. He caught up with the pilot before he left the room and asked if he could talk to him.

"About what, sir?"

"About the weather. About how you know so much about the weather."

"Well, sir, we have to know. We don't want to fly into dangerous conditions."

"But how do you get the information? You seem to know exactly where the storms are and what they are doing. I own a string of radio stations, and I'd like to be able to give my listeners that kind of detailed weather information. All we get from the Weather Bureau is that it's going to be warmer or cooler and that it might rain or snow."

"We couldn't fly with information no better than that," the pilot replied. "Come with me, and I'll show you the operations room where we get our weather briefings."

For the first time in his life, Jack saw a weather map. The young pilot explained to him the nature and significance of highs and lows, cold fronts and warm fronts. He pointed out isobars and isotherms and explained the other symbols on the map. A Teletype chattered, bringing in detailed weather reports from all over the nation.

"What's the *source* of all this information?"

"We do use the Weather Bureau reports. That's what's coming in on the Teletype. But the Bureau does not make complete forecasts, and a lot of their information is not current. There are weather instruments on every airport—barometers, thermometers, wind gauges—so we know what conditions are on every airport. Pilots and airlines share the information. If I hit turbulence I didn't expect or see a thunderstorm building where none was reported, I radio that information. Other pilots hear it. Of course, the boys here assemble as much information as they can get and draw these weather maps. If you know how to read them, you can pretty much figure out what the weather is going to do."

Back in Boston, Jack checked with the newspapers. Not all of them bothered to publish weather information. Those that did ran only the general information that the Weather Bureau provided. He went to the airport. There he found a weather station with even more detailed information than they'd had in Omaha.

He sent a memo ordering each of his station directors to visit his local airport, make a deal to get detailed weather information regularly, and broadcast the forecasts several times a day—in fact, every hour.

On September 20, the day before the century's most destructive hurricane struck New England and killed seven hundred people, the newspaper weather forecasts read, "Cooler, rainy tomorrow." Only the Lear stations broadcast a warning of the powerful storm racing toward Connecticut and Massachusetts.

The Lear stations were the first to broadcast weather forecasts that predicted the temperature, the amount of rain that would fall, and the time of day it was most likely to occur. The forecasts often proved wrong and became the butt of jokes. Even so, other stations followed suit, and shortly the newspapers began to publish the same kind of forecasts.

Three

JACK MET with Solomon Weisman in a small restaurant in Cambridge, a place frequented by members of the Harvard faculty. They sat in a booth of heavy dark wood with seats upholstered in red leather.

The owner of six shoe stores in the Boston area, Weisman was an active member of B'nai B'rith and was often its spokesman. He was a big, solidly built man, perhaps ten years older than Jack, whose black curly hair was beginning to thin out.

After they had saluted each other with their glasses and taken their first swallows of Scotch, Weisman spoke gravely to Jack. "Your grandfather Johann Lehrer was a professor of rational and revealed religion at the University of Berlin. He left Germany in 1888 because he didn't want to serve in the German army."

"I know all that," said Jack.

"Something you did not know, maybe, is that he had three brothers and a sister. None of them left Germany. You have an extended family of great-uncles, second cousins, and so on."

"I do know, in part. My grandfather exchanged letters

with some of them. I recall his saying he urged them to leave Germany. But they wouldn't. It was where they had their homes and businesses. Anyway, what are you driving at?"

Solomon Weisman smiled and nodded. "Let me come to that point by point," he said. "Did you know that a second-cousin of yours was murdered on *Kristallnacht?"*

"The Night of the Broken Glass. No—"

"Three other second cousins were arrested. We talk about people 'disappearing.' Your three cousins have disappeared."

"My God! I don't know these people. Except that they exist, I know nothing about them. But . . . of course there was nothing I could have done about it, even if I had known. There's nothing I can do now, about the ones who were arrested. Is there?"

Solomon Weisman shook his head. "There is nothing you can do about it. Except . . . except this, which is why I asked to meet with you. The more prominent Jewish businessmen affiliate with B'nai B'rith, the more effective we can be. All we can do now is try to make the world know what is going on in Germany, and seek help. You and your radio stations could do a lot. You've already done something by broadcasting the Hitler speech. You can do more."

Jack wrapped his hands around his glass of Scotch and stared into it for a long moment. "Mr. Weisman," he said quietly, "I have never denied I am a Jew. I am sympathetic with your cause—"

"Our cause."

Jack hesitated briefly, then nodded. "All right, *our* cause. I think I can do more to help it if I am not publicly identified with it."

"You don't want to be known as a Jew."

"I don't want to advertise that I am a Jew."

Weisman nodded. "I understand. Many feel that way. It has always been so."

Jack stared into Weisman's eyes. "If the Nazis had understood that Lear Broadcasting is Jewish-owned, they would never have consented to our broadcasting one of Hitler's harangues."

"I suppose you have a point."

"I may find other opportunities to inform the American public of what is going on in Germany. In fact, you can bring information to my attention. But even in this country, if my company is identified as a Jewish broadcasting company, what we put on the air will be less effective."

"The *New York Times* is known as a Jewish newspaper but nonetheless is quite effective."

"Not everywhere," said Jack. "In some parts of the country it is suspect."

"Well . . . I believe my effort to recruit a member has been rejected."

"Let's not put it so harshly. You put me on a hell of a spot. I'm serious when I tell you I'll broadcast information about Nazi persecutions. You hand me facts, and I'll broadcast those facts. Hand them to the other stations, too, and we'll see who uses more of them. Also, when I go back to my office I'll send you a check for a thousand dollars. I'll give B'nai B'rith at least a thousand a year from now on."

"That's generous," Weisman conceded. "I think we understand each other. You even arranged to meet me where none of your friends or associates would see us together. Didn't you?"

Jack flushed. "I . . . I wish I could deny it," he said. "I'm deeply embarrassed. No. Make that 'ashamed.' That's what I am: ashamed."

"So," said Solomon Weisman. "We really don't have to have lunch. If you can do more for us by not being identified with us, so be it."

"Identification would be counterproductive," Jack said quietly.

Four

JACK FOUND IT DIFFICULT to carry on his love affair with Connie Horan. She could not—or would not—arrange to see him more than once a month or so. Because she was practicing the rhythm method in hope of avoiding conception, she could see him only on those days when she was infertile—or so she hoped. She knew for a certainty that rubbers were sinful. When he offered to slip one on to be sure she would not conceive, she recoiled in horror.

"I've really fought with myself over this one," she told him one afternoon as she ran her tongue from the back of his scrotum to the tip of his cock. "I can't— I can't ask anyone for advice. Do you know what sophistry is? I've reached a conclusion that it's not a sin for me to lick you, so long as I don't take you inside my mouth. I mean, licking is affection, but—"

"Okay, baby. Okay."

He understood by now that she was willing to lick him for up to an hour at a time, running her tongue also over his belly and hips and even his backside. Unless he misunderstood her sighs and murmuring, she had developed a fondness for it. She would lick until her mouth became dry, when she would moisten it by sipping tomato juice laced with gin. This she could do at any time of month, and after a while she came to prefer it over letting him enter her and risking pregnancy.

"We're not risking pregnancy, and we're not doing anything to prevent it, either," she explained.

He decided to let her lick and not to point out the weaknesses in her rationalization. He was afraid that if she thought any more carefully about what they were doing, she might reach conclusions he would deplore.

"Connie honey, if I washed the old backside thoroughly with soap and water, would you run your tongue in there?"

"Well, I suppose I could try it. If it doesn't gag me. I do want to show you how much I care for you."

When he returned from the bathroom, she took a big sip of tomato juice and gin. Tentatively at first, she experimented with running her tongue into the crack of his anus. He grunted. The sensations were exquisite but short of orgasmic.

"So . . ." she muttered. "Well—"

She pressed her face hard against his backside and ran her tongue as far as she could make it reach.

"Ohh . . . *baby!*"

Connie pulled back and laughed. "You like, hmm. Okay. We can do *this* anytime you want."

Jack realized he had a serious problem on his hands. He had begun to care for Connie Horan.

Five

KIMBERLY, AT THIRTY-ONE, was if anything more ardent than ever. Having decided, though, that two children were enough, she announced her intention to undergo a tubal ligation. Jack expressed his unhappiness with the plan, but she said it was her choice to make. She made it, and the surgery was performed in the autumn.

Maybe relief from her anxiety about getting pregnant released new energy and imagination in Kimberly. She began to suggest to Jack that they become more adventuresome and conduct experiments in eroticism.

She kept a small library in the sitting room off their bedroom, where her books would not be seen by guests. For the first six years of their marriage Jack had paid little attention to the books she kept there. But, after her operation, when Kimberly told him that these books had whetted her appetite for sexual experimentation, Jack took a look at them. Somehow she had managed to import from France the forbidden Henry Miller novel, *Tropic of Cancer.* It had to have arrived hidden in someone's luggage; otherwise it would have been seized by Customs. Next there appeared on her shelves a scandalous eighteenth-century novel called *Memoirs of a Woman of Pleasure*—the notorious *Fanny Hill*—by John Cleland, first published in 1749. Then appeared a multivolume erotic autobiography, published in the nineteenth century, called *My Secret Life.* Jack was astonished to learn that his wife was reading these books; and of course he read them himself, to find out what was in them.

Then came something more interesting and influential —the *Kama Sutra,* a Hindu sex manual that described the pleasures of activities Jack would never have imagined could be pleasurable, such as biting and scratching.

One evening early in December Kimberly invited him to go to bed early. She switched on the bedside lamps and sprinkled cologne on the sheets. It was apparent that she had no intention of going to sleep. Their lovemaking was nothing unusual at first; then suddenly it turned extremely unusual. He was straddling her, and she had wrapped her legs around his back—one of her favorite positions. With her eyes wide open, she stared at his face. He reached his orgasm. As the first violent paroxysm shot his fluid into her, she ran her fingernails down his back, scratching him painfully. As long as his spasms continued, she scratched him. He knew she was drawing blood. He might have protested. But he couldn't. The pain on his back intensified the rapture in his loins. He experienced more spasms than he had ever experienced before. They exhausted him.

"Hmm, lover?" she whispered when he lay flat on top of her.

"God, Kimberly!" he exclaimed as he rolled off.

"The greatest you ever had, wasn't it?"

"Yes, but—"

"I know. We can't do it again. If you'd known what was going to happen, you couldn't have come. But aren't you glad you had it that way once?"

He lifted himself to kiss her breast. He sat up and looked at the sheet under him. It was stained with his blood. She rubbed his back with alcohol. It stung terribly, but somehow even that was vaguely stimulating and caused him to regain his erection.

Three nights later when he was on top of her and thrusting, she opened her mouth wide and whispered, "Slap me!"

Before, he would not have done it, but now he knew she meant it, and he slapped her cheek.

"Harder, for Christ's sake!"

He slapped hard. Her head jerked under the impact.

"*Again!* And keep it up till I tell you to stop."

Her head snapped from side to side as he hit her with the palm of his hand, first on one cheek and then on the other. She began to writhe and squirm and moan. Then suddenly she reached up and drew him down on herself, pinning his arms so he could not slap anymore. Her eyes were brittle with elation.

In the bathroom a little later she spit blood. Her teeth had cut the insides of her cheeks. Outside they glowed pink.

When he woke in the morning she was already out of bed. He found her in the bathroom, carefully applying makeup to cover the red marks on her cheeks. Her lips were a little swollen, but like an artist, she used lipstick to disguise the gleaming swelling.

He drew a deep breath. "Well, don't expect me to say I'm sorry. You wanted it. Harder and more."

Her words were a little slurred by her swollen lips. "I can take more than this. And you better be able to give it!"

NINE

One 1939

IN 1939, WHEN JACK was thirty-three years old, Kimberly arranged for him to be photographed in his office. She attended the photography session to make certain Jack Lear appeared as she wanted him to appear: as a distinguished young businessman on the rise, self-confident and handsomely dressed in a handsome office.

She chose the suit he would wear, a dark gray with a faint white pinstripe, double-breasted but tailored with narrower lapels and softer shoulders than the typical double-breasted suit of 1939. In some of the shots he held a cigarette between two fingers, not in a holder, which he insisted was an affectation.

She had refurnished his office not long before, in anticipation of these photographs. The yellow-oak desk that had suited him for years was gone, replaced by an ornately carved mahogany desk. All of the usual clutter had been removed. Sitting on the gleaming mahogany desktop were an onyx pen-and-pencil stand, a deep marble ashtray, and a microphone bearing the letters WCHS. On a credenza behind his desk stood three gleaming trophies he had won at bridge. For some of the photographs he did not sit at his desk but stood in front of green velvet drapes. In a few of those shots he was holding an Old-Fashioned glass filled with ice and what looked like whiskey but was actually tea.

Kimberly chose one of the color prints submitted by

the photographer and turned it over to a painter from Maine, who produced a portrait that she hung in the library of the house on Louisburg Square.

The painting did not flatter Jack. It looked exactly like him. He had given up on trying to comb his thinning hair to cover his widow's peaks; they were there, and he could only hope his hair would recede no further. His eyelids had developed a tendency to droop, giving him a sleepy-eyed look. His mouth in repose still settled into a natural smile, but he had developed a small second chin.

A caricature of him in *Fortune* magazine provided a more insightful likeness. It portrayed him smiling as if at some private joke, with sly, shrewdly appraising eyes.

The caption identified him as "Radio mini-tycoon, Boston-based owner of seven radio stations." The brief profile identified him as "the elder son of Erich Lear, a man who has hugely augmented the family fortune by buying and breaking up for scrap some of the world's finest old liners. Jack is apparently something of a chip off the old block. Owners of small East Coast radio stations hope he will not take notice of them, for what he covets he seems invariably to get."

When Jack decided he wanted an outlet in Washington, he sent Mickey Sullivan to scout the ground. Sullivan reported that WDIS, a Negro-owned station that broadcast chiefly to the Negro population of the city, had borrowed heavily to upgrade its power and studio facilities and was having difficulty making payments on its notes. The owners took great pride in the station, and it was not for sale. But its notes were. Jack bought them for eighty cents on the dollar from the D.C. bank that had made the loans. Then he sued the station to collect. Within five months after he'd identified the station, it was his. He kept its management, for the most part, but drastically changed its programming.

He acquired his Philadelphia station by hiring a score of Philadelphians to complain to the Federal Communications Commission that the station did not broadcast in the public interest. Then he retained lawyers to argue the point before the Commission. The FCC did not renew the station's license, and Lear Broadcasting applied for it and won it. Then of course he bought the station's facilities at a distress price.

His reputation for sharp dealing—dealing like a Jew, she called it to her father—troubled Kimberly. It was not the image she wanted to share.

Two

THAT SUMMER Kimberly leased a house on the Cape. It was across the road from a beachfront house her parents owned. The Lear children spent their summer on the beach, closely watched by their grandmother Edith.

Cecily Camden, the nanny, did not go with them. She said Great Britain would be at war before the end of the year and she had to go home to help her family with what she was certain would be a horrible ordeal. She stayed in the house on Louisburg Square for three weeks after Kimberly and the children moved to the Cape, which made it possible for Jack to take her to bed more often and for longer, more satisfying times than they had ever had before.

Because they were alone in the house, Cecily could strip naked for Jack, which she had never dared to do before. She loved the needle shower, and they made love in it half a dozen times.

"I thought you wanted to stay in this country."

"I had that in mind," she said blandly.

"You're twenty-nine years old. I know you don't want to be a nanny all your life. I thought that when the kids were a little older I'd offer you a job with the broadcasting company. Also, I could sponsor you for citizenship."

"I wouldn't need a sponsor. I could pass the test. And I've been here long enough."

"Well, then maybe you should change your mind. I could give you a job right now."

"There's another little problem," she said quietly.

"What's that?"

She smiled and kissed him on the neck. "Don't you know, really? You're not that insensitive. You know I'm in love with you. I mean, do you think I'd let you screw me just because I worked for you? Do you think so little of me?"

Jack drew a deep breath. "Well," he said, "all the more

reason for you to stay. I'll set you up in a job that will make it possible for us to be together often."

"And I'll be your mistress while you stay married to Missus? No, Jack, I don't think so. Anyway, I really feel I ought to be home, seeing what's coming."

He drew her into his arms. He realized now that he had not sufficiently appreciated this simple girl. "Cecily . . . I'm going to miss you. What can I do for you, say, as a going-away present?"

"Well . . . you can give me three hundred dollars."

"Three hundred? Okay. But why three hundred, exactly?"

She stared into his face for a moment, then lowered her eyes. "That's what it cost me to have your baby taken out of me before it was too late. I got a good doctor to do it, and I had to pay him three hundred dollars—just about everything I had saved."

"Why didn't you tell me? I'd have paid for it."

"You might have tried to talk me out of having it done. And . . . well, you might have decided you didn't want to risk having me again. And I looked forward to those times. I remember every time we did it, every single time."

He kissed her. "You're a wonderful girl, Cecily. You're right; you do deserve better than being a mistress to a married man. Of course I'm going to give you the three hundred. And what will your passage back across the Atlantic cost?"

"Well, I'm going third-class on the *Aquitania,* and—"

"No, you're not. You're going first-class!"

"Jack! I don't even have the *clothes* to go first-class!"

"You will before you leave."

Cecily knelt before him, took his penis in her hands, and placed it between her breasts. Then she pressed her breasts together around his hard shaft, capturing it in a soft, warm cleft. She moved from side to side and up and down until he achieved a unique orgasm: slow and rhythmic, reaching down into him and drawing up sensations from deeper inside him than ever before.

She kissed him fervently, on his eyes and ears, his cheeks and throat, as well as on his mouth. "There," she whispered. "Let the Missus try to do *that!*"

"I'm going to miss you terribly, Cecily," he said quietly.

Three

JACK WAS NOT FOND of the beach. But since this was the last weekend of the summer, he had agreed to drive out on Cape Cod as early as Thursday and stay through Labor Day.

Kimberly had chosen his bathing suit. For many years men had worn dark blue trunks with a white web belt and a white knit vest top. It had been all but a uniform. Now, she decreed, that outfit was passé, and she had bought for him a pair of maroon boxer-style trunks that did not include a vest. While it was true that the trunks covered more of his legs than the old ones ever had, he felt immodest exposing his bare chest, particularly since nearly every other man on the beach was wearing a white vest.

"I'm not sure," he remarked to Kimberly, "that a constable won't come along and issue me a citation for indecent exposure."

"He'll be issuing it to the best-dressed man on the beach," she said acerbically.

"To the husband of the best-dressed woman on the beach."

Jack was not entirely comfortable with the bathing suit Kimberly was wearing either. It was the first nylon swimsuit he had ever seen—the first one anyone on Cape Cod had ever seen. Her father's company did a lot of business with Du Pont, and Harrison Wolcott had been given a bolt of the new experimental fabric. It was white, the only color yet made, and Kimberly had employed a skilled seamstress, first to make her an evening gown of it, then to make this bathing suit. One-piece suits had been around awhile, but they were knitted in dull-color wool and tended to conceal the curves of a woman's figure. The elastic nylon clung like skin and gleamed. Kimberly had been wearing the suit for several weeks, but this was the first time she had worn it when Jack was with her on the beach. He wondered if both of them were not gaining a scandalous reputation.

He knew Kimberly didn't think so and didn't give a damn if they were. She thought they were by far the handsomest family on the beach. She was convinced that everyone else admired them. Probably she was right.

Little John came trotting toward them. "Mummy, Daddy! Is it all right if I run over and knock up Barbara? We can have such a good bathe together!"

Kimberly covered her mouth with her hand for a moment as she laughed. "John, you must not say you want to 'knock up' Barbara. That's not a polite thing to say. You can say you want to knock on her door and ask her to come out and play. Do you understand? You mustn't say you want to knock her up."

The boy glanced at Jack, who was laughing hard. "But Cecily said—"

"I *know,* John," said Kimberly. "I know. But you must understand that Cecily is from England, where they say things differently. Here it is very impolite to say you want to knock up Barbara."

"Well, is it all right if I go knock on her door?"

"Yes. But ask her if she'd like to come swimming, not if she'd like to have a bathe. Cecily said that, too, but that's not how *we* invite someone to come swimming."

John frowned, but he ran off toward the neighboring house where the girl two years his senior had become his summer friend.

Kimberly shook her head. "Cecily was a gem," she said, "but I have to be glad she's gone."

Jack wiped the tears of laughter from his eyes. "I suppose I should go in the water," he said. "It's silly to come to the beach and not swim."

"I have to confess something," said Kimberly. She patted her bathing suit. "This tends to get a little transparent when it gets wet. I'll stay out of the surf for today."

Walking down to the water, Jack wondered why she wore a bathing suit if she was afraid to get it wet. Then the answer came to him. He remembered that Kimberly had tennis clothes and didn't play tennis, and riding clothes and didn't ride.

He didn't ride either, because he didn't trust horses. But, growing up in California, he had become a strong swimmer, and he'd learned how to play a devilish game of tennis.

He had played a bit this summer and had developed a reputation for being a worthy opponent on the court. This had led to invitations to play at a couple of the local country clubs where otherwise he probably would not have been welcome.

He swam out through the surf. Someone had anchored a raft beyond where the incoming waves broke, and he climbed up on it.

Looking back at the shore, Jack watched John scamper down the beach, followed by his friend Barbara. John and Barbara romped happily in the surf.

Jack was so engaged in watching the kids that he did not immediately notice that Kimberly was no longer alone. When he glanced in her direction, she waved at him and gestured that he should return.

Curtis and Betsy Frederick were with her, neither of them dressed for the beach.

He swam in and strode up the sand toward them.

"It seems our pledge not to listen to the radio this weekend was a bad choice," said Kimberly.

Curt walked toward Jack. "Hitler invaded Poland this morning," he said gravely.

TEN

One 1940

ON DECEMBER 17, 1939, the damaged German battleship *Graf Spee* sat at anchor in Montevideo harbor. It had been pursued into Montevideo by British cruisers, which waited offshore. The government of Uruguay notified the German captain that unless he took the ship out of its neutral waters within the forty-eight hours allowed by international law, Uruguayan shore batteries would open fire.

The whole world waited to see what the German captain would do. Anticipating a spectacular naval battle, huge crowds assembled on the Montevideo waterfront. By great good fortune an American newscaster was in Montevideo, and he arranged to broadcast live as the drama unfolded.

In the event, Captain Langsdorff scuttled his battleship. The broadcaster breathlessly described the gripping drama to the American radio audience. Jack and Kimberly Lear were among the millions of Americans who listened with intense interest.

Until he heard that broadcast, Jack had been reluctant to station Curt Frederick in Europe. Occasional trips were enough, he'd thought. Seeing at last the impact of live descriptions of dramatic events, he authorized Curt to set up a news bureau in Paris and to go from there to the expected war front along the Maginot Line to broadcast personal impressions, live as often as possible.

Curt arrived in Paris in February—just in time to cover

what soon became known as "the Phony War" or "the Sitzkrieg." The real war was in Norway or on the Russo-Finnish front. The only story with any drama that he was able to cover was the meeting between Hitler and Mussolini at the Brenner Pass on March 18.

Since Paris was in no danger, Curt brought Betsy over to live with him in a flat on rue Saint Ferdinand.

They were enjoying something of a romantic idyll when Jack decided to call Curt home. It cost Lear Broadcasting far too much to keep him in Paris if he could produce only the stories he had been sending.

On Monday, May 6, 1940, Jack boarded the Pan Am Clipper in New York for the flight to Lisbon. Kimberly insisted she would go with him, but he argued that he would be in Paris no more than forty-eight hours, all of which time would be devoted to business. She acquiesced but said she would not stand for his making a second trip to Paris without her. Next time he was to arrange to spend two weeks.

Jack arrived in Paris on Thursday, May 9. Curt met him at the station and took him to the Royal Monceau, a huge traditional hotel a few blocks from the Arc de Triomphe, which loomed above rooftops and trees and was clearly visible from his windows.

Jack had never been in Europe before. Curt assured him that Paris had never been lovelier and that spring was the best time to see it. It had not rained for weeks, and the skies were high and blue. Fresh May gardens were in bloom. From the taxi between the station and the hotel, Jack saw Parisians—many of them fashionable women with long legs and colorful spring frocks—enjoying themselves in the famous sidewalk cafés. Though he also saw men and women in uniform, Paris did not look like the capital city of a nation at war.

"Well, Jack," Curt said as he sat down in the parlor of Jack's suite. "You cabled that you would like to see the Folies-Bergère. Every American does. Every American should. But I am told the Duchess of Windsor will be dining this evening at the Ritz. Would you rather see her?"

"Will the Duchess be as naked as the showgirls?" Jack asked mock ingenuously.

Curt laughed. "Well, then. And dinner afterward."

"With Betsy, of course."

The three of them went to the Folies. Jack enjoyed the show. Kimberly had taught him to think of himself as a sophisticated man—she probably would have insisted on the opera if they were to see any show at all—but Jack was not too sophisticated to love the spectacle and to delight in the nudes on the stage of the Folies.

They dined in a Russian restaurant not far from the hotel. It too offered a show, with balalaika music, cossack dancing, and saber dancing. The place was so noisy that Jack found it difficult to talk. He wondered if Curt had chosen this place precisely because it *would* be difficult to talk. When Curt went to the men's room, Betsy took Jack's hand and told him she was happy but missed their assignations of years past.

They walked to the hotel. Paris after midnight. Like New York, it was a city that didn't sleep. For a moment Jack was sorry that he had not brought Kimberly along. But . . .

"Curt . . . is there really going to be a war?" he asked.

"I assure you there is going to be a war. I'm so sure of it that I'm sending Betsy home next month."

Jack thrust out his arms to gesture at the songs and laughter echoing in the streets. "Not everyone thinks so."

"I know why you came to Paris," Curt said somberly. "On the other hand, should we have set up our operation in Helsinki or in Oslo? We've missed *sideshows,* Jack. The big curtain has still to go up."

"I can't afford to keep a correspondent in Paris and one in Berlin, one in London and one in Rome. *You're* not the problem, Curt. But we've got to find the damned war!"

"The French shook up their government today. *Paris* is the key city. It may be bombed, as Madrid was bombed. That's what I fear most, and that's why Betsy is going home to Boston. Imagine bombs landing on Notre Dame! On the Louvre! Bringing the Eiffel Tower down in a tangled ruin! There's going to be a great story here, Jack!"

"The question is, how long can we afford to wait for it?" Jack said glumly.

"Let's talk tomorrow. I'd like to take you out to the

Maginot Line. The world has never seen anything like it. Did you bring a camera?"

Walking back through the marble-floored lobby of the Royal Monceau, Jack noticed three women sitting in chairs in the hallway by the elevators. Even he, an American on his first visit to Paris could guess that they were prostitutes, waiting for a call to one of the rooms. Glancing over them, he decided that one of them, a faintly worn-looking woman no less than thirty-five years old might afford him an example of the legendary pleasures only a professional Parisian whore could offer. The other women were younger and more attractive, but he sensed that he would experience something special only with this conspicuously well used woman.

She said her name was Angélique—said it with a faint ironic smile that admitted it was not her real name and emphatically did not suit her. With sagging tits, smeared nipples, stretch marks on her belly, and a shaved pussy, she was just what he had expected.

And just as he had expected, he learned from her. First, they found that his French and her English were about equally weak. They amused themselves lying in bed, where she gave and he received French lessons.

He would touch her nipple and ask what was the French word for that.

"Le mot propre ou le mot vulgaire, Monsieur?" she would ask in her throaty Parisian accent—the polite word or the vulgar word, Sir?

And he would laugh and say, *"Oh, le mot vulgaire, Mademoiselle, s'il vous plaît!"*

She taught him the Parisian slang for cock, balls, cunt, tits, ass and for fucking, sucking, and what she called *"la manière grecque"*—the Greek style—fucking her in the ass, which she also taught him to enjoy.

She was an earthy Frenchwoman. Back home he would have refused her because she needed a bath. After their first penetration, from the rear, he suggested that they stretch out in the tub together, and she laughed. Then he told her he meant to pay her to stay all night. After that, she was willing to do anything, even take a bath. They agreed on a generous price, and she remained awake all night.

Two

THE TELEPHONE woke Jack the next morning.

Curt could not control his voice. It cracked as he spoke. He was in tears. "The Germans are attacking in massive force! I will be at your hotel by eight-thirty."

Angélique detected the urgency of the conversation. *"Les Boches,"* he said to her. She nodded, dressed quickly, and left.

Jack ordered breakfast for two brought to his suite at eight-thirty. His French was good enough to order breakfast but not good enough to understand much from the radio bulletins. Curt described what he had been hearing. The Germans had struck with overwhelming force. It was the blitzkrieg against Poland all over again, only ten times stronger. They were were attacking through Luxembourg and Belgium as they had done in 1914. Besides that, they were invading Holland.

On the streets, Jack and Curt found Paris still lighthearted. The day was fine, and people were going about their business and pleasure the same today as they had been yesterday.

Curt wanted to go to the Gare du Nord to arrange railroad travel to Arras.

"I want to go with you," Jack said.

Curt shook his head. "Not a good idea. It could be a very dicey trip. The Krauts will start bombing the railroads soon."

"I want to go," Jack insisted.

Curt bought tickets for Arras, on a train leaving the next morning.

Jack did not check out of the Royal Monceau, assuring the management that he would return within a week and wanted his suite held for him, with his luggage in it, so he could come back whenever he wanted to.

May 11 was another fine spring day. They reached the railroad station before they saw the first evidence of the major battle that was now raging in Belgium. Dazed Belgian refugees stumbled off the trains from the north. The station was crowded with grimly phlegmatic soldiers, trudging in ragged columns toward the trains that would carry them to the places the Belgians were fleeing.

Curt had brought with him a middle-aged Frenchman named Jean-Pierre Belleville, a communications engineer who was the other half of Lear Broadcasting's Paris "bureau." His job would be to patch through telephone communication so Curt Frederick could broadcast live reports to the States. Curt had described Belleville as an expert at improvisation, the aptitude they would most surely need. He was a sad-faced man in an olive-colored double-breasted suit, carrying a case filled with tools.

On the trip north, Jack, Curt, and Jean-Pierre were the only civilians in a car filled with French officers. A colonel and a captain shared their compartment. The officers were oddly confident, certain the Germans were making a major mistake.

At Arras, Jean-Pierre Belleville proved to be the improviser Curt had promised he was—and a consummate scrounger, too. He found them two rooms in a small hotel and a table in a restaurant that was still open.

Shortly after dawn Jack was awakened by the wail of air-raid sirens. He stood at his window and looked for the planes. He saw some: black specks slowly coming toward him. An antiaircraft battery located in a park a few blocks from the hotel opened fire. This was Jack's first experience of war.

When the planes came closer, Jack recognized them as Junkers-87 Stukas—dive-bombers. He had seen pictures of them. He counted six. They flew slowly over the town, apparently oblivious to the black puffs of flak that burst around them. When they went into their dives, the pilots turned on the infamous sirens meant to terrorize civilians below. They disappeared from Jack's sight, behind buildings across the street. He heard the thump of bombs and saw towers of yellowish smoke rising lazily into the bright morning sunlight. Finally he saw the Stukas again, in the distance now, flying away.

He dressed quickly and went downstairs. He spotted Curt in a telephone kiosk, talking earnestly. As Jack approached the kiosk, Curt raised his hand in a gesture to tell him not to speak. Jack stopped and listened. Curt was broadcasting!

The ubiquitous Jean-Pierre had somehow managed to put through a call to Boston, and Curt was on the air describing the raid. He had held the telephone instrument out and had caught the sounds of the antiaircraft fire, the Stuka sirens, and the explosion of bombs.

Jean-Pierre had been scouting for a car and had come up with a twelve-year-old Mercedes-Benz sports touring car, painted white. Though a tangled mass of folded leather behind the passenger seats suggested a top might be raised, the car was open. The front fenders turned with the wheels. The exhaust from each of six cylinders left the engine through a gracefully curved nickel-plated pipe. Not one but two spare tires hung from the rear. The owner-driver was a white-haired Fleming with whom only Jean-Pierre could communicate.

They ate quickly and left before seven o'clock.

As they drove east, the driver explained to Jean-Pierre that he was using secondary roads because all the main routes had been appropriated by the army. Jean-Pierre explained to Jack and Curt. The countryside impressed Jack as neat, in contrast to what he had grown up with in California. Fences were straight and orderly, houses were in good repair, fields and orchards were neatly tended.

An hour and a half east of Arras they crossed the Belgian frontier and began to encounter files of refugees on the road. Sleek Belgian horses pulled farm carts piled high with furnishings. People who had no horses pushed handcarts. The great majority of the refugees were women. Their men were in the army. Only elderly people, pregnant women, and tiny children rode in the carts. The rest walked, stolid and resigned.

Abruptly the Flemish driver shrieked and pointed at the sky. He ran the car off the road and charged through a field of newly sprouted grain, the car bouncing and twisting. He stopped only when they reached a row of poplars a hundred meters from the road. There he threw himself out of the car and tried to crawl under it.

Jack crouched behind the car and wondered if it would

stop machine-gun bullets. Thinking maybe the engine block would, he slipped forward and squatted as close as he could get to the car without touching the hot exhaust pipes. He saw two twin-engine airplanes. Before he heard the clatter, he saw the winking yellow lights on machine-gun muzzles.

The two planes swept along the road, strafing the refugees. First he saw horses rear and fall. Then he saw people blasted off their feet as they ran. He saw blood and flesh fly. He heard screams.

The Germans made just one pass and then were gone.

The driver rose, dusted himself off, and spoke to Jean-Pierre. Jean-Pierre spoke to Curt, and Curt translated: "He says we must move on. There is nothing we can do. We can't help those people."

"We can't leave them lying there!" Jack yelled.

Jean-Pierre translated Jack's protest, then the Flemings response. "He won't stay here. There are too many for us to help. Anyway, the Boches will be back. From now on, we stay as far as we can from refugees. They attract strafing."

Jack knew that what the Fleming said was true. He and his companions could not help the dying Belgians. They had nothing with which to help them: no medicine, no skills. Even if they tried to carry some to a village and a doctor, they could not take more than one or two. Anyway, the driver was determined not to take the risk.

They couldn't argue with him. If he left with the car . . .

Three

A LITTLE FARTHER along the road, the Fleming stopped to mount white flags on the Mercedes. There were nickel-plated sockets on either side of the hood, and into them he stuck what looked like flagstaffs cut from pool cues, to which were tacked square white rags.

The four men were silent as they drove on. Each one coped with his emotions as best he could. There was nothing to say.

They saw fewer refugees. Those they did see looked

stunned as they plodded impassively on. The Fleming scattered them with loud blasts of his horn and sped past. Twice they saw bodies lying beside the road.

"The Germans did the same thing in Poland," Curt observed, speaking at last. "They strafe the secondary roads to drive the refugees onto the main roads where they'll impede the progress of the armies. It's totally cold-blooded."

On a stretch of road where there were no refugees in sight, a Stuka flew over. It did not fire on them or drop a bomb —whether because the Flemish driver waved at the pilot, because the car flew white flags, because it was a German-made car, because it was heading east, or because the pilot just didn't want to bother, they could not guess.

Well before noon they reached the Meuse River at Dinant. There they stopped for lunch, and Curt hovered over a radio set, listening to the bulletins. The word was that the French and Belgian armies were moving toward the Meuse and would take a stand on its west bank. German armored columns were advancing steadily through the Ardennes. Important battles would be fought on the Meuse.

The last bulletin Curt heard before they set out again was that German tanks had been seen only forty miles to the east. At the bridge over the Meuse a Belgian officer tried to block them, saying it would be dangerous to go farther and in any case they might get in the way of Allied military operations. Curt asked him if the Belgians meant to move east of the river—knowing very well that they did not. As to the danger, he and Jack were neutrals, Americans, and would not be harmed by the Germans, particularly when they were seen driving a car flying white flags.

This raised a point. Jean-Pierre Belleville and the Flemish driver were not neutrals. They would have to stay in Dinant. The Fleming was not willing to let the two Americans drive his car, so Jack bought it from him, paying him cash— with the understanding that he would sell it back to him when he and Curt returned.

The Belgian officer pronounced them damned fools but made no further attempt to stop them.

Jack drove, going slowly, taking care not to appear to be in any purposeful hurry. It took half an hour to reach the village of Rochefort, which was nearly abandoned. A store had been looted, and some of its merchandise lay on the sidewalk. A café was open. Two men lay on the floor, passed-out drunk. Three others remained erect only by clinging to the bar. A forlorn woman, apparently a prostitute, sat at a corner table, drinking wine as if it were the last she'd ever taste.

The proprietor stood behind the bar. He too was drunk. He reached to a shelf behind him and handed Jack and Curt two bottles of red wine. "It is free," he said. "Today everything is free. Tomorrow I have no business." He nodded toward the prostitute. "*She* will have business. Her mother did, the last time."

They accepted the wine and put it in the car. There on the street before the café they heard for the first time the thunder of artillery.

At the edge of the village, Curt asked Jack to stop. "Let's talk about going back," he said. "The Belgian officer may be right—I mean, that we're a pair of damned fools."

"The Stuka flew right over us and paid no attention," Jack pointed out.

"The next one might not."

"Well, then, tell me something. If you were alone, if I weren't with you, would you go on or go back?"

"I'm a war correspondent," said Curt. "It's my *business* to go on. It isn't yours."

"In other words, I hire you, so I should send you out to face danger and go back myself," Jack said as he shoved the Mercedes in gear and drove northeast on the road to Marche.

The main road from Bastogne to Namur passed through Marche, and it was on the outskirts of the town that they met the Germans.

Jack turned a corner, and there, sitting at one side of the street, apparently not wanting to block traffic, was a German tank. It was a Panzer IV, as they would learn. Two men in black uniforms, wearing garrison caps, with their shirtsleeves rolled up in the spring sunshine, stood on their tank and were talking to two infantrymen in field-gray uniforms and bucket helmets. A school-age boy in short pants stood a short distance away, staring curiously.

One of the black-uniformed men, the tank commander,

turned and looked at the white Mercedes. His expression suggested that he had just wandered onto a circus lot and was confronting two clowns. With a firm, curt gesture, he ordered Jack to drive up to the tank.

He spoke to them in German. Jack understood enough to know that he was asking who they were.

"We are Americans," Curt told him in English. "Neutrals."

"What are you doing here?"

"We are journalists, foreign correspondents."

The tank commander jumped down and walked to the car. "Your passports, please," he said brusquely.

Curt handed him his passport. He examined it carefully, then asked for Jack's.

The tank commander was a muscular blond man of thirty years or so. He fixed a mildly contemptuous smile on the white Mercedes. "War correspondents," he muttered as he handed back the passports. "Wait here."

He returned to the tank and climbed up. A man inside handed him a radio microphone, and he communicated for a minute or so.

Jack and Curt waited. In ten minutes a car drove up, and an officer stepped out.

"I am Captain Hans Ritter," he said. "*Abwehr*—German military intelligence. We know who you are, Mr. Lear, Mr. Frederick. You left Paris, where you stayed at the Royal Monceau, Mr. Lear, then traveled to Arras, to Dinant, and—"

"You know a great deal," said Jack.

"We know something more, Mr. Lear. We know you are a Jew. And we are going to show you that we do not abuse Jews."

Four

JACK AND CURT dined that evening in Neufchâteau on bread and soup from a field kitchen, supplemented by their two bottles of red wine. Captain Ritter and an *Abwehr* colonel named Cassell were with them.

The archetype of a German professional military officer, Cassell spoke almost no English. Jack spoke imperfect German to him, explaining that his grandfather and grandmother had been German.

Through Ritter, Cassell told them, "You must forgive me, but I am very busy. I need hardly tell you what is about to happen. Within the next forty-eight hours this great war is won or lost. I assure you, gentlemen, it is won—by the German Reich."

Jack did not mention the strafing of refugees. He had something else in mind and did not want the Germans to decide he was hostile. "We would like to be able to observe your attack on the Meuse and broadcast a live account to the United States."

"You want to tell the story of this battle? I will arrange it."

"One thing more, Colonel," said Jack. "We left a French national and a Belgian national in Dinant. Employees of Lear Broadcasting. I would be most grateful if they could receive safe conduct from Dinant to wherever we may be."

Captain Ritter grinned. "The Fleming who rented you the car is in our employ. Your redoubtable Monsieur Belleville is ignorant of that fact. Dinant is in our hands now. The men you speak of are in our custody. They will be released to you. No difficulty."

A German lieutenant named Huntzinger drove the white Mercedes, which now flew German flags. A command car followed, carrying technicians and equipment. Their broadcast post was set up on a hill east of Sedan, from where they had a view of the river, the town, and the wooded hills behind the town where the French awaited the German assault.

The technicians arranged to transmit on an army frequency to a relay station in Bastogne, from which the signal was sent to Norddeutchsche Rundfunk in Hamburg, which transmitted to the same receiving station on Cape Cod that had received the interview with Hitler and his *Sportspalast* speech in 1938.

Lieutenant Huntzinger explained what they saw. The attack began with an hours-long artillery barrage, supplemented by incessant Stuka dive-bombing attacks on the French positions, particularly on the French artillery situated in the woods behind the town. By the time German infantry units began to cross the Meuse in large rubber boats, the smoke and dust from the explosions hung so heavy over the town and river that the French could hardly see the boats and sank very few. German infantry stormed through Sedan and up to the heights behind, where they drove the gunners away from the artillery that could have saved the French. By the middle of the evening it was apparent that the German army was crossing the Meuse at Sedan all but unopposed.

Curt was on the air. For hours, listeners to the Lear stations heard the sounds of the battle and his voice telling Americans what was happening in France: "Here at Sedan on September 2, 1870, the French Emperor Napoleon III surrendered to the German army in one of the worst military disasters in the history of France. Tonight, May 13, 1940, it appears that the equal of that disaster may be developing."

For the German army it was a military coup. For Lear Broadcasting it was a journalistic coup.

Five

EVEN AFTER FRANCE had fallen to the Germans, Curt Frederick could have stayed indefinitely in Paris. He and his network were regarded by the Germans as basically friendly. He had not been able to get Betsy out of town before the Germans arrived, but they were never in any danger. In fact, in many ways Paris was still Paris that summer of 1940, at least for the citizens of neutral nations. Still, any broadcasts from there would have been subject to strict censorship.

Jack ordered him to move his base of operations to London. Curt took Jean-Pierre Belleville and his wife with him, but anticipating a German attempt to invade the British Isles, he sent Betsy home. She was scheduled to cross the Atlantic on a Cunarder, but on its eastbound voyage it was sunk by torpedoes. She went instead on a modest American ship.

Back in the States, Jack spoke at three dozen dinners, describing what he had seen in Belgium in May.

"They cared nothing for the lives of those people. Children. Pregnant women. Old people. To drive them onto roads where they would impede the flow of Allied troops and supplies to the front, they machine-gunned refugees without mercy. I saw them lying on the ground. I saw their blood. I saw their torn flesh. I heard their screams. And I saw or heard no sign of regret from the German officers who so kindly helped us to broadcast descriptions of their victory."

America Firsters complained that Jack Lear was using his network to help Roosevelt drag the nation into war.

Time used his portrait on a cover and published an extensive account of Jack Lear's adventures in Belgium in May of 1940.

Time did not know and did not mention that he had invited Solomon Weisman to visit him and had joined B'nai B'rith.

ELEVEN

One 1941

THE MAN CURTIS FREDERICK had brought to Boston was not really his brother. His name was Willard, but it was not Willard Frederick. What was more, he was not working on a biography of William Lloyd Garrison. He had wept when Curt married Betsy, and he'd wept again when Curt left for Europe and said he could not take him along. He endured life in Curt's Cambridge apartment until January of 1941 when Curt wired him from London that he should come over and share a London flat with him.

Having felt he could not bring Betsy to London and subject her to the hazards of the Blitz, Curt had decided Willard had a renewed place in his life.

In fact, the two men had never ceased to see each other. Curt's marriage had not terminated their relationship, as Curt had assured Willard it would not. They did not live together in Boston, but they shared a satisfying intimacy at least once a week.

Curt's flat in Kensington was smaller and shabbier than any quarters either man had ever before occupied, although it was regarded by Londoners as a fortunate residence in a fortunate neighborhood the Germans did not bother to bomb. A retired major general and his wife had lived in it until the general was recalled to active service and sent his wife to Kent to live with her sister for the duration of the war. The flat consisted of one bedroom, a living room with dining alcove, a kitchen, and a bath. The upholstered chairs and couch featured antimacassars, and the windows were covered by yellowing lace curtains.

Willard, whose real name was Willard Lloyd, called his dominant partner Curt, which he pronounced "Coort." Curt called him "Cocky."

Cocky did not look like Curt's brother. He was a slight, spare man with only a little sandy hair remaining on his head. He painstakingly shaved off what little hair grew anywhere else on his body. Clothed he was nondescript, but when he pulled down his pants and shorts he released a memorable penis and happily displayed his sole distinction.

Cocky made it a point to be stark naked whenever Curt came home to the flat, except of course when cold weather made that impossible. When he was naked he displayed the penis that was the origin of the nickname Curt had given him. It was eight inches long and two-and-a-half inches thick. He loved to have Curt admire it and fondle it, and when the flat was too chilly for him to be naked, he pulled it from his pants and walked around with it hanging out.

Cocky would greet Curt with an account of what he had been able to buy that day for them to eat and drink. He spent all day, nearly every day, looking for whatever would relieve the spare, bland diet Londoners endured throughout the war. He found black marketeers and paid them exorbitant prices for meats and vegetables and spirits that almost no one else had.

Theirs was a domestic relationship: Curt earned their living; Cocky kept house.

Hot bathwater could hardly be had, but Cocky bathed Curt nearly every evening. He left water out in pans and a bucket all day, to become tepid. Then he warmed it more, using as much gas as he dared. He washed Curt lovingly, licking him too, especially behind the ears and between his toes, and, of course, in his crotch. Invariably he finished by sucking Curt's penis into his mouth and licking and nibbling until he induced a full orgasm. Some nights, when Curt was exhausted, Cocky worked on him as long as it took to coax a climax out of him. He didn't ask Curt to reciprocate, and Curt never did. The most Curt ever did for him was to masturbate him. Cocky was grateful for that.

Cocky was a most unselfish man. All he asked for, really, was warm appreciation. All he wanted was to feel affection from his lover. He loved to sit on a couch beside Curt when Curt was reading or listening to the radio and to have Curt casually fondle his big penis.

He begged for assurance, repeatedly. "You don't play our games with other men, do you, Coort? Please promise me you don't." On his knees and working Curt toward a fine orgasm, he pleaded breathlessly.

"The only other man I know who might tempt me is Jack Lear, and I assure you absolutely that I have never approached him and never will."

"If you did, I'd kill you both," said Cocky.

Two

KIMBERLY STALKED around the bedroom. Jack was all but ignoring her, which he knew infuriated her.

"You make a fool of yourself," she averred. "Half the people we know are outright laughing at you."

"To hell with them," he muttered.

"*To hell* with them? To hell with our friends? To hell with important people who've done things for us?"

Jack ran his hands down across his eyes. "I really don't care," he said. He slumped wearily in a small overstuffed chair, with his legs stretched out before him. He had not even untied his black bow tie.

Kimberly had thrown her dress in a corner of the room. She was wearing what she had taken to wearing regularly in the past year: a tight black corselet with long garter straps. She had the idea that her flesh was looser than it had been before she was thirty, and confining it inside what she called a foundation garment was an easy way to make herself sleek.

"I can recite it," she declared, throwing out her hands. "So can everyone we know. And they *do!* 'It was a pleasant spring morning. The women trudging along the road pulling their carts might have been picturesque if we had not known the grim reason that had impelled them to abandon their homes and set out in the bleak hope of finding safety. . . .'

Then you get *tearful!* People aren't sure if you're drunk or what. I *know* it made you sick to see people machine-gunned. Everybody knows it. But we don't have to hear about it again and again and again."

"Let some of them see a thing like that and see how soon they forget it. Anyway, I don't *want* to forget it, and I don't want anybody else to forget it."

She stood with her hands on her hips and faced him angrily. "You know what they're *saying* about you? They say you are obsessively anti-Hitler because you are a *Jew!"*

Jack put his head back against the upholstery of the chair and closed his eyes. "I am obsessively anti-Hitler because I am an eyewitness to Nazi inhumanity—just one small example, actually, of Nazi inhumanity."

"All right. But *enough!* Stop making yourself the spokesman for Belgians who get shot on roadsides and for Jews who get knocked around because they're Jews. Everybody knows you *are* a Jew, and they have accepted you—"

"In spite of it," he interrupted dryly.

"I've worked, struggled, to see us welcomed in the best— Jack! All I'm asking you to do is be more subtle."

"More the gentleman."

"You *are* a gentleman, almost. Do you resent it?"

"No. But how I react to seeing women and children machine-gunned on a Belgian road has nothing to do with being a gentleman, or sophisticated or unsophisticated, or Jewish or goyish."

"Oh, I know. *Kristallnacht* and all that."

Jack drew a deep breath and blew a loud sigh. "How do you want me to react?"

"As my father reacts" she said coldly. "As a citizen of the world. As a humanitarian. Not as a fanatic."

"Be specific, Kimberly."

She stepped over to the bed and sat down. "We married as a very unlikely couple," she said quietly. "Your father and brother hated the marriage. My friends couldn't believe it. You asked me to make you . . . worthy of me. Those are your words, Jack, not mine. 'Make me worthy of you, Kimberly.' All right. I have worked at it for ten years. And you're not the man you used to be. You're a *better* man. *Goddammit!* Did I make you a better man or did I not?"

Jack nodded, but he said, "It's a question of values, isn't it?"

Her face hardened. "Jack, gentlemen adopt causes. But they support their causes with gentlemanly restraint. If you want to help B'nai B'rith, help it. I don't object. But don't be identified with it. My father contributes generously to the support of Irish foundlings, but he's not a goddamned mackerel-snapping Catholic! Can you understand the difference?"

Jack nodded and said nothing.

Kimberly came toward him. "Husband . . . I try so hard to make you what you told me you want to be. *We are what we are, Jack!* Which is not— Okay, never mind what it's not. Think about what it is! A home on Louisburg Square! Even my parents don't have that. Don't blow it all! You can't defeat Hitler all by yourself. Don't get yourself identified with—"

"With what, exactly?"

"With FDR! With going to war. *Our* kind of people are rational. That's what we are: rational. Be rational, Jack, I *beg* you!"

Three

ON JUNE 4, Jack received a letter from Harry Hopkins, assistant to the President. Hopkins said the President was going to appoint a committee to encourage more complete and more accurate broadcast information about the war and about steps he was taking to strengthen hemispheric defense. He asked if Jack would serve on that committee.

Jack replied by telegram that he would be honored to serve on the Hemispheric Defense Information Committee.

He made no announcement of his appointment, but the White House did. On Thursday of the following week he stopped at the Common Club on his way home for the evening and joined his father-in-law at the bar.

Times had changed the Common Club. Ten years before almost every man at the bar after six o'clock was wearing white tie and tails. Even five years before white tie or at least black tie was de rigueur. Now most of the men were in business suits, as were Jack and Harrison Wolcott.

Jack had not been in the club since his appointment to the HDIC, and several men came up to him to offer congratulations. Some who knew him and might have congratulated him did not—rather pointedly, Jack thought.

Harrison Wolcott thought so, too, and commented: "Some of our fellow members are committed America Firsters. Some hate FDR so much they despise any man who helps him in any way."

Jack put his glass down on the bar. "To hell with them."

"I have to warn you of something: Kimberly is very upset."

"About the HDIC?"

"Someone sent her a copy of the Dearborn *Times*—you know: Henry Ford's newspaper. It translates HDIC as 'Hebrew Defense Information Committee' and says the committee is part of a plot to get the United States into a war to save the Jews of Europe from Nazi anti-Semitism." Wolcott shrugged. "That's what Mr. Ford's paper says."

"Does anybody take it seriously?"

"No one but semiliterate anti-Semites. Kimberly doesn't take it seriously in the sense of believing anything in the story is true. But she's upset that you're being attacked on this ground."

"She doesn't like the identification."

"I'm sorry, Jack."

"My father doesn't like it either," Jack confessed. "I got a wire from him asking if I'd lost my mind."

Four

THE HEMISPHERIC DEFENSE INFORMATION COMMITTEE met only twice. Its members conducted most of their business by exchanging letters and memoranda and by occasional telephone calls. After the second meeting, in September in Washington, Jack stayed in town an extra day, at the Mayflower.

He had not come to Washington alone. Betsy was with him and shared his suite. They lay together in bed, and Jack told her what the committee had said and done, acknowledging that it was probably a waste of time. No one of any great consequence in the administration had appeared at either of the meetings.

Betsy lifted Jack's cock and stared at it intently. Then she closed her fingers loosely around it. "You're hung," she said quietly. "I wish Curt had one as big."

Jack grinned. "He has other good qualities."

"He does, you know. He's a fine man. A trusting man. I should be in London, where he is, and instead I'm in Washington in bed with you. Does that bother you at all? I mean, aren't we betraying your friend, my husband, and a fine man?"

"Let's talk about that in parts. You say Curt's a fine man. He *is* a fine man. And he's your husband, and he's a friend of mine. But is 'betraying' the right word? You're lonely. You need a man now and again. I can be that man. There's no complication, because I'm married to Kimberly, for sure, and you're married to Curt, for sure."

"That's me, okay. I'm lonely. My husband's in London. But what about you? Your wife's in Boston."

"I'm just as lonely as you are, Betsy."

"She's shut you out of the bedroom?"

He grinned. "Not at all. She's developed a whole new set of interests. She wants me to spank her. She's actually suggested I use a riding crop on her backside."

"My God! So, then—"

"Bets, there is something more to a relationship than just— Put it this way: she *wants* me, but she doesn't *like* me. We're lovers, for certain, but I'm not sure we're friends anymore."

"Meaning?"

"Ten years ago we set to work to *build* something together. To defy my goddamn father. And we did it, too. That's what I call a friendship in a marriage. I don't think we could do it anymore. Her values—"

"I know, Jack," Betsy said quietly. "If it could have been you and me—"

"If not for the kids, it could have been."

"Do you mean that? If not for your children, you could have left her for me?"

"I'm comfortable with you, Bets. Nobody is ever comfortable with Kimberly."

Betsy gently squeezed his cock and balls. "I could have made you *so comfortable,*" she whispered.

"You'd have been proud of me, Bets. That's something she can never be: proud of me. She's not proud of anything I do. I bought two more radio stations this year. She's not proud of that. My fuckin' father's not proud of me—though about that I couldn't care less. Kimberly's not proud of me, and that hurts."

Betsy rolled off the bed and went into the bathroom. She did not close the door but let him hear her stream falling into the toilet. She was four years older than he was, which made her almost forty, but she was as playful as a girl. She had not boarded the train in Boston but had caught it at its first stop, in Dedham. As soon as she was in his roomette and had handed the conductor her ticket, she undressed and remained stark naked until the train was pulling into Penn Station. It was like the trip in the Duesenberg when she had kept her skirt pulled up all the way to her hips from Boston to White Plains. Betsy was bold, earthy, and fun.

She had a more generous figure than Kimberly or Connie had, and yet her underthings were designed not to confine and slenderize but to emphasize and show off. Her brassieres lifted her breasts and thrust them forward. Though she had a round belly and tush, she wore nothing tight around her middle. She wore very simple nylon panties, not panty girdles. That was what she was wearing now, with a white lace push-up bra.

"Well . . ." she said, tipping her head to one side and showing him a wicked little smile. "So she likes to be spanked, does she?"

Jack grinned. "I shouldn't tell it."

Betsy sat down on the foot of the bed. "I want an honest answer to an honest question. I want to know if you enjoy spanking her."

"Well . . ."

"C'mon. Tell the truth. Do you get anything out of it?"

He hesitated, then said, "I suppose I like it, sort of."

"Tell me. Describe it. I want to know how it goes."

"Bets!"

"C'mon, now, if you want me to be cooperative tonight."

"What do you want to know?"

"Let's start with, say, how does she— How does she, shall we say, *dispose* herself? Across your lap?"

"No. She gets on her hands and knees on the bed, pushes her face down into a pillow or two, and shoves her butt up in the air."

"Do you hit her hard?"

"Pretty hard. She's not satisfied if I don't."

"Does she *come,* for God's sake?"

"Sometimes."

Betsy shook her head and grinned. *"Jesus!* The elegant Kimberly Wolcott Lear, kneeling and taking a *spanking!* It's all I can do to believe it!"

"Believe it," Jack said dryly. He lit a cigarette. "Believe it."

Betsy chuckled. "Will you spank me?" she asked solemnly.

He frowned and shook his head. "You don't want that, Bets. You really don't."

"You're right," she said quietly. "I don't. My daddy spanked me once. I hated it. I hate the memory of it. I was twelve and thought I was too old to be treated that way. He was very angry. He pulled my skirt and petticoat up and my drawers down—we still wore drawers in those days, if you can believe it—and spanked me on my bare bottom in front of my mother and my brother and my sister. The pain wasn't so bad. What was intolerable was the *humiliation.* I never really forgave him, until the day he died."

"I'm not going to spank you, Bets."

"No, you devil, you're not. But I'll tell you what you are going to do. You're going to take your belt and give me a lacing on the ass."

"Forget it."

"No. I remember my spanking. The pain was— If he'd done it to me alone instead of in front of the family, I might have done something that would have made him *really* mad."

"Hey, Bets, drop it, will you?"

"What I'm going to drop is my pants. Give me just one whack. I want to see if I can take it. I've got to know if it will do to me what I think it might do to me."

"Betsy, *please* drop the idea."

"Hmm-mm. You're the only man I'd trust to do it, and you're not going to deny me. C'mon. That's a nice wide belt. It won't cut me."

Jack kept shaking his head, but he pulled his leather belt out of the loops of his trousers.

Betsy hunched on her hands and knees on the bed and presented her backside. *"Do it! Do it!"*

Reluctantly he swung the belt and snapped it against the soft flesh of her buttocks.

Betsy grunted, but she turned her head and complained, "Goddammit, Jack, if that's how you're going to do it, you might as well not do it at all. Now I want a *real* one! Wait a minute."

She grabbed her panties and stuffed them in her mouth. She glanced at him, then turned her face away from him and nodded emphatically.

He pulled the belt back over his shoulder and swung hard. She shrieked, but the shriek was muffled by her panties.

He threw the belt across the room and sat down to take her in his arms. She was crying. Her cheeks were wet. But as she settled into his embrace, she took his hand in hers and guided it to her crotch. She was very wet there, too.

TWELVE

One 1942

JACK AND KIMBERLY sat at their dinner table. The children had left with Mrs. Gimbel, their governess, and were upstairs finishing their lessons, which would be followed by their baths.

Jack rarely wore black tie to dinner anymore. Kimberly, just the same, made it a habit to dress for dinner, usually in a silk gown. Tonight she wore yellow, a color that did not become her, in Jack's opinion. She wore it because she believed it suited her new topaz necklace.

"I thought I'd heard everything," she said quietly, barely able to maintain an air of patience.

"Kimberly, I'm thirty-six years old. I'm subject to the *draft!* I could wind up as a basic rifleman in an infantry squad."

Her smile was acid. "You know that won't happen. Daddy can take care of it. He can keep you out or get you a navy commission. After all, the *navy* is where gentlemen serve. And he can see to it that you are assigned to Boston or New York or Washington."

"I'm not looking for a gentleman's commission. I don't want to go to war as an infantryman; I won't kid you about that. But this is something I can *do!*"

"What you are going to *do* is leave home," she said coldly. "Remember something. Remember the afternoon we got the word about Pearl Harbor. Do you remember at all how frightened little John was? He had a most vivid memory of your repeated accounts of the strafings in Belgium, and he wondered how long it would be before that would be happening here. Do you remember how you had to take him to his bedroom and explain to him that Pearl Harbor is thousands of miles away and that the war was not coming anywhere near Boston?"

"What are you saying?"

"I'm saying your place is at home with your family, giving your children comfort and assurance. Which they *need.* When that tanker was torpedoed off the coast two weeks ago, our children saw the red glow and in the morning saw the smoke. The war you told John would always be thousands of miles away was *right out there!* And I don't have to tell you that our John has a special reason to be afraid. He knows what the Germans do to Jews."

Two

JOHN, AGE TEN, had developed a child's fascination with airplanes, particularly warplanes. Not yet dexterous enough to build models from balsa and paper and dope, he built crude and simple ones from kits of solid wood. He had an aircraft spotters' handbook with pictures, silhouettes, and specifications of two hundred aircraft from all countries.

John studied the war aircraft avidly. He was proud that he, probably better than any other boy in his class, could distinguish a Henschel from a Heinkel, a Spitfire from a Hurricane.

John was sitting up in bed, studying a magazine with more pictures and diagrams of warplanes. Jack sat down on the foot of his bed.

"How goes it, Cap'n?" he asked, using the nickname he had given his son when he'd discovered the boy's fascination with airplanes.

"Daddy, will the war last long enough for me to fly? It won't be over before—"

Jack shook his head. "No, son. It won't last that long.

When it's over, you'll still be a little boy. But I tell you what. I'll see to it that you get flying lessons and learn to fly a peacetime plane."

John grimaced. "Not the same thing," he said.

Jack took his son's hands between his own. "My boy, we can't arrange wars just to suit you. Anyway, there are plenty of ways to be brave, besides flying in wartime."

John smiled weakly. "I s'pose."

"I have to tell you something, John. All your friends' daddies are going into the services. You know that. I have to do the same. I can't sit at home and take no part in the war."

"What are you going to do, Daddy?"

"Well, I'm not going to go out and fight with a rifle against German soldiers. It takes all kinds of activities and all kinds of people to win a war. What it takes, actually, is all kinds of skills. I happen to know how to run a network of radio stations. That's what I've done since before you were born. The War Department thinks I can be very helpful in London. I'll be working in an office over there, just as I do here. The only difference is, I'll be in London instead of Boston, and I'll wear a uniform instead of a blue suit."

The ten-year-old boy closed his eyes, drew a deep breath, and flexed his shoulders. "Daddy . . . if some way the Germans managed to get to London, they'd kill you, wouldn't they? I mean, you first—you before other people. I don't mean before *all* other people, but—"

"What do you have in mind, John?"

The boy focused his eyes on Jack's. "They'd kill you because you're a Jew," he said. "And if they ever got to Boston they'd kill me for the same reason. Wouldn't they?"

Jack tried not to let his son detect the shudder that went through his body. "Okay. That's why we have to do everything we can to make sure they don't get to Boston. Right? They're not going to get to Boston. I promise you. And not to London, either. But let's think this out. Suppose there was a chance they'd get here. What should I do? Should I stay home? Or should I go and do whatever I can do to fight them? John, even if I had to go into the line with a rifle, isn't that what I should do?"

John nodded, but he sobbed.

"It's not going to be that way. I'll be in an *office* in London, helping to broadcast information. That's the best thing I can do to fight them."

John cried, but he kept nodding.

"So what can *you* do? You give up your daddy for a little while. That's what *you* do to fight the Nazis."

"Okay."

Jack put his arms around his son. "We've never talked about being Jews. I never thought it made much difference until people started killing us. When I come back, we'll talk a long while about what it means, what it is. In the meantime, I promise you, John, that the Nazis are not going to kill you or me. Or your sister. Or your mother."

John frowned. "Why her?" he asked.

"Because she married a Jew and had children by him. In their judgment that makes her the worst of all. But nothing like that is going to happen. Look, Cap'n. If Hitler can't get his soldiers across the English Channel, he's sure not going to get them across the Atlantic Ocean. Right?"

John nodded.

"Okay. I'm going to go and do what I have to do. But it won't be for long, and none of us will be in any danger."

The boy nodded, but Jack could see that in his heart he remained unsure.

Three

INDUCTED INTO the United States Army with a commission as a captain, Jack once more encountered Kimberly's all-but-tearful scorn.

"Burke is a *commander,* United States Navy. That's the equivalent of a lieutenant colonel! And you . . . Do you have to go to boot camp?"

"Kimberly, I am assigned to OWI, the Office of War Information. I will go to an estate on Long Island and take a two-week orientation course. After that, as I understand it, I will fly to London. My assignment there will be confidential, but it will have to do with radio broadcasting."

"I know what you're doing, Jack. You're bored with your business, you're bored with your home, and you're bored with your wife. You are *escaping!*"

He did not answer her. If he had, he would have told her she was not altogether wrong.

Four

THE TRANSATLANTIC FLIGHT was acutely uncomfortable at first, then frightening toward the end.

Twenty officers, who had never seen each other before and would never see each other again, sat on their duffel bags in the fuselage of a B-24 bomber, bundled in long johns, wool clothes, and heavy overcoats but still feeling cold, comforted only by the jocular promise of the bombardier that he would not accidentally open the bomb doors and drop them into the ocean. Warmed a little by gallons of hot coffee and nourished by scores of stale doughnuts, the officers, who had nothing in common and nothing to talk about, tried to sleep.

Jack's discomfort was compounded by the understanding that he was the lowest-ranking officer aboard.

When the bomber landed at Reykjavik, the officers were welcomed inside a barren terminal building and told to use the toilets. They were given some thick, greasy soup.

Jack was paged by an American sergeant. "Captain Lear! Captain Lear!"

He took a radiotelegram from the messenger. It read:

YOU ARE ASSIGNED COMBINED OPERATION STAFF UNDER MY IMMEDIATE COMMAND STOP REPORT TWO DAYS AFTER ARRIVAL LONDON STOP CONGRATULATIONS YOUR PROMOTION RANK COLONEL UNITED STATES ARMY STOP OBTAIN APPROPRIATE INSIGNIA ETC BEFORE REPORTING STOP

BASIL COMPTON
REAR ADMIRAL
COMBINED OPERATIONS EXECUTIVE

How had that been arranged? Jack wondered. Harrison Wolcott? He would never know.

Somewhere over the sea and in gray fog the B-24 went into an abrupt turning and diving maneuver. Three officers simply vomited, either from fear or airsickness or both. They heard machine-gun fire, or thought they did. They felt their aircraft hit, or thought they did. It was all over in thirty seconds. The B-24 leveled and resumed its course. None of the crew elected to explain what had happened.

Five

AS JACK LURCHED into another bleak terminal, stiff from the cold and from hours without moving, Curt Frederick rushed toward him and seized his hand. In almost the same movement with which he took his hand, Curt passed him a pewter flask. It was filled with brandy, and Jack drank.

"Welcome to England! Yes, it's always this cold and always this wet."

Jack reached into the pocket of his overcoat and took out the wire he had received in Reykjavik.

"I know," said Curt. "Congratulations. You couldn't have hoped for a better assignment."

"Which will be to do what?"

"I don't know. They'll tell you. How tired are you?"

"Tired."

"Well, we've got to make a stop on our way to the hotel where you'll be living for the time being. See what he says? 'Obtain appropriate insignia, et cetera.' I have arranged for you to see a bespoke tailor this morning. You *have* to see him this morning if your 'appropriate' et ceteras are to be ready when you report. This kind of thing counts in London, old boy. I don't know how you got assigned to Compton, but I can tell you it will be very damned important to make a good first impression."

"Why the hell Compton?" Jack asked. "And who the hell's Compton?"

"Professional officer, Royal Navy. Took a piece of shrapnel in the leg in the Mediterranean about six months ago. His job is to try to make British and American operations work together. We don't have a similar officer yet, but we will shortly, you can be sure. Take Compton very seriously," Curt advised. "Washington does."

Six

ADMIRAL COMPTON was a diplomat as well as a distinguished naval officer. He received Jack in his office at the Admiralty.

He was tall and handsome and ineffably aristocratic. That element of his character and presence defined him. Although Jack was wearing a beautifully tailored uniform that displayed the solid silver eagles of a full colonel, his uniform paled in comparison with the elegant blue and gold of a rear admiral in the Royal Navy. As soon as they were seated, Compton opened a silver cigarette box on his desk and offered Jack a smoke.

"You see," he began, "until now it has been of vital importance to convince the American people that it is essential to their national interest to come to the assistance of the British. Now it becomes vital to convince the British people that the American personnel, who will be descending on this island in their millions, are highly civilized people—not just allies but *friends*. I want you to take charge of broadcasting to the people of the United Kingdom an honorable sample of what Americans hear on their radios, to let the British hear that we are very similar people with similar values and even, perhaps, a similar sense of humor."

"Yes, Sir. I believe I understand the assignment. I'll do the best I can."

"My subordinates will provide resources: offices and the like. And broadcasting facilities: those of the BBC."

Seven

JACK HAD SUPPOSED his office and staff would be supplied by OWI. Within a day after his meeting with Compton he learned otherwise and realized that he would need the offices the British had offered and that he would have to recruit his own staff. To the United States Office of War Information, Jack Lear's department was decidedly a sideshow on which it did not intend to waste its meager resources.

Jack moved into the offices provided for him, in what had been a small and modest hotel on Half Moon Street in Mayfair. His staff consisted of a secretary, a tall, spare woman of fifty or so named Mrs. Eunice Latshaw, who explained to him that he would be expected to pay her wages. He assured her that he would, though he had no idea where the money would come from.

Jack sent a wire to his father-in-law, Harrison Wolcott:

FIND I WILL BE BEATING MY HEAD AGAINST WALL HERE FOR WANT OF RESOURCES ASSIGNED STOP MOST URGENT NEED IS FOR FIRST CLASS SCROUNGER KNOWLEDGEABLE ABOUT PROCUREMENT STOP CAN YOU ARRANGE STOP WIRE ME AT DORCHESTER STOP

Wolcott replied the next day:

WAR DEPT HAS ATTACHED SCROUNGER TO YOUR STAFF STOP CAPTAIN DURENBERGER WILL ARRIVE SOONEST STOP GENERAL MARSHALL PERSONALLY ADVISING COLONEL DONOVAN TO EXTEND COOPERATION STOP KEEP ME INFORMED STOP

Eight

JACK GAVE an assignment to the resourceful Jean-Pierre Belleville, who was still in the employ of Lear Broadcasting, and the Frenchman carried out this assignment as effectively as he did any other. At seven the next evening, Jack heard a discreet rap on the door of his suite in the Dorchester. He opened the door, then opened his arms and fervently kissed Cecily Camden.

"What are you doing *here?*" she asked as he drew her

into the room. "And dressed like a soldier! Belleville did say I was to meet with *Colonel* Lear, but even when he told me that, I wasn't sure it would be you—couldn't *believe* it would be you."

She kissed him repeatedly. That was one of the things he had remembered about her—her great, generous, wet kisses. She hugged and kissed, and tears ran down her cheeks.

She had changed little. On the starchy diet of wartime Britain, her belly had kept its rotundity, and her breasts were even fuller than they had been before.

"Oh, Jack!" she sobbed. "Oh, Jack!" She had regained something of the London accent she had gradually suppressed while she was in the States. "I've *missed* you!"

"I've missed you, Cecily," he said earnestly. He meant it. He *had* missed her. He had missed her innocent enthusiasm. "Sit down. Whiskey? I'll call for our dinner."

"How are the kids? How's Missus?"

"Fine. They write to you, don't they? I mean the kids."

"Oh, yes. Every three, four months. John was very worried about the Blitz. Afraid I'd be killed. I almost was, one night. You know what happened at the Elephant and Castle station?"

"No, not exactly."

"We were down in the tubes, sheltering, and the fire was so hot above that they made us come out. They were afraid the heat would suck all the air out of the tunnels and we'd suffocate down there. I was out in the street during a firestorm! Hot coals came down from the sky and burned half my clothes off. A fireman squirted water on me. It was the last really big raid, the last really big one."

"I'm sorry, Cecily, and I'm glad you made it. What are you doing? Are you working?"

She nodded. "I teach in a school across the river, in Putney. The regular teacher's flying for the RAF."

"I want you to come work for me. I'm establishing an operation to broadcast American entertainment and information to the British people. I need help. I need people who know London well."

She sighed. "Oh, Jack! I can give notice. What will I be doing for you?"

"Can you drive a car?"

"I have done. My father is a taxi driver, and he taught me to drive. He owns a little old car of his own, but there's no petrol now, so it's just sitting in a garage."

"You know London pretty well, I imagine."

"Yes."

"One of the things you may do is drive for me. I expect to be assigned a car."

Cecily smiled impishly. "We can probably find other things I can do for you."

After dinner they did.

She remembered how well he had enjoyed having his shaft between her breasts, imprisoned between them by her hands holding them tight, and she did that. He did not come this time. She bent forward and put the tip of her tongue to his glans. He gasped and moaned.

"Ohh . . . So that's what you like. Well, I can't get pregnant that way even if I swallow it. Right?"

"Right," he whispered.

Her kisses had always been wet and enthusiastic, and they were no different now in this new situation. She wet him thoroughly with her saliva, and he slid smoothly in and out of her mouth. She didn't lick. She just sucked on him as he moved in and out, between her tight lips. When he came, she grunted and sucked harder and swallowed every drop.

THIRTEEN

One 1942

FIVE WEEKS after Jack arrived in London his American Information Service began a regular schedule of broadcasts over the facilities of the BBC. Combined Operations continued to supply office space and the services of one secretary, though she was supposed to be moved to the AIS payroll. The staff included the secretary along with Cecily, a second lieutenant, and a tech sergeant. Jack assigned responsibilities and established a small organization that would have run smoothly if only he'd been able to penetrate the labyrinth of army bureaucracy to obtain such basic supplies as another typewriter or even paper.

At first the AIS programs were one hour a day, five days a week. By late fall they were two hours a day, seven days a week.

Captain Emil Durenberger, the scrounger Jack had asked for, finally arrived. Durenberger was a career officer who had served with Pershing in pursuit of Pancho Villa in Mexico in 1916–1917, had been an assistant company commander in France in 1917–1918, had remained in the army between the wars, and had served here, there, and the other where, gaining a treasury of arcane knowledge about sources, regulations, forms, and especially the whole convoluted bureaucracy of the War Department. He was a diminutive man, almost bald, whose face was constantly wrinkled with the amusement he found in nearly everything around him. Someone had said of him that he might have been a general if he had been more serious.

The reputation that brought him an assignment to Jack Lear and the AIS had also probably impeded his promotion. He was widely known as a skillful and unscrupulous scrounger. The general who had assigned him to Jack in response to Harrison Wolcott's request knew two more things about him: that he drank too much and that he had an unparalleled talent for breaking through tangles of prescribed methods and finding a direct way to accomplish whatever he wanted to.

On his first day in the office Jack had promised the secretary, Mrs. Eunice Latshaw, that she would be paid. Until Captain Durenberger arrived, he had been paying her himself. The captain chuckled and within two days had established Mrs. Latshaw as a civilian employee of the United States Army.

He did the same for Cecily Camden. Then he had her assigned a room in the Park Lane Hotel, not adjoining Jack's suite but on the same floor. He had moved Jack to the Park Lane because it was a three-minute walk from the AIS offices on Half Moon Street and also because the army would pay the rental of a suite in that hotel, which was entirely comfortable but less luxurious than the Dorchester. Jack paid Cecily's rent himself.

Finally, Captain Durenberger obtained an olive-drab 1938 Ford for Colonel Lear and the American Information Service.

Two 1943

CECILY RARELY USED her own room. She slept with Jack and took her meals with him, either in his suite or in a nearby restaurant. The only times she didn't stay with him were when visitors came from the States.

Harrison Wolcott was the first to visit. Jack entertained him in the suite, and Cecily stayed in her room. Then Dan Horan, Connie's husband, arrived. He was a captain in the

Army Air Corps and was adjutant for a bomber squadron. At first Jack feared he might be stationed in or near London and might drop in from time to time, unannounced. In fact, he turned out to be stationed on a field in Kent, and he never came in to London without calling first. Probably he surmised that Jack did not live alone in the hotel suite.

Anticipating that Dan or someone else would tell Kimberly that Cecily was working for him, Jack told her himself in a letter, saying he had been fortunate to find her and to be able to hire her as driver and factotum.

Kimberly wrote constantly that she should be allowed to come to London. Her father settled that as firmly as Jack did, by reminding her that she could not leave the children alone.

Connie also wrote that she hoped to arrange a visit to England, to be with her husband for a few days. Dan must have discouraged it, even though travel restrictions would have allowed it.

Jack's expertise at bridge made him a welcome guest in many homes, and he soon developed a circle of friends. Until Lord Mountbatten went out to Burma, he occasionally invited Jack to dinner and bridge. So Jack played cards with General Alan Brooke, Chief of the Imperial General Staff; Foreign Secretary Anthony Eden; press lord Max Beaverbrook; Randolph Churchill; and General Bernard Montgomery. He also met General Charles de Gaulle and Prime Minister Winston Churchill, though he made no claim to be friends with them.

Cecily shared Jack's taste in theatrical spectacles. The theaters remained open, and Jack especially enjoyed the Windmill Theater. In accordance with British law, girls could appear on stage stark naked so long as they did not move. Naked girls stood on pedestals and posed while scantily clad ones danced around them. Jack and Cecily went as often as the show changed.

Curt arranged a standing relationship for Jack with the bespoke tailor in Savile Row. From then on, the tailor would see to it that Mr. Lear had such suits as the seasons required, billing him only annually. In those years, the clothes were mostly uniforms, spring and fall weight, and winter weight. Each one was tailored from the finest fabrics and made to fit.

When General Eisenhower arrived in London and was seen in the short, tight jacket that came to be called the Eisenhower jacket, Jack asked the tailor to make him one of those. The man covered his eyes with his hands and protested, "Mr. Lear! You *wouldn't!*" And Jack never did.

Three May 1943.

KIMBERLY PULLED a last drag from the Herbert Tareyton in her cigarette holder, then put it aside. The radio beside the bed was tuned to the midafternoon news on WCHS, and this afternoon the news was of the American recapture of Attu, an island in the Aleutians.

It was early afternoon, and she was lying on her bed, letting the radio play but paying it minimal attention. She could not remember a time in her life when she had been more bored. She could not recall a time when she had been more dissatisfied.

Part of the trouble was her self-image, which was badly damaged. She was thirty-six years old, and she smoked, drank, and ate too much. Her body, which had once been spare and taut, was now heavier, and her flesh was looser. When flat chests were fashionable she had not been compelled to strap her breasts down, for they were small and firm. The current style was to wear brassieres that molded breasts into conical shapes and thrust them up and forward à la Lana Turner, the sweater girl. Kimberly was not comfortable with that style—in fact, she thought it was demeaning—but lately she had the flesh required. Her friend Betsy, on the other hand, who was five years older, gloried in showing off her boobs and was elated that fashion now dictated that she should.

Kimberly identified generosity of flesh with advancing age. She was not ready to turn forty, but forty was coming.

Another reason for her dissatisfaction was that she was idle. She did her committee work, as every patriotic woman was expected to do, but she did not find it challenging.

Herb Morrill and Mickey Sullivan ran Lear Broadcasting Company, along with a staff somewhat diminished by the draft. Kimberly had supposed at first that she would move into Jack's office and assume considerable responsibility. But he had arranged things differently. He was never really out of touch; Morrill and Sullivan sent him a constant flow of reports, and Jack still made all the really important decisions. For example, a Baltimore station became available in April. Kimberly was a member of Lear Broadcasting's board of directors, as was her father. In a board meeting she had asked to see the balance sheet and profit and loss statement of the company that owned the Baltimore station, and she had suggested she could not vote on the acquisition until she'd had time to study those documents and maybe let the family accountant check them. Herb Morrill had told her she was welcome to look at the documents but that Jack had already communicated his decision to buy the stock of the company and the tender offer had already been made.

Jack wrote regularly, but Kimberly found his letters bland and far from satisfying. It irritated her that he dictated them to a secretary, who typed them.

Even though he added a handwritten note to each typed letter, telling her he loved her and the children, she always felt as if she were reading a business letter.

When the doorbell rang, Kimberly breathed a happy sigh. She pulled on a light blue negligee and went downstairs. The maid had already opened the door and was welcoming Dodge into the house.

"Dodge! How nice to see you," she said, trying to sound surprised. She doubted the maid was naive enough to believe there was anything surprising about the arrival of Dodge Hallowell. The girl probably knew that Mr. Hallowell would spend the next two hours or so in Mrs. Lear's bedroom and would leave just before Mrs. Gimbel arrived home with the children.

"Rebecca," Kimberly said to the maid. "See what you can do to dry Mr. Hallowell's coat and hat."

The maid took his dripping raincoat and left them alone.

Kimberly nodded toward the stairs. Dodge took her arm as they climbed to the second floor and headed to the master bedroom suite.

Dodge Hallowell was a handsome and distinguished man. If the Wolcotts had had their choice, Kimberly would have married him instead of Jack Lear. The only reason she had refused him was that he was seven years older than she was, which had seemed an insuperable obstacle when she was twenty-one. Now the age difference didn't bother her at all.

Dodge was the president of Boston Common Trust, which was by no means the largest bank in Boston but was still a powerful bank with major assets and formidable lending capacity. He was a tall man with broad shoulders and a bulky body. He had thick graying hair, a ruddy complexion, and a strong, square chin. He wore an exquisitely tailored single-breasted dark blue suit. Like Curt Frederick, he never wore double-breasted jackets, even though they were in style. He didn't like them, and what he did not like he did not wear.

He despised cigarettes and all but despised people who smoked them. Kimberly had to remember not to light up when she was with Dodge. If they hadn't established a routine of sharing the needle shower at the beginning of their trysts, she would have showered to wash the cigarette stench out of her hair and off her body before he arrived.

But the first thing they did was shower together, even before they had a drink. She tossed away her negligee and, feeling slightly embarrassed to be seen in her long-line brassiere and panty girdle, helped Dodge undress. At forty-three, he was muscular and in better shape than Jack. His penis—which at times he called his "pecker"—fascinated her. It was long, curved, thin, and uncircumcised. She had seen only two others and was not sure if his was unusual.

He knew how to use it well. Again, she had a very limited basis for comparison, but she found that Dodge satisfied her as much as Jack did, no matter that his penis was not nearly as long as Jack's and certainly not as thick.

Kimberly had not yet ventured to introduce Dodge to her *Kama Sutra* techniques. After six months of making these afternoon visits, he was still troubled by the idea of having sex with a woman who was not his wife—who was, in fact, another man's wife. He was troubled, but he was also very grateful. He had never married, though Kimberly was certain she was not the first woman he'd ever had.

After their shower they often sat naked together on the

settee in the sitting room of the master bedroom suite and drank Scotch. The first time they did this, Dodge had wanted to pull on his undershorts, but Kimberly had said no, no, no. This was one of the best parts of their relationship: these moments when they sat together and sipped whisky and she fondled his penis and he fondled her breasts.

"I received an interesting letter," said Dodge. He had a bad habit of introducing irrelevancies into conversation when they were being intimate. "A colleague of mine, now in the Pacific, writes that he was supervising the unloading and unpacking of a shipment of small machine guns when he suddenly realized the weapons were stamped with the words 'Kettering Arms, Inc.' They were manufactured under license by your father's company. He inquired around and learned that the guns with that stamp are well regarded by the men who use them."

Kimberly smiled and tugged on his penis so hard he grunted. "*You* tell Dad," she said. "I'd be hard put to explain how I knew the contents of a letter you received."

"Harrison doesn't know—"

"Of course not. Nobody knows. Oh, maybe Rebecca, my maid. Nobody can keep things from servants. And I think Connie has probably figured it out."

"Connie!"

"Trustworthy as the day is long. Hey—I'm wet."

Dodge drew a deep breath. "I'm on the verge of a premature ejaculation. I'll make up for it in a little while."

He did come fast—too fast. But ten minutes later he reentered and this time kept her in ecstasy for thirty minutes.

When they lay together in bed afterward, Kimberly tentatively suggested to him a couple of variations on the theme. His eyes widened. But he did not say he wouldn't hazard a try.

Four September 1943

THE BEDSIDE TELEPHONE in Jack's suite in the Park Lane Hotel rang at 2:33 A.M. Cecily picked it up and handed it to him.

"Hello?"

"Colonel? Durenberger."

"What the shit in the middle of the night, Durenberger?"

"Fuckin' big problem, Colonel, and thank God I found out about it first."

Jack struggled to sit up. Cecily switched on the lamp. "What's the big problem?"

"You awake, Colonel? Have Cecily get you a sip of brandy. We got a *big* problem."

"So you say. What the shit is it?"

"Two employees of Lear Broadcasting are in the nick and scheduled to appear in Bow Street Magistrate's Court in the morning."

"Who and why, for God's sake?"

"Well, Curtis Frederick, to start with. And a man you know as Willard Frederick, whose real name is Willard Lloyd. He's *not* Curt's brother."

Jack beckoned to Cecily to bring him a cigarette. "In slow, simple words, what the Christ is going on?"

"Okay. A friend of mine at the BBC called. It appears that Curt Frederick and the man who calls himself his brother were on their way home tonight from dinner at Café Royale. Drunk. Just couldn't wait to get home, it seems, and started doing dirties in the taxi."

"Started doing *what?*"

"In clinical terms, Willard started fellating Curt in the taxi. The driver turns out to be a Christian sort who's not about to tolerate that kind of conduct in *his* taxi, and he pulls up at a police station. The two of them are in durance vile and are to appear in court in the morning."

"It's the driver's word—"

"No. They were still at it when a constable came out and took a look."

"Where are you?"

"I'm at the police station. Might be a good idea if you came. I have the impression it would not be altogether impossible for us to work something out."

"I'll try to get someone from Combined Operations to join me," said Jack.

"I've done that," said Durenberger. "Captain Harvey is on his way."

"Okay. While I'm getting dressed, tell Cecily the name of the station. She'll probably know where it is and how to get there."

The city was dark, of course, blacked out, and the shielded headlights of the Ford cast only a dim yellowish glow on the pavement. Jack always marveled at how Cecily could find her way around at night.

She parked wherever she wanted to. Civilian-type cars, painted olive drab and marked with big white stars, signified important officers and were never ticketed. Tonight she parked directly in front of the police station.

Durenberger was waiting, with a tall, distinguished-looking British naval officer whose face showed both annoyance and amusement.

"Colonel Lear, this is Captain Harvey."

The two officers shook hands.

"What can we do about this, Captain? Anything?"

"It has been done, Colonel. The two men will be released in your custody. The charges have been dropped."

"Well, I certainly thank you."

"It's part of my job," the captain replied crisply. "I spend a good deal of time getting American officers out of scrapes." He smiled faintly. "I must say, though, this is the first time I've had to cope with a charge of buggery."

Jack heaved a loud sigh. "One of them is going home. Can we arrange transportation?"

"*One* of them is going home?" the captain asked.

"We need Curtis Frederick here, Captain. He's doing a remarkable job of making the American people understand what's going on, specifically of making them respect your people. I don't think we want to give him up. How soon can we get the other one aboard a plane?"

"Not tomorrow, obviously. P'raps Wednesday, p'raps Thursday."

"In my custody . . ." Jack mused aloud. "I'd like the one who's going home to remain in jail until he's taken to the airport."

"Your choice, Colonel."

"That's my choice, then. I'll take Curt Frederick with me now, if that's all right."

No man was ever more humbled and abashed than Curt Frederick when he was brought from a cell and handed over to Jack Lear. He was disheveled, and his breath smelled, not of alcohol but of vomit. He glanced at Captain Harvey, whom he recognized, and at Captain Durenberger; then without a word he followed Jack out to the car, where Cecily waited.

Only inside the car did he mutter, "What about Willard?"

Jack spoke coldly. "He'll be put on a plane to the States later this week. Until then he stays where he is."

Frederick said nothing. He hunched inside his raincoat, with the brim of his hat half covering his face.

Jack sat in the front seat beside Cecily. He turned and stared into the darkness, barely able to make out Curt's figure. "What have you done to Betsy?" he asked sharply.

"Nothing," said Curt. "She doesn't know."

"*I did,*" said Jack. "I was warned. I didn't believe it."

"Betsy doesn't even suspect," Frederick said, his voice breaking.

"Well, let's get something straight, Curt. From now on, there will be nothing *to* suspect. Your former friend is not going back to Boston. He'll be flown to Washington. He'll be told not to come to Boston and to stay away from you. Durenberger will explain it to him. If he fails to obey his marching orders, somebody will use a baseball bat on him."

"*Really, Jack!*"

"And on you, too, Curt. Don't doubt it. You better put together a box of Willard's stuff to go with him. Durenberger will pick it up. I suppose you'll have to send some money with him. Do you have some?"

"Yes."

"I don't give a damn about you, Curt. What I give a damn about is Betsy. If you hurt Betsy, I'll have you *killed.* Do you understand?"

"I don't understand, but I believe you."

"Let me explain it this way: I'm a son of Erich Lear."

FOURTEEN

One 1944

General Dwight Eisenhower had arrived in Britain to take command of the operation code-named Overlord. He worked long, hard hours. In the little time he had for relaxation he loved to play bridge and arranged for challenging players to be available. Someone told him there was a colonel in charge of the American Information Service who played a tough game and was welcome at the best tables in London. The general had Colonel Jack Lear included on the list of players who would be welcome at his table. In fact, Jack played with General Eisenhower only once, but his standing invitation brought him often to the general's headquarters, where he played bridge with a number of distinguished officers, British as well as American.

In January Jack received word that he had been promoted to the rank of brigadier general. A few evenings later, General Eisenhower grinned at him and congratulated him. Later, other officers saluted his promotion with a champagne toast served at the bridge table.

In bed later, Cecily said to him, "I never thought I'd someday open my mouth to the privy member of a bleedin' *general!*"

To have found Cecily was great good fortune for Jack. She satisfied his manly needs with enthusiasm and without making many demands. She was an engaging companion as well, ready to do whatever he wanted to do. And she never spoke a critical word.

Letters from Kimberly were not so agreeable:

> A Boston man returning from a short visit to London says you have a reputation there for drinking a good deal of Scotch. If there is anyplace in the world where a man can enhance his status as a *gentleman,* that place is London. If you take every advantage of that opportunity, make the right kind of friends, and don't sit around sucking on a bottle at night, you will return to Boston with a new polish that everyone will envy . . .
>
> Two handsome suits arrived from your London tailor. I cannot overlook the fact that you have gained an inch around the waist. *Really, Jack!*

Two

In January 1944, Curtis Frederick, who had not been home since 1940, asked for a leave of absence. Jack refused and told him to take vacation time, since he would be paid for that.

When Curt arrived at home, Betsy greeted him with all the enthusiasm she could command. She had not changed; she was his wife in every sense, as she had always been.

A few days after his return, Curt confessed the September incident.

"It wouldn't have happened if I had been with you," Betsy said with quiet simplicity.

"It might have. I'm going to be entirely honest. You see, Willard—"

"I always knew what Willard was," she interrupted. "Always. I knew your . . . predilection, too. I knew about it before we were married."

"Betsy . . ." he whispered.

"I tolerated it. I figured you were worth it. When Willard left here and went to London, I knew why. You were afraid to risk my life in the Blitz, but you were willing to risk his. I liked that."

"Yes. It wasn't a choice between— You are absolutely right. I was *not* willing to risk your life." He stopped. His eyes filled with tears. "You are the best thing that ever happened to me, Betsy. I've always thought so, but I didn't until this moment realize how much you knew and tolerated."

"Can you stop it?"

"Yes."

"I'm going to London with you if you go back."

Curt drew a deep breath. "I'm not in Jack's good graces."

"Saint Jack? If he wants to moralize, let him moralize with somebody else. Jack and I committed adultery before you came along. He's done it with Connie, too."

"Well, between us, he has a live-in girlfriend in London. I feel sorry for Kimberly."

"Don't. She sleeps with Dodge Hallowell. She thinks nobody knows it, but in fact *everybody* knows it."

Curt managed a weak smile. "I'll say this much for Jack. What he really resented was that I might hurt you—that is, that you might find out. He told me if I ever hurt you, he'd kill me."

Betsy looked amused, then turned serious again. "Okay, and let's say something for you. You've made a fine nationwide reputation for Jack's broadcasting company. It's quid pro quo on all points."

Three

HAVING BEEN OUT of the country since 1940, Curt had no American ration books. Without his red points and blue points, Betsy could not buy the extra meat and other food she needed for the two of them. What was more, he needed shoes but could not buy them without a shoe coupon. So on a Tuesday afternoon he appeared at the office of the War Ration Board to request a temporary supply of ration books and coupons. The staff at the office knew who he was and issued to him what he needed.

He stepped out onto the street afterward, wearing the rumpled raincoat and battered hat he'd worn in London. He didn't see a cab and decided to walk home.

"Curt!"

He turned around. It was Willard.

"Been a long time, my friend," Willard said almost tearfully.

"Yes. A long time."

"But you're home now!"

"Briefly."

"Well . . . uh, can we . . . ?"

"No, Willard, we can't."

The smaller man drew a deep breath. "I guessed we couldn't . . . when you didn't write. So . . . just one thing, Curt. They let you leave that wretched jail. Couldn't you have gotten me out, too?"

Curt shook his head. "I couldn't do a damned thing about anything."

"They kept me in that cold little cell. Then they took me to the airport *in handcuffs!"*

"I'm sorry. I would have helped you if I could have."

"I've missed you," Willard said sorrowfully.

"Are you with someone else?"

"Well, yes! You can't expect me to *pine awaay!"*

"No. You take care of yourself, Willard."

He reached for Curt's hand again. "Still friends?"

Curt smiled and nodded. "Still friends."

"Could you let me have a little money, for old times' sake? I'm shabby. Don't you see?"

Curt gave him fifty dollars and told him to write his address on a piece of paper so he could send him more later.

Four

ONCE DODGE HALLOWELL understood what Kimberly wanted, he got into the spirit of things beautifully.

They made a love nest in the attic of the house on Louisburg Square. The third floor had unfinished walls and sloping rafters and was furnished with quaint pieces that had been banished by former owners of the house. Kimberly and Dodge worked together up there, vacuuming up the accumulated dust of decades, going over the furniture with damp cloths, then with oiled cloths, until, in the light of two Tiffany bridge lamps, the old sofa and chairs gleamed in a simulacrum of past luxury. They rolled out a threadbare Oriental rug to cover the unfinished wood floor.

The Victorian settee was upholstered with red velvet and looked, Dodge said, as if it had come from an elegant whorehouse. Two graceful chairs, one with arms, one without, were covered with black horsehair. They tacked up old velvet drapes to enclose a dormer, making a dressing room out of it. They tacked up another drape over the window in the dormer to ensure privacy there, and they furnished the dormer with two wooden chairs.

The entrance to the attic was through a door in the second-floor hallway. It could be secured by a primitive lock, but Dodge drilled holes in the door and the frame and installed a heavy bolt to ensure their privacy. He also changed the lockset, so no key in the house, except his and Kimberly's, could open the door.

No one but the maid guessed that they had set up a love nest in the attic. If the governess, Mrs. Gimbel, suspected anything, she was circumspect and gave no indication that she knew what was going on.

The attic, which was not insulated, could become cold in the winter and hot in the summer, but for most of the year it was ideal for its purpose.

One day in March, when it was still a bit cold, Dodge warmed Kimberly up with a bit of exercise. She was naked except for the steel handcuffs that held her hands behind her back. A loop of rope circled her neck. Dodge stood in the center of their room, holding the end of the rope in his left hand. In his right he held a riding crop. Kimberly trotted in a circle around him.

She did not just trot. She trotted as he required, raising her knees as high as she could. Her breasts flopped, which was what he wanted. If she did not raise her knees high enough, or if she slowed down, he stung her backside with the crop.

Around and around she went until she was panting and her body gleamed with sweat.

She had stopped smoking. No matter how much she washed, she could not entirely remove the stench of tobacco smoke from her body, and Dodge had a preternatural sense of smell. He whipped her when he detected tobacco smoke on her breath, and the pain was real.

She had lost seventeen pounds and had promised Dodge that she'd lose more. To do it, she'd had to cut down on eating and drinking. He took her for long, vigorous walks and for rides on horseback. He had lugged a scale up the stairs, and each time they visited their attic room she stripped to be weighed, knowing he would use the crop on her backside if she had regained a pound. They had also cleaned off a tall mirror and set it up so she could look at what she had achieved. She had almost reacquired the sleek figure she had gloried in until recent years.

"Okay," he said, unlocking the handcuffs and putting them aside. "Get a towel and rub yourself down."

Five

AS SPRING CAME and warmed England, the buzz bombs began to fall. They were a terror weapon. The German bombers had had targets, but the buzz bombs had none; they could fall anywhere in London. They flew faster than any fighter aircraft, but the RAF had developed a technique for tipping them over in flight and sending them down in rural fields. Antiaircraft fire got many others, but still too many reached the city.

One night as Jack and Cecily lay in bed a buzz bomb exploded near enough to their hotel to shatter the glass in their bedroom windows. Cecily shuddered and snuggled closer to Jack.

At first he thought she clung closer to him because she was afraid. Then she began to whisper to him, and he realized there was a different reason. "Our time is running out, Jack. The war will be over soon, and you'll go home."

He'd thought about that. What if he went back to Boston, ended his marriage to Kimberly with some kind of generous settlement, and imported Cecily as his second wife?

He knew he couldn't. First, there would be the matter of custody of the children. Kimberly would win it. Besides, when he reviewed the situation in the cold, hard glare of daylight, he saw that Cecily was just a plump, pleasant English girl. She would give him a second family of children, no doubt —she was just thirty-four—and would be a supportive, admiring wife. But she would contribute nothing to the plans he had for his life in the postwar world. In fact, she would be an impediment.

Some nights, when Cecily was asleep, he thought about the nights he'd spent in bed with Kimberly. She had become very adventuresome in the last few months before he left for London. He couldn't help but compare her to the accommodating creature who currently warmed his bed and snored gently beside him. He'd told Connie he was capable of loving more than one person at the same time. Well, he couldn't help but love Cecily. But he loved Kimberly, too.

She was a nag and worse. But he had not stopped loving her.

Oh, what a gorgeous war! he thought darkly. But it would end, and he would have to go home.

FIFTEEN

One — May 1944

DURING THE FINAL STAGES of preparation for Operation Overlord, General Eisenhower moved his headquarters to Southwick House, some sixty miles southwest of London. There he worked eighteen-hour days, but when he did find time to relax briefly he still liked to play bridge with players who could challenge him. Jack Lear was called to Southwick House four times, but on none of those occasions did the general find time to play bridge.

It was at Southwick House that Jack met Anne, Countess of Weldon.

She was the widow of a British officer General Eisenhower had known and respected. She played bridge aggressively and, like Jack, was occasionally invited to the general's table.

Jack was smitten with her from the moment he saw her.

Even in the baggy uniform of the Auxilliary Territorial Service, a women's service organization for the armed forces, she looked every inch the aristocrat. Nobility was in her mien and bearing. Quite obviously she entertained no doubt that she was an exceptional person. Yet she didn't flaunt it. She didn't have to.

She was a tall, slender blond with prominent cheekbones and a slightly pointed chin. She wore her hair in a casual style that required little attention, and she wore almost no makeup.

Naturally, she and Jack played bridge on the evening they met. The games were kept going so that General Eisenhower could appear and sit in when he had half an hour to spare. As the date of the invasion approached, he had fewer opportunities to play. Sometimes he just stood behind someone, thoughtfully smoking a cigarette and watching how that man or woman played the hand. The guests enjoyed these evenings. They sipped whisky and nibbled on light snacks and played for fun, never for money.

At midnight General Eisenhower appeared for a moment and said he was sorry he hadn't been able to join the game that evening. Kay Summersby asked if everyone had transportation back to London. When the Countess said she did not, Kay Summersby suggested that she go with General Lear, whose car was waiting.

On the way back to London, with Cecily driving, Jack's fascination with Anne, Countess of Weldon increased. From their conversation he learned something about her but not nearly as much as he wanted to know. He did not learn that she was widowed and assumed she had a husband somewhere in the forces. When he took her to the door of her flat at York Terrace, a very distinguished address, he saw that she was not just an aristocrat but quite well off, too.

Jack could not get her out of his mind. Two weeks later he ran into Captain Harvey, the British naval officer who had arranged to spring Curt Frederick from jail, and he mentioned the countess to him. The captain knew of her. She was a widow, he said. Her husband, the Earl of Weldon, had been killed about six months ago.

Two

JACK ASSIGNED his scrounger, Captain Durenberger, the task of learning all he could about Anne, Countess of Weldon. As always, Durenberger was resourceful but probably not subtle. His report was more detailed than Jack could have expected.

Brigadier Sir Basil Fleming, Ninth Earl of Weldon, had been killed in Italy in January 1944. He was thirty-nine years old. His widow, Sarah Anne Helen, Countess of Weldon, was thirty-one. She called herself, and was called, Anne.

Though Anne's father was not titled, he was descended in one of the several junior lines from the Sackvilles, Earls De La Warr; she was remotely related to Vita Sackville-West and mant blue bloods considered her lineage superior to that of Sir Basil. Besides, she was brilliantly beautiful and had been courted by a dozen distinguished men.

Anne had married Basil in 1935. Their wedding had been the social event of the year, eclipsing everything else. At that time, Basil had not yet inherited his title and had been a member of the House of Commons. The marriage ceremony took place in St. Margaret's Church, the small church adjacent to Westminster Abbey—the church of the House of Commons, where Winston Churchill had been married in 1908. Churchill was, in fact, present for the ceremony, as were David Lloyd George, Anthony Eden, Duff Cooper, and many others.

When the Eighth Earl of Weldon died in 1938, Basil inherited the title and could no longer serve in the House of Commons. Though they kept their London town house and Basil took his place in the House of Lords from time to time, he and Anne began to spend much of their time at their country place in Bedfordshire, where Basil studied agricultural management and determined to make the old estate a profitable enterprise. His efforts were interrupted in September of 1939.

No one asked, though many wondered, why Anne did not become pregnant. When Basil died, the earldom passed to his brother, though of course Anne remained Countess of Weldon—Countess Dowager, a title she hated.

Three

JACK TELEPHONED Anne and asked if she would have dinner with him. She agreed to meet him on the evening of Monday, June 5.

They met in the dining room of the Ritz. Jack came in

his tux. Anne wore a pale green silk-satin gown, that suited her aristocratic mien far better than her awful uniform had.

"I am pleased you came in mufti, General."

He grinned. "I am pleased that you did, too," he said.

Anne laughed.

"And please, don't call me 'general.' The rank is temporary at best."

"Mr. Lear?"

"No. Jack. And that's my name. For me, Jack is not a nickname for John."

"Well, then. I am Anne."

"You will perhaps forgive me. I am by profession a journalist, and I did a bit of checking into your name and background. That was terribly unfair of me, but I did it."

"Not unfair at all. I have resources, too. You are Jack Lear, the son of the American salvage operator Erich Lear and the brother of the film producer Robert Lear. You own a string of broadcasting stations in America, and you have been married since 1931 and have two children."

He nodded. "That's me, I'm afraid."

She smiled in a way that he thought was aristocratic. "What is more, you have an intimate relationship with that charming, plump English gel who drives you. Which means that a woman such as I—one who sees you socially—is safe from your more, shall we say, lubricous instincts? Those are taken care of."

"You are entirely safe from those, Anne. Even *without* Cecily, you would be safe from those."

She laughed. "Come now, Jack! Even though you have Cecily, no woman is entirely safe with you. You've a reputation, you see."

"God help me!"

Four

GETTING AWAY from Cecily to go to Anne became a problem for Jack. He began to drive the car sometimes. Although it was very awkward for him to drive on the left side of the road through blacked-out streets, he made excuses to Cecily and drove himself to York Terrace and the exquisite flat that belonged to Anne, Countess of Weldon.

When they were alone there, he and Anne kissed. That was the extent of their intimacy. Gradually he kissed her more fervently. She accepted it.

"I went down to the USAF field in Kent again today," he told her one evening. "The bombers are meeting no Luftwaffe fighters and little flak. Our smaller planes are bombing and strafing at will. It's over, Anne. We've won."

She nodded. "Too late for many."

He held her. She was wearing a simple cream-white linen dress. "I know, Anne. I know what you mean," he said somberly. "And a lot more men are going to die. But there's no doubt anymore. God, when I saw that attack in Belgium in 1940—"

She kissed him, running her moist lips gently over his. "Why couldn't you have helped us sooner?"

"God, we wanted to! I mean, Roosevelt wanted to. *I* wanted to. Anne . . ." He glanced around her sumptuous living room. "Do you have any brandy? I'd have brought some, but—"

"I still have some of yours. A lot of yours."

He sat down, and she poured.

"Obviously we must be glad that the war is over, or nearly over," he said. "But it's going to be like it was after the last war. The problems of the peace will be as great as those of the war."

She handed him a snifter. "I have a sense that you are not talking about politics but about your personal life."

He sipped brandy. "You've been hurt by the war. I haven't. But you are going to be just as bored as I'm going to be when it's over. In wartime, we've known who we are and what we have had to do. Circumstances have made our decisions for us. Now we are going to have to make decisions for ourselves again, and it isn't going to be easy."

"What decisions are you going to have to make, Jack?"

"Business decisions. I've let them slide since 1942. Then . . . personal decisions."

Anne put her hand on his. "You've got one hell of a

problem, Jack. So does General Eisenhower. I'm going to be very interested to see how you both solve them."

Five Sunday, June 18, 1944

LATE AT NIGHT Jack lay in bed in his suite in the Park Lane Hotel. He was listening to the BBC, trying to match the place-names he heard to the names on a board-mounted map he had propped up against his knees.

Forces of the American Seventh Corps, under the command of General Bradley, were reported to have taken a port city named Barneville. If that was true, it meant that the Cotentin Peninsula had been cut in half and that the great port city of Cherbourg was isolated from the German lines.

He would have liked to be in touch with Curt, who, as of their last contact, was in a French town called Carentan, which couldn't be far from Barneville. This news had to be significant.

Cecily would not let him ponder it. She had smothered his scrotum in her big wet kisses and was now licking her way up his shaft.

Jack closed his eyes and let the map fall.

His hours with Anne were nothing like that.

He usually visited Anne on Sunday afternoon, when she had time off from her work at ATS. Cecily welcomed the opportunity to spend that time with her family. Jack would drop Cecily at home, giving her some story about where he would be during the afternoon, and then would pick her up before sunset.

On the afternoon of Sunday, June 18, he dropped Cecily in the Elephant and Castle neighborhood south of the Thames and drove immediately to York Terrace.

Anne was not alone. A man and a woman were with her—Arthur, the new Earl of Weldon, and his wife, who had just finished having lunch with Anne. Jack couldn't help but notice that they were put off by him. They kept glancing at the small woven hamper of cheeses and lunch meats he'd brought. Obviously they were wondering about the nature of the relationship between Anne and this American general whose name they had never heard before. They stayed only long enough to be civil, then hurried away.

The nature of the relationship between Jack and Anne was affectionate, even amorous, but not erotic.

Jack moved to the sofa where Anne sat and embraced her. They kissed fervently. They sat together and kissed during much of the time he spent there. Occasionally he would very tentatively touch her breast or her leg, and she would firmly—though in no great hurry—push his hand aside. He was careful not to press her too much, out of fear that she would simply dismiss him.

London came under buzz-bomb attack again that afternoon. Anne poured whiskies, and she and Jack stepped out on her south terrace to see what was happening. Others were out on adjacent terraces, staring half apprehensively and half curiously at the sky.

The V-1s had what were called pulse-jet engines and made a staccato noise as they approached. London Defense put up a storm of antiaircraft fire, but it was not very effective. Jack and Anne and her neighbors on the other terraces saw one bright flash in the sky and realized that the flak had hit one of the buzz bombs. Others came on and dived to the ground. Dark yellowish columns of smoke and dust rose over the city.

Anne took Jack's hand. "So damned *random,*" she said. "Where would you go to hide? I understand these bombs can even blast open the shelters."

"I'm going to try to persuade Betsy Frederick to go home to Boston. She's in greater danger here than Curt is in on the Continent."

Anne squeezed his hand. "For a time I was almost sorry the Blitz had ended. I thought maybe I could go out and walk along the river and wait to be hit. But now I don't want to die. I've gotten over that."

"I haven't suffered what you have," Jack said quietly, "but I think I can understand why you felt that way."

"Let's go back inside. At least we can be in each other's arms if one of them comes down here."

Inside, Jack pulled her against him and kissed her so

passionately that he bruised their lips. "If it had to happen, would you want it to happen while you were in my arms?" he asked in a hoarse whisper.

Anne nodded.

Six

AT FIVE-FORTY that evening Anne's doorbell rang. When she opened the door, she was surprised to find Jack standing there. He'd left her flat less than a half hour ago.

He staggered into the foyer, stopped, and turned to Anne. "Cecily is dead!"

She embraced him and found he was shaking. "Oh, Jack! How?"

"One of those goddamned flying bombs. Her whole family, plus two or three other families. When I drove into the neighborhood I could see a bomb had hit. When I reached her street, all that was left was a crater and wreckage. Wreckage of houses—no legitimate target anywhere near. *What the hell kind of war is this?*"

"That *is* the kind of war it is," said Anne. "You saw them strafe the Belgian refugees. You should have seen what happened here during the Blitz. Legitimate targets? Buckingham Palace? The House of Commons? And Oxford Street, for God's sake—stores! Not a factory within miles. I'd walk out on that terrace in the morning and find that ashes had drifted down in the night and turned the whole thing gray. I'd find shreds of charred fabric and wonder if they were from the stock in some shop or the clothes of someone who'd died during the night. That's what kind of war it is. And— Oh, forgive me, Jack, for lecturing you. Poor Cecily!"

She took his arm and led him into her living room, where he sank down on the sofa and covered his face with his hands while he shook with sobs.

She poured him a whisky. She sat beside him and put her arms around him.

Two hours later he still sat slumped and, for the most part, silent.

"Jack, I want to say something to you."

He lifted his head and focused his attention on her.

"Thank you for coming to *me,*" said Anne.

Seven July 22, 1944

JACK SAT BESIDE Anne in her living room. They were going out to dinner shortly. He reached into his pocket and pulled out a letter. With a solemn shake of his head, he handed it to her.

THE WHITE HOUSE
WASHINGTON, D.C.

Jack Lear
Brigadier General
American Information Service
London, U.K.

Dear General Lear,

First, let me extend to you my personal gratitude for the magnificent job you have done as head of the American Information Service. Your broadcasts to the British people have achieved every objective we had in mind for them, and more.

It is precisely because they have been so successful that the decision has now been made to discontinue them.

Within a few days you will receive from the War Department orders to disassemble your operation. That done, your orders will be to return to the United States, where you will be discharged from the armed forces.

I know you must be eager to return to civilian life, to your family, and to the management of your business, so your new orders will be good news to you.

Once again, my personal thanks for your sacrifice and service.

It was signed by Franklin Delano Roosevelt.

"I've dreaded this," said Jack.

"Something else the war has done to us," Anne said sadly. "And you know there's nothing we can do about it."

"I dreaded having to go home and leave Cecily. And now . . ."

"We never had a chance, Jack. We deceived ourselves if we thought we did."

"So what do we do now? The noble thing?"

"Name the alternative," Anne murmured sadly.

He bent over and kissed her. "I'll be going home without one wonderful memory I had hoped to take."

She sighed. "Not . . . necessarily, I suppose." She glanced toward the bedroom door. "I am not unwilling to give you that memory. So . . . not necessarily."

Jack shook his head decisively. "Necessarily," he said.

SIXTEEN

One — September 1944

KIMBERLY RAISED HER HEAD and smiled lazily at Dodge Hallowell. He put his foot against her chin and gave her a gentle shove. She had no balance, no control of herself whatsoever, and fell over on her side. She was wearing two pairs of handcuffs, one pair attaching her right wrist to her left ankle, the other chaining her left wrist to her right ankle—behind her back. It bound her in a painful and awkward posture, and she had just struggled up on her knees when he shoved her and she toppled over.

"Don't kick me, you bastard!"

"That was no kick."

"Okay. Kick me and let me see the difference."

He stood up and gave her a sharp kick on the hip. *"Oww!"* she cried as she rolled over. The sole of his shoe left a smudge on her hip but not a bruise. "You *hurt* me, dammit!"

"I gave you what you said you wanted."

"Well . . ."

"You want loose from those?"

"I want you to hook me up in front, so I can get my butt up in the air and you can give it to me doggie-style."

He took a tiny key from his pocket and unlocked the handcuffs from her ankles. "Uh-oh," he said. "Bruises. Jesus Christ! They'll be there when Jack gets back."

"Put the cuffs on a little looser."

"They don't *go* on looser around your ankles. They weren't made for ankles."

"Well, I'll take care of Jack. But— Okay. Cuff me to the rafter."

"Then what?"

"Then anything you want!"

As she stood with her hands fastened above her head, he took her from behind. She wailed in ecstasy.

After he let her down, he put both pairs of handcuffs in his briefcase, along with some lengths of chain and half a dozen little padlocks. On top of those he put two pairs of crotchless panties, a brassiere with holes cut to expose her nipples, and a strip set: a transparent bra and a G-string.

Kimberly sat nude on the couch and watched him sadly. "I don't intend to give up these times," she said simply. "We just have to find someplace else."

"I don't know where," he said resignedly.

"Rent a place, for Christ's sake! Is it unheard of for a couple to have a love nest? We just can't have ours in the attic of this house anymore."

"What would Jack do if he found out?" Dodge asked.

"What will I do if I find out what he's been doing in London the past two and a half years?"

Two

THE NIGHT of his homecoming was all that Jack could have imagined. The family sat down to a dinner that Kimberly and Joan served, having sent the cook and maid home. Jack put the children's presents on the table. For John he had brought a set of authentic USAF identification models, painted black and made to aid American pilots in identifying German aircraft, an assortment of shoulder patches and other insignia from the USAF, the RAF, and the Luftwaffe, and an Iron Cross taken from a shot-down German pilot. For Joan he had brought a gold bracelet hung with miniature medallions of the Victoria Cross and other British decorations, also a white silk scarf taken from a downed German fighter pilot.

The two children sipped champagne and later a distinguished Bordeaux that Kimberly had bought and saved for the homecoming dinner. They dined on caviar, then slices of roast beef with Yorkshire pudding.

The only sad note of the evening was sounded when John said, "Tell us about Cecily, Father."

Jack glanced at Kimberly. He frowned and said, "All I can tell you is that what happened to Cecily happened instantly. She suffered no pain. One second she was alive, and the next second she was . . . gone. And there was nothing anyone could have done to prevent it. The same thing could have happened to me that afternoon."

In their bedroom an hour later, Kimberly lit a cigarette—the first she had smoked in weeks—and said, "You may as well admit it. You loved Cecily. You had her, even when she worked here; and in London she became very, very convenient. But you're not the kind of man who humps women he doesn't care about. You cared about Cecily."

Jack hung up the Savile Row suit he'd worn for dinner and turned to face Kimberly. "All right. I cared about her."

"You *loved* her."

He nodded.

"I'm prepared to forget it. Circumstances—"

"Fate took care of it, right?" he asked crisply.

"*I* didn't suggest any such thing."

"You didn't. That's right, you didn't. But I'm not going to kid you. I cried. I shed a lot of tears."

"War . . ." said Kimberly. "What we have to do now is forget it. No, not forget it. But live with what it did to us."

Jack gave Kimberly the presents he'd brought back for her: an emerald bracelet and a personally autographed photo of King George VI and the Queen.

The night was everything he could have expected.

Three

KIMBERLY INSISTED that Jack appear in uniform at the welcome-home party she gave for him in the house on Louisburg Square. She seemed much more pleased with the uniforms he'd had tailored on Savile Row than she'd been with the hastily made uniforms he had worn before he left for London —apart from the fact that he now had stars instead of captain's bars on his shoulders.

She was in fact eager to show him off. He had attained a higher rank than any of their friends or acquaintances. As she prepared for the party, Kimberly found herself wishing he'd won some kind of decoration. He'd had the President's letter to him framed, and it would hang in his office, but he couldn't wear it on his uniform. All he had was the modest ribbon that indicated he had served in the European Theater of Operations. But even that, she conceded, was a distinction some men they knew had not achieved, because they had spent the entire war in Boston or Washington.

"Jack did see something up front and personal of the war," she told a friend at the party. "He *was* in Belgium, you remember, and witnessed the strafing of Belgian civilians, plus the German attack across the Meuse at Sedan. Besides, his personal driver was killed in a buzz-bomb attack on London."

Dodge Hallowell shook Jack's hand firmly and declared himself overjoyed to see that Jack had returned safely. "You know, it's been a source of considerable embarrassment to me that I was too young for the old war and too old for this one."

"War is a young man's game, Dodge," Jack said. "I was too old for any real part in it, too, except for the kind of office job I did."

"But you were *there*. You saw something of it, *experienced* some of the tragedy, I understand. I can't say I envy you, but I have a sense that I have lived my life on the periphery."

"I'm glad to be back on the periphery, Dodge," Jack assured him, clapping him on the back and then moving on. He had just laid eyes on an irresistible sight.

Connie Horan extended both her hands and clasped his warmly. "I've been so worried! About Dan and about you. They've shut down the buzz-bomb sites, haven't they? I mean we've overrun the places where they came from."

Jack ignored her question. "When am I going to see you, Connie?" he asked earnestly.

"We don't dare!" she whispered. "Oh, no, we don't dare!"

Four

IN A MEETING with Mickey Sullivan and Herb Morrill, Jack decided the time had come to let the world know that Betty—Carolyn Blossom—was a Negro, provided she agreed.

She did *not* agree. That year, for the fourth time, she won an award from *Broadcast* magazine as the best radio comedienne in America—an award that Gracie Allen had won nine times. Jack wanted Carolyn and her husband to accompany the Lears and the Sullivans to the awards dinner and let the world see that Betty was Carolyn Blossom.

"No!" she declared when he proposed it. "No! Let that crowd call me a nigger? Even if they didn't call me that, that's what they'd think. A long time ago you and I decided we'd make a buck, not a point. The time for makin' a point was a long time ago, Jack. We didn't make it then. I'm not going to try to make it now."

"It's a matter of principle," said Jack.

"If it wasn't before, why is it now?" She shook her head. "You told me once that the big thing is to have a fat bank account. Well, I've got one. Me and my man gonna live in the south of France. We'll be neighbors of Josephine Baker, which is who told us to come."

"Well, I'm damned sorry. I should have stood up for what's right a long time ago."

"I've had a fun time for thirteen years, and you've paid me generously. I'm grateful to you."

"I'm grateful to *you.* You've been a mainstay of our entertainment programming for a long time. I'm really sorry that—"

"Jack . . . neither one of us was big enough to stand up and be counted—you to do it, me to insist on it. We pocketed dollars out of our cowardice. We may have to account for that someday. But for now I'm going to take mine and go away and enjoy them."

Five

THE WARTIME YEARS had not dampened Herb Morrill's infectious enthusiasm. He had never managed to convince Jack Lear that Jack Benny was funny, but he had convinced his boss of a lot of other things.

"I swear to you, this thing is going to work," he said to Jack, to Mickey Sullivan, and Emil Durenberger. Durenberger had obtained a discharge from the army and come to work for Lear Broadcasting. Jack had begun to call Durenberger "Cap," after the rank he'd had when they met. They were together in Jack's office late in January. "Not just technologically. I mean commercially."

"Where do I have to go to see it?" Jack asked.

"Just out to Cambridge. They've got one set up in a lab at Harvard. A Professor Loewenstein is the expert who will demonstrate the thing to us."

That afternoon Herb, Jack, and Cap stood in a darkened lab and stared at a curious little bottle with a faint and fuzzy image on its bottom. Oddly, the image was a moving picture of *them.* The camera that produced it was pointed at them.

Jack was fascinated. He gesticulated and watched himself gesticulate on the face of a cathode ray tube, which was the name the professor had given the bottle. The camera, he said, contained an image orthicon tube. The orthicon tube converted light to electrical impulses, and the cathode ray tube converted electrical impulses back into light.

Dr. Friedrich Loewenstein spoke with a heavy German accent. He was a young man, tall, blond, and intense.

"The point, Mr. Sear—"

"Lear."

"Oh. Yes. Sorry. The point is that the picture signal can be transmitted on a radio frequency, the same way a sound signal can be transmitted."

Jack smiled. "Fifty years from now."

"No, sir," said Dr. Loewenstein. "It has been done. Pictures from the World's Fair in 1939 were transmitted from the fairgrounds to receivers in downtown Manhattan. It was done in England some years earlier. If not for the war, stations would be in operation today, sending pictures and sound. During the war we have given all our technological resources to things like radar and sonar. This technology was put aside for the time being. Everyone's interested in getting back to it as soon as possible."

"What's it called?" Jack asked.

"No one knows for sure. Since sound transmission is called radio, maybe this is video."

Jack pointed at the receiver. It was a tangle of wires and glowing tubes, not enclosed in any kind of case. "Suppose a family wanted to have one of those, like they want a radio. What would it cost?"

"This is a guess, Mr. Lear," said Dr. Loewenstein, "but some of us think they can be manufactured for less than a thousand dollars."

"It will cost more than a *car,*" Cap Durenberger pointed out.

"And may be worth more," said Jack. "A family could sit in front of that thing and see pictures of anything in the world—news events while they were happening. Think of one of Roosevelt's fireside chats, with his face there as well as his voice."

"That is very possible," said Dr. Loewenstein.

Cap shook his head. "A long way down the road," he said.

"This could put us out of business somewhere down that road," said Jack. "Professor, let me ask you something. Would you be willing to accept a fee to become an adviser to my company, to keep us informed of the development of this technology—including the names of other companies who are taking an interest?"

"I should have to give that a great deal of thought," said Dr. Loewenstein.

A week later Dr. Loewenstein phoned Jack and said he would sign a consulting contract with the broadcasting company. "You are a difficult man to say no to Mr. Lear."

Jack had talked with Solomon Weisman about Dr. Loewenstein. Weisman, who had recruited Jack for B'nai B'rith, knew Dr. Loewenstein as a Jew whose family had fled Germany in 1934 when he was twenty. Weisman had told the professor of Jack's services to the cause of American understanding of Nazism and America's entry into the war.

"I am not ready to invest much in this video thing," Jack told the professor. "But I want to be kept fully informed of its development."

Six Wednesday, February 14, 1945

"THIS IS WHAT she does to me," Jack said to Connie. He used his thumbs and index fingers to pinch little rolls of flesh at his middle. "Do you know what she's done? She's quit smoking. She's quit drinking. She's gone on a regimen to lose weight. She weighs almost as little as she did when we were married. I weigh twenty pounds more, and I'm supposed to be ashamed of it."

They were in Connie's bedroom. It was midmorning, and her children were in school.

"You *are* huskier than you used to be," she said.

"You want to pinch me too?"

She rolled over against him. "You're a comfortable man, though," she said. She sighed. "And a persuasive man. Jack, do we dare have a sip of Scotch in the morning?"

"Why not? Why live by rules?"

She put on a robe, went downstairs, and came back with a bottle of Black & White, two glasses, and a bowl of ice.

He didn't need to encourage her to put the robe aside. When she first undressed, she had said she wanted him to judge her body. She was thirty-four and had put on a little weight while he was away. Her legs were long and slender, as always, but her breasts were newly sumptuous and inviting. He judged her improved and told her so.

When she put her glass aside, she took his penis in her hands and explored it all over with her long, delicate fingers. It was as though she wanted to renew her acquaintance with it. She lifted his scrotum and gently massaged his testicles.

"I am going to *sin* with you, Jack," she whispered. "May the good Lord forgive me!"

"Going to lick? That's what you seemed to like best when—"

"Lick you? I said I'm going to *sin!*"

"I'm for it. But don't forget there's a certain risk."

"Jack . . . Just lick you? I couldn't be happy with just that. Not now. You taught me to like having a man inside me. Before you, I didn't know I *could* like it. You remember. I didn't think I was supposed to. But now, *Jack!* I haven't had a man in a year and a half!"

He reached for his jacket and took a condom from his pocket. "Well, we'd better—"

"No! Oh, no! To do it at all with you is sin enough. To do it with that on you—"

"Connie, you could get pregnant."

"No. I've counted the days very carefully. Now is the time when I can enjoy it and not conceive. And I *want* to enjoy it."

Seven

THAT FEBRUARY, Jack acquired another station, in Atlanta. This made eleven stations on the Lear network. Pointing out that "Lear Broadcasting" was not an appealing name, the ever-astute Cap Durenberger suggested they call the string of stations LNI, for Lear Network, Incorporated. Jack bought the idea, and Durenberger hired an artist to devise a logo for LNI.

It became apparent to Durenberger that the network needed more than a logo that could be used only in print advertising; what LNI needed was a catchy *sound* signature, something like NBC's three notes—pumm-*pumm*-pumm.

Jack knew something about radio sound signatures. Government-sponsored shortwave stations all over the world opened their daily schedule of broadcasting by sending out repeatedly a phrase of music, usually the opening notes of their national anthem. The United States did not use the opening notes of "The Star-Spangled Banner" but those of "Columbia, Gem of the Ocean." For LNI Jack chose the opening notes of "The Star-Spangled Banner," tapped out on a xylophone: "Oh-oh, say, can you see?"

Eight

CAP DURENBERGER hated to fly, so in March he took a train to Los Angeles, where he signed the hot movie comic Sally Allen to a five-year contract with LNI. He committed LNI to pay her half a million dollars a year to do twenty half-hour shows. This left her time to do at least two pictures a year. It was an unheard-of amount of money for that number of radio shows on an eleven-station network. For her release, she was to pay LNI 10 percent of the salary she received from the pictures she made.

Only after Jack and others expressed outrage at the generous terms of the contract did someone find time to read the hundred clauses of the contract and discover that LNI had the right to accept or reject her film contracts. What was more, LNI had the right to *sell* its acceptance.

"Perfectly simple, *mi jefe,* Durenberger told Jack with a devilish glint in his eye. "Her radio shows make her a bigger star than ever, film studios clamor for a picture contract, and we sell that contract to the highest bidder, thereby recovering a major part, if not all, of our half million."

Nine

Tuesday, April 17, 1945

CONNIE'S DIGNITY never failed her. Neither did her style. She looked stunning when she met Jack for lunch in the ladies' dining room at the Common Club. Jack still held the opinion that Connie was the only woman in Boston who could matched Kimberly in beauty and elegance.

When their drinks were before them and he had saluted her with his glass, Connie made a calm, simple statement: "I've seen my doctor, Jack. I'm pregnant."

SEVENTEEN

One

"IF YOU THINK you are going to live in this house and share a bedroom with me, you are out of your mind."

Jack had expected that, just as he had expected that Connie would call Kimberly and tell her she was going to have his baby. What he had not expected was that she would call Kimberly immediately, probably from a telephone in the Common Club. He had wanted to be the one to break the news to Kimberly, but he did not have the chance. Now, he wasn't confronting hysteria, only cold hard fury.

"Connie! Connie, for God's sake—who was reared like a nun and had no idea 'what evil lurks in the hearts of men.' If you had to fuck somebody, why didn't you fuck Betsy, who— Why do I ask that? You probably did!"

Jack poured two stiff Scotches. He handed her one, half expecting her to throw it at him. She didn't. He sat down in the living room. She paced.

"Do you know what this town is going to think of you? Apart from the fact that you screwed Constance Horan, of all people? It's going to know you as the cheap little California kike—"

"That's enough, Kimberly!" he snapped.

She gritted her teeth. "As the crude, vulgar . . . son of his father, who came here and made himself a parasite on the Wolcotts and then spectacularly *betrayed* them!"

"It isn't spectacular," he muttered.

She twisted her mouth into an evil, mocking smile. "Oh, it's *going* to be," she threatened. "Everybody in Boston is going to know every detail of your treachery."

"That can only hurt the children," he said quietly.

"*That's* going to hurt them? What about what *you* did?"

"It will hurt Connie, too."

"Well, isn't that too fuckin' bad! *Poor* little Connie! Poor little innocent virginal Connie. One look at that cock of yours and she couldn't wait to get it in her cunt."

Two

JACK LEAR and Harrison Wolcott sat together at the bar in the Common Club. Other members kept a distance from them, as many knew what the two men would be discussing.

"She's retained lawyers. They will be filing for divorce," Wolcott said. "She has the one ground that's valid in Massachusetts, and she's not in a forgiving mood. The worst of it is that she feels she's been humiliated. Constance Horan is one of Kimberly's closest friends. Kimberly thinks everyone in Boston is snickering."

"Guffawing," said Jack grimly

"If only you hadn't gotten her *pregnant!*"

"Try having sex with a devout Catholic girl and *not* getting her pregnant."

Wolcott smiled. "I know. A lot of us got Irish maids pregnant in the old days. It was a Boston thing, I suppose."

Jack had moved into the Copley. He was allowed to see the children for two hours every other Saturday afternoon.

"Kimberly's lawyers are advising her to ask for just about everything," Wolcott informed him.

"I could be very nasty," Jack said soberly. "I humped Connie a few times, true; but Kimberly had an ongoing relation ship with Dodge Hallowell during most of the time I was away."

"They'll deny it."

"I can prove it."

"Really Jack? How could you prove it?"

Jack stared for a moment into the apparently innocent eyes of his father-in-law. "Maybe I shouldn't tell you."

"I am hoping you and I can talk things out in a friendly manner," said Wolcott. He signaled the bartender to bring a fresh round of drinks. "I thought maybe I could act as an honest broker between you two."

"All right. I appreciate it. You won't like what I'm going to tell you. You see, Harrison, in spite of the beautiful veneer Kimberly thought she put on me, I'm still my father's son and my brother's brother. Kimberly should have wondered why, within two weeks after I came home, the maid quit. She—"

"The maid, too?"

Jack chuckled. "No. The maid who worked in the house all through the war—during my absence, that is—was actually a private investigator I had hired. I doubt very much that you want the details of what she found out. She took photographs."

"My God! What—"

"She took risks I would not have authorized her to take. The photographs are fuzzy, but you can tell who the subjects are and what they're doing, Harrison. In three of the pictures Kimberly is wearing handcuffs."

"Handcuffs?"

"Yes. I'm afraid so."

"Kimberly . . ." Wolcott whispered.

"That element of it didn't surprise me," said Jack. "I knew she had all-embracing tastes. My detective reported to me by letter. All she said was 'Things are as you suspected. Do you want details?' No, I didn't want details. I didn't want the details entrusted to the mail. I didn't even know who the man was until I got home and heard the detective's report in person."

"Do you propose to make these things public? I mean, do you expect to bring them into court as evidence?"

"Not unless Kimberly is totally unreasonable."

"May I tell her you have this evidence against her?" Wolcott asked gravely.

"Use your own judgment," Jack advised.

"I'm going to urge Kimberly to be reasonable. I hope we can remain some kind of friends, Jack."

"I hope so too. Very much. I am deeply indebted to you, Harrison—probably for acts of kindness I don't even know about, as well as those I do."

Three

DURING THE MONTHS since he had returned home, Jack had exchanged weekly letters with Anne. They were filled with news. The lights were on again in London, but the nation suffered from shortages of everything. Jack wrote to Anne that he missed her, and she wrote that she missed him. That was all they could say.

The morning after his talk with Harrison Wolcott, Jack sent a wire to Anne:

KIMBERLY IS FILING FOR DIVORCE STOP I WOULD LIKE TO COME TO LONDON AT AN EARLY DATE TO EXPLORE IMPLICATIONS THIS MAY HAVE FOR US STOP PLEASE WIRE TO LNI BOSTON STOP

JACK

He received Anne's return wire the next day:

WILL BE GLAD TO SEE YOU STOP ADVISE DATE STOP

ANNE

Jack wired her the same day, saying the divorce would take several months and that it would be unwise for him to come to London until it was final. He hoped everything would be concluded before the end of the year.

Kimberly demanded to see the photographs Rebecca Murphy had taken. Jack supplied copies to her father, who took them to the house on Louisburg Square.

Kimberly blanched at the sight of the photographs.

Her bitter comment to her father was "Well, obviously, no matter what you do, you can't make a gentleman of a cheap little kike."

Harrison Wolcott flushed with indignation. "I think you had better amend your vocabulary, Kimberly. If Jack is a kike, so is John, and so is Joan."

Kimberly instructed her lawyers to draw up a separation agreement. They resisted, saying they could get her better terms, but she was adamant that they draft the agreement as she'd said, incorporating the terms her father had negotiated with Jack.

Kimberly was to receive two radio stations: WCHS, Boston, and WHFD, Hartford. Jack would buy her stock in Lear Network, Incorporated, for $200,000. She would receive the house on Louisburg Square. Jack would pay child support of $500 a month for each child until that child reached the age of twenty-one. He would pay tuition and expenses for each child's college education.

At the suggestion of Jack's lawyer, Kimberly flew to Nevada, where the divorce was filed and granted. It became final on Friday, September 14. The separation agreement was incorporated in the decree.

Four

JACK CALLED ON Dodge Hallowell in his office at Boston Common Trust.

Though conspicuously tense and pallid, Dodge affected a hearty welcome and invited Jack to have a seat. His office, while not as large as Harrison Wolcott's, was handsome and ornamented with antique models of whaling ships. A collection of scrimshaw was displayed on a shelf behind his desk.

"Well, Jack, I . . . I don't know what to say."

"That's okay. I do."

"I hope you appreciate the circumstances."

"I do. What I can't appreciate is how damned stupid you two could be. My God, man! Even after she demanded I leave the house, and I did, you two were making whoopee in that little apartment you rented across the river."

"Your detective followed us even there?" Dodge asked, alarmed.

"I'm no gentleman, Dodge. Didn't Kimberly tell you?"

Dodge's face darkened. "She showed me the pictures."

"You going to marry her now?"

Dodge swallowed visibly. "We've talked about it."

"Okay. That will make what I'm about to propose a good deal more palatable. Under the terms of the divorce, she's to get $200,000 for her stock in my broadcasting company—"

"We'll lend you that," Dodge interrupted quickly. "Boston Common Trust will lend you $200,000 at a low rate of interest. A *very* low rate of interest."

Jack smiled. "I had a different idea in mind. Since you two are going to get married, a transfer of funds from you to her would zero out in terms of your joint assets. You give me $200,000, I give it to her, you marry her, and your money is back in your joint account. I'm sure you've got that much cash, but if not, you can borrow it from Boston Common Trust at a *very* low rate of interest."

"That would be most irregular," Dodge said somberly.

"Think of the other advantage to yourself," said Jack. "A reputation for probity is a valuable asset in the banking business."

Dodge Hallowell stood. "There is an ugly name for this," he said stiffly. "But I accept. I'll write the check now."

"Thank you, Dodge," said Jack. "You're a gentleman—and a practical man of affairs."

Five

ON SATURDAY AFTERNOONS, twice a month, Jack could go to the house on Louisburg Square to pick up the children.

"Where's your mother?" he asked the children one Saturday.

"She's upstairs."

"What would you like to do this afternoon?"

"We'd like to see a movie: *Anchors Aweigh*" said John. "But there isn't enough time. We wouldn't be back in time."

"Your mother won't mind if we're a little late."

Joan shook her head. "Yes, she will."

Another Saturday afternoon John told Jack that Kimberly was very angry. "She said you are *never* to take us up in an airplane again!"

"But you had such a good time. If we do it again, we won't tell her. Okay?"

"Something else, Daddy," Joan said hesitantly. "Last Sunday Mother took us to the Congregational church."

"That's okay."

"But, Daddy, she had us *baptized!*"

Jack frowned hard but subdued the frown as fast as he could. "Don't worry about it, kids," he said gently. "It didn't hurt anything."

"It hurt your feelings, I bet."

"Maybe. But *you* didn't do it. She did. Don't feel bad about it."

Joan grimaced. "It was icky."

In addition to Kimberly's venom, Jack had to deal with Connie's decision about their baby, which was due in November. When Dan Horan returned home from England in July, Connie spoke to Jack on the telephone.

"Dan will raise the child as if he were its father."

"Express my most heartfelt thanks to Dan, Connie. He's a generous, big-spirited man."

"The child is never to know that Dan is not the real father. That means you can't see it or have any contact with it. No cards or presents. Nothing. Dan and I will bring the child up as we see fit. You know what I mean. You must not interfere."

Jack's eyes were closed, and there were tears on his cheeks. "I understand," he said quietly. "I'll go along with your wishes."

"And one more thing, Jack," Connie added before she hung up. "I will never see you again. Not even in public."

Late in November, Harrison Wolcott called Jack. "Connie gave birth yesterday to a baby girl. They are naming her Kathleen."

Six December 1945

"WE SHOULD MARRY at Weldon Abbey," Anne told Jack. "Arthur is emphatic about it. Rose says she will hear of nothing else." Arthur was of course the Tenth Earl, the younger brother of Anne's late husband, and his wife, Rose, was Anne's successor as Countess of Weldon. "He insists that nothing else would be appropriate."

"Let's do what's appropriate," said Jack.

They arrived at Weldon Abbey two days before the ceremony. The Abbey was not one of the grandest English houses, but it was old and distinguished, built chiefly in the seventeenth century on land that had belonged to a monastery closed by Henry VIII. The Fourth Earl had been a connoisseur of art and had bought paintings all over Europe. A minor but distinctive Rembrandt hung in the hallway that the Fourth Earl had made his gallery. The collection also included a portrait by Sir Anthony Van Dyck of a subject no one had been able to identify, a domestic scene by Vermeer, a plump teenage nude by Boucher, and a portrait of the Fourth Earl's wife by Sir Joshua Reynolds.

Though Jack and Anne had said they wanted a small wedding and had suggested a short invitation list, the Earl and the Countess had a different idea. They invited an assortment of peers and knights, most of whom Jack could not confidently identify. Anthony Eden came, as did Duff Cooper and Lady Diana. Vita Sackville-West, who was a distant relative of Anne, attended the wedding with her husband, Harold Nicolson. Max Beaverbrook and Randolph Churchill came, as did Kay Summersby.

Jack had suggested only a few names—Curt and Betsy Frederick, who were still in London; Mickey Sullivan and Cap Durenberger; and Mr. and Mrs. Herb Morrill. He would have liked to invite Harrison Wolcott but decided that would be inappropriate.

He put no California names on the invitation list.

On the day before the wedding, Anne took Jack on a tour of the estate.

"I had expected to spend most of the rest of my life here. God *damn* the goddamned Krauts!" She grabbed Jack's hand and squeezed it. "I'm sorry. If . . ."

He kissed her gently.

They walked along the gallery, and she identified each of the paintings. When they reached the Boucher, the teenage nude, she asked Jack what he thought of it.

"Erotic . . ." he murmured with a little smile.

"You're going to see a lot of this painting. It's our wedding present from Arthur and Rose."

Tradition had it that Jack was not to see his bride before the ceremony on the day of the wedding. The Tenth Earl took him for a drive. As they drove in the rain, the earl gave him an extended lecture on the history of his family and Anne's.

"Her lineage, you see, is in most respects more distinguished than mine. It's a century older, at least. Historical records show that an ancestor of hers was beheaded on Tower Green by warrant of King Henry the Eighth." The Earl smiled broadly, showing his teeth. "We Flemings, Earls of Weldon, can claim no such honor."

"I know nothing of my ancestry beyond my grandfather, who was a professor in Berlin and fled Prussia to avoid military service."

"Anne's a fine gel, Jack. She'll make you the best of wives."

"I am honored that she's accepted me."

"I should be amiss if I did not tell you certain facts," said the earl. "This match astounds a great many people, and they explain it variously. Some say the earldom is bankrupt and faces the loss of Weldon Abbey and that therefore *I* arranged the marriage and demanded a great deal of money from you. That is, of course, not true. I shouldn't think of asking you for money."

"If it should become necessary, it's not outside the realm of possibility . . . within limits," Jack said.

"Oh, no! God forbid! There is nothing mercenary about this match. You love each other! Rose and I saw that when we first met you at York Terrace."

"I do love her. You can be sure of that."

"Some say you are a great seducer."

"Arthur," Jack said, using the earl's Christian name for the first time, "I will be as forthright with you as you have been with me: Anne and I have had no intimate relations."

"My God, man! You didn't have to tell me that!"

"Why not? It's the truth. We are deeply in love, and for the first time in my life I have not asked a woman to prove her love."

The sun set early in England in December, and it was dark outside when Jack came down from his room and accepted a small whisky just before the wedding party assembled in the art gallery.

Jack and Anne had agreed on a semiformal wedding. He appeared in a new dark-blue suit, and she wore a simple pink silk dress with an ankle-length gathered skirt and a hat of pink chiffon. Jack whispered to Curt, who stood beside him, that he had never seen anything so lovely. The stone-floored gallery was lighted by a hundred candles and decorated with banks of poinsettias flown in from America. Except for two elderly ladies who were seated in chairs, the guests stood to watch the ceremony.

The wedding service was performed by the rector of the parish church who, the day before, had questioned Jack closely about his religious beliefs and secured a promise from him that any children of the marriage would be baptized and reared as Christians.

After the ceremony, dinner was served in the dining room, on a table built in 1687 that was large enough to seat the entire wedding party and all the guests. Portraits of all the Earls of Weldon, including Basil, the Ninth Earl, looked down solemnly from gilt frames onto the candlelit scene. The meal was turtle soup, followed by venison from two stags killed on the estate a few days before, followed by a plum pudding as big as a washtub.

At ten o'clock the Tenth Earl and his Countess led the bride and groom to their bridal chamber, which was lit by the flames in a huge fireplace. The great bedroom was still uncomfortably cold, but they soon discovered that heating pans had just been run over the sheets on the immense curtained bed where, as they were told, King Edward VII had once slept with his mistress, Mrs. Keppel. They made love without emerging from under the big down comforters—an extraordinarily intimate way to couple.

Seven

THEIR WEDDING NIGHT was all that either one of them had expected, and more. That they had deferred their ultimate intimacy to this night, and had so often thought of it and dreamed of it, gave it a piquancy it almost surely would have lacked otherwise. Jack made love to his bride as if she were a virgin: tenderly, with elaborate care for her, as though she were a delicate creature he could bruise by his ardor. She followed his lead and accepted him demurely, letting him imagine if he wanted to that he was deflowering a maiden. It became very plain, though, in a little while that she was a fervid lover, who wanted him as much as he wanted her.

They stayed at Weldon Abbey through Christmas. Anne was going to America with Jack and had a wistful feeling that she might never see the old house again. She took Jack on a walk around the grounds, showing him the ruins of the monastery and of the abbey church, which the first earls had allowed to crumble. To Jack's great surprise, a peacock strutted in the ruins of the church. He had not supposed this exotic species could survive the cold climate of England, but Anne told him this was by no means the only estate that kept a flock of peafowl.

On December 27 Jack and Anne left Weldon Abbey and were driven to the airport in London, where they boarded a flight for Majorca. They would stay there ten days, their honeymoon.

EIGHTEEN

One 1946

ANNE HAD NEVER visited the States, but she believed New York was where she wanted to live. Jack agreed. He emphatically did not want to live in Boston. They leased a brownstone on East Fifty-fifth Street, and he took office space in the Chrysler Building.

Mickey Sullivan was with him when one of the lease agents asked Jack if he could provide credit references. "Certainly," said Jack. "You can check with Mr. Harrison Wolcott, president of Kettering Arms, Incorporated." Then he glanced at Mickey and showed a trace of a smile. "And Mr. Dodge Hallowell, president of Boston Common Trust." Mickey turned away until he could choke down a laugh.

Jack did not have to seek sponsorship for a club. As a graduate of Harvard, he was welcome at the Harvard Club.

Curt's broadcasts would now originate from a studio in the Chrysler Building and go out by telephone line to the LNI stations. Curt and Betsy also moved to New York.

Two

IN APRIL, Anne flew to London and from there traveled to Berlin. Beautiful homes had been blasted to pieces in both cities, but many distinguished pieces of furniture, antique silver, and even china had survived and were for sale. She spent much of her own money and some of Jack's, not guessing that money was scarce for him. She shipped thirty crates of treasures to New York. Few of them arrived before autumn, but when they did and were unpacked, the Lear house on Fifty-fifth Street became a showplace of the city.

The furniture Anne had shipped to New York was of fine eighteenth-century workmanship, but none of it was delicate; the antiques were not museum pieces; they were meant to be used.

"Most of these pieces are from Berlin," she explained to Jack as they worked together, unpacking her purchases and arranging in them in their rooms. "I bought them at distress prices. If your house gets knocked about, you salvage what you can and sell it to buy food."

"I guess you have to feel sorry for the people who owned some of these things," Jack suggested.

"*I* don't feel sorry for them at all. They made war and lost. Basil and Cecily were just two of the many millions of fine, innocent people they killed. If their treasures are picked up by the victors, that's just too bad. I'm sorry I had to pay anything at all for these pieces. I'd have stolen them if I could."

The house could not *all* be furnished with 18th-century antiques. The library was not. The master bedroom was not.

Also, while Anne was in Europe, Jack had contracted with a firm of plumbers to replace all the fixtures in the four bathrooms with more modern fixtures. He could not find a marble shower stall with a needle shower and a bidet, but he did have installed a tiled stall big enough for two people to shower together.

Before she left for Europe, Anne had told him to go ahead and hire a maid; she would be satisfied with his choice. He hired a thirty-year-old Negro woman named Priscilla Willoughby, who had worked for Tallulah Bankhead until the actress's idiosyncrasies became too much for her. She came with good references, including one from the redoubtable Tallulah herself.

Three

BY DECEMBER the Lears considered themselves sufficiently well established in their new home to throw a party.

They invited guests to a dinner party, to be held on Friday evening, December 13. It was to be a small party, nothing grand—a dress rehearsal for something bigger they would do later.

The invitation list was limited to old friends and associates: Herb Morrill and his wife, Esther; Mickey Sullivan and his wife, Catherine; Curt and Betsy Frederick; and Cap Durenberger and his girlfriend. Anne suggested this would be a good opportunity for her to meet Jack's family. When he demurred, she insisted. The invitations went out, and on the Tuesday before the Friday-night party, a wire from Los Angeles advised that Erich Lear and a friend, plus Robert and his wife, would be pleased and honored to attend Jack's housewarming.

The Lears arrived and checked into the Waldorf only hours before the dinner party, so Jack had no opportunity to introduce them to his new wife before the other guests arrived.

"All I can tell you, darling, is that I warned you. I hope you can still love me after you see what I come from."

The guests were due in less than half an hour. Anne kissed Jack as she straightened his tie.

He was wearing a single-breasted tuxedo that had arrived unordered and unexpected from his Savile Row tailor, as had a tweed jacket and two pairs of slacks. Curt had explained to Jack that the tailor regarded it as his obligation to see to it that his gentleman was properly outfitted for all occasions. Indeed, he had helped Jack to write a letter to the tailor, explaining that he would not be riding, hunting, or fishing and would not require clothes for those activities, nor would he be coming to England for the races at Ascot or doing any upland shooting in Scotland. Curt had explained also that there would be no point in asking for a bill; the tailor would submit an annual statement, as he had done during Jack's years in London. Curt also advised him to visit the tailor each time he was in London so the man could check his measurements.

Anne and Jack left their bedroom and checked the living room and dining room. Everything was ready. Priscilla, who wore a black uniform with white apron and white cap, plucked up from the floor a leaf that had fallen from a pot of gold chrysanthemums. Since there would be only twelve at table, Priscilla had suggested that Mrs. Lear need not hire a butler for the evening. The cook would take care of everything in the kitchen, and Priscilla would serve. By now Anne was confident that the maid would handle everything to perfection.

Curt and Betsy were the first to arrive.

Anne waited for them in the living room, where she stood before the fireplace. Behind her, a huge mirror half shrouded in drapes hung above the mantel. She wore a full rose-colored silk taffeta skirt, calf-length, and a black cashmere sweater with mid-length sleeves and a scoop neckline that displayed the Arthur Emerald in a setting of diamonds and white gold.

Jack greeted Curt and Betsy in the foyer. "Anne looks . . . regal, Jack," Curt observed.

"I'm very proud of her," Jack said simply.

"My God, what an emerald!" Betsy exclaimed when she took Anne's hand.

"It's the only significant piece of the Weldon family collection I brought with me," Anne explained. "I have it on loan, so to speak. It has to go back, eventually. King George the Third gave this emerald to Arthur, Fifth Earl of Weldon, who had supported him in some political dispute or other. The Eighth Earl commissioned the present setting, with the diamonds."

Jack nodded toward the voluptuous teenage nude hanging on the wall to the right of the fireplace. "Don't think the Earl and Countess of Weldon are cheap for wanting the emerald back. The painting is a Boucher, and it was their wedding present to us."

"I've never seen a Dürer quite like that one," said Betsy, pointing at a framed sketch.

Anne explained. "Albrecht Dürer didn't like to go to the doctor, so he did sketches like this of himself nude, pointing to the place where he hurt—hoping the doctor could diagnose from that."

"The painting on wood over there—of the Annunciation—is a fragment of a Grünewald altarpiece," said Jack. "Anne looted Europe."

"Just Berlin," Anne said with a sly smile.

The Morrills arrived, and the Sullivans. Then came the California Lears.

Erich, at sixty-one, was now completely bald and heavier than the last time Jack had seen him.

He was accompanied by a nineteen-year-old girl with flaming red hair, big blue eyes, and a red-painted mouth. "Jack," he said, "let me present a gal with a great future in pictures. Miss Barbara Tracy."

Barbara Tracy was wearing a black sequined dress that clung to her. Jack sensed that she was embarrassed—though for which of several possible reasons he did not try to guess.

Erich stared into the living room and saw Anne. "Well, Jee-zuss Christ! You seem to have a talent for one thing, anyway. And a *countess* no less."

"She's very beautiful," said Dorothy Lear, Jack's dowdy sister-in-law. Like Eleanor Roosevelt, she was not an unattractive woman but one with an uncanny knack for choosing unflattering styles. Unfortunately, she was entirely without Mrs. Roosevelt's winning personality.

"Oh, is that a Christmas tree I see?" Bob asked. "And a menorah, too. Aren't we broad-minded?"

"Eclectic," said Jack.

Anne greeted her in-laws with skilled and practiced warmth. If Erich expected to detect any suggestion of approval or disapproval or even of surprise, he had to be disappointed. She gave nothing away.

"How do I address you?" Erich asked with a slightly sardonic smile. " 'Your Ladyship'?"

"Really, Mr. Lear, why don't you try 'Anne'? I've been known to respond to it."

Erich grinned and tightened his grip on her hand. "You're gonna make a great American!"

"With all due respect, Sir, I am going to try to avoid doing so."

"Okay. Right. Jack didn't become an Englishman when he spent some time in England, and you're not going to turn into an American."

"Precisely."

Erich nodded. "I, uh, I've never seen a home furnished with such taste."

"It wouldn't suit everybody," said Anne. "But it suits us."

"I hope you come to California soon and see the California style. It wouldn't suit everybody either."

"I'm sure I'll admire it, Mr. Lear."

"I hope you will. Everybody calls me Erich. Why don't you?"

Anne nodded. "Erich. I'm so glad we've met at last."

A little later Jack spoke with his father. "Some girl you brought," Jack said dryly.

"Don't kid yourself," said Erich. "What you're lookin' at is *talent*. That gal's got talent. She's a natural."

"Natural redhead?" Jack asked with a grin.

Erich laughed. "She's no redhead!"

"Bob have her under contract?"

Erich pointed a finger at Barbara Tracy. "If I bang 'em, he signs 'em. Family obligation. He may even put her in a picture."

At dinner, Curt was seated beside Erich.

"How many radio stations does my son own?" Erich asked Curt.

"You'll find this hard to believe, Mr. Lear, but I don't know for sure. I'm a journalist and a broadcaster. Mickey knows. Herb knows. I *think* LNI has twelve stations now. I understand we may pick up one more in January and another a month or so later."

"He's a damned aggressive corporate raider," said Erich grimly. "I know something about the Richmond station. Jack went to the stockholders. Their stock could bring $15.25 a share. He offered $17.00. Management found another investor who was willing to bid $17.25. Jack stuck at $17.00 and sent a mailing to the stockholders. He told them their stock was not worth even the $15.25 but he had offered $17.00

because he knew he could make the station more profitable and increase their dividends. When the stockholders met, he owned 38 percent. The owners of 14 percent voted for his management, and Jack took over. He fired every damned executive in the house, as a warning to others who might resist him sometime. He even fired their goddamned *secretaries!* He fired two *announcers* because he didn't like their voices. He put the word out that southern accents were out; the station was to sound like a station in Washington or Philadelphia, if not a station in Boston. The local congressman had been getting free political ads. Jack told him that was illegal and from now on he'd have to pay for any ads he ran. The congressman told Jack he'd give him trouble with the FCC. Jack told him to go screw himself. In the 1946 election, the congressman scraped through with less than seven hundred votes. He ain't going to give nobody trouble, now. My son's a chip off the old block."

"I've heard that," Curt said blandly.

"He never learned a damned thing from me," said Erich, who was a little fuzzy from what he'd had to drink. "He ignored me, never figured I knew anything he needed to know. But guess what. It was *born* in him! He's just as big an asshole as I am."

"With a different style, I believe you'll admit."

"Yeah, but style doesn't count. What counts is *results,* and my son knows how to get results."

After dinner Barbara Tracy, the redhead, talked with Betsy Frederick. "Erich tells me Anne is his second wife and that the first one was just as beautiful and refined as this one. Erich says that the first wife—what was her name?"

"Kimberly."

"He says Kimberly disliked him."

"I think there was mutual antipathy between them," Betsy remarked.

"I got the impression there were bad feelings between father and son, but they seem to get along all right."

"Each of them would gladly kill the other," Betsy said mordantly, with a trace of a smile on her lips.

Four

IN PARIS, Anne had found two superlative etchings by Mario Tauzin that had apparently been taken from a portfolio and professionally matted and framed. They were deftly executed line drawings of an innocently nude pubescent boy and girl. In one the girl smiled lazily as she welcomed the boy to use a finger to explore her spread-open furrow. In the other drawing the boy grinned as the girl gripped his shaft in one hand and lifted his balls with the other. Anne had bought the etchings for their bedroom, and they hung there now.

She and Jack had showered together and now lay on their bed and talked.

"I don't like to say anything negative about Basil," she said, "but he never did appreciate anything like the Tauzins. He was a man of very straightforward tastes and wouldn't really have appreciated even this. . . ."

She meant what she was doing: gently fondling Jack's penis with her long, slender fingers.

"Englishmen have many admirable qualities," said Jack. "They make bold soldiers, not bold cooks or lovers. Now, English girls, on the other hand—"

"Bawstard!" Anne laughed, and she bent forward and kissed his glans. She flicked it with the tip of her tongue. It seemed never to have occurred to her to do more, and he had decided not to suggest she should. If she found her way— He would let her find it.

She turned on her back and spread her legs. With her fingers she stretched her cunt open and showed him her delicately colored folds. She rolled her hips and smiled as she watched him stare at her cunt flower.

No woman had ever done this for him before. Tonight, for the first time, he bent forward and kissed what she was showing. He couldn't resist doing that. He touched her folds, then the little finger of her clitoris, with his tongue. She moaned.

"Come in, Jack! Come in! I *want* you. Hey! No rubber. Let's make a baby! It's time we made a baby!"

NINETEEN

One 1947

JACK FLEW to New Orleans because Cap Durenberger insisted it was important, and he had learned to place some trust in Cap's judgment. He had asked Curt to come with him. At about six o'clock he sat down with Cap and Curt in the living room of the hotel suite Cap had reserved. Cap poured drinks.

"What's the deal, anyway?" Jack asked Cap. "Let's get specific. We can acquire nine stations all at once?"

"Not *acquire,*" said Cap. "Affiliate. They've got nine stations—Dallas, Shreveport, Memphis, Lexington, Kansas City, and so on. Their stations are not for sale. The company's not for sale. But they might listen to a proposition for a merger. They play a lot of bluegrass and country music, and they broadcast a stream of market reports—pork bellies, cattle, grain, and cotton. They're losing market share in some of their cities because the population wants to hear just so much bluegrass and then wants something more. On the other hand, they don't want network affiliation, even if they could get it, because they'd have to give more time to network programs than they want to give. We could offer them a looser relationship. They—"

"Well, what's the deal tonight?" Jack interrupted. "How come we—"

"If your flight had arrived earlier, they'd have asked us to meet in their lawyers' offices. But since you got here after four in the afternoon, they seem to figure an evening meeting in a club, where we can all get better acquainted, is a good idea."

"What kind of club?"

"Ray l'Enfant is taking us to his club. For dinner and . . . whatever."

"What's 'whatever'?" Curt asked.

"I'm not really sure. Anyway, he's picking us up at seven."

L'Enfant came to the hotel for them in a sixteen-cylinder Lincoln Continental. Billy Bob Cotton was with him.

Since no one but Ray knew the city at all, they had no real idea where he was taking them. For a while Ray l'Enfant drove along the river, chatting blandly about the weather and about the varying scents that reached them through the open windows of the car, particularly the unique smell of the lower river: the stench of death on a saltwater tide combined with the singular oily stink of Mississippi mud. Then he turned into a neighborhood of what looked like antebellum mansions, though it would have been difficult to describe the houses in any detail, since each was hidden by a tall hedge or a wall and by thick oaks festooned with Spanish moss. The scents there were stronger, so much so as even to be oppressive, like heavy perfumes.

"This is an area of myths and legends," said l'Enfant. "Some of the houses are said to be haunted . . . some with things worse than ghosts."

"Like?" Jack asked.

L'Enfant chuckled. "Zombies. Vampires. Werewolves. All the things simple minds can imagine when they hear strange noises or see unexpected lights."

"Like Christians." Cap laughed. "When they can't explain something, they figure Satan has been at work."

"I take Christianity a bit more seriously than that," Billy Bob Cotton said reprovingly.

Billy Bob Cotton had appeared for their evening meeting in a light gray suit,with a champagne-colored Stetson, and snakeskin boots. If to an easterner he looked and sounded like a country boob, he needed to say only a few words to disabuse anyone of that notion.

"We are not going to see any ghosts or devils, vampires or saints, tonight," said l'Enfant.

Raymond l'Enfant was the youngest man in the car. He was tall and slender and had shiny burn scars on his left cheek and left hand. As Jack would learn, he had flown a P-47 Thunderbolt in Europe during the war and had been burned over much of the left side of his body when he landed his flak-damaged plane on a field in France. He had won the Distinguished Service Cross and wore the ribbon in his lapel.

Somewhat abruptly he pulled off the street and drove up to a Gothic wrought-iron gate, where he stopped and blinked his headlights.

A big Negro emerged from the shadows. "Monsieur l'Enfant. Welcome," he said.

L'Enfant got out of the car and beckoned his guests to do the same. The Negro slid behind the wheel and backed the car into the street. He would park it somewhere out of sight.

The five men walked up a short driveway bordered by lush and malodorous shrubbery, then mounted the wooden steps to a broad veranda.

A woman, probably alerted by a buzzer the Negro had sounded, opened the double doors of the mansion.

"Messieurs . . ."

"*Bon soir,* Antoinette," said l'Enfant. "We'll sit in the big room tonight and see the show."

Antoinette, who was fifty years old at least, and wearing a clinging red dress, led them to a table in a dining room with about twenty tables. A quartet—trumpet, saxophone, piano, and drums—played New Orleans jazz, but not so loud as to inhibit conversation.

The big round table was set for six, but a busboy quickly removed the sixth setting, almost before the five men were in their chairs. The linen was thick, the silver heavy. A crystal vase in the center of the table held a dozen white roses.

A waitress appeared. "Ah'm Polly," she said. "What's your pleasure, gentlemen?"

Except for red shoes and dark stockings held up by red garters, Polly was stark naked. She had an angelic face, light brown hair, and a fleshy body with swelling breasts that seemed to stretch her skin almost to the breaking point. L'Enfant ordered a bottle of bourbon and one of Scotch, and Polly hurried off to fill the order.

"Nevah git enough of this place," said Billy Bob.

"I don't think I ever will either," Cap added.

"I'll propose each of you for membership," Ray said. "It costs $1,500 initiation fee and $150 a month minimum. 'Course, out of *town* guests pay only $25 a month minimum."

"I'd be honored to be a member," said Jack. "What's the name of the club?"

"That's one of the beauties of it," said Ray. "It's got no name. Your monthly statement will come from the New Orleans Cotton Exchange Club, but don't ever ask a cabdriver to take you to that. Tell him to take you to the No-Name Club."

Jack laughed. "The No-Name Club. Curt, don't we have anything like this in New York?"

Curt shrugged, but Cap grinned and said, "I can introduce you to a place on West Forty-seventh Street. But my suggestion is, it's a dumb dog who shits in his own bed. You want something like this, find it out of town. Right, Ray?"

"Or find it in N'Awleans, where we know how to keep secrets."

Cap spoke to Ray. "I won't make any decisions for him, but I'll suggest to you that Jack may not want to take advantage of the best the No-Name Club has to offer. He's recently married to the most heavenly creature you could ever hope to see—an English countess."

Jack laughed. "In return for the favor, I'll report that Cap recently married a heavenly creature of his own. A girl from Lubbock, Texas, which is his hometown."

"I'll suggest we don't take advantage of what the club offers in that respect," Ray said. "I'd rather have mine in circumstances a good deal less public. 'Course if our waitress gives you a hard-on—"

"I come to look, not to touch," said Billy Bob. "The two are to some extent mutually exclusive."

"You can do your touching back at your hotel," said Ray. "I can arrange something if you want, but you can arrange for yourselves easy enough."

"The food here is out of this world," said Billy Bob.

"If you'll allow me, I'll order," said Ray. "I warn you, though. It won't be what you're used to."

Jack smiled.

"Give me escape from what I'm used to."

They drank sparingly from the bourbon and Scotch, because Ray put in an order for their appetizer and entrée, with the appropriate wine—a musty red Bordeaux.

"We might talk a little business," Ray suggested. "You must understand, Mr. Lear, that my partners and I are not interested in selling our stations or our company. There are nine of us. We call ourselves partners, but in fact Broadcasters Alliance is a corporation, and each of the nine partners owns one-ninth of the stock. The stations and their licenses belong to the company. Of course, if five of us sold our stock to you, you could take control of the company. But I don't think any five of us will."

"I hope not," said Jack. "I didn't come to talk about buying your stations or taking control of your company. Frankly, I couldn't raise the capital to absorb nine more stations this year. You call your arrangement an alliance. I came to explore with you the possibility of a different kind of alliance: one between your company and mine. My general idea is that all of us would retain ownership and control of our stations. LNI would provide you with a certain amount of programming, which you would get without having to surrender any control to a network. Broadcasters Alliance would provide some programming to LNI. We would pay each other for the programming we exchange. Or maybe we could trade to some extent—that is, trade some programming on a barter basis, with no cash changing hands."

"It'd be a complicated deal, with lots of issues to decide," said Billy Bob Cotton.

"Absolutely," Jack agreed.

Their meal was brought by a tall, dignified Negro man with white hair, who expertly served their food with pairs of spoons manipulated in his right hand. Polly served just two tables, hovering between them, moving in to fill wineglasses, hurrying away to speak to the waiter when she saw that a gentleman might want more of something. Once when she was pouring wine, Curt patted her gently on her bare bottom. She smiled warmly and suggestively raised her eyebrows.

The appetizer was oysters skewered between slices of smoked sausage and cooked in a wine sauce. With the oysters came a bowl of roasted pecans. This was followed by a peach-

and-pepper salad. The entrée was broiled alligator tail in lemon butter sauce, served with red beans and rice.

"My God, this is *exquisite,* Ray," Jack said.

"Enough to make us think about getting together in N'Awleans from time t' time," said Billy Bob.

Then the entertainment began. A small low stage was hidden behind a red velvet curtain. The curtain was drawn back by Antoinette, revealing a narrow bed in the glare of bright overhead spotlights. The jazz quartet played louder.

"Polly and Amelia!" Antoinette announced.

Polly trotted across the room, climbed up on the stage, and lay down on her back on the bed. Amelia, another waitress who was blond and had a spare figure, followed Polly to the stage, knelt, and pressed her face into Polly's crotch. She pushed Polly's legs farther apart, so the men at the tables could see what she was licking. Polly writhed and moaned.

When after some ten minutes the pair broke off, Polly was flushed and sweating. As the men at the tables applauded appreciatively, she left the room.

"Deirdre and Marie!" Antoinette called next.

Two more waitresses climbed onto the bed. They embraced each other and rubbed their crotches together. They sucked on each other's nipples. Deirdre, a thin young girl, rose on her knees, presented her backside to Marie, and used her hands to spread her hinder cheeks as wide as she could. Marie, who was a handsome redhead probably more than thirty years old, shoved her tongue into Deirdre's anus and began licking vigorously. At the same time she reached through between Deirdre's legs and inserted her middle finger into her slit.

After a few minutes they reversed positions, and Deirdre returned the favor.

"God!" murmured Jack. "I may wind up arranging something at the hotel after all."

Now the lights went off, leaving the room dark except for the lights on the stage, which were themselves dimmed.

A single spotlight shot a bright circle on a hole in the curtain behind the bed. Marie, the handsome redhead, climbed up on the stage, pushed the bed aside, and knelt on the floor. In a moment a man's parts were shoved through the hole in the curtain. Marie seized them and sucked the penis into her mouth.

"He's of the members," Ray explained. "They turn off the lights so no one but the others at his table know who's gone behind the curtain."

"Damned hard to resist," said Billy Bob.

"*Too* damned hard," said Jack. "Polly?"

"If you want," Ray said.

Ray snapped his fingers, and Antoinette made her way to the table. "Who?" she whispered.

"Polly."

" 'Kay. C'mon, whichever one of you it is."

She led Jack by the hand through the dark room to a tiny bathroom behind the stage curtains. "You'd be doing the girl a favor if you'd wash it off first," she said blandly.

Jack went inside the little bathroom and used warm water and soap and paper towels to wash himself. He heard a knock on the door and opened it. Antoinette pointed to the eight-inch hole in the curtain, where the light shone through.

"Drop your pants and stick it through. She's waiting."

He heard applause as he shoved his cock and balls through the red velvet curtain. He could not see the girl. He could not be sure it *was* Polly. He felt her hands on him first, then felt her licking him, then felt her suck his penis into her mouth. She didn't have to work long. He came sooner than he wanted to. His pleasure was quick, but it was deep and complete.

When he returned to the table, another man's parts were displayed in the hole, and little Millie was on her knees and ready to go to work. Thank God, Jack thought. That meant the room was still dark and everyone's attention was focused on the stage.

No one else went behind the curtain. The room remained dark until the third man was back at his table. Then the lights came up, and all the performers stood naked on the stage or on the floor in front of it and took their bows. Men wadded up money and threw it to them.

The party of five stayed at their table and drank brandy and coffee. None of the others said anything to Jack, not even to ask him if it had been good.

When they left the club, the naked waitresses were standing by the door, saying good night. Jack stepped over to Polly and slipped a fifty dollar bill into her hand.

Two

NEGOTIATING THE COMPLEX CONTRACT between Broadcasters Alliance and LNI took several months. In the end, the Alliance conceded more influence over its operations than Jack had thought it would. He was not surprised, though, when *Time* described the deal as "in effect a merger, giving Jack Lear and his associates control over twenty-three radio broadcasting stations and making LNI a more powerful voice than it has ever been before, or than anyone ever dreamed it would become."

Three

ON OCTOBER 21 Anne gave birth to a healthy little boy they named Jack Arthur.

They hired a live-in nanny for the baby. She was Mrs. Gimbel, who had served as nanny for John and Joan and had come to love the family. Jack's confidence in the woman eased Anne's concern that Mrs. Gimble was too old to be a nanny.

The first confrontation between mother and nanny occurred when Anne informed Mrs. Gimble that she would breast-feed the child for a year. Mrs. Gimbel did not approve, saying a formula would provide more complete nutrition. Priscilla, the maid, weighed in on the side of breast-feeding. Jack just smiled and refused to take sides in the argument.

In any event, Little Jack, as he was inevitably called, thrived and became a plump, effervescent baby. Jack loved him, even though little Little Jack reminded him that John would be sixteen before long and that they rarely saw each other.

TWENTY

One 1948

IN 1946 KIMBERLY had married Dodge Hallowell. In March 1948 she wrote to Jack saying he could not have the children for a month in the summer, as usual, because she and Dodge would be taking them to Europe for the entire summer. Jack telephoned Harrison Wolcott.

"I'll speak to her, Jack. She ought to know by now that she can't just ignore the terms of the decree any time it suits her."

"I most emphatically don't want to do this, Harrison, but I will hire a lawyer and go back to court if she forces me."

"She'll calm down. I'll talk to her. While we're on the phone, I'd like to raise another subject. Would you have any interest in buying back WCHS and WHFD? Kimberly would be better off with some money. Neither she nor Dodge has any inkling about how to manage a radio station."

"I'll think about it," Jack said, "but frankly, Harrison, I couldn't afford them right now. I've bought other stations, you know—and mortgaged my ass to do it. We're selling more advertising time. Revenues are up. But—"

"Suppose *I* buy them. Let Kimberly and Dodge think you bought them. You manage them. Real ownership will be in a trust I will establish for the benefit of John and Joan. So far as the world will see, you will just have added two more stations to your network."

"That's very generous of you, Harrison. I'm sorry Kimberly has to be kept in the dark about things like this. You know, I *did* love her. I loved her deeply. In a sense I still do. But, Harrison, she *smothered* me. Now she tries to keep the kids from seeing me."

"Kimberly's problem with the children is that she worries about their living in your New York townhouse. Won't it be a little crowded?"

"I'll rent a summer place."

He leased a rambling house with a swimming pool, in Greenwich, Connecticut, for July and August.

To the residents of Greenwich, Anne was the Countess of Weldon even though she was married to Jack Lear, son of the notorious Erich Lear. Within two weeks the Lears were invited to take summer membership in the Greenwich Country Club and to attend services at Second Congregational Church and Temple Shalom. They joined the country club, though neither of them played golf, but they attended no religious services.

The children arrived from Boston on July 3. John was almost six feet tall, muscular and tanned and without hair on his body. His eyes were blue. His hair had been bleached by the sun. Joan was fourteen but looked as old as her brother. No longer a child, she was developing into a beautiful young woman with her mother's regular features and smooth dark-brown hair. She tended to be solemn and to avoid the horseplay of the other teenagers at the country club pool and at the beach. She was self-conscious about her figure, embarrassed by her swelling new breasts and the sleek curves of her hips and her long legs—embarrassed, yet proud.

John told his father on the day he arrived that he would like to be taken to Westchester County Airport, which was only about five miles from the house. The next day Jack took him there. The boy's fascination with flying had continued unabated. At the airport they walked out on the flight line and looked at airplanes.

A pilot came out of the shack and walked toward them. He looked like a man who had flown during the war. "Like to go for a ride, gentlemen?" he asked.

Jack shook his head. "No. Not what I had in mind."

"Mom doesn't need to know," John muttered.

"What I had in mind was that you might give this young

man flying lessons. He's going to be in town, in Greenwich, all this month. Maybe he could get in—what?—a dozen lessons, fifteen?"

"How many depends on a lot of things," said the pilot. "Mostly the weather. How old are you, son?"

"Sixteen."

"In that case you couldn't get a license this year. You have to be seventeen. Anyway, we couldn't get in all the flying and studying you'd have to do in just one month. But you can get a student certificate and start logging flight training. You'll have to pass a medical exam, too. My name is Fred Dugan. I'm a licensed instructor. 'Course, there are other instructors. You might want to shop around."

"What kind of plane would he fly?" Jack asked.

Dugan nodded toward a low-slung, high-winged little yellow airplane. "That one. That's a Piper Cub. Perfect little airplane to start out in. You say he'll only be here a month. When will he be back?"

"Next summer."

Dugan cocked his head and regarded John skeptically. "What's your name, son?"

"John Lear."

"Okay, John Lear. Don't expect to solo this summer. But if we get in some good hours this month and you study your materials all winter so you can pass the written exam next summer, I figure we can get you a license next year."

Two

ON HIS FOURTH TIME OUT in the Cub, Dugan required John to fly a maneuver called a turn about a point.

They were somewhere north of the airport, over New York or Connecticut.

"Okay, son, see that right-angle road intersection down there."

"Yessir."

"Put your left wingtip on that intersection and fly a three-sixty, keeping your wingtip right on it."

John tried, but the Piper Cub drifted off the point.

"Why's that?" Dugan asked.

"The wind, I suppose," said John.

"You got it. The wind blew you off the point. So how you gonna correct for that?"

"Gotta turn my nose into it a little."

"Right. Go at it again."

It was one of the most difficult maneuvers for student pilots to master. John worked on it. He succeeded on his fourth try, coming around to his original heading with the wingtip hanging firmly on the intersection.

"Now, son," said Dugan. "Look at your altimeter. What was your altitude when you started the turn?"

"Eighteen hundred feet."

"And what is it now?"

"Uh-oh. Fourteen hundred feet."

"How can you correct for that?"

"Add power," said John.

"Exactly. Do it again. You gotta keep your wingtip in place and keep your altitude constant. You see what this is for? You gotta make precise turns like that to fly the landing pattern."

Jack couldn't always drive John to the airport. Anne did. Priscilla did. The boy who was working on his pilot's license didn't yet have a driver's license.

Fred Dugan took Jack aside as John was filling out his logbook. "Mr. Lear, I wouldn't want the boy to hear this, but he is a natural-born pilot. He's got a *sense* of flying, a *feel* for the airplane in the air that most of us work years to acquire. He's the best student I ever instructed. I sent him up with another instructor the other day, and that guy agrees with me."

Jack shook hands with Dugan. "I don't know what to do about it," he said quietly.

"He wants to fly a bigger plane so you can come along and see him fly. Don't do it. We've been working on stalls. Mr. Lear, he stalls a plane and sends it over into a spinning dive that almost makes *me* upchuck—then recovers and comes out level like nothing had happened."

Three

DURING THE SECOND WEEK in July, Jack and Anne traveled to Philadelphia to attend the Democratic National Convention. They were in the hall when Harry S. Truman was nominated and at 2:00 A.M. when he made his acceptance speech.

Jack's new associates at Broadcasters Alliance were happy with Curt Frederick's live coverage of the convention. Curt sat in a glassed-in booth overlooking the convention floor while three men with microphones wandered through the crowd interviewing delegates.

Curt himself went out on the floor occasionally. He scored a broadcasting coup when he thrust a microphone at a group of Dixiecrats angrily abandoning the convention and picked up the voice of a South Carolina delegate growling, "Truman! Truman! That nigga-lovin' cocksuckah!" Since the feed was live, the words went out on sixteen Lear Network stations and seven of the nine Broadcasters Alliance stations and were heard by millions.

Shrieks of protest went up from the Dixiecrats, especially the South Carolinians. Some of them charged that a hidden microphone had been used to pick up private conversation. The South Carolinian whose voice was heard on the air charged that Curt Frederick had spoken the words himself in a fake southern accent.

Asked about the incident, President Truman laughed and said, "My! Such language!"

LNI received thousands of letters saying it should not have let the words go out on the air. Jack himself read a network editorial, which was broadcast three times on all the stations. He said LNI had no wish to air such words, but since the broadcast was live there had been no way to stop it. He apologized to those who were offended.

The incident was a highlight of LNI's exhaustive convention coverage, which was on the whole an acknowledged triumph of broadcast journalism.

Four

FRIDAY WAS Priscilla's day off. She took the train into New York early in the morning and would not return to Greenwich before midmorning on Saturday. In the afternoon Mrs. Gimbel took Little Jack to the beach. Big Jack and Anne would not be home from Philadelphia until tomorrow. This left John and Joan alone in the house.

They swam in the pool, but the water was still a little cold, so they felt clammy when they came out. They decided to go upsatairs and take a warm shower—together.

Both nude, they went in Joan's room and stretched out on the bed. John began to fondle her.

"Hey, Joni," he whispered in her ear. "Let's . . ."

She grunted. "Well . . . I'm still scared about that, John. If we ever got caught—"

"We aren't gonna get caught. If Gimbel comes home, we'll hear the crunch of the gravel in the driveway. If *anybody* comes, we'll hear them, and we'll have plenty of time to get dressed. Hey, you *do* like it, don't you?"

"You know I do. I just figure we're taking chances. The more times we do it, the more likely somebody will figure it out."

"Not if we're careful. And we've been very careful."

"You're sure I can't get pregnant?"

"Right. You can't. A guy can't get his sister pregnant. I don't know exactly why. It's . . . something in the way it works. It's something in the genes."

"We're not supposed to."

"Yeah, but who could you trust more? Who could I trust more. C'mon, Joni. You like it as much as I do."

"Yeah, I do."

Five

"ONE OF THE REASONS Sally Allen is no tremendous success on radio," Cap said to Jack, "is that radio's not *visual.* She's a comedienne chiefly, and she's damned funny, but in every picture she does she has a role that lets her show off her legs. In her radio show she's a housewife. We give her funny lines, but . . ."

Jack frowned. "Let me ask you something. Has she ever smoked a cigarette on-screen?"

"Not that I recall."

"Well, she smokes on the radio show. Every goddamned episode has some line like 'Hey, Harry, I need to relax. Light my Amber for me. Ah . . . thanks. That's better.' "

"Hell, I know," said Cap. "And Harry probably says something like 'Yeah. Relaxing. Sure tastes great.' The sponsor demands it. Which makes our comedienne sound like a vacant-headed idiot."

"Why do we let sponsors—or sponsors' advertising agencies, actually—dictate to us?" Jack asked angrily "Why the hell should Sally Allen's show start with a breathless idiot yelling into a microphone, *'The Amber Cigarettes Hour, Featuring Sally Allen!'?* Why? Why not *The Sally Allen Show,* sponsored by Amber Cigarettes!?"

"Because the bastards will desert us," said Cap.

"No they won't. They need us as bad as we need them."

Six

JACK DECIDED to fly to Los Angeles to see Sally Allen. They met for lunch at the Brown Derby.

Sally Allen was distinctive. In a Hollywood that still insisted on bland conformity in leading ladies, she was different. Her eyes were too big. Her teeth were too prominent. Her voice was high-pitched and nasal, except when she held it in tight control. On the other hand, her figure was one that any leading lady would envy. She was twenty-eight years old.

They chatted about nothing much for a while, but when she was halfway through her third martini she told him she was sorry she had signed a five-year contract. "Cap Durenberger's a sharp, persuasive guy," she said.

"You want out of the contract?" Jack asked.

"Well . . ."

"I'll let you out. I don't want anyone working for me who's unhappy with the deal."

She tipped her head to one side and regarded him with skeptical curiosity. "You're not the kind of guy your brother says you are."

"You know my brother?"

Sally grinned and opened her big eyes wide. "Everybody knows the Lears, father and son. I understand you refused to release me from my radio contract to make a picture for Carlton House."

"We've released you to do four other pictures. I was trying to protect you from my father, who inisists on doing you-know-what with every actress Bob hires."

"This kid can protect herself."

"Don't kid yourself. Erich doesn't play fair."

"I don't have to either."

Jack put his hand on hers and stared hard into her eyes. "Sally, you can't compete with him. Don't even try."

Sally blew a loud sigh. She stared at her drink, as though considering ordering another, then visibly decided not to.

"Listen," said Jack. "I've got a couple of ideas. Let me explain them. Don't say no until you've heard me out."

She shrugged. "I wasn't doing anything else this afternoon."

"All right. The fall season has started, and it's the same old shit. Sally Allen, batty housewife, star of *The Amber Cigarettes Hour.* What have we got in the can? Enough to last till January?"

"I suppose."

"Okay. Suppose we announce shortly that *The Amber Cigarettes Hour* is cancelled for the balance of the season. We—"

"The sponsors may cancel themselves. They can jump the gun on us."

"Not if we announce tomorrow."

"What are we gonna announce tomorrow, Mr. Lear?"

"Call me Jack. Suppose you and I call a press conference tomorrow. We announce that we are unhappy with *The Amber Cigarettes Hour, Featuring Sally Allen* and that we are going into production immediately with a new mid-season program called *The Sally Allen Show!*"

"Which will be different how?"

He snapped his fingers and ordered another round of drinks. "Sally Allen is no situation-comedy housewife, prattling about how much she loves her Amber cigarettes and her Flo laundry soap. She's a showbiz girl! The comedy is built around her adventures putting together a vaudeville act, a nightclub show, a . . . whatever. Some of the lines are jokes about how brief her costumes are. The audience has an image of this hardworking, sharp-talking gal struggling to make a career on the stage and frustrated by every prosaic, cliché-ridden—"

"Who's gonna write this?" asked Sally.

"We can find a writer. Got somebody in mind?"

"I might."

"Well, if you want a release, you got it. You want to try something different, you got that."

"Who's gonna sponsor?"

"I am. For a while. But I'll bet that Southern Tobacco will be back, offering money for commercial spots, before the opening half-season ends. That's the way my network is going to operate from now on. Sponsors can buy commercial time, but they'll buy it on shows *we* create and produce. Nobody is going to own us."

"You'll go broke," Sally said flatly.

"Even if I do, you won't. I can fund my obligations under your contract until it expires. Something else, Sally. In the bitter end, you know, you're not really a radio performer. You're too *visual.* Suppose we get into this thing called video—"

"Television," she interrupted.

"Okay. Whatever. Suppose Sally Allen appears on the face of a tube—singing, dancing, showing her legs. Hey, all we have to do is not lose too much capital in the spring of '49."

Sally Allen turned down the corners of her mouth and shook her head. "You and Durenberger," she said. "Okay, boss. Let's give it a try."

Seven

IN OCTOBER Jack returned to Los Angeles unexpectedly.

"Siddown, kid." Erich Lear pointed to the couch that faced his desk. "What the hell are you doing here?"

Jack let himself down heavily on the big leather-covered couch. "I've got a big problem," he said.

"What are you saying?" Erich's Marsh Wheeling stogie had gone out, and he snapped a Zippo and touched flame to it. "What kind of problem could you have that you'd want to talk to me about it?"

"This is goddamned serious."

"I figure. You wouldn't be here if it wasn't."

"All right. You can screw me to a fare-thee-well on this. I've come to you for help. You can shit me or not shit me."

"Runnin' out of money?"

"I wouldn't call that serious. I could handle that. I have something a hell of a lot more serious than that."

Erich clasped his hands behind his head and leaned his chair back, letting the stogie hang from a corner of his mouth. He was wearing a madras jacket over a golf shirt. "Jesus . . . to think of it. My son coming to me for— What's the deal, Jack?"

"Confidential. You and I have never been the best of friends, but I always figured your word's good."

"They figure that in this town. I screw broads, not business guys. *They* watch their chances and screw you back."

"All right. When you need something out of the ordinary, you go to the guy who knows how to do it. Dad, I need the services of a damned good, damned secret doctor."

Erich's face lit up. He grinned. He brought down his arms and pulled the stogie from his mouth. *"An abortion!* Christ the Lord, who have you got knocked up? Don't tell me it's Sally Allen!"

Jack choked on his words. He wiped his eyes and shook his head. "That'd be a joke. This isn't. This is *serious!"*

Erich put his stogie aside in an ashtray. "A kid . . . ?"

"Not by me! I don't know who the guy is. She absolutely refuses to say."

Erich frowned. "Who?" he asked darkly.

"Joan. My daughter."

Erich gaped. "What's she . . . ? *Fourteen fuckin' years old?"*

"Yes."

Erich reached for a button on his desk, then pulled back his hand. "You gotta get somebody killed, son."

"Yeah . . . when I find out who. Right now what I need is a one hundred percent trustworthy doctor."

Erich nodded. "Okay. I know one who can do it. When?"

"The kids are coming to me for Thanksgiving. They'll arrive in New York on Wednesday, but they have to be back in Boston Sunday night."

"You tellin' me her mother doesn't know?"

"I'm telling you her mother doesn't know."

"But you do."

"My son called me."

Erich blew a loud sigh between the fingers that covered his mouth. "Chartered plane," he said. "Fly her out here on Thanksgiving Day. Operation that evening, Friday morning at the latest. How far along is she?"

"Maybe two months, ten weeks."

"It's not a serious operation, but it'd be better if we could get it done sooner."

"Dad, I'm not responsible for this. Not in any way."

"Well. Something that makes you call me Dad is pretty important. I'll set it up. You get her out here. Does the Countess know?"

"Anne knows."

"Why don't you tell Kimberly you're celebrating Thanksgiving with the California grandparents?"

Eight

JOAN MANAGED to hold back her tears until the chartered twin took off from Teterboro Airport. Then, in the air, she broke down.

Anne hugged her. "The operation is easy, Joni," she whispered. "It'll be over in five minutes."

"I believed it couldn't happen," Joan wept. "I didn't *want* it to happen! I was afraid."

She was very careful not to stare at John, who sat opposite her. The passenger cabin was configured as a sort of little living room.

"The big point," said Jack, "is that we keep a family secret. I'm not going to press you about who it was. But could it have happened when you were visiting us in Greenwich?"

"It happened then," Joan wept. "And that's all I'm going to say about it. Don't try to figure it out."

"We're not going to say we don't care who it was," Anne whispered to her. "But you don't have to say. What difference would it make?"

Joan sobbed and nodded. "A whole lot of difference!"

"But you don't want to tell us?" asked Jack.

"I'll *never* tell!" Joan shrieked. "I'll never tell!"

"Well, answer one question," Jack said grimly. "Was it Dodge Hallowell?"

"No!"

Anne hugged the girl tighter. "When we fly back, you'll feel better."

"But I'll have *killed my baby!"* Joan screamed.

Anne nodded. "Just remember, there's nobody with you on this trip who doesn't love you."

TWENTY-ONE

One 1949

CURT FREDERICK'S contract came up for renewal in 1949. He was by now one of the most respected broadcast journalists in the United States. Jack had released to him all copyright claims to his wartime broadcasts, so he could make an LP record, which was called *As It Happened.* Such cuts as his 1940 broadcast from Sedan, with the roar of German artillery behind his voice, won him brisk record sales and millions of new listeners who still did not have LNI stations in their communities.

Jack also released to him some snippets from more recent broadcasts, including the South Carolina Dixiecrat yelling "Truman! Truman! That nigga-lovin' cocksuckah!" Many thousands of records were sold to people who had not heard the broadcast and still had to be convinced that the words had actually been spoken on the radio.

"I hardly need tell you I'm grateful to you," Curt said to Jack over lunch at the Harvard Club, "but I've also got to tell you I'm a little tired. Doing a nightly news show five times a week is wearing me down. Betsy keeps telling me she doesn't want me to have a heart attack, and she says we don't need the money."

"I can't imagine you'd actually retire," said Jack. "What are you looking for, Curt?"

"Maybe a weekly show, a whole half hour exploring some topic in depth, with interviews and so on."

"I've got a different idea," said Jack. "Sooner or later we're going to start telecasting. Suppose you did a television show, maybe twice a month. You'd make a hell of a fine appearance on television."

"Maybe. Or maybe I'd look like an idiot. Anyway, how soon do you plan to go into television?"

"Let's think in terms of next year. In the meantime, do me a favor and continue the nightly radio news for one more year. Right now, let's suppose you take a month's vacation. We'll put that in your contract: a month off every year. Of course," Jack added, "we can also work a little more money into the deal."

Two

IN APRIL Jack called a meeting in the offices in the Chrysler Building. With him in the conference room were Cap Durenberger, Herb Morrill, and Mickey Sullivan—the three long-time members of the management team of LNI—plus Ray l'Enfant of Broadcasters Alliance and Professor Friedrich Loewenstein.

The meeting was held early in the evening.

Jack presided. In 1949 he was a new man. Exuberantly happy in his marriage to Anne, he had cut down on drinking and smoking and had lost a few pounds. Anne had measured him meticulously and sent the new dimensions to his Savile Row tailor, who kept him handsomely clothed. Jack was not the proper conforming gentleman Kimberly had wanted to make of him, but he was a gentleman in a better style.

"The purpose of our meeting, obviously, is to talk about this thing called television," he said. "I think we have to get into it. We have no choice."

"That's going to be a little difficult," said Herb Morrill. "The FCC has frozen the issuance of new television broadcasting licenses. RCA owns most of the stations now operating. CBS has a few. The independents are—"

"For sale," Jack finished the sentence. "Five years from now a television license is going to be worth ten fortunes. Right now they're not. In the first place, there's not much programming. What is worse, the cost of sending out the signal, to only relatively few receivers, is prohibitive. How many television receiving sets are there in the United States? Cap? You know?"

"Half a million, maybe," Durenberger said. "Almost all of them within fifty miles of New York City."

Jack nodded. "Okay. Suppose we acquired a license in St. Louis or, say, Dallas. Suppose we put up a broadcasting tower that reached halfway to the sky. Suppose we sent out a signal that could be picked up for two hundred miles—by people who were interested enough to raise their receiving antennas high, maybe as much as fifty feet. Professor Loewenstein?"

"You could reach *sree* hundred miles, Mr. Lee-ar."

"Okay," Jack went on. "Forgive me. I've thought this through. Maybe too much. Maybe my enthusiasm is running away with me. What good's a television receiver in Tulsa? It's worth nothing because there's no signal for it to receive. But suppose we were sending a strong long-distance signal out of Dallas or St. Louis—"

"Or Kansas City," said Cap. "Look at your demographics. Look what you could reach from Kansas City."

"You overlook something, gentlemen," said Professor Loewenstein. "You could have a broadcasting station in Kansas City, let us say, but with *satellite* transmitters in Dallas, Tulsa, Wichita, and so on. You could send the signal from Kansas City to those transmitters by *wire*."

Jack turned and stared at the professor. "Are you willing to join our company, Professor Loewenstein?"

"Yes, I guess so. And we must look into something else. There is a good technology coming along called microwave transmission."

Three

THOUGH THE COMPANY was called Southern Tobacco, its offices were in New York—in fact, in the Chrysler Building a few floors above Jack's offices. Jack had seen Luther Dickinson in the elevators, though they had never met until now.

After they had exchanged pleasantries, Dickinson went straight to the point. "Mr. Lear, my advertising agency is recommending we drop sponsorship of *The Sally Allen Show* and, indeed, of anything you broadcast."

Jack smiled wryly. "Mr. Dickinson, you need a new ad agency."

"I've had six of them over the past fifteen years. I sometimes wonder, quite frankly, if we sell Amber cigarettes because of the commercials or in spite of them."

"Have you considered trying to sell cigarettes without advertising?"

"We're not considering dropping advertising, just dropping advertising *with you.*"

Jack smiled. "Because I won't let you call the new Sally Allen show *The Amber Cigarettes Hour.*"

"My advertising agency says we shouldn't accept that. They insist on identification."

Jack shook his head. "I won't do it. It will be *The Sally Allen Show,* sponsored by . . . whoever. That's enough identification. Also, I don't know if your ad agency has told you this, but we won't allow a sponsor to inject product mentions into the scripts."

"The ad agency also insists we have script approval."

"Out of the question," Jack said.

"We've done it our way for many years."

"But you're not happy with the results. Why else would you have had six advertising agencies in fifteen years? I'm serious when I say you need a new agency. You need somebody with new ideas."

"Easily said," Dickinson remarked dryly. "Can *you* give me a new idea?"

"Yes, I can," said Jack. "Ambers are identified with *The Sally Allen Show* and with a couple of shows you sponsor on other networks. Each week the same people tune in to Sally Allen and are exposed to your commercials. A substantial part of that audience already smokes Ambers. Another substantial part will never smoke Ambers. I'm going to suggest to you that your advertising dollars will be better spent if you *diversify.* Advertise on various programs at various times and reach different audiences. For example, I can open a place for you on *The Curtis Frederick News."* Jack paused and smiled. "You wouldn't ask for script approval on that program, would you?"

"You are a persuasive man, Mr. Lear."

Jack smiled. "You run a successful business, Mr. Dickinson. Maybe I'm presumptuous in telling you what to do. But I do know something about broadcast advertising."

"I'll review your suggestions with my people," Dickinson said. "So . . . would you care to have lunch at the Yale Club one day soon?"

Four

JACK AND ANNE were so pleased with the house they had leased in Greenwich that, in the spring of 1949, they bought it. With a second child coming, the brownstone in New York began to seem confining. They decided to keep the brownstone and not move its elegant furnishings into the country house, where they would have looked out of place anyway. The Greenwich house, which stood on an acre and a half of land, had been built in the 1890s as a reproduction of the eighteenth-century New England Colonial style. The Lears bought it furnished and agreed they would not spend a great deal of money decorating it. The purchase itself had placed a strain on their finances, and Anne had to put the last of her Weldon inheritance into it. It was to be a comfortable retreat from Manhattan when they needed one.

In June they sent Mrs. Gimbel and Little Jack to Greenwich. The little boy, now two, loved the beach and was encouraged to romp on it all he wanted. Priscilla went out to take care of the house and to get it ready for Jack and Anne, plus John and Joni, who would take up residence the first of July.

In the town house, Jack and Anne reveled in their newly regained privacy, which they had cherished in the past.

On a Friday night late in June, Jack broke away from the office early and reached the townhouse by six o'clock. Anne was waiting for him, dressed in an ivory brocade satin short teddy, which she wore with a matching G-string. Garters attached to the teddy supported sheer black stockings.

"God!" Jack exclaimed.

"While I can. Next month I'll start to swell."

She had Johnnie Walker Black on the coffee table, with a bucket of ice. Because she was pregnant she would drink nothing more than a glass of white wine. After he poured a Scotch and soda for himself and wine for her, they stood at the window looking down on the FDR Drive and the East River.

"It seems," Anne said, "that I may be named one of the ten best-dressed women in the world."

"No doubt you're the one who spends the least for the honor," he said.

"The honor should go to someone who knows how to do it without spending a fortune. I've got eleven pairs of shoes, including tennis and beach shoes. I counted them today after I read that one of the candidates has *sixty* pairs."

"What would anyone do with sixty pairs of shoes?"

"Damned if I know."

"Is the honor for conspicuous consumption or for taste?" Jack asked.

"I won't comment." She laughed.

They stood close together, far enough back from the window so that someone below wouldn't see them. His arm was around her.

Anne put her hand in his crotch and felt for an erection. She found one. "The honor is partly for appearing at the right places at the right times," she explained. "Which reminds me that we have two appearances to make before we retreat to Connecticut. A dinner at the English-Speaking Union and one at the Lotos Club. By the time the fall season opens, I'll have an incontrovertible reason for failing to appear at the right places and times."

"And I won't go without you," he said simply.

"Well, we have to think about that. There will be places you need to go, need to be seen. You are not just an ordinary businessman. You are becoming something of an institution, Jack. Some functions will not be complete if you're not there!"

He turned and kissed her very gently. He still acted like a new husband in awe of his wife's pregnancy and afraid of injuring her.

She thrust her tongue into his mouth and made the kiss

erotic. "Maybe you're right to be so cautious," she whispered. "Maybe I'm already at the stage where I shouldn't let you inside me. I've got so I enjoy the other, though. I would not have believed I ever could. But I do . . . a little anyway. And I know you enjoy it immensely, husband!"

He nuzzled her throat. "You don't have to, darling."

"I *want* to. I don't want to let my pregnancy interrupt everything. Trousers off, please. Sit down."

Putting his pants and shorts aside as well as his jacket, but still wearing his white shirt and necktie, he sat down on a velvet-upholstered chair and spread his legs. Anne knelt before him. She had a tissue handy. She spit on it, then used it to wipe him.

She glanced up at him, giving him a devilish, lascivious look. Then she lowered her head and took his penis into her mouth. For a minute or so she slipped it in and out, back and forth; then she withdrew it from her mouth and began to lick it. This was what she did best. She had an instinct for it, for the way to generate in him the most exquisite sensations.

It did not take her long to bring him. She swallowed his come and licked him clean, swallowing the last drops.

Jack dropped to his knees in front of her, to embrace and kiss her. "One of the ten best dressed or not," he whispered hoarsely, "you are *the* best. For sure. I love you beyond anything I ever thought I was capable of."

"I love you. You know it. But I want you to understand something. The first time I did what I just did, it was a sacrifice—because I loved you so much. Now I like to do it almost as much as you like to get it." She grinned and twisted her shoulders. It's great for pregnant times, isn't it?"

Five

IT WAS GREAT ALSO for a brother and sister who were genuinely in love with each other but did not dare risk another pregnancy.

Kimberly and Dodge had reestablished their attic love nest, this time securing it with a heavy cylinder lock. They didn't think John and Joni knew what was up there; but John was seventeen years old, Joni was fifteen, and they did know. They knew that when their mother and Dodge noisily attached the chain inside the attic door and went up those stairs they would be up there for at least an hour. Also, the sound of their footsteps on the uncarpeted, creaky stairs would give plenty of warning that they were coming down again. The two young people had privacy to do anything they wanted.

Right now they wanted to love each other, and they did. John used his tongue on her and brought her to ecstasy. Then she took his hard cock into her mouth. Joni never swallowed. She spit into a Kleenex, which she immediately flushed down the toilet.

She returned from the bathroom, where she had also rinsed out her mouth. They began to dress.

"What in the world are we going to do?" she whispered.

"I don't know. There's nothing we *can* do for a while. Then . . . who knows?"

"You should find another girl."

John shook his head. "I don't *want* another girl. I love *you,* Joni."

"I love you, too. But, *Jesus!*"

Six

BEFORE THE END OF JULY, John received his license as a private pilot. Jack rented a high-wing two-seater Cessna and sat in the right seat while John proudly took off, flew up the Hudson River for a view of West Point, then crossed over toward Long Island Sound and flew to Greenwich. As he passed over the Lear house he wagged his wings. Anne and Joni were sitting by the pool and waved at the little airplane circling a thousand feet above. The following day John took Joni for the same flight.

Over dinner two nights before John and Joni were scheduled to go to the Cape to join Kimberly and Dodge at their beach house, Jack asked John when he would make his application to Harvard.

"This fall," said John. "Grandfather Wolcott got the papers. I guess it's all settled. I'm not at all sure I want to go there, though."

"What he'd really like to do is go to M.I.T. and study aeronautical engineering," Joni added.

John shook his head. "What I'd *really* like to do is get an appointment to Annapolis."

"And after graduation go to Pensacola and learn to fly the navy way?" Jack asked.

"Yes."

"Are we to understand that you want to fly, not design or build airplanes?" Anne asked.

"I want to fly," John affirmed.

"Have you spoken to your mother about Annapolis?" Jack asked."

"I wouldn't dare. She doesn't even know I can fly."

"I think you had better talk to your grandfather. Or would you like me to call him?"

John's face brightened.

"I'd appreciate it if you'd talk to him. Then I'll try to make him understand."

Seven

IN OCTOBER Anne gave birth to a little girl they named Anne Elizabeth.

In November Jack flew to Houston. Cap Durenberger and Herb Morrill went with him. In a private dining room in the Petroleum Club, the three of them met with Billy Bob Cotton and Raymond l'Enfant, two of the partners in Broadcasters Alliance, and a man named Douglas Humphrey, who was president of—among other things—Humphrey Petroleum.

Jack and his friends knew what the meeting was to be about. They were prepared.

They met over drinks and hors d'oeuvres, and before lunch was called in, Humphrey opened the discussion.

"You gentlemen call me Doug, please. Jack, you know

that Billy Bob and Ray and I have been giving a good deal of thought to your company. Our nation—hell, our *world,* for that matter—stands on the threshold of a communications revolution. On the threshold of an *entertainment* revolution. This thing called television is coming on, and . . . well, I won't be surprised if it closes a lot of movie theaters. I happen to own forty-two drive-in theaters. Seemed like a big thing when I decided to invest in them, and it's been a big thing; but what do you want to bet that in a dozen years I won't have ten of them open anymore? When people can sit home and watch shows on the little screen, they won't be as interested in the big screen."

Douglas Humphrey exuded strength and self-confidence. He was perhaps sixty years old, probably a little older. His powerful face was tanned and deeply lined. His abundant hair was white. He had loose jowls, and the tight knot of his necktie pinched a wattle. His blue eyes were a bit sleepy and droopy. His wide mouth was expressive. His dark blue pinstripe suit was faultlessly tailored, probably by a Savile Row tailor, Jack guessed. His breast-pocket handkerchief was folded into two points. His white shirt was undoubtedly handmade. He wore on his lapel a red, and white and blue ribbon emblematic of the Distinguished Service Cross, which he had earned in France in 1918.

"You and your company are, in one sense, admirably situated to play a leading role and make an immense profit in this coming business," he told Jack. "In another sense, you are not. You are not because you are inadequately capitalized." He paused and thrust out upturned palms. "Am I right?"

This was precisely what Jack had expected to hear, and he had decided there would be nothing to gain from denying the point. "You are right," he said simply.

"Okay. This is a preliminary, exploratory meeting. And here is a preliminary, exploratory proposal. Are you willing to listen to a proposal?"

"That's why I'm here."

Humphrey's lips curled into a faint amused smile, then quickly turned solemn. "At present you own 82 percent of the common stock of Lear Network, Incorporated. You have distributed 18 percent to certain of your associates. And that,

Jack, is why you are undercapitalized. You need a broader base of stockholders. I myself don't own anything like that percentage of any of my companies. The vast majority of the shares are owned by investors. That's where capital comes from—*investors.*"

Jack nodded. "I'm not sure I could sell off much of my stock. The balance sheet doesn't look that good."

"Right. Your profit-and-loss statement looks very good. Your balance sheet— You're carrying too much debt. You've got valuable assets, but you're strapped for cash. And that's where I may be able to interest you in a proposition."

"I'm listening."

"We take your company public. Dallas Trust—in which I own a substantial interest—will buy all but 20 percent of your stock at book value. It will buy the 18 percent your friends hold, but each of them can retain 1 percent. And the bank will put the stock on the market, with the understanding that I can buy 10 percent and Billy Bob and Ray can buy 5 percent each, but no other investor can buy more than 1 percent. Then we offer a big issue of preferred stock. I'll exchange half of my 10 percent of common for preferred. You exchange half of your 20 percent of common for preferred. Preferred stock in a widely held corporation will attract investors. I know a dozen men who will snap at it."

Eight

ANNE SAT PROPPED UP against pillows. Jack sat on the edge of the bed, sipping on a light Scotch and soda.

"You're giving up control," she said quietly.

Jack shook his head. "Suppose he'd gone to the banks and bought my notes. Then I wouldn't have *given* up control; I'd have *lost* control. For some reason I trust the man. Maybe I have to."

"But—"

"I stay as chairman of the board and chief executive officer. I get a new executive vice president, designated by Doug. I keep control of programming. I—"

"You've never shared control of your business with anybody. Your father doesn't share control of his."

Jack bent over and kissed her nipple. "Something more," he said. "When Dallas Trust buys all but 20 percent of my stock, I will be wallowing in cash. After taxes we'll have something like twelve million dollars in the bank. *In the bank,* Anne! I've worried about . . . well, you know. That money will be ours, and not a dime of it is going to be churned back into the business. Even if Doug Humphrey takes the whole damned thing away from me, you and I are going to be comfortable for the rest of our lives."

Anne shook her head. "You'll never be comfortable watching someone else running the business you built."

TWENTY-TWO

One 1950

THE COMPANY was completely reorganized. Jack remained chairman of the board and chief executive officer, as Humphrey had promised. And he got a new executive vice president, also as Humphrey had promised.

Richard Painter was ten years older than Jack. He was bald and wore a succession of hairpieces that had been designed to make it appear as if his hair were still growing—until he supposedly had a haircut and started the sequence over again. Casual acquaintances didn't know about the hair pieces; people who knew him well did. His facial expressions were never casual or bland; they shifted from dark scowls to exaggerated toothy grins. He was a careless dresser who favored rumpled off-the-rack suits and ugly neckties. Nevertheless, Jack had to admit that Painter was a shrewd and aggressive executive who seemed to have achieved success by expending a great deal of nervous energy and always moving at a trot.

Although Painter was a Chicagoan by birth, Douglas Humphrey had recruited him away from a Dallas-based company that owned eleven radio stations and one television station. He bought 1 percent of the stock in Lear Network.

He brought two assistants with him: gofers who made no particular impression on anybody. He also brought his personal secretary, the strikingly handsome Cathy McCormack. She had a flawless face, stylishly short coal-black hair, and a spectacular figure. She dressed the same way every day, probably as Painter required, in long-sleeved white silk blouses buttoned up to her throat with collars fastened by an oversized gold safety pin, tight black skirts that ended just above her knees despite the current fashion of lower hemlines, and black patent-leather shoes. The other secretaries found her formidable. Everyone called her Miss McCormack, including Painter. She did not encourage familiarity. She ate lunch alone, someone discovered—and not at the Automat or Schrafft's but in a secluded booth in a good restaurant on Forty-third Street, where she drank two glasses of wine with her meal. People suspected after a while that she was more to Painter than his secretary.

Jack still occupied the same office in the Chrysler Building and still sat behind the ornate mahogany desk Kimberly had bought for him. He still had his onyx pen-and-pencil stand and the old WCHS microphone that he had retrieved from a closet in the Boston office when he repurchased the station. But Anne had made a few changes. Dealers in Berlin remembered her and kept her appraised of choice items whenever they appeared on the market. The Matisse they offered her was almost certainly stolen from a family that would never lay claim to it, and she was able to buy it for a bargain price. The painting was of a nude woman lying on a couch, with a vase of flowers in the background. Though the nude was voluptuous, the style of painting was so linear and bold that not even the most prudish visitor could see anything erotic about it. It hung above a standup reading desk Anne had also bought. She had found the office lighting too bright and had arranged new lighting, by lamps only. Jack was proud of the office and very comfortable in it.

He discovered to his horror that Richard Painter had nothing better in his office than a gray steel desk, behind which he sat in a vinyl-and-aluminum swivel chair. The room was lighted with glaring fluorescent tubes. His desk was cluttered with piles of paper, paper coffee cups, and doughnut wrappers.

Jack didn't like Painter, but he tried not to show it.

Two

THE BOARD OF DIRECTORS consisted of Jack Lear, Douglas Humphrey, Richard Painter, Emil Durenberger, Raymond l'Enfant, Curtis Frederick, and Joseph Freeman. Freeman was a Chicago banker who had participated in the company's recapitalization.

Jack was well aware that his management team was a minority of the board. Freeman might be a swing vote if a dispute arose. He was interested in money, not power. Actually, Jack was not sure Humphrey or l'Enfant would oppose him. It would depend on the issue. In any case, the composition of the board dramatically underscored that fact that he was no longer in control of the company.

At the first serious meeting of the board, Painter made a move he probably knew Jack wouldn't like.

"What we have is a somewhat loosely organized partnership between Lear Network and Broadcasting Alliance," Painter said. "I understand that Broadcasting Alliance is willing to tighten that relationship. I'm wondering if it wouldn't be wise to reorganize into a parent corporation with subsidiaries. The Lear broadcasting operations and Broadcasters Alliance could become subsidiaries of the parent. As we grow and perhaps enter other enterprises, the parent could acquire other subsidiaries."

"How do you feel about that, Jack?" asked Humphrey.

"It depends on how we own it," Jack answered. "We worked out some rather careful arrangements about who owns what. It's a little early to be changing them, isn't it?"

"Absolutely," Painter said. "My suggestion is that the parent company be Lear Network, Incorporated. Then we switch its radio broadcasting *functions* to a subsidiary we form for that very purpose."

Jack looked toward Humphrey. "Doug?"

"Efficient arrangements. Efficient arrangements are important."

"A rational corporate structure is certainly helpful when you set out to raise money," said Freeman.

"My suggestion is that we convert Lear Network, Incorporated, into . . . let us say, Consolidated Communications, Incorporated," Painter explained. "Its officers and board will remain in place. This board will be in a position to appoint the board and officers of the subsidiaries. We—"

"There's one element of that that I don't like, Dick," Humphrey interrupted. "I don't think we should take the Lear name off the basic corporation. After all, Jack built this whole thing. I'd rather see us call it Lear Communications, Incorporated."

Painter frowned for an instant, then nodded. "Right. Sure. Lear Communications."

"Jack?" asked Humphrey.

"Let's see the details," Jack replied.

Later, when the board assembled at 21 for lunch, Jack, Cap, and Curt went to the men's room together.

"Well? What do you think?" Cap asked Jack.

"We're in the presence of masters, gentlemen," Jack said as he washed his hands. "They played white hat–black hat. And they threw me a bone. It was all rehearsed and orchestrated. That's the way it's going to be."

Curt shrugged. "They've made us all rich, though. If things get shitty, I'm going to retire."

Three

JACK SAT in a motel room outside Boston with Rebecca Murphy, the private investigator he had hired to watch Kimberly during the war.

He'd brought a bottle of Johnnie Walker Black to the room, and they were sipping it from bathroom water glasses. She was smoking a Camel; he had almost quit smoking.

Jack stared at a series of 8-by-10 black-and-white prints he had pulled from the envelope she'd brought him. His eyes were damp with tears. "She's beautiful," he whispered.

Rebecca Murphy nodded. "She really is."

The pictures were of Kathleen, his daughter by Connie Horan. She was a towheaded five-year-old, romping happily in a park, photographed by Murphy with a big telephoto lens.

"How do they treat her?"

"Mr. Lear, I can't find even a *suggestion* that they treat her as anything but their darling daughter. I'll be frank with you: there's no way you're gonna get custody away from them. The Horans are—what would you call them?—*prosaic* people."

"Where could I see her?"

"Except through a big lens, I don't think you could. I mean, it's like they expect you to show up someday."

"I'm sure they do," he muttered. "I expect they do. *And I will, too, by God. Someday.*"

Rebecca Murphy was in her early thirties, a solid-looking woman with tightly curled light brown hair and a craggy, acne-marked face.

Jack tossed back his Scotch and poured more. "You have any idea what it's like to—"

"Yes, sir, I do. I lost custody of two children. I'm allowed to see them for an hour every two weeks. They keep a careful separation from Mommy. They've been told I won't go to heaven. I know they wouldn't see me at all if they didn't have to."

"Rebecca . . . May I call you—"

"Call me Becky."

"Life shits, doesn't it, Becky?"

She smiled. "Here sits a man with . . . how many million? Married to the most beautiful woman in America. Father of two fine children here in Boston, plus the one you can't see. Father of two fine children in New York." She shook her head. "Have you ever missed a meal, Jack? I went out on the street when I was fifteen and turned tricks to make the money for something to eat. The worst part was having some drunk decide to beat on me. And that happened more than once."

"I'm sorry, Becky. That's rotten."

"Yeah. So I got married. And guess what? My husband, the wonderful father of my kids, used his fists on me too. When I went after a divorce, it was denied on the ground that he hadn't committed adultery. Then he went for exclusive custody of the kids on the ground that I'd been a hooker, also on the ground that I wasn't home all the time. I was working as a private investigator, but my husband's lawyers suggested that what I was really doing was turning tricks again." Becky

Murphy would not sob. Her face turned harder as she spoke. "The court gave my husband custody and ordered me out of the house. There I was, still married to him and couldn't live in the house or see the kids."

Jack reached out and took her in his arms. "What I said. Life shits."

"Finally I went to Reno and got a divorce, not so I could get married again, God forbid, but so that bastard couldn't lay claim to my earnings."

"Becky . . ."

She kissed him and asked, "You want something?"

He nodded.

"Me too. From a gentleman. You won't use your fists, will you? Or bite? Don't worry about anything. I got tied off years ago. But don't hold back! I want all you got, as hard as you can do it!"

She undressed. Her body was spare and hard. Her belly was concave and rose from her prominently defined pelvis. He could count her ribs. A line from Gilbert and Sullivan came to Jack's mind, the self-description of the Mikado's daughter-in-law-elect: "tough as a bone, with a will of her own."

She tuned him up with her tongue and then spread to take him in. He plunged and plunged, and no matter how hard he did she grunted, "More! More!"

He took her to dinner that night. "I doubt we'll ever see each other again, Jack," she said. "You should forget it. It's not a part of your life. It was an incident, that's all. That's what it was for me, too. You're damned good. I hope Mrs. 'America's-Ten-Best-Dressed appreciates you."

Back in the motel room, Jack found on the sheets a strange mixture of odors: sweat, cigarette smoke, and some kind of perfume or cologne he hadn't noticed before. He placed a call to Anne and talked to her for ten minutes. He told her he loved her, and she said she loved him.

Except for the time in New Orleans when he had stuck his penis through the hole in the curtain—an occasion he deeply regretted because he'd allowed four associates to see him do so stupid a thing—this incident with Becky Murphy was his only adventure outside his and Anne's marriage bed. He resolved it would be the last. Married to a woman like her, he would be a fool to risk losing her.

Four

JOHN WOULD NOT COME to Greenwich that summer. He had won his appointment to Annapolis and would report there in June to begin his summer of orientation and to learn to sail before classes began.

Jack took Anne to Boston to attend the boy's graduation from high school. Inevitably, they met Kimberly and Dodge. It was the first time the two women had met, and it was inevitable that they would size each other up very thoroughly.

Kimberly was now forty-three years old. She remained an elegantly beautiful woman with an impressive style. Though she was the very image of self-confidence, the truth was that she was no longer self-confident. Dodge badgered her constantly about keeping her weight down, as he had always done; but Kimberly found it impossible to do unless she dieted so strictly that it made her irritable. The result was that she was twenty pounds overweight, and she carried the weight where it showed. Confronting the exquisitely beautiful Anne, Kimberly was instantly envious of her gracefully slender figure.

Anne wore a dress of Shantung silk, draped so that it covered her left arm almost to the elbow but left her right shoulder bare. She wore a simple bracelet on either wrist, three strands of pearls on the left and a delicate gold chain on the right. She carried a crocodile handbag and a pair of black gloves, which Kimberly never saw her put on. Her makeup was subdued. She wore her hair in a smooth, careless style and let a wisp fall over her forehead.

Kimberly too was handsomely dressed in a cream-colored linen jacket over a black linen sheath, but she wondered if she looked frumpy in the presence of one of the ten best dressed.

At the beginning of her relationship with Jack Anne had been curious about Kimberly and had been anxious to meet her. But when she finally met her face-to-face, she found that Kimberly simply made no impression on her, good, bad, or indifferent. Kimberly was no longer a factor in Jack's life, or in hers, and Anne had no sense that she was in competition with her.

Kimberly on the other hand, was quick to make judgments. She detected that Anne regarded her with indifference, and that angered her.

But she remained under control. "I've looked forward to meeting you," she said to Anne. "I've seen your picture in magazines, but the photographs don't do you justice."

"That's very kind of you," said Anne. "I'm glad to meet you too, at last."

Later that afternoon, talking with Jack away from the crowd in the Louisburg Square house, where Kimberly and Dodge were giving a party for John, Harrison Wolcott rubbed his hands together and shook his head. "I can't tell you I'm not surprised, because I am surprised. Jack, they'll take the company away from you."

"They already have. But they paid me handsomely for it. Besides, they've given me a big opportunity. Harrison, the glory days of radio broadcasting are over. Television is going to steal the audience."

"I see *The Sally Allen Show* is going on this fall. Do you think she can compete with, say, Milton Berle?"

"She can't. We won't have enough stations to begin to compete with Berle. But she doesn't have to. We won't put her on opposite Berle."

"How many stations will you have?" Harrison asked.

"Four, when the season begins. We're going to get all the radio stations to talk constantly about what a funny woman Sally Allen is. We'll have articles published about her. We're going to create an intense curiosity about her. People will want to see her. Then we'll get more stations."

"You're going to have a hell of a time competing against the networks."

"Granted. We'll never get ratings as high as theirs. But there's something else down the road—way down the road. Someday we won't *broadcast* television. The signal can be sent out over a wire. The day will come when you'll look up at the utility poles on your street, and you'll see electric wires, telephone wires, and *television wires*."

Harrison Wolcott smiled. "In the year 2000."

Jack shook his head. "A long time before that."

Anne was approaching, and before she could reach them Wolcott lowered his voice and said, "Your wife is beautiful."

Five

JONI SUCKED on John's penis and wept at the same time. "We'll never— Why couldn't you have just gone to Harvard?"

He ran his hand through her hair. "A lot of reasons."

"One of the reasons is so that we can't go on loving each other," she sobbed.

"One of the reasons is that I have to escape from our mother. And so do you. She smothers us, Joni."

"That lout Dodge encourages her."

"Joni, have you read *The Late George Apley?*"

She shook her head. "I saw a copy of it downstairs."

"Well, read it. It explains why we have to get out of Boston."

"Boston?"

"Boston. Biloxi. Any confining place."

She licked him, from scrotum to glans. "John . . ." she sobbed.

"Hey, it may be— Hey, I can't promise you this. But suppose someday we meet someplace like San Francisco, Miami, Chicago, where nobody knows us. And we just introduce ourselves as mister and missus. Or one of us uses a different name and we *do* get married."

Joni sighed. "You'll find another girl."

"And maybe you'll find a guy."

"But I love you, and I always will. Nobody's ever going to compare to you."

"Nobody's going to compare to you, Joni."

He used his hands to spread her legs and pushed his face into her crotch. He had learned the special sensitivity of her clitoris and how to stimulate it with his tongue. He did it only for a minute before she writhed and shrieked.

"Nobody, John! Nobody!" she cried as she fumbled for his penis and drew it in between her lips and deeper into her throat than he had believed she could do without gagging.

TWENTY-THREE

One 1950

JACK SAT IN THE BACK SEAT of a car driven by Cap Durenberger. They had flown to Tulsa. Billy Bob Cotton had been waiting at the airport and was sitting in the front beside Cap. Jack had thought to catch a little sleep on the drive to Okmulgee, but he'd found the countryside so interesting and the weather so threatening that he had remained awake.

The skies to the west were a purplish gray, the darkest he had ever seen while the sun still shone in the east. The contrast between the sunlit leaves on groves of trees to the west and the surly clouds behind them gave the trees a juicy green color. Jack wondered if he was going to witness a tornado, but he didn't ask.

As he stared in fascination, the dark finger of a tornado stretched toward the earth from the clouds; but after a minute it retreated and disappeared.

Billy Bob switched on the radio and found a station broadcasting a weather warning. A tornado watch was in effect for Okmulgee County. A tornado *warning* was in effect for Okfuskee, Seminole, and Hughes Counties.

"Storm's movin' south," Billy Bob said casually, and he switched off the radio.

The countryside through which they were driving was rolling, with low hills and shallow valleys. Herds of cattle grazed. A crop with pale green leaves grew in fenced-in fields. Billy Bob explained the crop was peanuts.

They stopped at a farm five miles from the town of Okmulgee. As they drove up the driveway toward the house, Jack appraised the place as a prosperous working farm. Standing behind the garage was what they had come to see —a fifty-foot steel tower topped by a wide-armed television antenna. Towers just like it stood on nearly every farm they had passed.

"The Martins are fine people," said Billy Bob. "I've known Ed and Martha for many years. A bank I own part of, in Tulsa, lent them money for this place. They paid off their mortgage ahead of time."

A huge black-and-brown German shepherd trotted out and stood a short distance from the car, alert and wagging his tail only tentatively.

Mrs. Martin came out of the house. "Well, hi there, Mr. Cotton! Nice to see you." She had an accent and actually said, "Haa there, Mista Cotton! Nass t' see ya." She was a pleasant woman, wearing a simple cotton dress that she had probably made herself.

Jack climbed out of the back seat and offered his hand to Mrs. Martin. "Hello, Mrs. Martin. My name is Jack Lear. It's nice of you to let us come see your television," he said.

She shook his hand with a firm grip. "Well, it's not so much, really. Some get better reception than we do. That storm goin' down the west there may interfere some."

Jack offered his hand to the dog to sniff. The dog checked him and seemed satisfied.

Mrs. Martin shook hands then with Cap and invited the men into the house, where she had coffee and homemade doughnuts waiting. "Ed'll be in right smart," she said. "He'll have seen your car."

The living room floor was covered with new linoleum and furnished with a couch and two chairs upholstered in maroon plush. The room, perhaps the whole house, was heated by a large cast-iron coal stove which stood on a piece of tin-plated steel that protected the linoleum from its heat. Their television was a seventeen-inch Sylvania set. Pictures of children sat on top.

Ed Martin came in. "Well, hi there, Billy Bob!" he said, reaching out to shake hands. "Long time no see." He turned and extended his hand to Jack and then to Cap. "Welcome, gentlemen."

Martin was no overalled farmer. He wore sturdy blue Levi's, almost new, and a khaki work shirt with a pack of cigarettes in one pocket and a yellow pencil in the other. He was a rawboned outdoorsman.

"Well, y' come to see the TV," said Martin. "Let's see what we can pick up this mornin'."

He switched on the set. It warmed up, and a picture appeared. It was a bit fuzzy and had some snow in it, but there it was: a black-and-white picture of some overexuberant master of ceremonies playing to a studio audience of women.

"That there comes from Dallas, and that's about as far as we can git it," said Martin. "Lemme show ya Tulsa, which comes in a whole lot better."

First he changed channels, and a different picture came in, not clear at all. Then he turned the dial on a box controller on top of the set, and the picture became much clearer, all but perfect. "See, what I did was turn the antenna toward Tulsa. Before there, it was turned toward Dallas. A TV antenna is what you call directional."

"In other words," said Jack, "you've got an electric motor on top of the tower, which turns the antenna."

"That's exactly what we got."

In the course of a few minutes he showed them he could tune in Kansas City, which like Dallas was at the far reach of their antenna, and Oklahoma City, though that signal was broken up by the storm between here and there.

"There's talk they're gonna start a station in Wichita, and that'd be nice. That'd give us five channels. Once in a while, if we're lucky, we can get St. Louis, but y' can't count on it."

"I guess my question," said Jack, "is how important is television to you?"

"Oh, it's *very* important," said Mrs. Martin. "I tell you somethin'. Our oldest son lives in Dallas. And sometimes when we're watchin' something, I get to thinking, by golly our boy is watching the same show, 'cause we got the same favorites, and it makes it seem like he's not so far away."

On the way back to Tulsa, the three men talked in the car.

"I've done some numbers," said Billy Bob. "If we set up a powerful station in Kansas City, we're going to cover a market with a minimum of five million people."

"I've done the same numbers," said Jack. "St. Louis doesn't work nearly as well. Neither does Dallas. The only other city that might reach a bigger market is Columbus, Ohio. But much of the terrain in Ohio is hilly, and you'd have to put up a hell of a tall tower to reach Pittsburgh, for example, and Detroit. In the East you've got another problem, which is that people aren't accustomed to the idea of putting up a fifty-foot tower to get their television. Many of them couldn't, anyway."

"I agree with Billy Bob," said Jack. "Kansas City."

"We can't live with one station," Cap pointed out.

"Right," Jack said. "I've done some looking. There's an independent station in Dallas. We can lease a wire from Kansas City to Dallas and broadcast simultaneously from these two. We may be able to reach an independent station in Minneapolis the same way. After those, we'll have to kinescope. I think we can slot *The Sally Allen Show* on independent stations in Atlanta and Indianapolis. The show won't come in as clearly, and it will be a day late, so we have to make *The Sally Allen Show* something people want to see."

Two

"KANSAS *CITY?*"

That was Sally Allen's reaction when she was told her show would originate in Kansas City. "You gotta be kiddin'! Somebody wants me to go live in— Out of the question!"

Jack himself explained to her why the initial shows had to originate in Kansas City. Sally told him she hated him, she hated the whole goddamned deal she'd made, and she'd walk out on it and let him sue her.

Ten days later she was in Kansas City, walking scornfully around the dusty warehouse that LCI—Lear Communications, Incorporated—was converting into a television studio.

She was placated a little when Jack named the supporting actors who would be working with her. "You spent a lot of money," she said.

He had, for salaries and perks, but everything else had cost far less than it would have in New York or Los Angeles. He leased an apartment for Sally. He leased a suite in the Muehlebach Hotel for himself and the other members of the management team when they were in town.

Over dinner at an excellent French restaurant, Sally acknowledged that Kansas City was a very pleasant little city. "I like this place," she said, glancing around the restaurant. "I figured I'd have to live on bar-bee-kew. And, hey, they got a nightclub you wouldn't believe. Female impersonators! Those guys are *good.* We ought to figure out a way to slot the best of them in on the show."

They did. On the second show a young man named Burt Wilson, who called himself Gloria, appeared in a comedy sketch. At the end of the sketch he turned his back to the camera and pulled off a sweater, exposing his bare back. As he turned to face the camera, he jerked off his wig. Gloria was Burt.

With that episode alone, *The Sally Allen Show* achieved much of what Jack had hoped for it. It was, of course, denounced as indecent. A Texas congressman demanded that the FCC revoke the license of the LCI station in Kansas City. Churchmen condemned the show. Newspapers and newsmagazines reported the controversy. LCI provided photos of the bare-chested Burt.

Audiences all across the country demanded to see *The Sally Allen Show.* Stations all over the country asked for the kinescope.

The recapitalized Lear company bought the independent stations in Minneapolis and Indianapolis.

Three

SALLY ALLEN rarely displayed temperament. Usually she was an easygoing, cooperative actress who accepted direction and caused few problems on the set. She did make some demands, though, and one of them was that her dressing room be something better than one of the plywood cubicles that had been built into the warehouse studio. Jack ordered the production manager to buy a house trailer and tow it into the warehouse.

He sat on a couch in the trailer and watched Sally being fitted for one of the costumes she would wear on the eighth show. It was a dance costume, a black satin corselet decorated with hundreds of glittery spangles. She would wear dark, sheer tights with it, but for the fitting her legs were bare.

Sally grabbed the corselet at her hips and tugged upward on it, drawing it higher and exposing more of her hips. She spoke to the seamstress. "What say, Bertha? Can I wear it pulled up like this?"

The seamstress nodded. "Lace it so it'll stay up like that."

"Okay. But you'll have to trim it or fold it over and sew it down at the top. Gotta have cleavage. Audience expects it."

Bertha laughed. "The director will want to stick a flower down in there."

"To hell with that," said Sally. "What are boobs for? The secret of my success, is what. Right, Jack?"

Jack lifted his Scotch. "They get a lot of comment," he said.

" 'Kay, Bertha. Let's take it off."

The seamstress began to unlace and unhook the corselet.

"I've got a deep secret in my past," Sally said to Jack. She let the seamstress take the corselet. She was wearing nothing under it. Naked, she reached for her own Scotch and took a sip before she reached for the red wrapper that lay on a chair. "Not bad for an old gal of thirty, huh?" she asked before she pulled on the wrapper and covered herself.

Bertha left the trailer.

Sally sat down facing Jack. "Deep secret," she said. "I did an apprenticeship nobody seems to remember. People talk about my comic timing, about how I can mug with funny lines, and all that. How do they think I learned my business?"

"Tell me your secret," said Jack.

"Burlesque. When I was seventeen years old I became a stripper or, as they liked to say, an 'exotic dancer.' I worked on a circuit. Towns like Detroit, Toledo, Cleveland, Columbus,

Cincinnati, Pittsburgh. Just in theaters, never in clubs. I took off as much as the cops would allow, which in some towns at some times was everything. But half of a burlesque show, you know, is the baggy-pants comics, and some of their sketches have a girl in them. Lots of times I was the girl. I watched their routines and techniques, saw the faults in them, and did my part better than they did theirs."

"I bet you did."

"I remember some of the lines. I'm playing like I'm hot for sex, and I say to the guy, 'I want what I want when I want it!' Then I do a bump. And he says, 'You'll get what I got when I got it!' Of course, they play language for all it's worth, and more. In one routine the straight man says, 'She was coming across the street, and I *scrutinized* her!' The baggy-pants rolls his eyes and asks, 'Y' mean you scrutinized her before she even got across the street?' 'Why, of course. Sometimes I scrutinize them when they're clear on the other side of the street.' Now baggy-pants rolls his eyes some more, turns and leers at the audience, points at the straight man's crotch, and asks, 'How you got it in there—rolled up like a hose?' "

Jack laughed. "We couldn't do it on television."

"More's the pity," she said. "In those old routines the situation almost always managed to get my boobs out. I used to think it was sexier being bare-titted on the stage and doing a sketch under full lights than it was to strip down to a G-string."

"I agree."

"The reason I bring it up is, I got a letter. It's from . . . well, I guess it's from my husband, 'cause I never divorced him, really, just left him. He saw me on TV and realized for the first time that Sally Allen was the girl he remembered as Flo."

"Does he want money?" Jack asked.

"Just a little. A couple hundred. He says times are tough. The old burlesque houses are closing all over. He was a straight man, and his top banana died. He's been working as a candy butcher. He's also got a girl, a stripper named Marilyn, who works a comedy routine with him. She broke her leg and went on stripping and doing the routine with her leg in a cast. Can you believe humanity? The guys in the audiences liked her *better!* I mean, they liked seeing her strip with a cast on her leg."

"Makes her seem more human," said Jack.

"Anyway, his name is Len Leonard, and he's asking for two hundred dollars. What do I do?"

"How'd you break up, if you don't mind my asking?"

"I didn't want to be a stripper my whole life, that's all. I wanted to leave the theaters, and he didn't; he didn't know what else he could do. So one day I just packed my little suitcase and left."

"And went on to fame and fortune," Jack said with a smile.

Sally tossed back her Scotch. "I'll tell ya what I never did. I never turned tricks. I had a lot of chances, from guys who offered a lot of money. Let some of your Hollywood queens make that statement."

"You want me to take care of the problem for you?"

"By doing what?"

"By getting you a secret divorce. You send the two hundred to keep him quiet for a few weeks, and I'll take care of the rest of it, if you want me to."

She sighed. "I'd appreciate it, Jack."

Four

ON A NOVEMBER EVENING Jack sat down in what had to be the shabbiest theater he'd ever been in, a burlesque house in Toledo. The house was probably best characterized by the chicken-wire cage that enclosed the trio of musicians to protect them from whatever members of the audience might throw at them.

The performers were limp and devoid of talent. One of the strippers was a teenage girl who managed to look embarrassed. The others were women in their late twenties or their thirties, all long past being embarrassed by anything.

The top banana was a man of at least sixty who had left his dentures in the dressing room. His signature line, delivered with a smirk at the audience, was "Gotta *eat!*" His second banana was Len Leonard, who fed him his lines woodenly and waited for his responses, knowing the men who filled the seats in the front rows of the theater could not have cared less about what the two comics said.

The only comedy sketch that generated any reaction was the one done by Leonard and a woman Jack guessed was Marilyn, Leonard's girlfriend who had performed with her leg in a cast. She played a female suspect being interrogated and searched by a detective played by Leonard.

"I understand you carry a forty-four," Leonard said.

"No way! No way. Thirty-nine, maybe."

"Thirty-nine?"

"Well, mebbe forty."

"Show me."

The woman pulled off her blouse and bared her breasts. "See? Thirty—"

"—two. Huh-uh. Where's your *big* one?"

The woman did a bump and grind. "Where's *yours,* baby?"

And so on.

The star of the show was a woman whose name Jack had heard before: a huge redhead with immense breasts. She stayed onstage longer than any of the other strippers. She had a better costume and showed a minor talent for dancing.

At intermission Leonard worked the crowd, trying to sell them boxes of candy for a dollar, making impossible claims. "A pound of this candy ordinarily sells for five or six dollars. Well, this box is not a pound, just enough good candy to eat and enjoy during the show. But this week, to introduce this special candy to Toledo, we have put a special gift in each box. In . . . two, three, four . . . boxes there is a Hamilton wristwatch! In others—"

The job was actually a little perilous. From time to time Leonard would yell breathlessly that one of the wristwatches had just gone. A shill would scream that he'd won a watch. By the time the lights went down for the second half of the show, a few drunks were ready to rush Leonard and demand their money back, having paid a dollar for three or four pieces of cheap taffy and realizing there were no watches or other gifts in the boxes. Leonard dashed backstage, and one or two menacing toughs kept the drunks at bay.

About midnight, Leonard and Marilyn sat down wearily in a booth in a bar next to the theater. They'd done three shows. He'd done three candy scams. They looked tired and depressed.

"Mr. Leonard?"

The man looked up at Jack. "My name is Jack Lear. I'm the president of Lear Communications. May I join you for a moment?"

Leonard pointed at a seat. He was an overweight man with oily hair slicked down against his head. He wore a shabby gray suit. Marilyn's pupils were dilated. The needle tracks on her arms told the story.

"I have something for you, Mr. Leonard," Jack said. He pulled out of his raincoat pocket and placed on the table a neat package wrapped in brown paper and tied with white string. "What's in there is yours if you sign a paper I'm going to hand you."

"What's in there?" Leonard asked dully.

"One hundred one-hundred-dollar bills," said Jack. "Ten thousand dollars."

Leonard was not stupid. "From Flo," he muttered.

"No. From me."

"This paper I sign. Divorce?"

"That's right."

"Okay. I never asked her for anything like ten thousand."

"I know. Just sign the paper. There are three copies. Sign three times."

"Sure. Lend me your pen."

Jack handed Leonard a Parker 51 fountain pen, and Leonard signed the documents without reading them. He pulled the package across the table toward him.

"Want to open it up and count it?" Jack asked.

Leonard shook his head. "You're a gentleman, Mr. Lear—what I could never afford to be."

Marilyn had stared dully throughout the conversation. Jack doubted she understood what had happened.

"One final thing, Mr. Leonard. Do you know the meaning of a major headache?"

Leonard nodded. "It's what I get if Flo ever hears from me or about me again."

Five

ON A SATURDAY MORNING Sally Allen appeared in a courtroom in a county in northern Alabama. Her head was covered by a scarf, and she wore dark sunglasses. A local lawyer stood up beside her.

In her papers Florence Stanwich Leonard swore she was a new resident of Alabama but intended to be a permanent resident. (She had been a resident for twelve hours, since she'd checked into a motel the evening before. She would remain a resident until almost noon, when she would drive out of the state forever.) Leonard's sworn affidavit said he knew his wife was a bona fide resident of Alabama and that he consented to her obtaining a decree of divorce from him. The lawyer handed the papers to the judge, who signed the decree without reading it or any of the other papers in the file. The process took less than a whole minute and was one of fifty decrees entered in that court that morning.

TWENTY-FOUR

One 1951

ERICH LEAR put his stogie aside in the ashtray on his desk. He lifted his glass and took a sip of gin. It was not his favorite drink, but it was what he had at the moment, and he didn't want to interrupt this moment by sending out for anything else.

"Well?" the nude blond asked.

Erich grinned. "Yeah. You're everything anybody ever said you were. And more."

The blond tossed her chin high and thrust her breasts forward. "I'm a first-class actress, Mr. Lear," she said. "Hey! I'm playing a role *right now.* But I can play others. I'm not just—"

"A plaything."

"No, I'm not. I can play around as well as any girl, but I have more to me than that. Help me get the right part. I can make you proud you know me. I really can."

"I have a strong feeling you can at that," said Erich.

"Hey, it's not that I don't have credits, you know. I got real good notices for *Savage City.*"

She was called Monica Dale, though her name was Phyllis Dugan or Phyllis Frederickson, depending on whom you asked. She had appeared briefly in one or two films, then got a lot of attention for her role as the kept girl in *Savage City,* and now was waiting around for another contract.

"What I'm not is a lady," she said. She sat down in the

chair opposite his, hooked her heels in the rungs of the chair, and spread her legs as wide as possible, displaying her shiny pink parts. "I'm willing to play the game."

"I've actually heard you glory in the game."

"Mr. Lear," she said with a faintly mordant smile, "one of these days I'm going to be so big a star that I'll never have to suck another cock." She tipped her head. "Except yours."

"Okay. Let's see what you can do, kid."

She knelt before his chair, unbuckled his belt and opened his pants, and pulled his underpants down so she could lift his penis and scrotum over the waistband. Then she set to work on him. She licked. She didn't take him into her mouth yet; she just licked, stroking, then flicking, with her tongue.

Erich groaned.

Monica looked up and grinned.

"One hell of a girl," he said. It was the famous line used about her in *Savage City*.

She began to nibble with her lips.

He grunted as if in surprise. She looked up. His eyes bulged wide. His mouth hung open. He gasped and then slumped.

As quickly as she could, she tucked his parts back into his underpants and pulled them up. She zipped his fly, buttoned him up, and buckled his belt. She grabbed her panties and pulled them on, then pulled her simple white dress over her head.

She left the office. As she passed the secretary's desk, she said, "You better get a doctor quick. There's something wrong with him."

The doctor arrived in ten minutes. Erich Lear was dead.

Two

"I CAN'T IMAGINE WHY, but he left you half of Carlton House Productions. I get everything else, including the salvage company. But you get half the movie company. You and I are partners, *brother.*"

"I didn't even know the old man *owned* Carlton House,"

Jack said. "I was dumb enough to think it was yours. So tell me something. Who was the broad who ducked out of the office when he died?"

Bob Lear grinned. "You ever hear the name Monica Dale?"

"Jesus Christ!"

Bob glanced around. They stood a little apart in the mausoleum where Erich's body was being entombed and spoke in subdued voices. For this funeral neither of them wore a yarmulke. Almost no man did. Anne was there, looking like a reigning queen. Joni was there, looking like a princess. Mickey Sullivan had come. The stars present had drawn an army of reporters and cameramen.

"The word is that Monica gives the best blow job in the business. We hired a little blond gal to say *she* was with the old man when he had the seizure. A script consultant. Looks about right. The town has bought the story. The secretary knows better, but I paid her off. She was loyal to the old man anyway. She'd played his skin flute herself at least a hundred times. Except for morbid curiosity, there's no big concern about what happened. He died of a heart attack, and that's that. I have to feel sorry for the poor old bastard. There he was, with the sexiest broad in Hollywood going down on him, and he ups and dies before she finishes him."

"How do you know that's what she was doing?"

"He had lipstick on his cock."

"What a way to go!" Jack put a hand on Bob's shoulder. "Brother, we have a great opportunity looking at us. With my television deal and your—our—motion-picture deal, we can build an *empire.*"

"Fuck you. You just want to take the business away from me. I mean, all the business, including the ship-breaking company."

"If I'd wanted to take it away from you, I'd have taken it twenty years ago. You could be working for me as an office boy, right now. The old man wanted me to have it. But I'd have had to pay for it by being his flunky since 1931. Well, I didn't do that. You did. I'm not without gratitude for that. But you're going to work *with* me, Bob, not against me. Or I'll put your ass out on the street."

"Think you can?"

"In six weeks. But"—He patted Bob's shoulder—"why would I do a thing like that to my own brother?"

"The old man thought you had smarts," said Bob. "I suppose that's why he left you half the showbiz end. You know, lately that was all he was interested in, really. He let hired guys run the salvage operations."

"Can we be sure that Dale broad will keep her mouth shut?"

Bob's grin was broad and derisive. "Big brother, you don't know *shit* about how things go! You got it all backwards! What do *we* care if she talks?"

"Why did you hire a blond to say *she* was the one who was with him? Why'd you pay off the secretary?"

"For Wolf Productions, big brother! They own her. She's a valuable property that could be damaged bad if the word got around that she was giving head to Erich Lear when he died. Now Wolf owes us one, for sure, for covering up the deep, dark secret behind their new star. The new Jean Harlow, some say!"

"Okay, so Wolf owes us. How they gonna pay it off?"

"Who knows? We want the loan of one of their stars, say . . . Hey! I'll tell you what's been offered. I didn't take it, but maybe you'll want to. They've offered to send Monica around to finish the job she was doing for the old man."

Three

MONICA DALE sat where she had been sitting naked in front of Erich Lear moments before he died.

"I can't tell you how important it is to me to have this secret kept," she said to Jack. "When I went down on your father I didn't know that Wolf was about to offer me a marvelous new contract! I was hoping to get a contract with Carlton House." She rubbed a tear from the corner of her eye. "Every girl does what I do, Mr. Lear, for the sake of getting someplace in this business."

"You don't have to tell me that," Jack said. "My father didn't have a casting couch, really. He wasn't really in the business. But—"

"You know, he almost never fucked anybody," she whispered. "All he wanted girls to do was give him blow jobs."

"Some of the biggest names in the business," Jack suggested.

She blinked and nodded. "I suppose so. And for nothing, most of the time. Mr. Lear, I may be on the verge of a wonderful break. If the word got out that I— Goddammit! Why *me?* Half the female Oscar winners of the last twenty years went down on Harry Cohn, and there they are, big stars. But if the word gets out that I—"

"It's not going to get out, Monica. Not through Carlton House Productions, it's not. Now, if you should choose to show me your gratitude . . ."

He had resolved not to do anything like this with anyone. But *Monica Dale!*

She wiped away more tears, then smiled. "Sure. Sure, Mr. Lear. Why not? I told your father I was going to quit blowing guys, except for him. Okay. You inherited the exception."

She pulled her dress over her head. She had a spectacular body; there was no doubt of that.

As she worked on him, he wondered what his father's last thoughts had been—if maybe they'd been that she was not really very good at it. Monica didn't want to do this, really, and she couldn't conceal her disgust for it. She was making a sacrifice, doing a duty, and she performed woodenly. Some men probably exulted at being sucked off by a girl obviously nauseated by it. Jack didn't.

When she stood up and reached for her dress, he took her gently in his arms and kissed her lightly. "Thank you, Monica. I'll never forget this afternoon. But I'll never ask you to repeat it."

She returned his kiss. "You're a gentleman, Mr. Lear."

Four

RICHARD PAINTER waxed rhapsodic. "That's wonderful! We merge Carlton House Productions into Lear Communications, and we have an entertainment powerhouse."

Grinning, he glanced at the three other directors of LCI, who were present at the meeting.

"We buy part of Jack's stock and part of his brother's," Painter went on. "You're already a rich man, Jack. This will make you—"

"You're getting ahead of things, Dick," Jack interrupted him. "My brother won't sell. And he owns half."

"All right," said Painter, his enthusiasm undiminished. "We buy part of yours, and you vote with us. He can't do anything with Carlton House without our consent."

"And we can't do anything with it without *his* consent," Douglas Humphrey said pointedly.

"There are ways to bring him around," Painter replied.

"I wouldn't count on that," Jack said. "Anyway, we've got something else to talk about. Something my brother will consent to. Our chief problem with our television stations is finding programming. Aside from *The Sally Allen Show* we've got only two shows that are anything but local—*Bet a Buck* and Art Merriman running around a studio audience in the morning, trying on women's hats. Both of those shows make me sick, but they get decent ratings. Apart from that, our stations broadcast kinescopes of old network shows, *Victory at Sea,* and local amateur hours. Now—"

"Quality is not essential," Cap Durenberger interrupted. "A substantial part of the TV audience will sit with eyes glued to the test pattern. That's why the thing is called the boob tube."

"Well, it won't always be," said Jack. "Now look. Over the years Carlton House has made more than a hundred feature films. When Carlton House acquired Domestic, it acquired their archives—everything from English-country-house comedies to swashbucklers of the Spanish Main. It acquired Bell in 1944, with a hundred horse operas in cans. Carlton House has something like four hundred fifty pictures in storage. That's a huge film library. We can contract to broadcast all those old movies on television. Some of them feature the great stars. Some are Oscar winners. They can fill hours and hours and hours of broadcast time, with something people will want to see."

"What about the most recent films?" Painter asked. "Like *The Weed.*"

Jack shook his head. "Not until there's no more demand for theater rentals. But look at something else. Carlton House has half a dozen important stars under contract. At the very least, they could become guest stars for *The Sally Allen Show.* And maybe, just maybe, we could start a live drama show."

"These are the things I'd hoped to do with the merger," Painter explained.

"We can do them without the merger," said Jack.

Five

CATHY McCORMACK was on her hands and knees on the floor of her living room. Except for her white garter belt, her dark stockings, and her shiny black patent-leather shoes, she was nude. Her head and shoulders were down, and her bare bottom was thrust up. A big cruet of olive oil stood on the coffee table within reach, and three layers of bath towels were spread out beneath her to protect the rug.

Dick Painter poured oil on the palm of his left hand and used the fingers of his right to oil the cleavage between her hinder cheeks, pressing it well up into her. Then he poured more and spread it generously on his penis.

She grunted as he slipped his oiled shaft into her anus. She was used to it, and his entry was not as painful as it had once been. Even so, it did hurt. No matter how many times they did it, her body instinctively closed against this invasion, and only when he was in and slowly stroking did her muscles gradually loosen so she could stop gritting her teeth and sweating.

" 'Kay?" he asked.

"Okay, honey. Easy, though."

She had given him everything, and if this was what he liked best, it was okay with her.

She wondered how it felt to him and why he liked it better than putting himself in the regular place. He could feel her body slackening to let him in, and he began to thrust harder and deeper. The sweat came again, on her forehead.

He came explosively. She could feel the violent paroxysms of his ejaculation. She was grateful when he went limp and dropped over on his back, moaning in ecstasy.

Dick was a strange man, some ways, Cathy thought. They could not live together. She had never seen the inside of his apartment. They would have sex, go out to dinner or eat here, and spend the evening together; but he would go to his own apartment and sleep alone. At first she had wondered if he had another woman, maybe his mother, living with him. But he didn't. A man of habit, he wanted to sleep alone, rise to shower and shave when he wanted to, fix his own breakfast, and read his morning papers at the table—alone.

He lived by rules he made for himself. He made rules for her, too. He prescribed what she was to wear—the white blouses and black skirts she wore every day. She was not to take off her garter belt, stockings, and shoes when they had sex. She was not to wear panties, any time. He was not to see her in slacks or jeans, only in skirts. Whenever they were alone together, she was to keep her breasts bare. He would not complain or sulk if she broke a rule, but she saw no reason not to accommodate him. His rules were no burden on her, and she benefited too much from their relationship to put it at risk.

He was intensely jealous and did not want her to have friends. That was all right with her. There was no one in the office she wanted for a friend.

Her little white poodle was the only friend she needed. She called him Whitey. It was funny to see him sit, watching alertly as Dick pumped away behind her. Sometimes Whitey tipped his little head to one side, as if he could get a better perspective that way. Cathy imagined he was trying to make sure the man wasn't hurting Mommy.

Now, Dick sat up and reached for one of the towels. He wiped the oil and ejaculate off himself, then wiped Cathy's backside. He kissed her there—the signal that he had finished wiping. He rose from the floor and dressed, except for his tie and jacket.

Cathy pulled on her half-slip and her black skirt. She put her blouse and bra aside on a chair, leaving her breasts bare, as Dick wanted. She was glad he liked them, because in her own judgment they were the mature breasts of a woman of forty, too big and too soft.

"Drink?" she asked, knowing he would want one.

"Well," he said after he'd taken a sip of rye, "the goddamned Lears are going to hold out on us."

"You have a problem, Dick. You knew you were going to have a problem."

"Inheriting half of Carlton House Productions gave the bastard his independence, and today he issued his declaration."

"Is that how Doug feels about it?"

"Not as strongly as I do, I suppose. But he has the same agenda I do—to take over and run the goddamned company as we see fit. I'm going to have somebody look into Carlton House. It may be carrying a load we don't know about. I hope so. I'd like to have both companies."

TWENTY-FIVE

One 1952

HOME FROM ANNAPOLIS, John sat at the dining table in the house on Louisburg Square. He studied his mother subtly but critically, and he was appalled. She was forty-five years old, an age when a woman might well be at her prime, but she had deteriorated dramatically. Since he saw her only every now and then, when he came home for holidays, the change in her shocked him.

He remembered being proud of her. He remembered when she was called the most elegant woman in Boston. Now, in *his* judgment, she was thick and coarse, a caricature of what she had been. She smoked and drank more than ever before, and she wore more makeup than he had ever seen her use, which did nothing to disguise the lines around her eyes or the two deep, curving lines at the corners of her mouth. She had her hair dyed darker than was natural and puffed up in a bouffant style. She wore big beaded bracelets, but they shifted and did not entirely hide the dark bruises on her wrists, which Joni said were from the handcuffs she wore when she and Dodge were in the attic. Joni said their mother had white scars on her back from lashings. She couldn't wear swimsuits anymore when they went to the beach on the Cape.

Dodge seemed resistant to aging. He was self-contained and placid. He was affectionate, and kissed and fondled Kimberly in the presence of her son and daughter and the servants.

"How much of the summer will you be home, John?" Dodge asked.

"Not much, I'm afraid. I'm going on sea duty this summer. Midshipman, you know."

"Do you know what ship you'll be aboard?"

"Well, I asked that it be an aircraft carrier. I'd like to know my way around a carrier."

"Why that, especially?" Kimberly asked. "Are you still obsessed with *flying?*"

"Well, Mother, you have to know this. I'm going in the navy air training program. I'm going to fly."

Kimberly sneered. "A boyish obsession. The first time you *go* up, you'll *throw* up. I really wish you'd *grow* up."

John looked for a moment at Joni. "I won't throw up," he said. "I already know how to fly. I have my license."

"Who paid for—*Oh, shit!* Your father!"

"John's a skilled pilot," said Joni.

"How would *you* know?"

"His instructors have said so. Anyway, I've been up with him. I've never been in the least afraid, with John flying."

Kimberly stared at Dodge. "Both of my children," she said, barely containing her fury. "I might have lost both of them. Jack is a consummate *ass!*"

"No, he isn't," Joni protested.

"No? Well, you're not going to see him anymore. You won't go down there *this* summer!"

"Mother, I'll be eighteen years old in August. I'm going to spend the summer in Greenwich . . . whether . . . you . . . like it . . . or not."

"Then why don't you go now? Pack up your stuff and go to your father. Now . . . Tonight!"

Two

JOHN DROVE Joni's car, the Buick convertible that her father had bought for her a year ago. On the way down from Boston to Greenwich, Joni took John in her mouth twice. She told him it had been too long since she'd last had a chance to do it and that she'd missed it terribly. He admitted he'd missed it, too. They arrived in Greenwich at two in the morning. They had telephoned from Louisburg Square, so Jack and Anne were up, waiting for them.

"She's lost her mind," were John's first words to Jack. "I didn't say it on the phone. I figured she was listening on an extension. But she's lost her mind. Joni can't live with her anymore."

"Well, of course she doesn't have to," said Anne.

"Wellesley—" Jack started to say.

"I don't want to go to Wellesley. That's too close to her. She'll harass me."

"But you're admitted," said Jack. "It may be too late to get admitted somewhere else."

"If it is, I'll work for a year."

"Doing what?"

"Daddy, I'll be a *waitress* if I have to!"

Anne interrupted. "We shouldn't try to make decisions in the middle of the night. You're very welcome to stay with us. We'll work something out. One thing that may help is that your father and I are building a house here in Greenwich. We're going to make it our chief residence, though we're not giving up the townhouse in New York. So there'll be a place for you here, or there'll be a place for you in New York. One way or another, it's going to be just fine, Joni."

"Unless you get pregnant again," Jack laughed, slapping his daughter gently on the shoulder.

Three 1952–1953

JONI DECIDED she would work for a year before she went to college. She said she was too disorganized to settle into any program of study and wanted a year to think.

She wept inconsolably when John left. Anne found that a little curious but did not guess the reason. She tried to involve the girl in the planning for the new house. Joni was enthusiastic but was conspicuously distracted. She began to look for a job.

Finding one was not easy. She had no secretarial skills

and didn't want a secretarial job anyway. Jack offered to find a place for her in the company. She responded with a blunt question: "What could I do?" For a while she drove her car around in Greenwich, Stamford, and White Plains, answering employment ads in the local papers. When she turned eighteen, in August, she went to New York and moved into the brownstone. She came to Greenwich only on the weekends. Jack gave her an allowance, but she was embarrassed to take his money.

Finally, in October, she told Jack and Anne that she had a job and asked if she could continue to live indefinitely in the brownstone. They said yes and asked her what kind of job she had. As a model, she said. For Macy's. She would be photographed in clothes the store wanted to feature in ads in the *New York Times* and other papers.

Joni was pleased. This kind of modeling was not glamorous work, and the pay was meager, but she could live quite well without taking an allowance—as long as she lived in her father's luxurious apartment.

Before long Jack and Anne began to recognize Joni in advertising spreads in the *Times*. She modeled dresses and coats for a time; then she began to appear in bras and panties.

Just before Christmas a telegram arrived from Boston:

> DEEPLY HUMILIATED BY TIMES PHOTOS OF JONI IN HER UNDERWEAR. TRUST YOU ARE HAPPY ABOUT TURNING OUR DAUGHTER INTO A WHORE. TRUST SHE IS HAPPY BEING ONE.
>
> MRS. DODGE HALLOWELL

Jack and Anne did not show Joni the telegram. They didn't need to. Joni had received one of her own:

> YOU HAVE THOROUGHLY HUMILIATED YOUR GRANDPARENTS AS WELL AS DODGE AND ME BY ALLOWING YOURSELF TO BE PHOTOGRAPHED ALL BUT NAKED FOR PUBLIC DISPLAY IN NEWSPAPERS. SUGGEST YOU NEVER AGAIN APPEAR IN THIS CITY.
>
> MRS. DODGE HALLOWELL

Joni did not show that telegram to Jack or Anne. She answered it with a wire to her mother:

GO TO THE DEVIL.

JONI

Her mother's telegram only made her more determined to find success in the work she had chosen to do. When the time came to apply to colleges and universities, she did not apply. Instead, she had a portfolio of photographs taken of herself and began to visit modeling agencies.

In April 1953 she was accepted by the Rodman-Hubbel Agency. Her assignments then became more varied, and she appeared in slick magazines instead of department-store ads in newspapers.

Four October 1953

JACK AND ANNE had two children: Little Jack, who was now six, and Anne Elizabeth, who was four. Jack was forty-seven. Anne was forty. They talked about having more children and decided they should not.

Anne went to her gynecologist in the spring and was fitted for a diaphragm. She found it uncomfortable, and Jack could feel it when he was inside her and didn't like it. They relied on condoms instead. But neither of them liked those, either. Both were bothered by the feel of rubber between them.

In bed one night in the Manhattan townhouse, where they had come after a formal dinner honoring Curt Frederick, they talked about what they had come to regard as a problem.

"I love you so much, Jack," Anne whispered to him as they lay together. "I want to *make* love with you. All the time. I . . . have been thinking that maybe I should have my tubes tied. It's not a big operation. It—"

"I have a better idea," he said. "The operation that *I* can have is much easier."

"Oh, but, baby!"

"It's much easier. It's not painful. And it doesn't change anything, as far as feeling is concerned. Curt had it done when he was fifty and Betsy was forty-seven. He assures me he cannot tell the difference. He says it's just as good for him as it ever was."

"You wouldn't feel you were . . . How can I say it?"

"Less of a man? I'd feel I was *more* of a man, for having done something . . . responsible. Why should you have to undergo surgery when I can have this done as an office procedure?"

Ten days later he lay on a table in a surgeon's office and submitted to the procedure. It was not painless, but it was not major surgery, either. The discomfort was gone in a week.

Three times Anne used her hand to make him ejaculate into a glass and went with him when he took the sample to a lab, where it would be examined under a microscope. The third time, the lab found no sperm cells in his semen.

He and Anne made love with a new freedom. She offered him more, as if she wanted to make it up to him for having had the operation. She had never withheld anything from him, but now she welcomed him with new fervor.

Five

DR. LOEWENSTEIN had been right. Not every television station had to be a separate entity. A station could be connected by wire to satellite stations. What was more, local commercials could be inserted in the commercial breaks in a program. During commercial breaks in a Carlton House movie, local businesses could advertise their goods and services.

Late in 1953, LCI began an experiment in transmitting signals from its major stations to satellite stations by using a series of microwave transmitters. A microwave transmitter could send its signal only on line of sight, not over the horizon. Even so, a properly situated microwave transmitter could send its signal for twenty-five or thirty miles. A series of stations could send a program from a major television station to a community of satellite stations for a fraction of the cost of leasing wires.

Frequency allocations were another problem. With only twelve VHF channels available, competition for them was aggressive. For a time, the seventy UHF channels were all but ignored. Independent and public television stations took them. So did LCI.

Most television sets received only the twelve VHF channels. Sets that could receive the UHF channels cost a little more money. Also, the UHF channels did not reach such great distances. The solution, said Dr. Lowenstein, was to make consumers *want* to receive the programming on UHF.

In many areas—rural areas, especially—people could watch Milton Berle and *Your Show of Shows* on their VHF sets but had only heard of the interesting, risqué *Sally Allen Show.* They wanted it. They bought UHF sets and put up the additional little antennas that were needed to bring in the UHF stations.

By the end of 1953, the Lear Network was being called the fourth network. It was a status Jack Lear would not claim, but he was pleased with the result of his adventure in television.

Six

IN THE AUTUMN of 1953 Jack and Anne returned to London. They spent a week seeing shows and visiting shops, then drove to Weldon Abbey for a three-day visit, bearing gifts and also photos of the home they were building in Connecticut. The Countess put them in the bedroom where they had spent their wedding night.

A big fire burned in the fireplace. Tonight it warmed the room.

"The fireplace didn't do much for us *that* night, did it?" Jack remarked. "The bed had been warmed for us, but this room was *cold!*"

"I'd intended to wear the white negligee," said Anne. "Remember it? I bought it for our wedding night. But this room was so cold that night that we couldn't come out from under the covers."

"Without frostbite," he chuckled.

She smiled. "It was a wonderful night for snuggling, though, wasn't it? The bed was warm, but you'd have kept me warm even if it hadn't been."

"We were in Majorca before you could wear the negligee. I wish we had it now."

"We do," she said with a playful smile. "I brought it. Give me a minute to put it on."

The white negligee consisted of a sheer pleated skirt and a snug lace bodice that scooped under her breasts, leaving them bare. It was held up by narrow silk straps that ran from her armpits and over her shoulders. She modeled it for him, the way she'd done in Majorca. The pleats stirred as she walked, yielding glimpses of everything the skirt covered.

She sat down on an eighteenth-century settee that faced the fireplace. While he took off his clothes and pulled on a knee-length black Japanese silk robe, she poured cognac into two snifters. He sat down beside her, and before he took a sip of the brandy he kissed her, first on the mouth, then on each nipple. Then he dipped his tongue in the cognac and transferred a few drops to her lips and a drop or two to each nipple, where he knew it would tingle.

Anne dipped her tongue in the brandy and transferred a few drops to the tip of his penis.

They laughed.

"Can I ever express to you how much I love you?" he asked.

"Maybe not with words," she said. "Anyway, you don't have to express it. I know it. I feel it."

They moved to the bed. In one respect, Anne was a woman like none he had ever known before. She was *wet!* Sometimes, with others, he had put saliva, even Vaseline, on himself to effect a smooth entry. Never with Anne. From the time he began to kiss her, she became wet. Entering her had never been difficult; she was ready and slippery as soon as he approached her.

The only sexual difficulty they ever experienced was a minor one. Well hung though he was, Jack could never seem to penetrate Anne as deeply as she could accept. She could be satisfied without deep penetration, but she loved to feel him as far inside her as he could reach. They achieved the best penetration when he lay on his back and she mounted him. She would spread as wide as she could and lower herself on him.

She had a joke: "Oh, lover! I feel you in my *throat!*"

As she impaled herself on him, she grunted, "You didn't get in like this on our wedding night. Damn that cold night and those down comforters!" She began to pump. "Damn!"

He looked up and studied her closely. She kept her chin high, her eyes tightly closed, and drew her lower lip back between her teeth. She grunted and sometimes squealed, as she raised her hips and slammed them down, driving his shaft into her. Her breasts bounced, and sweat began to gleam on her lithe body. Who could have guessed *this* of the polished, dignified, aristocratic Countess of Weldon? Nobody, he judged. Besides every other wonderful thing she was, Anne was a carnal animal.

Seven

AT THE SAME TIME that his father and stepmother were reenacting their wedding night in rural England, Midshipman John Lear was exulting in one of the most memorable experiences of his life. Tense but alert, he took his turn at the wheel of the venerable aircraft carrier *Essex.* It was midafternoon in California, and the *Essex* was cruising off San Diego, launching and recovering F9F Panther jets. The pilots were in training for carrier operations. The midshipmen were getting their first sea experience.

Keeping an eye on the compass, hoping he wouldn't let the ship wander off heading, John could not watch the air operations, even though they were what interested him most. The jets roared off, hurled by steam catapults. Returning to the deck demanded the maximum skill and steely calm of every pilot. It was surely the most difficult flying anyone would ever be asked to do.

The wind was shifting.

"Bring the ship to two-eight-five degrees."

"Two-eight-five degrees, aye, sir."

John spun the wheel.

"Twenty right rudder will be enough," muttered the regular quartermaster. "Then ten left when she's within five degrees of course, to stop the turn."

Watching the turn of the compass, feeling the huge ship turn in response to his steering, John had to brace himself to keep from shuddering.

His turn at the wheel lasted only half an hour, but he knew he would never forget the experience. Leaving the bridge, he was able to linger for a while at a vantage point where he could see the flight deck operations. There was no doubt in his mind that in another three years he would be flying from a carrier.

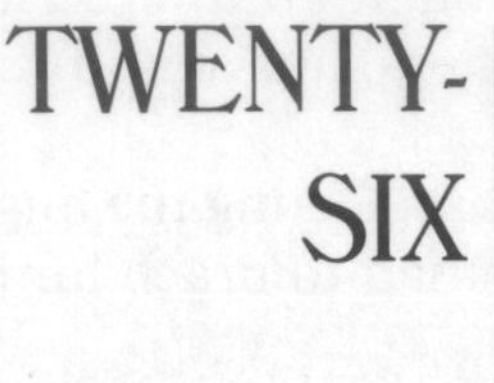

TWENTY-SIX

One 1954

"I'M GLAD to make your acquaintance, Mr. Lear. I've wanted to meet you for a long time."

Dick Painter saluted Bob Lear with a glass of rye. They sat together in the living room of a suite at the Mark Hopkins Hotel in San Francisco. They had chosen this place because they didn't want Jack to learn they had met.

Dick had made all of the arrangements. Two girls in black panties and bras, with black garter belts and dark stockings, sat in chairs by the bar, ready to bring fresh drinks to the two men on the couch.

"I can't help but feel that your brother has made a point of keeping us from meeting. Do you have that feeling too?"

Bob shrugged. "Jack's a devious guy."

Dick leaned forward and stared into Bob's eyes. "Your brother is one of the most intelligent and effective men I've ever known. And 'devious' is not a word I would use to describe him. Since you used it—"

"He has a lot in common with our father. You know much about my father?"

"Everyone knows of your father. He was a tycoon. Whatever he touched turned to money."

"Well, my father and my brother have got something in common. When my father wanted something, *he got it!* Whether it was a piece of ass or a contract. But he ran up against one guy he couldn't break—Jack. Jack just walked out on him. My father hated him for it. Still, he had to recognize that Jack was just like him."

"A chip off the old block," Painter suggested.

"Like that. Me, I'm more a business-type guy. I had to be. That was what the old man wanted."

Dick Painter was glad he had arranged this meeting. He'd had no idea what Bob Lear might be like. Now Bob sat there in a light-gray double-breasted suit with a bright, splashy necktie, the archetypal envious younger brother, unable even to *aspire* to his elder brother's achievements.

In Bob's own suite, before they came here for their business meeting, Dick had met Dorothy Lear. My God! Married to that, Bob would have had to be blind and illiterate not to have been envious of his brother's marriage to the exquisite Anne, Countess of Weldon. And before her, there had been the most beautiful Boston debutante of 1929.

"Bob, some of us at Lear Communications have been exploring for almost four years now the idea of merging Carlton House Productions into LCI. We think there are immense advantages. Jack has blocked us at every turn, saying *you* would never accept such an arrangement. Has Jack seriously presented the proposal to you?"

Bob shook his head. "I never heard of the idea," he said. "He never said anything to me."

Dick glanced at the two young women waiting beside the bar. "Why don't you girls call down and have dinner sent up?" he said. "Tell them to give us, say, forty-five minutes." Then he lowered his voice. "Bob, do you have any idea how much Jack is worth?"

"A hell of a lot, I figure."

"Have you seen the home he's built in Greenwich, Connecticut? A fuckin' *museum,* Bob! And where did the money for something like that come from? He sold most of his network to the gentlemen who now own the controlling interest in LCI. In short, he cashed out! But he won't with Carlton House, and he won't let you. Maybe, uh . . . You get my point?"

Bob Lear nodded.

"Okay. Maybe that's as far as we can go this evening. Tell you what, maybe we should look a little closer at the two young ladies over there. I can promise you one thing. They're *artists!* You take your choice. Maybe a little before dinner, then a little after."

Bob Lear frowned. "I've been . . . Well, I've never been what my father was—what I guess my brother is."

Dick laughed. "Then here's your chance to expand your horizons, Brother Bob. Pros, those girls. Absolutely discreet. They don't know who you are. I'll take care of them, money-wise. Enjoy!"

"Well . . . the one with red hair."

"Good! Good choice, Bob! Uh . . . figure half an hour before dinner comes up. Save a little of yourself for later. Okay? Know what I mean?"

When Bob Lear had gone into a bedroom with the red-head, Dick and the other girl shared a laugh. Then Dick slipped into a closet to make sure the cameraman caught everything that happened in that bedroom.

Two

JACK HAD NO HESITATION about calling Monica Dale to ask her if she would appear on a special television show he was producing. He was surprised and pleased when she said she would, depending on her schedule and the script. He told her he wanted her to appear on a special two-hour broadcast of *The Sally Allen Show.* It would be a variety show, built around songs and dances, with perhaps some sort of flimsy plot in the background to tie it all together.

She did not ask the question her agent would have asked: did the Lear Network have enough stations to cover the nation and get worthwhile exposure for his star? Very soon the agent called to ask just that—plus, of course, how much Jack proposed to pay. The answer was that Lear Communications, Incorporated had just acquired WNNJ in Newark, New Jersey, whose signal could be received in all five boroughs of New York City and even in Westchester County and well up into Connecticut, as well as all over northern New Jersey. WNNJ was a Lear satellite station. Most of its broadcasting came in by microwave transmission from Kansas City, which continued to be the pilot station of the network.

Sally Allen surprised Jack with an odd request.

"I got a letter from Len," she told him. "Jack, I can't help still having some kind of feeling for the guy. He's not asking for money. But could I help him find a job? Is there anything in the world we could do for the guy? I guess I'm too tenderhearted, but I hate to see old Len on the curb."

"Doing what? What could he do?"

Sally closed her eyes and smiled. "Believe it or not, Jack, the stupid son of a bitch is a not-bad comedy writer. He wrote all our old routines, plus a lot of routines for other people. He's not a bum. He really isn't."

"Are you telling me you want him to write for *you*?"

"We've got worse guys."

"To be perfectly frank with you, Sally, four years ago he looked like a shabby bum."

"I'll be just as frank, Jack. If you had to live on what he's had to live on, you'd look like a shabby bum, too. When I married him, in 1938, Len was a good-lookin' guy and a sharp dresser. He made a hundred a week. So did I. In those days plenty of people were working for twenty a week."

"What about his girlfriend, the one who stripped with her leg in a cast?"

"Gone to the slammer. Ten to twenty for possession of heroin. His letter says he doubts he'll ever see her again."

"And you want him for a writer. Seriously?"

"Give him a chance, Jack."

"Well, let's see what he can do."

The show was built during the spring and summer, for fall broadcast. Leonard submitted a script to the producer, and the producer hired him—whether because Sally had promoted him or because the script was good, Jack would never know. He let production people handle production.

Three

JOHN GRADUATED from Annapolis in June and was commissioned an ensign in the United States Navy. His application to be admitted to flight training was approved, and he was given two months' leave before he was to report to Pensacola.

Kimberly did not come to Annapolis for his graduation. But his seventy-three-year-old grandfather did. Harrison Wolcott told John that Edith, John's grandmother, had become too frail to travel but sent her congratulations and highest regards.

Jack and Anne were there, as were Curt and Betsy Frederick and Cap and Naomi Durenberger.

And of course Joni came. She had always been tall and leggy and busty. The training she had received at the modeling agency had given her new self-confidence and grace. The new ensigns abandoned their families for the privilege of being introduced to her. John confided to her that he had shown clippings of her ad layouts to some of his friends. The ads had became collector's items among the midshipmen. The early ones, in which she had modeled bras, were especially prized and kept under lock and key.

John spent his leave in Connecticut. He went into the city every week and stayed for two or three days with Joni in the Manhattan place. They slept together.

They were in bed, in fact, when Joni received a telephone call from a young man who reminded her that John had introduced them on graduation day. His name was Frank Neville, and he was calling to ask if Joni would allow him to take her to dinner or maybe to a play, or both.

She was holding the phone a little distance away from her ear, to let John listen in. She looked at him, grimaced, and shrugged. John nodded vigorously.

When she had agreed to the date and hung up the telephone, John said, "Frank is a good guy, and I mean a *very* good guy. To have a date with him— Well, Joni, as much as I love you, we both understand for sure that we can't . . . You know what we can't do. You've got to see guys."

"Then you have to see girls," she said defiantly.

John nodded. "Yes. I suppose I do."

Four

THE MOST VALUABLE ARTWORKS and furniture from the Manhattan townhouse were moved out to the new house in Greenwich. That house became the new Lear family showplace.

Jack never said so to Anne—or to anyone else—but he was determined that the Greenwich house should exceed in every respect the house on Louisburg Square. Even though it was new, he didn't want the house to look as if it had just been built. He had insisted that every old tree should be preserved and that the construction crews should work around them. New plantings were not of raw young shrubbery but of mature shrubs bought from all over the area. His architect's staff had visited sites fifty miles around, looking for old lumber and especially for old bricks. Bemused farmers accepted surprisingly high prices for their old brick walks that ran between farmhouse and gate or farmhouse and barn. The worn and sometimes slimy bricks were hauled to Greenwich and laid to form new walks and the patio behind the greenhouse conservatory. The floor of the library was meticulously assembled from oak that had formed the hayloft floor of a barn built in the 1770s.

The electrical circuits and plumbing, hidden inside the walls, were absolutely modern. The house was centrally air-conditioned, which was almost unheard of in Connecticut.

Jack had insisted that the architects find him a duplicate of the marble-enclosed shower he had enjoyed in Boston. They could not, but they employed people who could build one. Jack had his choice of marble and chose white with black streaks. The showerhead was as big around as a sunflower. Plumbers drilled nickel-plated pipe to make the needle shower. The bidet swung out from the wall, just like the one in Boston. Even Anne had never seen a shower like it before and declared it a "Yankee extravagance." She loved it. When they were at home together, they never showered alone.

They built a swimming pool, but downhill from the house, at the edge of the woods, lay a small natural lake. They did not touch it, except to arrange filtration of the water and to plant cattails and water lilies. Anne swam in the lake; she preferred it to the pool. When she was satisfied about her privacy, she swam nude at dawn in midsummer.

In late July, Joni came to Jack with a request. "Daddy, could Frank and I use the shower?"

Jack reached for her hands and took both of them in his. "The two of you are that close?"

She nodded.

He smiled and told her yes, any time. He wrote to John, who was now at Pensacola, that Joni seemed to be in love. He had no idea what kind of impact that news would have on John.

Five

WHEN CAP DURENBERGER asked Jack if he could have a private conversation with him, Jack told him to come to the townhouse that September evening. Both of them had begun to wonder just how much notice was paid to who talked to whom in the office.

Joni had replaced some of the furnishings and decorative pieces that had been taken to Greenwich, and the place now looked very different. Joni's prints were bright and cheerful, but they were nothing like the original Boucher and the Dürer that had once hung in the living room.

Joni was out of town, modeling. The only household help she had was a cleaning woman who came in once a week, so Jack and Cap had complete privacy tonight.

Jack poured drinks from the bar, which Joni kept stocked.

Cap sipped, then leaned back in his overstuffed chair and closed his eyes. "Shit's in the fan, boss," he said. "One way, anyhow."

"What is it?"

"Sally Allen."

"What's with Sally?" Jack asked, concerned.

"She's pregnant."

A week later Jack and Cap met with Sally in Kansas City.

"So I'm knocked up," she said. "I'm a woman. I'm entitled. We'll do the Monica Dale special before it begins to show."

"Can I ask who's the daddy?"

She smiled at Jack. "Len, of course. Who'd you suppose? Hey! He's not the shabby bum you remember. Now that he's got a respectable job, he—"

"I understand he writes good comedy," said Jack. "But this is something else. So, okay, we get the special on the air. What about the rest of the season?"

"Len has written a sketch about my being pregnant."

"Unmarried and pregnant?"

"The script doesn't say."

"But that's the whole point! If the scripts don't say it, the news people will. Look, we just went through the battle over *The Moon Is Blue—"*

"Yeah! What a *horrible* film! It dared to use the word 'pregnant.' It dared to—"

Cap interrupted. "The Legion of Decency—"

"Legion of *Crap!"* she yelled angrily. "Fuck the Legion of Decency!"

"We can't—"

"Wanta bet? Everywhere that film plays it makes big money! *Big* goddamned money! The *audiences* don't give a shit about—"

"Wait a minute," Jack interrupted. "How will you do energetic dance routines?"

"Very simple, Jack. I *say* I'm pregnant. I tell 'em I can't dance like an idiot right now. So here's a kinescope of a dance routine I did last year. Or, better yet, here's the new young dancer, so-and-so. I can still sing. I can deliver funny lines. The movie studios have notified me they're canceling my contracts, under the so-called morals clause. And you can do the same. In which case I'll take my pregnant body to Europe and appear before audiences who don't give a shit about the Legion of Decency."

Sally clapped her hands over her face and began to cry.

Jack stared at her for a moment, then at Cap. "Okay," he said decisively. "Okay. We'll do it your way. Tell Len to write a line into the special, announcing that you're pregnant."

She drew her hands down her face, streaking her tears.

"It's already written," she said. "Goes like this: Monica says to me, 'Hey, Sally, I hear you're gonna have a baby.' I rub my belly with both hands and say, 'Feels that way.' Then she says, 'Uh, can I ask the pregnant question?' And I say, 'Ask me no questions, I'll tell you no lies.' That's also what I say to the reporters."

Six

"I THINK YOU'LL AGREE—I think you *have* to agree—that we were entitled to be told," Dick Painter said at a meeting of the board of directors. "Lear Communications is not your private fief anymore. We should *consult* on major decisions."

"I am chief executive officer of this corporation and am entitled to make decisions," Jack said coldly. "I wouldn't refinance the company without consultation and action by the board. But decisions about the content of a program are within my executive purview. I made the decision, and the decision was carried out. Besides, if we'd consulted, we wouldn't have done it. Committees—and I don't care what kind of committees they are—are not noted for courage."

"You did take one hell of a risk," Douglas Humphrey observed.

"I don't think so. This is 1954, gentlemen, not 1934. Audiences are sophisticated today. They're sick of the tired old pap that passes for television comedy and drama. I saw a film the other day. It's called *On the Waterfront,* with Marlon Brando. There's a scene where Brando tells a priest, played by Karl Malden, to go to hell. In those words. 'Go to hell.' So how does the priest react? He doesn't go cow-eyed and wring his hands like 'Father' Bing Crosby. He clenches his fist and slugs Brando. Have any of you looked at the ratings for *The Sally Allen Show* since she announced she's pregnant?"

"It could have come out the other way," said the Chicago banker Joseph Freeman. "And may yet. Some powerful people are shocked and offended."

"And what are these powerful people going to do?" Jack asked.

"Catholics in Columbus, Ohio, have been ordered not to watch our station for the next six months, under pain of sin," said Ray l'Enfant."

"So? *Are* they not watching us? Look at the numbers."

"We've lost some sponsors—"

"And picked up others."

"The question is," said Painter, "will this board of directors have any influence on programming decisions?"

"The answer is no."

TWENTY-SEVEN

One 1955

Joni was not intimidated by the big photo studio she was working in today. She had been photographed here before and had confidence in the photographer, Clinton Batchelder. Anyway, her agent, Muriel Hubbel, was with her. They had discussed the project at length and decided it was worth a try. The magazine was disinclined to use photographs of professional models—or so it said—but Joni was so conspicuously unspoiled and youthful that the publisher might make an exception.

The project had been initiated by Batchelder. *Playboy,* he had explained to Joni and Muriel, was a new magazine, but it had a rapidly growing circulation and received an immense amount of attention. Its Playmate of the Month photo spread could send a model's career soaring. Besides, the magazine paid generous fees to both model and photographer.

Robin Rodman, the president of the Rodman-Hubbel Modeling Agency, had issues of *Playboy* in his office. After looking over the centerfolds in those issues, he and Muriel and Joni had agreed they were professional and tastefully done. The final decision was Joni's, and she agreed to be photographed in a set of pictures that would be submitted to *Playboy.*

The studio was cavernous. The room was so large, and the ceiling so high, that Batchelder said he flew his radio-controlled model helicopter around inside it, though no one

Joni had talked to had ever seen him do it. The expanse of empty space made it possible for the photographer to move cameras, lights, props, and models around without interference.

There was no dressing room, not even a screen behind which models could undress, and many did so because Batchelder shot a good deal of lingerie advertising. He photographed nudes occasionally but not often. When he did, they were only for photography shows, where in fact some of his nudes had won prizes. He had some kind of connection with a Manhattan ballet school, and almost all of his nudes were young ballerinas. Joni's admiration for his ballerina prints was another reason why she had agreed to this session.

Clinton Batchelder was about forty-five years old, not memorably handsome but not unattractive, either. Joni knew him to be a very businesslike photographer, brusque in manner and abrupt in his movements when he was working. He was wearing a white shirt with a yellow necktie and tan slacks. He smoked a pipe, which he would put aside when the shoot began.

"Well, Joni, all set?"

Joni smiled weakly. "I guess," she murmured.

"How 'bout a Scotch to settle your nerves."

Joni glanced at Muriel, who nodded and said, "One for me, too."

"We'll all have a Scotch," said Batchelder. His liquor bottles sat among the bottles of chemicals in his darkroom, and he took ice and soda from the darkroom refrigerator. They sat in three wooden chairs behind the lights and toasted each other.

Joni drank about half of her Scotch, then said, "Well, I guess I better, huh?"

Batchelder nodded. "You can finish your drink afterward."

Joni nodded. She drew a breath and reached behind her back to unzip her white knit dress. She stood up, pulled it over her head, and folded it on the chair. She was wearing a half-slip and a bra, and she took those off. She unhooked her stockings from her garter belt and pulled them off. She unfastened the garter belt and dropped it on the chair.

She was wearing sheer white bikini-style panties that exposed her hips and bottom, though not her pubic area because they had an opaque panel in front. "Clint . . . Since *Playboy* doesn't show the lower part, I was wondering if I could keep the panties on."

He smiled faintly. "I'd very much rather you didn't," he said soberly. "It's true that we won't submit pictures that show your down-below hair, but we probably will want to submit some that show your bare bottom."

Joni nodded and pulled off the panties.

"You know Laurie," said Batchelder.

Laurie was the body-makeup girl who now approached Joni and would smear parts of her with greasepaint to give her an even skin tone all over, hiding the pale stripes left by her swimsuits. Laurie would also cover the red marks made by the elastic in Joni's clothes. Joni had been made up by Laurie before, when modeling bikini panties or appearing, as she occasionally did, with arms folded over bare breasts.

Laurie also gave her hair a final brushing. It hung around her shoulders, smooth and glossy.

While Laurie worked, Joni finished her drink. Batchelder took her glass and poured her some more Scotch.

"We'll work with the neutral background first," Batchelder said. He pulled a sheet of light-gray paper down from a roller that hung on one wall of the studio. "Just step over there and let us see what *you* think might be effective poses."

Joni handed her glass to Muriel and walked out in front of the gray background. Batchelder's two lighting men switched on powerful lights.

Suddenly the situation struck Joni. She was standing in front of the photographer and his assistant, her agent, the makeup girl, and two lighting technicians. She was naked. Six clothed people were staring at her. Her mouth dried up. For an instant she felt as if she might lose her balance.

She stared down at herself. It had seemed so cute to trim her dark pubic hair and not allow a thick bush to grow over her crotch. Now the piercing lights exhibited her pudenda and even outlined the dark stripe of her cleft.

Batchelder's assistant began to shoot pictures with a Rolleiflex twin-lens reflex camera.

"How do you want to pose, Joni?" Batchelder asked.

She recovered a little and raised her hands to clasp them behind her head.

"I love it," said Batchelder, "but that's a little too bold for the magazine. Let's turn to your left. Turn . . . a little more. Now bring your hands down. Now look back over your shoulder. Hey!"

He went to the big camera, hooded himself with the black cloth, and studied the image she was making on the ground glass. He began to order changes in the lighting. They spent three-quarters of an hour shooting pictures that would show the profile of Joni's left breast and all of her backside while she looked over her shoulder with various expressions that Batchelder suggested.

They sipped at a new round of drinks. Laurie patted Joni with Kleenex, to remove the sweat from her skin.

In the pictures they agreed to submit to *Playboy,* Joni was sitting on an antique wire chair, the kind that had been common in soda fountains in past decades. The neutral background had been turned dark maroon by floodlights, which dramatized the outline of her brightly lighted body. She was completely naked, but her right heel rested on one of the wire rungs of the chair, raising her right leg high enough to cover her pubic area. She clasped her hands behind her neck and lifted her chin. Her eyes were turned up and to the right. She smiled. Her lips were parted, showing her teeth. She looked young and fresh, proud and joyful—and maybe a little defiant. Even so, something subtle in her expression also revealed that she was more than a little embarrassed.

Two

BOB LEAR flew up to San Francisco to meet Dick Painter again in a suite at the Mark Hopkins. The scene was the same as before. Two girls sat by the bar, well out of earshot of the men's earnest conversation. One of them was the redhead who had gone with Bob into a bedroom.

"Let me get right to the point, Bob," Painter said.

"We've done our homework, and we know that the book value of each of your shares of Carlton House Productions, Incorporated, is $211.75. My associates have authorized me to offer you $250. Sell to us, and you've got a personal fortune of $12,500,000. Free of capital gains tax because the value of your shares has declined since you inherited them. And it's entirely possible they're going to decline some more."

"Are you offering Jack the same?"

"We're talking to you first. Jack's a little difficult to talk to on this subject. He will be much easier to persuade if he knows you've sold."

"I'll have to discuss it with my wife."

"Of course. Why don't you call your wife and have her come up here for dinner tomorrow night?"

"Uh . . . well."

Painter grinned. "Of course the girls won't be joining us."

Three

INVITED TO VISIT the control tower at Pensacola, Jack and Anne listened to the radio talk and watched John approach and land an advanced trainer. They knew next to nothing about aircraft, but the trainer was sleek and conspicuously powerful.

"He'll be leaving here shortly, you know," said Commander Hogan, a flight instructor who was acting as the Lears' host during their visit to the base. "Next stop, San Diego, where he'll start flying the blowtorches. Jets."

"Off a carrier, I suppose," said Jack.

"Well, eventually—after a thousand touch-and-goes on San Diego Naval Air Station."

"I can't hide the fact that I'm apprehensive," Jack said. "When I bought him his first flying lessons, I didn't guess he'd one day be flying jets off carriers. That's got to be dangerous."

"It *is* dangerous, Mr. Lear. I can't deny it. But John is good at it. Look at this landing. Look at the precision. He comes in over the threshold, and his wheels touch the pavement in the first ten yards. He's already thinking in terms of carrier landings."

"It's all he ever wanted to do," said Jack. "From the time he was a little boy, he was fascinated by airplanes." Jack smiled weakly. "More than by girls."

"He's got one of those," said Commander Hogan. "You know, almost all our young men here are handsome, romantic types: young officers, naval fliers. Girls have a choice. From the young men's point of view, the competition is fierce. Well, John has impressed one girl very favorably. *Very* favorably."

"I'm surprised you know that much about the trainees' personal lives," said Anne.

"In this case, I have to," said Commander Hogan. "The girl he's made the impression on is my daughter."

"He's a gentleman, I assume," Anne said with brittle precision in her voice.

"Oh, absolutely. But this is why I took for myself the duty of showing you around the base. I wanted to get to know you."

"I'm glad you did," said Jack. "Maybe you and your wife and daughter can join John and Anne and me for dinner."

"Our plan was to invite you to our house."

Anne and Jack met Linda Hogan on the screened-in front porch of a large white frame house. She was beautiful. She was a blond with perfect features in a perfectly shaped face. Though she was wearing a loose cotton dress, her figure was obviously perfect too. She was just twenty years old and was a student at Florida State University at Tallahassee.

The Hogans were amiable people. They had seen much of the world. The commander had graduated from Annapolis in 1933. He had been stationed in San Diego and had married there. During the war he had flown a Wildcat off the U.S.S. *Hornet*.

Though the cocktail hour and dinner were pleasant, it was apparent that the Hogans' purpose was to study and assess the people who might become their daughter's in-laws.

On the way back to quarters, Jack asked John what his relationship was.

"I wanted you to meet her before I ask her to marry me."

"That's plain enough."

"So what do you think of her?"

"I can find nothing to object to," said Jack.

"Good. I'm going to ask her."

"We have something else we want to talk to you about," said Jack. "It seems that this Frank Neville you introduced to your sister has made an even greater impression on her than you've made on Linda. I don't know what else they do, but they take showers together; I know that."

"Good," said John. "Frank's a first-rate fellow. Serving on an antisubmarine destroyer in the North Atlantic right now. Then he's going on to law school. Going to stay in the navy and be a sea lawyer."

"So you'd say he's the right kind of guy for her?"

John grinned. "Even my insane mother will accept him."

Four

IN 1954 PABLO PICASSO began to sketch variations on the famous Manet painting, *Le déjeuner sur l'Herbe,* Luncheon on the Grass, in which two young men and two young women are seated at what appears to be a picnic. The painting caused a scandal in the nineteenth century because one of the young women is nude. Picasso's variations continued for years as he filled sketchbooks with pages of line drawings, some colored with crayon, some realistic, some entirely abstract.

One of the European dealers who kept in touch with Anne wired her that a drawing from this series had somehow escaped the Picasso studio and was for sale in Paris. Would she be interested? The drawing was of an erotic nature and had been colored with crayon. Anne wired that she would be interested. A series of wires ensued until she beat out the other bidders and bought the drawing. It was so valuable that the dealer flew to New York to deliver it in person.

Almost all the Picasso drawings based on the Manet painting were bound in spiral sketchbooks, with pages 23 by 32 centimeters in size. This one was not bound and was twice that big. It was already sealed behind glass, where nitrogen had been injected to prevent the oxidation of the paper. Anne had it framed and presented it to Jack on his birthday.

The drawing was not something they would display in their living room. Against a yellow and green background that was the only suggestion of the inspiration from Manet, two distorted couples copulated. The men were bearded, bald, and lecherous, and their phalli were hugely exaggerated. The plump women looked frightened but offered little resistance.

They hung the Picasso in their bedroom, beside the etchings by Tauzin. The insurance agent was totally flustered when he tried to appraise it, but his company investigated its value and ultimately agreed to insure the Picasso for $200,000.

Anne was forty-two years old. Jack did not detect it, but she had gained a few pounds. She enrolled in a ballet class and danced strenuously three times a week. She asked Jack to build a glass enclosure over their swimming pool, so she could swim all year 'round. He did, and she swam a mile every day.

She began to wear knit pants with stirrup straps that emphasized her long, trim legs. She wore them with loose, casual sweaters. The style suited her well, and Jack decided she was more beautiful than ever.

She gave a good deal of thought to what she wore in the master bedroom suite, too: diaphanous negligees, sometimes over nothing, sometimes over lingerie that was both tasteful and erotic.

Jack loved her immoderately. He was confident she loved him, too.

Five

PLAYBOY BOUGHT Batchelder's pictures, and Joni became a Playmate of the Month. The text with the photo spread identified Joni as Jack's daughter and mentioned that she lived in a handsome Manhattan town house. The centerfold picture was one of the shots that showed her sitting nude on the soda-fountain chair. Several black-and-white photos—the ones Batchelder's assistant had made with the Rolleiflex—were printed on preceding pages. Also, the magazine ran two pictures of Joni modeling bras.

> When New York model Joni Lear agreed to pose for us, we were elated. Whether modeling the latest Paris fashion or just bras, as seen here, 21-year-old Joni is a very welcome departure from the spare, boyish models typically seen in fashion ads. With her 36–24–36 figure and her smiling young face, she is an ideal Playmate.

The picture chosen for the centerfold suggested precisely what Clint Batchelder had hoped it would suggest—that Joni was comfortable with being seen nude but still, as betrayed by a subtle hint in her expression, a little embarrassed, too.

A segment of the centerfold photo—her face and shoulders—appeared in a montage on the cover, with a blurb:

SUPERMODEL JONI LEAR NUDE!

Six

JACK STOPPED by the town house.

"My only negative comment," he said once he was seated and she had poured him a Scotch, "is that I wish you had told me about it. I mean, there I am, sitting at lunch in the men's bar in the Waldorf, and in comes Greg Hamilton with a copy of the magazine and asks me if I've seen it. I may have been the only man in the bar who hadn't yet seen it. *That* was a little embarrassing. Someone asked me if you really have staples in your navel. Well, you do look very nice."

"Thank you, Daddy. And I agree, I should have told you."

"I bought five copies. They're in my briefcase. Do people ask you to autograph your picture?"

She grinned and nodded. "I'm afraid they do."

He reached for the briefcase.

"Oh, don't take them out! I don't want you looking . . . when we're together."

"Okay. Well, you're the most famous member of the family now." He paused and frowned. "I'm not sure it was a good career move, though."

Joni went to her bar and poured herself a little Scotch. "Let me tell you how good it was," she said quietly. "My per-hour fee tripled when the magazine appeared. The agency began to ask three times what I was being paid before, and advertisers are paying it. I'm getting different kinds of jobs now, not so much fashion layouts as ads for cigarettes, liquor, an automobile . . . *And* I've been invited to Hollywood for a screen test."

"By which studio?" he asked grimly.

"MGM."

"Well, okay, but don't test for anybody else before you check with me. There's still a lot of hanky-panky in film casting."

"Uncle Bob called and asked me to test for Carlton House."

Jack shook his head. "The word would go around that you got something only because you're my daughter. I'll talk to Bob."

Joni smiled warmly. "Thank you, Daddy."

Jack stared at her thoughtfully. Twenty-one years old. Drinking Scotch. A nude centerfold. Little Joni. Her mother would go into hysterics.

Seven

Kimberly did go into hysterics, but that was not the worst reaction Joni got. Frank Neville called from Boston. His ship was in.

"Oh, Joni! How *could* you? What in the world ever possessed you to show yourself off naked to half the men in the United States? Do you have any idea how embarrassed I am? That magazine was brought aboard the ship at Reykjavik by a seaman who'd carried several issues of it from the States in his duffel bag. One of the officers saw it and recognized the name and face as *my* girl, whose picture was on my desk. The whole damned crew, officers and men, including the skipper, saw that god-awful spread of pictures. I don't understand you."

"You know I am a model, Frank. Whether you understand it or not, doing that centerfold was an *opportunity.* I'm more in demand than before, and—guess what?—I've been asked to Hollywood for a screen test!"

"For what, a nudie flick?"

"Nothing of the kind! For MGM. What's the matter with you? Have you been drinking?"

"Yes, I have. Everywhere I go, guys shove that thing in my face. I've actually been asked to autograph it—'Ensign Frank Neville, boyfriend of Joni Lear.' "

"All right, all right. When does your train leave? When will you be here?"

"I don't really think I should come, Joni. I can't afford to be associated with a . . . Playmate of the Month."

"Oh, really? Okay. Then, fuck off, you cheap little prig!"

TWENTY-EIGHT

One 1956

Bob Lear rarely came east. He thought of himself as a man with a West Coast style who was in some way out of place east of the Mississippi. He was uncomfortable in Jack's house. He was uncomfortable in the presence of Jack's wife, constantly fearful that he would make a grammatical error in conversation with her or would pick up the wrong fork at the table.

Jack understood that if Bob came here he had something significant on his mind. When the two brothers sat down in the library after dinner, Jack learned what it was. At first he was not surprised.

"They've increased their bid to $275," said Bob.

"I don't give a damn if they raise it to $375."

"That's easy for you to say. You cashed out of Lear Communications and are a millionaire many times over. I'm not."

"Why aren't you?" Jack asked. "You own half of a company they're offering $27.50 a share for."

"But it's all in stock! If something went wrong—I mean, if something went badly wrong—I'd be . . . broke. Look. Carlton House is my bread and butter now. The salvage business is in decline. It was for a long time before the old man died. The truth is, he didn't pay much attention to it the last ten years of his life."

"You want cash? Are you going to invest in something else?"

"Diversify. I need to diversify."

"Okay. I'll buy ten percent or twenty percent of your stock. Then you'll be a millionaire and can diversify. Buy an assortment of blue chips. Treasury bonds. Municipals. You want security—"

"Jack . . . I can't." Bob's lips trembled, and tears came to his eyes. "I have to sell to *them.* I've agreed to sell to them."

"Why? Why do you *have* to sell to them? God, man, there are *all kinds* of alternatives if you want to cash out."

"They've got me by the short hairs!" Bob wept.

"What short hairs? What the hell are you talking about?"

Bob reached into the inside breast pocket of his jacket and pulled out an envelope. "Look . . . Those are frames from a movie film!"

The black-and-white prints showed Bob in bed with an attractive young woman. They were fuzzy, but they were good enough for Jack to recognize him. He knew the projected film would be a lot clearer. The pictures were like outtakes from the cheapest 1940s stag films. Bob was naked except for a vest undershirt and ankle-length black socks. In three pictures he was taking head from the girl. In four others he was astride her.

"Who took these?" Jack demanded.

"Painter."

"What are you saying? Is that bastard *blackmailing* you?"

"Jack, it's a movie. I've got the whole reel . . . a copy."

Jack reached for the telephone with one hand and for a pocket notebook with the other. He dialed a number.

"I'd like to speak to Mr. Humphrey, please. This is Jack Lear in Connecticut. The matter is urgent."

Two

A STATION WAGON marked HP, meaning Humphrey Petroleum, was waiting for Jack and Bob at the Houston airport. The driver, who said he was a geologist, stowed their luggage in the rear and held the doors open for them. He drove them to a Houston suburb west of the center of the city, where he said Mr. Humphrey was expecting them. They were to be guests in his house for the night.

The one-story beige stucco house sat in the middle of a grove of great old trees. From the road it did not look prepossessing; but as the car approached, the dimensions of the house became more impressive. It was in fact a mansion.

Douglas Humphrey was waiting for them at an umbrella table beside the kidney-shaped swimming pool. He had been swimming and wore a white terry-cloth robe.

"Jack! And you must be Bob. Good to see you. Sit down. Mary! Emily! Come out and meet the Lear brothers."

A woman in a yellow bikini came out of the pool. She looked about thirty years old, and was blond, tanned, and handsome. The girl, who was eight or nine years old, was nude. Though she showed no sign of being particularly embarrassed, she did not come out of the water.

"This is my daughter, Mary Carson, and that's my granddaughter, Emily. Mr. Jack Lear and Mr. Bob Lear."

"We've heard your names often," Mary Carson said smoothly.

Jack had remained standing. "I'm happy to meet you, Mrs. Carson, Miss Carson. Don't let us interrupt your swimming."

"We've got lots of spare trunks, if you'd like to come in," said Mary Carson.

"Maybe we'll do that a little later."

The mother returned to the pool by diving gracefully from a low board. Jack sat down. A houseboy in white coat and black pants approached. The three men ordered a round of drinks.

"Let's deal with this thing," said Humphrey. "I want you to understand that Dick Painter acted totally without authority from me or Ray or Billy Bob. I talked to him today while you were flying down. I told him I want that reel of film burned, along with any copies or prints taken from it."

"Doug, I want his ass," Jack said bluntly.

Humphrey nodded. "I thought you would. And I don't blame you. But let's look at something. You and I know that in this broadcasting season the Lear Network has some of the most popular shows on television. We don't get the ratings because we don't have stations in every market—"

"We do all right where we do have stations," said Jack. "Some hours, we're the top station in Boston, top in Cleveland, top in Atlanta . . ."

"Exactly," said Humphrey. "And what shows are doing it for us? *The Sally Allen Show,* first and foremost. But besides that—*Doin' What Comes Natcherly, Thirty-Eight Special,* and *'Round the World.* Right?"

Doin' What Comes Natcherly was a situation comedy featuring a family of West Virginia coal miners and moonshiners who inherited a Park Avenue apartment building and came to Manhattan to live in it, thinking it would be their obligation to do all the cleaning and maintenance work themselves—to the horror of their wealthy and snooty tenants. *Thirty-Eight Special* was a police show. The title was a double entendre that could refer to the revolver carried by the policewoman heroine or to her prominent breasts. *'Round the World* was a quiz show in which, at the end of a series of several appearances, the winning couple won a luxury trip around the world.

Jack shrugged. "That's the backbone of it."

"And what do those shows have in common?" Humphrey asked. He answered his own question. "You had *The Sally Allen Show* going before Painter came on board. The other shows were developed for us by Dick Painter."

"The man has an unmatched instinct for vulgarity," said Jack.

"And the public has an insatiable appetite for it."

"All right. But I want something, Doug. I want a letter of resignation from him. I want a letter that apologizes for attempting a low and dishonest trick, which he need not name. I'll keep that letter for the day when I might need it."

"I'll see to it that you get the letter," Humphrey said grimly. "Would you like to take a swim before dinner?"

Jack shrugged. "Why not?"

Three

DINNER WAS FOR FIVE: Humphrey, Jack, Bob, Mary, and Emily.

"I saw your daughter in *Stage Lights,"* Mary Carson said to Jack. "She made a fine impression."

"Thank you. It was a bit part, but it was something she wanted very badly."

"Did you see her pictures in *Playboy?"* Bob asked.

Jack couldn't tell if Bob was being ingenuous or if he was being nasty, because he resented having had to be bailed out by his brother this afternoon.

"No," said Mary Carson.

"I did," said Humphrey. "She's stunning. I think we should arrange an appearance for her on *The Sally Allen Show."*

"Wouldn't that look as if she's there only because she's my daughter?"

"The fact that she's your daughter shouldn't deny her an opportunity," said Mary Carson.

"I don't know if she can *do* anything," said Jack. "She's a model. In *Stage Lights* all she had to do was look good."

"At which she's an expert," said Bob.

"It's your call, your judgment," Humphrey said to Jack.

Jack nodded. "I'll talk to her."

After dinner Mary and Emily left the table. The men stayed, with brandy and cigars, and Humphrey raised again the subject of merging LCI and Carlton House.

"It's a perfect fit. You could move production of *The Sally Allen Show* out of that Kansas City warehouse and onto one of the CH soundstages."

"We're thinking of leasing at least one of those soundstages to another television production company," Bob explained. CH doesn't make as many films as it used to, and we can't afford to maintain unused facilities."

"Why lease to a competitor? Whether we merge the companies or not, you could lease the facilities to LCI."

"A sweetheart deal?" Jack asked.

"No. I happen to know Carlton House can use cash. This would be a way of transferring some from LCI to CH."

"Why not bring in some cash from outside?" Jack asked.

"I think Mr. Humphrey is right," said Bob.

Four

JACK WOKE AT 7:45 A.M. Someone was knocking on his bedroom door. It was Humphrey, who told Jack he had a telephone call from Anne. He could pick it up on his bedside phone, line two. His hand trembled as he reached for the phone.

"Jack, something perfectly horrible has happened. Kimberly is dead! So is Dodge Hallowell."

"How? What happened?"

"I don't know. Harrison Wolcott called. He said they'd had heart attacks."

"Both of them?"

"That's what he said. He was very upset, of course. He asked us to get the word to John and Joni."

"Joni's in the apartment in New York, I suppose. Would you mind calling her? I'll try to reach John. I'll try to reach Harrison, too."

Five

ANNE REACHED JONI just as she was leaving the apartment to keep a modeling appointment.

"Joni, I have terrible news. Your mother is dead. So is Dodge Hallowell."

"That's too bad . . . I guess."

"It *is* too bad. It comes as a terrible shock to your grandparents, both of whom are rather fragile."

Joni was silent for a moment, then said, "Anne, I am not going to the funeral. That may as well be understood."

"That's your decision to make, Joni. But I wish you'd consider this. Not going will not be a statement to your mother, who won't know what statement you're making. On the other hand, you'll hurt your grandparents' feelings, and you'll be letting down your father and brother. Will you be home this evening? I'll call to tell you what the arrangements are."

Six

NEVER IN HIS DREAMS had John seen himself at the controls of an aircraft like this one, and he was aware that the navy had conferred a significant honor on him when it assigned him to one of the first F4D Skyrays to be delivered aboard an aircraft carrier. It was a delta-wing interceptor, propelled by so powerful an engine that it held a world speed record, having flown in excess of 750 miles per hour. It was also capable of climbing almost vertically and held world records for rate of climb.

Naturally, the F4D was a demanding aircraft. He had been assigned to it only five weeks ago, had trained in it at the San Diego Naval Air Station, and was now practicing carrier operations.

The ship was ahead of him and below. Five miles ahead of him another F4D was about to land—a tiny silvery bird hard to make out at this distance. The carrier was the *Yorktown,* the second U.S. aircraft carrier by that name, the first having been lost during the Battle of Midway. It was an Essex-class carrier. John had served aboard the *Essex* as a midshipman, so the layout of the ship was familiar to him. Sort of. Most of the Essex-class carriers had been modified. The landing deck had been angled 8 degrees off the line of the keel, an arrangement that made for more efficient and safer operations.

The aircraft ahead of him was being waved off. Something was wrong with his approach. The signal lights went blank and now came on again. John realized the signals were now for him. He was three miles out and too high. He cut power and felt the Skyray settling, losing altitude. He felt it was settling too fast, so he adjusted his power. The signals hadn't told him that; he had felt it in the seat of his pants. Pilots were urged not to fly by instinct but by the book, but

John knew his feeling for what his aircraft was doing was almost always right.

The lights indicated he was at the proper altitude for the distance. He was slightly to the right of course, which meant the wind had shifted. He did not turn the nose into the wind but lowered his left wing into it and added some right rudder—cross controls. The wings were a little less efficient that way, so he added a bit more power. The lights changed, indicating he was on the glide slope and lined up on course. Good. Now all he had to do was hold it that way.

For some reason, an approach to landing always seemed slow, even leisurely, with plenty of time to fly the airplane—time to make corrections. He knew, though, that from the time he turned on his approach course until the instant he hit the deck he had only two minutes.

Now he had ten seconds. It was too late to be waved off. He was committed. Crossing the threshold of the deck, he chopped his power and raised his nose. The Skyray fell like a rock and hit the deck with a bone-jarring jolt. He pulled the stick into his crotch until he felt the little tailwheel bang on the deck. The arresting hook caught a wire. He was thrown forward in his harness.

Deck crew surrounded the plane. They towed it off the landing deck. Another Skyray was less than a mile out.

"Lieutenant Lear," called a crewman who climbed up to help him out of the cockpit, "you are to report immediately to the Protestant chaplain, sir."

Whatever that meant, John knew it could not be good news.

"Sit down, son. I'm afraid I have very bad news for you. Your mother has died. And your stepfather as well. Get your gear together. A chopper will take you in to San Diego. A navy flight for Washington is taking off within the hour. You can be on it. When you get to Washington, there'll be a flight to New York. Your wife has been notified and will be waiting at the airport in San Diego to go with you. You've been granted thirty days' compassionate leave. Is there anything I can do for you?"

John shook his head.

The chaplain put both his hands on John's. "Why don't we share a moment of prayer?"

Seven

JACK AND ANNE had flown to San Diego for John and Linda's wedding two months ago. Until now the couple had not had time to come east, and Linda had never seen the house in Greenwich. Also, she had never met Joni.

"She's very beautiful, John. I'm glad for you,"

"You told me to find a girl."

"And you did. Wonderfully."

"It didn't work out between you and Frank Neville, I guess."

"He's a little prick." She grimaced dramatically and then hugged her brother.

Joni made a point of finding a time to be alone with Jack. They sat down in the library, behind closed doors.

"Simultaneous heart attacks, huh?" Joni said skeptically. "If you believe that, you believe in the tooth fairy."

"I don't believe it."

"Are you going to try to find out what happened?"

"I'm not sure it's any of my business," Jack said softly.

Joni lifted her chin and blew an impatient sigh. "If there's some kind of horrible scandal being covered up, we ought to know what it is. Anyway, John needs to know."

"I'll see what I can do," Jack promised.

Eight

DAN AND CONNIE HORAN attended the funeral. Jack hadn't seen them in more than ten years. When he spoke to them, they shook his hand and were cordial.

"Could we have a little private conversation later?" he asked them.

"About what?"

"About what happened here."

Dan drew a deep breath. "Why not? You and I can slip off and have a drink after the service."

Anne, John, Linda, and Joni went to the Wolcott home

when the funeral was over. Jack said he would join them in an hour and left the cemetery with Dan Horan. They sat at the bar in the Common Club. Jack had not been in the club for many years but paid his dues every year and was still a member.

"You've been decent about Kathleen," Dan said. "She has no idea who you are, and you've never forced yourself on her or us. We appreciate that."

"I'm capable of being decent," said Jack dryly.

"We . . . have different values."

"Granted. Understood. All right. Tell me something. How did Kimberly die? It's obviously a secret."

"More than a secret," said Dan. "It's a monumental scandal. I don't know the details, but the Boston police have covered it up under six layers of obfuscation. The world has changed, but the Wolcotts still have the power to cover up a scandal."

"The simultaneous heart attacks—"

"No one believes that. Murder and suicide maybe. Maybe there were drugs involved. Alcohol. Carbon monoxide. But . . . not simultaneous heart attacks."

"Okay. I don't really have to know the details. John wants to know. He . . . has a sense of— I don't know what you'd call it. Anyway, he's grieving. His wife is pregnant, and she is very curious about the mother-in-law she never met. Joni, frankly, doesn't give a damn. She's sorry her mother is dead, but— Well, I'm not going to pursue it. Did you see Joni's *Playboy* pictures?"

Dan nodded solemnly.

"Kimberly's reaction destroyed anything that remained of their relationship. Dan, I appreciate your seeing me. Give the little girl a kiss for me—without telling her it's from me, of course."

Nine

TWO WEEKS LATER Jack sat in the living room in the Manhattan townhouse. Joni was in California. Rebecca Murphy, the private investigator, sipped Scotch and talked.

She had not aged. After fourteen years she remained the solid, acne-marked woman who still wore her light brown hair in tight curls. Jack had always wondered what kind of private life she had, but he had never asked. He'd told her he would be going home to Greenwich for the night and that she could sleep in the townhouse.

"Yeah, I found out what happened," she said. "It's not pretty."

"I was afraid it wouldn't be."

"The maid and cook arrived about seven-thirty, their usual hour, so they could have a hearty breakfast ready when Mr. and Mrs. Hallowell came down a little after eight o'clock. But something was wrong. The maid found the door to the master bedroom suite open. The door to the attic was locked. She understood the significance of that. She knocked on the door. No response. She went down and told the cook, and the two of them came up and knocked again. When they got no answer, they called the police."

"And . . ."

"The police found Hallowell stretched out on the floor. The autopsy said myocardial infarction. Mrs. Hallowell was hanging from two pairs of handcuffs on her wrists and locked on two big screw eyes in two rafters, arms spread like Christ on the Cross. Stark naked. She had screamed, probably—and screamed and screamed and screamed. Eventually she just hung on the handcuffs. That cut off her circulation. Blood clots formed and went to her heart. She died about three A.M., after hanging there maybe five hours or more. Her back and her bottom were laced with ugly welts. A whip was found beside Hallowell's body. He'd been whipping the hell out of her. The exertion or— Anyway, he had a heart attack and died, leaving her hanging there with no way of getting loose."

"*God!* I—"

"Mr. Wolcott didn't have to ask the detectives or the coroner to cover it up. They didn't want to release the story."

Jack closed his eyes. "I'll tell my children you managed to confirm the simultaneous heart attack story."

TWENTY-NINE

One 1956

JACK AND ANNE decided to celebrate the holidays with an extended party. They invited John and Linda to come and stay as long as they could, and John managed to get ten days' leave. Anne called Linda's parents in Pensacola and invited them, too. They expressed their gratitude but did not come. Joni said she could take a few days off and spend them in Greenwich. Bob and Dorothy Lear were invited but chose not to come. Anne called Harrison Wolcott to invite him and Edith, but he said Edith could not travel that far.

So the household for a week included Jack and Anne; Little Jack and his sister, Anne, who was called Liz; John and Linda; and Joni.

For a noon-to-midnight party on the Saturday before Christmas, they invited Curt and Betsy Frederick, Cap and Naomi Durenberger, Herb and Esther Morrill, Mickey and Catherine Sullivan, and several neighbors. Jack also called Sally Allen and invited her to come and bring Len.

Priscilla took charge of party arrangements, as always, and suggested that for Saturday night a houseboy be added to the staff. She and the cook could use help that one night.

Every year Anne lit a menorah on the days of Hanukkah. She had bought their menorah, on her trip to Berlin in 1946. It had tiny oil lamps instead of candles, so was more nearly in the tradition of the holiday than were the ones with candles. Guests observed, some of them with a little surprise, that both a menorah and a Christmas tree were alight in the same room. On the days of Hanukkah, Anne and Jack exchanged small gifts and on Christmas Day, much grander ones. Joni was familiar with this holiday tradition. It surprised Linda, but she told John she loved it and would follow it in *their* home.

The arrival of Sally Allen was the highlight of Little Jack's holiday. He was ten years old and had watched *The Sally Allen Show* many times, though he had remained skeptical that his father knew the star or had anything to do with her show. His sister Liz accepted the arrival of a television star in their home as something entirely normal and to be expected.

Little Jack and Liz were were not to be regarded anymore simply as "the children"; they were young people who already had ideas about who they were and who they wanted to be. They had been allowed to see the *Playboy* spread of Joni. Little Jack had screwed his eyes shut and said, "Ooooh!" Liz had said, "Lovely, lovely! Am I going to have boobs like hers someday?"

Both of them were handsome children, and their parents were proud of them. No part of the holiday celebration was off-limits to them. They went to bed whenever they felt sleepy and not a moment before. Their governess, Mrs. Gimbel, remained with the family, not so much because she was needed as because she had become a member of the household.

Len Leonard, Sally's former husband and the father of her child, bore only a slight resemblance to the burlesque comic Jack had encountered in Toledo. He looked healthier and happier and was well dressed, as Sally had said he would be when he had money, but he still slicked down his hair with oil. He approached Jack when he saw him standing alone for a moment.

"I can't express my gratitude to you, Mr. Lear."

"You're a writer because you are a writer," Jack replied. "I didn't take you on for any other reason."

"I've written what I hope is a good introduction to television for Miss Lear. I put my all into that, Mr. Lear."

"I'm sure you did, Len. If the show bombs, it won't be your fault."

Betsy Frederick also caught Jack for a private moment. "What do you think of Curt's retiring?" she asked.

"He can't."

"Why not? He'll be sixty shortly. He says he's tired."

Jack shook his head. "Retirement will make him more tired than he ever thought he could be."

"Jack . . . We know how Kimberly died. I mean, it nearly killed me. I—"

"My children don't know."

Betsy blinked away tears. "What a way to go! There's gotta be some kind of fuckin' *dignity* someplace!"

"Well, dignity is in doing, in achieving. And in satisfaction, too."

"Curt doesn't want to spend the rest of his life in the saddle."

"There's no dignity in retirement. What would Curt do? Play golf? Fish? I'm fifty, close to fifty-one. I want to work until the last five minutes. I allow myself that much time for the heart attack. Five minutes. And when they stuff me into the body bag, I may sit up and say, 'Wait a minute! We've gotta do something about—' "

Betsy forced a weak smile. "Anne may have different ideas."

He spoke a little later with John. "You're a married man, with a child coming. Have you thought about asking the navy for a less dangerous assignment?"

John shook his head. "The navy has spent millions of dollars training me for what I do. I don't see how I could ask to be relieved of the duty."

"Besides, you love it."

"I love it a little less now."

John and Joni talked. "How's it feel to be a celebrity?"

"John . . ."

"Two pilots sent their copies of *Playboy* along and asked me to get your autograph on the centerfold."

She shook her head. "That's embarrassing."

"You *will* do it, though?"

"Oh, sure."

"I'm sorry Neville turned out to be an ass. Would you like to date a pilot?"

Joni shrugged. "Casually. If I'm in California."

"Aren't you going to be, actually? I thought you were going to do a TV show."

"Yes, I am. I'll be in Los Angeles for a month, I suppose."

"What will you be doing on *The Sally Allen Show?*"

"Believe it or not, I'm taking dancing and singing lessons. I'm going to dance with Mac Reilly. I'm petrified."

Sally Allen, who was approaching them, overheard. "So am I," she said. "That's something you learn to live with. The first time I went onstage, I had to take my clothes off in front of two or three hundred men, and I was petrified. I don't have to take my clothes off anymore, but I'm just as petrified every time I go in front of an audience. You'll do fine."

Two 1957

AT FIRST, Mac Reilly did not appear for rehearsals. Joni worked with one of the dancers from the chorus. Then Reilly did show up. Bone thin and loose-jointed, he was an easy, supportive man to work with. He encouraged Joni to relax, to adopt a loose, sinuous style, that matched his own.

Just before they went on the air he stopped by her dressing room.

"Scared?" he asked.

"Yes."

"So am I. Part of the game. Just remember this: you're gonna do what you've rehearsed. The routines aren't too demanding. I know you can handle them. Cyd Charisse you're not, but you don't have to be. We're going to have a good time."

The first dance routine took place at the beginning of the show. Reilly appeared in white flannel slacks and a turtleneck sweater. Sally Allen wore red tights, and Joni Lear wore a black leotard and dark sheer stockings. Joni danced the more strenuous parts of the routine. Sally was happy to save her energy for the other things she had to do during the hour. Joni was a little stiff at first, until Reilly winked at her; then she remembered what he had taught her. She got through the routine and left the stage and the cameras just before the sweat began to show on her leotard.

"Good work, kid," Reilly said to her, and he slapped her lightly on the rump.

In the middle of the show Joni had a few lines to speak in a sketch. After that, she went back to dress in a pair of black tights for the second dance routine. But the assistant director knocked on her door, stuck his head in, and said, "Never mind, Miss Lear. The show's running long, so we have to drop your other dance bit."

She was relieved but also disappointed. The second routine was less demanding than the first, but she would have been alone with Mac Reilly, which would have been a far more impressive credential than having appeared with him and Sally Allen.

Just one columnist mentioned her:

> Showbiz insiders supposed that the appearance of Playmate Joni Lear on *The Sally Allen Show* was attributable solely to the fact that she is Jack Lear's daughter. She acquitted herself competently, however, in a dance routine with Mac Reilly. She is lucky she was dancing with Reilly and not the perfectionist Fred Astaire, but on the whole she had an impressive first outing.

After Joni returned to New York, Sally called her. "Don't forget that second routine you learned. We'll slot it in on another show."

Three

IN MAY, Linda gave birth to a daughter, Nelly Linda Lear. Jack and Anne flew to San Diego to see her. John was at sea, off the Philippines, and would not be able to see his baby daughter for some months.

That month Joni made her second appearance on *The Sally Allen Show,* dancing two routines, both solo. Her singing did not impress the producer or director, but she was written into a sketch and given good comedy lines.

Within a week MGM assigned her a supporting role in a movie. She played the part of a Las Vegas showgirl, an understudy to the star of the revue. She appeared in a form-fitting spangled pink corselet and a feathered headdress, in a spectacular production number that she was supposed to be doing because the star was absent in the desert, in a love nest. The notices referred to her as a "starlet." The studio publicity department arranged for her to be photographed poolside at the Beverly Hilton in a swimsuit, in studio shots wearing shorts and a tight sweater, and in a satin slip à la Elizabeth Taylor as Maggie the Cat.

The studio arranged dates for her, mostly with aging or fading male stars. One night at the Brown Derby she excused herself to go to the women's room, located the flack who had arranged the date, and asked if he had the photos he wanted. When he said he did, she walked out and hailed a cab, abandoning a drunk, egomaniacal, and boring Errol Flynn. Three of the men asked for sex, which she had been promised would not happen. She refused two of them bluntly and firmly, the third gently, because he had asked her gently. He thanked her for not taking offense and returned to offering her some suggestions about acting. That was Orson Welles.

Next, the studio arranged for her to be seen with David Breck. He was a remarkably handsome thirty-one-year-old Welsh actor, though some described him as pretty rather than handsome. He had studied acting with the Royal Shakespeare Company, had played the role of Algernon Moncrieff in *The Importance of Being Earnest* at the Old Vic, had played the part of Biff in a London production of *Death of a Salesman,* and had played roles in several English films, including another screen adaptation of *Pygmalion,* in which he had the role of Freddy. His Hollywood career had been less than spectacular. Hollywood producers saw him as a body, not as an actor, and his roles had been nothing but heroes in three costume pictures.

Breck had been divorced two years and was often photographed escorting actresses, some of them substantially older than he was, to premieres, to the track, or to dinner. He granted interviews and encouraged reporters and columnists to believe he was having affairs with at least some of these women.

Joni expected him to be a shallow egomaniac. And so he seemed, spending most of the evening talking about how far superior West End theater was to anything done in America.

Toward the end of their dinner he turned to her, smiled, and in a quiet, matter-of-fact voice said, "I suppose you give the best head in town."

"I wouldn't be surprised if I do," Joni answered casually.

"Then . . . will you?"

Joni shrugged. "Why should I?"

"Well, I'm doing you a favor. You can do me one."

"What favor are you doing me?"

"Being seen with you," he said ingenuously, as if it were the most evident thing in the world.

"Mr. Brecknock," she said, using his real name, "when did you last make a film that amounted to crap? Considering the state of your career, I'm the one who's doing *you* a favor, *allowing* you to be seen with *me*."

"La belle dame sans merci," David said with a small, sad smile.

"That's graceful. You could almost seduce me. But not quite."

Four

JOHN WAS ALMOST SATISFIED he had tamed the beast. The F4D was not to *be* tamed, of course; no pilot could ever tame it, and overconfidence equaled death. Of the six F4Ds that had been delivered to the *Yorktown,* two were gone, and two pilots were dead. One of them, a young man who had graduated from Annapolis a year after John and had become a close friend of his, had died only a month ago, in the trickiest of all carrier operations: a night landing. They continued to practice night landings. One of the smaller fighters was lost, too.

The *Yorktown* was part of a task force cruising in the

South China Sea. The United States Navy was in Vietnamese waters to show the flag. President Eisenhower wanted to warn the Communists that America would defend South Vietnam if necessary.

Night operations were different. You could see all the other planes in the air, by their flashing lights. Seen from a distance, the carrier was like a gleaming, glittering jewel. As you approached, it took on something of the aspect of a great stadium brilliantly lighted for a night football game—except that it lay against the total darkness of the sea, with no other lights around except those on the destroyers.

John was angry. Fifteen minutes ago he had taken a wave-off. He'd come in too high—or so the landing officer had signaled, though John had thought he could put the wheels on the deck perfectly. He couldn't argue, though; the signal lights were orders.

He meant to land this time, for sure. He had enough fuel to go around more times if he had to, but he had a sense he would look ridiculous. He eased back on the throttle, letting the turbine spin down. The signal lights indicated he was squarely on the glide slope and on course.

He drifted slightly below the glide slope. He corrected for that by lowering the nose a little. The aircraft rapidly gained speed, which increased the pressure on the airfoil and caused a climb. Now he was back on the slope. The speed was a little too high, but he would correct for that when he raised the nose as he crossed the threshold of the deck. It looked good.

Then it didn't. The plane slipped below the glide slope again. He was too low. The signals blinked frantically. Too low! Too low! He needed power and shoved in the throttle. He knew he wasn't going to get power. The turbine in a jet engine, having spun down to a low speed, takes fifteen to twenty seconds to spin up again and generate full power. That's why you have to fly ahead of a jet. It's not like a prop-driven plane that can regain power in an instant. He didn't have twenty seconds.

The signal lights disappeared! He was below the level of the deck and couldn't see them.

Then all the lights in the world went out.

Five

JACK SENT a chartered plane to California. It picked up Joni in Los Angeles, then Linda and Nelly in San Diego, and flew them to Westchester County Airport. The Hogans arrived from Pensacola. Seventy-six-year-old Harrison Wolcott was driven down from Boston by Mickey Sullivan. Friends gathered at the house in Greenwich.

A navy plane arrived at Westchester, carrying a casket and an honor guard.

Anne made all arrangements, because Jack was utterly grief-stricken. With the help of a navy chaplain, she arranged for the casket to be set up on an improvised catafalque in the living room, where it remained for twenty-four hours while friends and neighbors, Annapolis classmates, and other naval officers moved in and out.

On Tuesday, September 10, an ecumenical service was performed by the navy chaplain, the pastor of the Second Congregational Church, and the rabbi from Temple Shalom.

As the rifles cracked over John's open grave, Joni fainted.

Six

LATER IN THE AFTERNOON, the families gathered on the patio by the swimming pool. Jack remained hardly able to speak. Joni sat pale and silent. Anne took charge.

"Jack and I would like to make a proposal," she said quietly. "We would be very grateful if Linda would live here with us. We have a big house. Mrs. Gimbel has little to do now that Little Jack and Liz are growing up. She's been with us for many years and is very good with children. Linda, you may want to finish your education, maybe pursue a career. You can be certain little Nelly will be well taken care of whenever you are away from her."

"I don't ever want to be away from her," Linda sobbed.

"In which case, you have a secure home here that we would like to share with you."

"There will be an inheritance, Linda," Harrison Wolcott added softly. "You will never want for resources."

"Here you'll have alternatives," Anne went on. "You can choose to do whatever you want."

Linda stared into the faces of her mother and father. Both of them nodded.

Linda sobbed and buried her face in her hands, but she nodded too.

Seven

"DADDY . . ."

Jack had walked down to the lake at the edge of the woods. The sun was setting. He stood there staring at the water, seeing nothing.

Joni threw herself into his arms, weeping, and he embraced her.

"Daddy! *I loved him so much!*"

"We all did."

"You don't know. You don't know how I loved him."

Jack tightened his embrace on his lovely daughter, who now cried softly, her body heaving gently.

"Daddy, I'm going to tell you something that nobody but John and I knew. You mustn't tell anyone, not even Anne."

"Joni?"

"You remember my abortion? I was only fourteen. You said you'd kill the boy who did it if you ever found out who he was, but I wouldn't tell you. God! how I wish I'd had that baby! He or she would be nine years old now. And we'd love that child like we loved John. 'Cause, Daddy, *it was John's baby!*"

Jack flinched as if he'd been struck. He began to sob, out of control, and he fell to his knees on the damp earth. Joni knelt beside him and clutched at him and kissed him on his neck and on his cheeks.

Anne had come out of the house, looking for them. She saw. She turned and went back inside.

THIRTY

One 1958

DOUGLAS HUMPHREY had been right when he said Dick Painter was the originator of the most successful television programming on the Lear Network. Other ideas came from Cap Durenberger. Jack himself acknowledged that he did not have an instinct for what the public would enjoy. He still did not think Jack Benny was funny.

For his understanding of the technology of television he relied heavily on Dr. Friedrich Loewenstein. The young scientist managed to persuade Jack and the board of directors to invest money in technology he promised would control the future.

Beginning in 1956, LCI had invested in Ampex television tape recorders and retired the old kinescope equipment. Curt Frederick did the evening news in New York at six-thirty. It went out as a live broadcast to stations in cities in the Eastern Time Zone—except in New York, where viewers preferred to have their news at seven-thirty. The taped broadcast was transmitted in New York and by stations in the Central Time Zone at seven-thirty. Three hours after it was made, the tape was seen in Los Angeles, San Francisco, and other Pacific Time Zone cities. Only when important news broke during that three hours was the 6:30 tape modified for California broadcast.

LCI opened twenty more satellite stations, in cities like Huntington, West Virginia; Harrisburg, Pennsylvania; and Toledo, Ohio. At first these little UHF stations originated no programming at all but were truly satellites of bigger stations, receiving their programs by wire or microwave and simply relaying them out to an expanded audience. It was Jack himself who suggested that the satellite stations should be able to inject local commercials. Why should a Huntington station broadcast commercials for a tire store in Pittsburgh? So the satellite stations began to make and broadcast their own local commercials. If they could do that, Jack figured they could also broadcast their own local news.

Two more major developments loomed in the future of the whole broadcast industry, and Dr. Loewenstein told the board of directors the company must have an enormous infusion of capital in the next few years.

"Within five or six years, everyone will want color television," he told them.

"I'm skeptical of that, Doctor," said Ray l'Enfant. "Color is available. The public is not rushing out to buy color sets."

"Why should they? There is little broadcasting in color. But there will be. The other networks will increase their number of color hours until in a few years they will broadcast nothing but color. We must do the same if we are to compete."

"What else, Doctor?" Jack asked grimly.

"Cable," said Dr. Loewenstein ominously. "Right now cable television is almost exclusively for small towns so distant from any station that they can't get good-quality reception. But it won't always be that way."

"Why not?" asked l'Enfant. "Why will people pay money to be wired up to a system when they can get good reception on rabbit ears or small rooftop antennas for free?"

"Because," said Dr. Loewenstein, "a cable television provider will be able to offer twenty-five or thirty channels, maybe more. Broadcasters will beam their programs up to satellites, which will relay the signal back to big dish antennas aimed by the cable operators. All reception will be equally good."

"How soon?" Jack asked.

"The color, immediately. The cable system, fifteen or twenty years. But we must plan for it."

Jack grimaced. "Doctor, I'm sure you're right. But it's depressing."

Two 1959

ANNE AND JACK found that Linda was a joy to have in the house. Gradually she recovered her cheerful, positive personality. She decided she should finish the education she had interrupted when she married John, and in the fall of 1958 she enrolled at Fordham University.

A Floridian, she spent as much time as she could in the sun. She would lie on a chaise longue by the greenhouse-enclosed pool, wearing a bikini and sunglasses, and study for her exams. Jack could not help but notice that she was a voluptuous young woman. Whereas Anne was elegantly slender, Linda was generously endowed with big, soft breasts, jiggly buns, and a convex little belly.

Nelly, too, was a joy. The towheaded toddler ambled about the house, often laughing, sometimes crying when she fell and bumped her head.

Jack and Anne decided to invest in a vacation home, where they could go in the depth of winter and bask in the sun on a beautiful beach. They found such a place on the island of St. Croix, where they bought a house large enough for whole the family, including Linda, Nelly, and Joni, in the hope that all of them would go there together.

They went for five days, between Christmas and New Year's. Joni, however, pleaded to be excused. She had acquired an agent in Hollywood, and he was telling her she had a good chance of winning a starring role in a picture. She'd had three small roles with MGM, but now her contract was expiring. Her agent was advising her not to renew if they offered. He could do better for her.

Three 1960

"I'D SAY it's now or never, kiddo," Joni's agent, Mo Morris, told her.

He was the agent who had turned Consetta Lazzara into Connie Lane twenty-six years ago. When Joni told her father she was going to be represented by the Mo Morris Agency, Jack had laughed and told her Mo was an old friend of his and an effective agent but that she should be careful of him. He did not tell her he had sent Consetta to Mo after she —had given him an afternoon he would never forget.

Mo was sixty-six years old, a veteran agent who had represented some of the biggest names in Hollywood. He had always been a small man, and he was wizened now, with dark-brown liver spots on his tanned bald pate. Ever a flashy dresser, he was wearing a blue-and-white checked jacket over a black golf shirt. He made a point of telling people that his wristwatch had been given to him by Spencer Tracy. He was a jolly man who seemed to take nothing seriously—until a producer made what he considered a skimpy offer for a client's services, at which point Mo could become very sharp and sarcastic.

"Meaning?" Joni asked.

"You're twenty-six, right? You need a breakout picture. You're not a starlet anymore. MGM built you up, but they never broke you out of the pack. What's more, television didn't do it for you either. What I'm talking about is making you a star."

"Okay. What's holding us up?"

"Question: are you willing to play the game? It's not played as much as it used to be, but there are powerful guys in town who still play it."

"What do I get if I play—besides screwed?" she asked.

"Nobody can ever guarantee these things, but I can almost promise you a starring role in an important dramatic picture."

"Who do I have to . . . service?"

Four

THE PRODUCER was Harry Klein. Joni knew the name very well —and she knew his reputation. The director was Benjamin Lang. The male lead was Trent Ambler. The three of them were in Klein's office when she arrived.

Klein stood, grabbing the hand she had extended to

shake hands with him, and used it to draw her close to him. He kissed her on the cheek and patted her on the rump. "Joni Lear!" he rumbled. "We're gonna do great things together!"

He was an exceptionally big man with a great strong face. His hair was black and wavy, and he wore horn-rimmed glasses. The other two men were casually dressed, but Klein wore a dark-blue suit, a white shirt, and a blue polka-dot bow tie.

"You prob'ly recognize Trent. And Ben Lang will be director."

Ambler was a handsome, well-built man. He was not just a body, not just a screen presence; he was an *actor,* whose status was only a little lower than Humphrey Bogart's. One reason Joni had accepted this challenge was that Mo had told her she would be playing opposite Trent Ambler.

Benjamin Lang was a small bald man about fifty years old whose eyes swam behind thick steel-rimmed eyeglasses. His directorial credentials were outstanding.

"Mo tells us you know how to play the game," said Klein.

She nodded.

"Well, we would like for you to take your clothes off, Joni. Do you understand why?"

"So you can look at my bod."

"That, too. But it is essential that an actress not lose her professionalism and aplomb in—how shall we say?—in stressful situations. You've read the script. You know a degree of nudity is part of the role. We need to know you will not break down when you must do your lines in front of camera and crew and you are the only naked person on the set. All right?"

"I was a Playmate of the Month," she said.

"This is a little different. Will you accommodate us, please?"

It *was* a little different. More than a little different. But it was, as Mo had said, now or never. For a brief moment she reminded herself that she would inherit a lot of money and didn't have to do this, didn't have to do what they were going to ask for next, either. But what she was doing here would be an achievement of her own, and this was how it was done.

She took off her clothes and put them aside on a chair. Naked, she sat down and faced Klein.

"Have you reviewed the contract?"

"Mo has. I will accept his judgment."

"We're going to make you a star, Joni. If you're as good a girl as we think you are, you will be a big star. We're going to do a fine picture. A year from now you come in here and *I'll* take off *my* clothes to get you on another contract."

"I won't ask you to, Mr. Klein."

"Hey! I'm only forty-two. The sight of me wouldn't make you sick."

Joni smiled. That was a sufficiently ambiguous response.

"Ben—"

"Okay," said Lang. "We asked you to memorize pages sixty-three through sixty-five of the script. You've done?"

"Yessir."

"Okay. Sit down on the floor, which is how you'll be positioned when the cameras are rolling. Trent picks up with line four on page sixty-three, and you join in from there."

Ambler moved to stand facing her, and she looked up into his face. They acted out the scene, about two dozen lines.

"Good enough!" said Lang. "More than good enough. I'm satisfied. She can act. She is emotionally stable."

Joni smiled wanly.

Ambler reached down and gave her his hand to help her stand. "Sign her, Harry," he said. "I want to work with her."

Klein grinned. "Now . . . One more thing. Mo told you what. We, uh . . ."

She glanced back and forth. "*All three* of you?" she asked.

He nodded. "All three of us."

Joni flushed. She raised her eyebrows and drew a deep breath. "All right," she whispered.

Trent Ambler unzipped his pants and pulled out his penis. Joni knelt and took it in her hands. He reached for a box of tissues and put them beside her on the floor. With her lips and tongue she worked on him for three or four minutes, and he came strongly and copiously. She spit his ejaculate into a wad of tissues.

Lang was next. He was so excited from what he had seen that he almost experienced premature ejaculation. She hardly got him into her mouth before he went into his spasms.

Then Klein. It took twenty minutes of licking and sucking and vigorously pumping her head up and down before he finally came. Her lips and cheeks ached, and her body gleamed with sweat. He generated little fluid, and she suspected he'd already been sucked off by some other hopeful, not long before.

Trent Ambler offered her a snifter of brandy, which she gratefully accepted. She sat on a chair and lowered her head a little, until her hair hid her face.

"The part's yours, Joni," Klein said. "You're a trooper, and you're gonna be a star."

Five

BOB LEAR telephoned Jack. "Guess who Joni's making a picture for."

"I know. She called me."

"Harry Klein. Five'll get ya twenty she—"

"Bob! Mind your own business."

"Don't you care?" Bob yelled.

"Of course I care, but what can I do about it?"

"Talk to the money guys. Block the funding for the flick."

"Oh, sure. If she did what you think she did to get the part, she's already done it. So you want me to fix things up so she did it and then doesn't get the part after all?"

"I'm just trying—"

"Keep out of it, brother. I got your certificates. The funds were transferred."

"Congratulations," Bob said bitterly. "You now own controlling interest in Carlton House."

"And you're the millionaire you always wanted to be."

Six 1961

BRAVE MICHELLE had its premiere at Grauman's Chinese Theatre.

Jack and Anne flew out on a chartered plane, bringing with them Little Jack and Liz, Linda, and the eighty-year old Harrison Wolcott. Curt and Betsy came on a different plane with Cap and Naomi, Mickey and Catherine, and Herb and Esther. Douglas Humphrey flew in from Texas with Mary and Emily Carson. Billy Bob Cotton came, as did Ray l'Enfant and his wife. Sally Allen and Len also attended the premiere. Bob and Dorothy Lear did not.

The Los Angeles group included Mo Morris and his wife, Harry Klein and his wife, and Ben Lang and his wife.

The star of the picture, Trent Ambler, escorted his wife, a girl of nineteen who had been sewn into a spangled white dress.

Joni's escort was David Breck. Mo had arranged that. David was told that he was not forgiven for his boorishness. He was asked to escort Joni only because as a pair they would attract extraordinary attention—which would probably be more to his benefit than hers. When he was alone with her in the limousine on the way to the premiere, he told her he was grateful to her for allowing him to be seen with her. He was attentive and deferential.

As they emerged from the limo, Joni was startled, then blinded, by the camera flashes. A crowd cheered. Joni could hardly see them but realized that bleachers had been put up on the sidewalk. She smiled and nodded to both sides, at people she could hardly make out.

Mo had also seen to her dress and hairdo.

Because her glossy brown hair was one of her most attractive features, Mo had sent around a stylist who had clipped it a little, exposing the back of her neck, combed it down over her forehead halfway to her eyebrows, and curled it smoothly under her ears. It was new style for her.

A designer who worked for many important stars had created her dress. Made of rose-colored silk embroidered with gold and silver thread, it was not tight but hung smoothly. The skirt was slit to the knee, and she wore no stockings on her tanned legs. Her décolletage was deep and wide. The designer had made her stride around, lift and swing her arms, and bend over deeply, until both of them were confident she would not fall out of it.

The picture was the star vehicle Mo Morris and Harry Klein had promised her. She had taken singing and dancing lessons, but no acting lessons. Nonetheless, she proved herself a talented actress—aided by Ben Lang's patient and meticulous directing. She played an ingenuous girl abruptly forced to mature in the face of tragedy and betrayal.

In two scenes she appeared nude. In one her breasts were shown, in the other her backside. The script made it plain that she was naked unwillingly and was painfully embarrassed. Lang's direction of the shots was such that she looked modest in spite of her nudity.

David's whispered comments on the film and her acting were respectful but insightful. At the post-premiere dinner he told Jack that Joni was an emerging talent and might become one of Hollywood's all-time greats. When Joni left him at the end of the evening, she kissed him in a sisterly way and told him he had redeemed himself.

The next morning Hollywood columnists described her as a major new star. Two of them said she would surely be nominated for an Academy Award.

Seven

JACK AND THE FAMILY stayed in Los Angeles for two days after the premiere. He looked for an opportunity to talk with Joni alone, and found it.

"I can't tell you how pleased I am for you," he said. "I could have helped you, but you didn't ask me. You did it alone. I respect your reasons."

"Thank you, Daddy," she whispered.

"John wasn't relying on me for anything, either. Both of you went out and found your places in life."

"I don't think you ever relied on my grandfather for much," she said.

"No. We didn't like each other. What I wanted to say to you—besides how happy I am for you—is that I know Harry Klein's reputation and I can guess what he demanded of you. I don't want to know if you met his demands."

Joni shook her head. "He didn't make the demand. I expected him to, but he didn't. I can't say what I would've done if he had."

"Well, don't. If it ever comes to that, let me help you."

"I will, Daddy."

THIRTY-ONE

One 1962

Having bought 25 percent of his brother's stock in Carlton House Productions, Jack was firmly in control. In spite of Bob Lear's defective character and occasional stupidity, Carlton House had made some fine films. Jack set these aside to be broadcast as "super specials," meaning that they would be broadcast uninterrupted by commercials, except for a fifteen-minute intermission when all the commercials would be broadcast together. These shows earned very high ratings but lost money. Sponsors surmised that during fifteen minutes of commercials the audiences would depart in droves. Jack insisted, even so, that a few quality films be broadcast without interruptions and without cuts.

He tried a gimmick to prevent that loss of audience. At some time during the intermission a question based on the film would appear on the screen. The first viewer in each city to phone in the correct answer to the local station would win $1,000. It didn't work.

He held back the great Civil War epic, *Cameron Brothers,* because it was in color and he was not willing to broadcast it in black and white. For months he ran teasers, promising that *Cameron Brothers* would be broadcast in color soon. Grateful set manufacturers estimated that Jack Lear's campaign sold a hundred thousand color sets.

The Sally Allen Show, now in its thirteenth season, was broadcast in color. Sally was one of the most popular stars on television. Joni made two appearances a year on her show, and her success on the big screen brought those two Allen shows exceptionally high ratings.

Doin' What Comes Natcherly had lasted six seasons, until the joke wore out. *Thirty-Eight Special* remained one of the top twenty shows on television. The original heavy-breasted policewoman had been replaced by another, and the coming of miniskirts had put her legs on display as well. *Blue Yonder,* a semidocumentary drama based loosely on the Strategic Air Command began in 1960 and a year later was one of the top ten shows.

Though scandals had ruined the big quiz shows, Dick Painter judged that the public still loved them. He had always had a fascination with them and believed he could revive them. All he had to do was find a format. Jack told him to look into the idea but to be careful.

"Right," said Painter. "The big networks thought they could get away with anything. We'll be careful—and subtle."

Two

WITH JONI spending most of her time in California, the Manhattan town house was reclaimed by Jack and Anne. During Joni's time in New York, they had become guests in what she had made *her* place—though she had never paid rent on it—but now when she came to New York *she* was the guest. Anne had the rooms repainted and the floors refinished and replaced some of the furniture.

She bought a Calder mobile and had it hung from the living room ceiling. In an obscure gallery in Lower Manhattan she came upon a collection of pre-Columbian pottery, much of it explicitly erotic. She was well aware of Jack's appreciation of high-quality erotic art, so she bought a piece of Chimu pottery, from Peru. It depicted a female figure sucking off a male. The piece stood about five inches high, and she put it on the small Empire writing table that faced the window.

Their children were teenagers now, and Jack and Anne felt at liberty to stay in town two or three nights a week. Often they met for lunch.

One Wednesday in spring he met her at Lutèce. He was

not entirely surprised to find someone with her; she often brought a guest to their lunches. Sometimes she called and told him who would be there, and sometimes she didn't. Today she hadn't.

"Jack. Let me introduce Jason Maxwell."

Jason Maxwell was the author of the current best-selling novel, *Voices from the Belly.* He'd had another best-seller, too, though Jack couldn't remember the title. Neither of Maxwell's novels was the kind of stuff Jack cared to read, though Anne had read both of them and had talked about them.

"It's a real pleasure to meet you, Mr. Lear," said Maxwell, extending his hand for a limp handshake.

"I'm happy to meet you, too. I've heard your name often."

Jason Maxwell was twenty-nine years old. He was a pretty little man, and the skinny on him was that he was a homosexual. If he wasn't, he was the caricature of one; he possessed every characteristic the straight community supposed homosexuals had: a high-pitched voice, girlish mannerisms . . . all of it.

"Jason is a flowing fountain of gossip," said Anne. "He knows everything about everybody."

"God forbid," said Jack.

"I'm catty," Jason warned.

"Fortunately," Jack said, "we have no secrets."

"Oh, everybody does. If you really don't, we should create some for you. I mean, what would life be without secrets?"

"You mean, scandals," said Jack.

"Yes, of course!" Jason piped. "Delicious scandals."

"Jason has confessed," said Anne, "that some of the characters in his novels are real people, thinly disguised."

"They recognize themselves," Jason said happily.

"How do you learn their secrets?"

"Oh, they confide in me! I don't know why. They *know* I'm a writer."

"It's lucky you didn't know my father and never told anything on him."

"Oh? Why?"

"He would have killed you," said Jack.

"How *thrilling!*"

Three

CATHY MCCORMACK put her eye to the peephole in her door. Ah. It was Dick in the hall. Quickly she pulled off her blouse and bra, then unchained and unlatched the door and let him in. He kissed her firmly on the mouth, then bent down and lightly kissed each of her nipples.

"I feel like going out to dinner tonight," he said to her as they walked hand in hand from the foyer to the living room. "I'm feeling faintly celebratory."

"Wonderful! What will we be celebrating?"

"Pour us a couple of drinks, and I'll tell you."

While she was pouring drinks, he picked up her *New Yorker* and riffled through it, glancing at a few of the cartoons.

"Cheers," said Cathy as she handed him his rye and lifted her glass of bourbon. "So what will we be celebrating?"

"The new show, *You Bet!* It's gonna work. I've already got three first-class contestants lined up. Hey! Listen to this. We got a guy from Queens who works behind the counter in a deli, cutting sandwiches. He speaks fluent English, Russian, German, Hebrew, and Yiddish. He can speak a little Polish, a little Lithuanian, a little Hungarian. Everybody knows him for a linguist. He reads his neighbors' foreign-language letters for them. He's a cute little guy, too. He's gonna win $100,000 on *You Bet!*"

"You're sure of that," she said skeptically.

Painter grinned. "Of course I'm sure. We start off with simple stuff that he already knows. Like 'Now, Mr. Abraham, you know that the word "lungs" is the name of an important part of the human body. What's the word for that part of the body in Russian, German, Hebrew, and Yiddish?' He knows. If he doesn't, we'll help him a little."

"You'll make sure he knows?"

"Damned right. I'm not gonna take chances."

"You're gonna feed him answers? Dick—"

"This son of a bitch is gonna know the Swahili word for penis."

"Careful."

"No. We won't use Swahili. Or Chinese. But he'll know

the Arabic word. A man who knows Hebrew could reasonably know Arabic. We'll be careful to stick to things he could reasonably be expected to know, has a reputation for knowing."

"Well—"

"There's a seventeen-year-old girl in Scarsdale who knows more about baseball than Red Barber. Think of this: Cute blond kid. She chews gum and giggles. 'What was Babe Ruth's batting average for the 1924 season?' She'll know."

"Because you fed her the question in advance?"

"Gimme a little credit, Cathy. For *some* smarts. She's got a hell of a reputation for knowing more about baseball than anybody. She's got that reputation already. That's why it'll be believable. If we used some kid who wasn't known for a freakish knowledge of baseball, we'd fall on our face. With this kid—"

"It's still risky. What if somebody blows the whistle?"

"Every winner that we coach will wind up with $100,000. The losers that we don't coach will win, say, $10,000. Small winners won't resent big winners. It's not a competition. They'll play against the questions, not against each other."

"Who's going to know?" she asked. "Lear?"

"Sort of. He doesn't want details."

Four

IN OCTOBER Jack met Rebecca Murphy, his private investigator, in a suite in a motel in Lexington, far enough from Boston so that it was unlikely he'd be seen or recognized. They sat together in the parlor, sipping Scotch and talking.

"Her parents saw the show last night. I can't promise you they won't come again tonight. I can go in ahead of you, save us two seats, and watch for them. If they don't show, there'll be nobody else there who'll know who you are."

"Can't be sure."

"Well, all right. Are you willing to be melodramatic?"

Jack thought the more appropriate word was "foolish." Still, Rebecca, had to use disguises often in her work and was good at what she did. She darkened his hair and eyebrows. She glued on a mustache, promising him it definitely would not slip askew or fall off if he kept his hands off it. She pushed two pieces of gummy plastic between his gums and cheeks, which puffed out his face and completely changed its shape. She dressed him in a brown houndstooth-check jacket that did not fit him well and in a pair of dark-brown slacks. Over all this she put a rumpled raincoat and shoved down on his head a floppy khaki hat, supposedly rainproof.

When he looked at himself in the mirror he was all but ready to risk entering the auditorium even if Dan and Connie Horan *were* there.

If anyone recognized him, he would look like the biggest fool ever born.

Rebecca drove him to the Convent of the Sacred Heart School. He waited in the parking lot while she checked the auditorium. She came out and beckoned him to come in. Their seats were halfway back. No one took any special notice of him. The audience stirred and buzzed.

He read the program:

THE MUSIC MAN

An Original Play

by

Meredith Willson

Featuring

Professor Harold Hill........... Brad Duncan

Marian the Librarian .... Kathleen Horan, E.C.

"What's E.C. mean?" Jack whispered.

Rebecca put her mouth to his ear. "It means Child of Christ. It's an honor given to girls who are most faithful in their religious duties."

He could be certain Kathleen was everything Connie wanted her to be: pretty, an achiever, something of an athlete, and, of course, a devout Catholic.

This was her class play. She would turn seventeen next month, and in the spring she would graduate. Nearly every year Rebecca photographed Kathleen at a distance and sent Jack the pictures. He had seen copies of her school annuals, copies of her school newspaper when it carried something about her, and even a *Globe* account of a girls' track meet where she had won a red ribbon in the hundred-yard dash.

The curtain went up. He knew the play, so he knew when to expect Marian the Librarian on stage. She appeared, in a powder-blue dress. Oh, God! Jack thought. So beautiful! Blond. Mature of face and figure. Graceful. Self-assured. Happy.

And of course she had no idea that the seedy-looking old man in the center of the audience was her father or that she was the daughter of Jack Lear, the media baron, as he was now sometimes called.

Rebecca saw the tears shining in his eyes and took his hand.

Five

"COULD YOU SPARE TIME to have dinner with me?" Jack asked as Rebecca drove him back to Lexington. "On your hourly rate, of course."

"Not on my hourly rate," she said quietly, staring intently at the road. "On the house."

They went back to the suite, so he could remove the mouth disguise and change his clothes.

She poured Scotch for them. He slumped on the couch and shook his head. "What she couldn't *be* if—" He sighed loudly. "Look at Joni. Look what she's become! John might have— But little Kathleen hasn't got a chance! Not a *chance!* Connie and Dan think a young woman is a baby-making machine, and that's what they want of her! God *damn!*"

"Jack . . ."

Rebecca reached for his hand again. She moved closer to him, leaned toward him, and kissed him on the side of the neck. Jack put his arms around her. They kissed for a full minute, running their tongues inside each other's mouths.

When he drew back at last, he grinned. He pointed at her forehead. The darkener from his eyebrows had rubbed off on her. "I think I've got to wash all this makeup off before we go to dinner," he said. "You want to help?"

They showered together.

"My God, it was twelve years ago!" he said to her when they lay down on the bed.

It had been twelve years since they made love before. She had been thirty-one years old then and was forty-three now. It was a good memory. This one would be better. Rebecca Murphy threw herself into making love with him, without reservation, again and again and again. They never did go to dinner. Early in the morning they ate some chips from a vending machine.

Six 1963

JACK AND ANNE flew down to St. Croix three days after Christmas. Joni and David Breck joined them for part of their two-week holiday as did the inimitable Jason Maxwell.

Joni had signed a contract with Harry Klein to do another picture—this time without a nude audition or even the suggestion of a casting-couch performance. She had suggested that David Breck play opposite her, but Klein had said no, because Breck spoke with a finely tuned stage accent that would not fit in the western they were going to make. The role went to Trent Ambler, who could affect a cowboy drawl.

She brought the script with her to St. Croix. Jack had some reservations about her doing a western, but when he read the script he saw that the film would be like very few westerns ever released.

Joni's role was that of a woman condemned to life at hard labor for the murder of her father. In a desert prison, she suffers cruelty and deprivation, until she escapes. The escape is hopeless because she's alone in the middle of the desert. Fortuitously, she encounters a craggy gunman-drifter, played by Ambler, who is escaping from a robbery he'd committed a few days earlier. He takes her on as a sex toy, but ultimately comes to love her. Their escape becomes an odyssey.

David said that her being chosen for this role was a measure of the respect she had won from Harry Klein and

Ben Lang. She hadn't gotten the hoped-for Oscar nomination for *Brave Michelle,* but if she brought this one off, the Academy could hardly deny her.

Jason Maxwell read the script. He pronounced it "slick," which offended Joni until she realized that in his lexicon that was a compliment. He asked her permission to use a pencil and suggest amendments to a few lines of dialogue. David told her in confidence that the changes suggested by this precious little man actually did make the lines more effective.

Joni sat on the beach that evening, wearing the red bikini she had worn all afternoon. Jack sat down beside her, and the others, sensing there was going to be a father-daughter talk, kept their distance.

"Why Jason?" she asked bluntly.

"Anne picked him up. She met him at an antiques auction, I understand. He's a best-selling writer, the darling of the critics."

"He's darling, all right," she said, nodding down the beach toward where he was cavorting in the surf. "You're not afraid that he and Anne—"

"Hardly. He's as queer as a three-dollar bill. Anne thinks he's amusing. I guess I do, too. He knows more about more people than anyone I've ever met, and I'm inclined to believe a lot of his gossip is true."

"Let me warn you about something, Daddy. Don't trust him. Tell Anne not to trust him. It's all right to have him around, but don't tell him anything you don't want the public to know. Remember, cute little lapdogs have ears, and this one's got a voice, too."

THIRTY-TWO

One 1963

HER work as Maggie in *Prisoners of the Rocks* was more arduous than Joni had imagined. None of it was shot in a studio. The first scenes took place in a jail, and they were done in an actual old jail in a desert county. When they shackled her wrists and ankles for the scenes of her being transported to the desert prison, the chains were real, heavy, and secured with real locks. She sat chained in the back of a wagon in the sun for three hours, while cameras on trucks followed and shot the film. Joni's ordeal was only a little less unpleasant than Maggie's. She sweated through the ragged clothes that were her costume, and by the end of the three hours she was sunburned and wet and exhausted, which was how she was supposed to look.

The worst she had to endure was the shaving of her head. Some players were allowed to wear flesh-colored rubber caps. The star could not do that, because there were many close-ups of her and because the director wanted to show her hair growing back—it was a metaphor for Maggie's recovering her personality.

Her hair was cut off and her head shaved by an actress in the role of one of the guards. Though the woman was as gentle about it as she could be, her role called for her to be brusque, rough, and profane. First, she cut off Joni's hair, not with barber shears but with a pair of big scissors. When she shaved her, she was not allowed to use lather, only to soap

Joni's head with a bar of laundry soap, after which she scraped her scalp with a straight razor. The scene was painful. The woman accidentally nicked her three times, and blood showed. Joni did not need any skill as an actress to cry. The cameras rolled and caught every wince and sob.

Ben Lang had not wanted David Breck on the location, but he relented and actually sent for David before Joni asked for him. David comforted her. He caressed her head and told her she was beautiful even without her hair.

Mo Morris came out to the location and saw what was developing between his star and the Welsh actor. He told Joni she would not have to date around anymore. Instead, he would build up David.

Two

EDITH WOLCOTT DIED at age seventy-nine. Joni wanted to go back to Boston for the funeral. Ben Lang readily agreed. He said he needed to take a break anyway, to give her hair a chance to grow in a bit. Harry Klein had supplied a wardrobe of wigs. Joni hadn't worn any of them in the location camp; she had simply made a turban of a towel or worn a scarf over her head. But now she chose a wig and settled it on her head, testing carefully to make sure it would not turn or fall off. David helped her. They drove to Las Vegas, where Jack and Anne were waiting on the LCI company plane.

"God, I'm tired," Joni said. "I can sleep all the way to Boston. And the damned wig itches like a hair hat. Excuse me." She pulled off the wig. "So what the hell? It'll grow back. Somebody offer me a drink." She had less than a quarter of an inch of dark stubble on her head. "Looked better when it was smooth," she said. "Stare and get it over with."

"I'm tempted to do it myself," Anne said lightly. "What a style!"

"If you do, have it done by a barber," said Joni. "Don't let an amateur do it."

To Jack's surprise, the Horans came to the funeral and brought Kathleen with them. Apparently they had decided to let him have a look at her. He pretended he had never seen her before.

They introduced her to him, and she shook his hand politely. She was more interested, though, in Joni, who was after all a famous film actress.

Anne knew who Kathleen was. Joni did not. Anne suggested to Jack that he had better tell her, and she made an opportunity for the two to be alone together on the flight to Westchester.

"*You're* in a mood," Joni said to him. She ran her hand over her stubble, a gesture she repeated again and again, as if she needed to reassure herself that her hair was growing. "I didn't know you cared that much about Grandmother Wolcott."

"What did you think of Kathleen?" he asked.

"Kathleen?"

"Kathleen Horan."

"Oh. Well. Pretty girl. She has some growing up to do. Why?"

"She's your half sister."

"*Daddy!*"

"She doesn't know it."

Joni frowned. "Do you have other secrets, Daddy?"

He returned the dark frown. "You told me yours. I've told you mine."

Three

LEAR COMMUNICATIONS sold off its radio stations. Most of the commercials on radio now were for local businesses: furniture stores, carpet stores, car dealers, tire stores, restaurants. Recorded music filled most of the hours broadcast by most radio stations. Some stations still broadcast daily hypochondriac hours, in which people with complaints from cancer to ingrown toenails phoned in for advice from anyone and everyone but real doctors. Listeners began to hear about holistic healing and natural medicines. Programs giving ostensible investment advice were mostly just bucket shops touting penny stocks.

It was not the kind of business Jack Lear wanted to be in anymore.

Four

LITTLE JACK, at sixteen, was a student at Brunswick Academy, a day school in Greenwich. The boys were encouraged to take part in athletics. Jack needed no encouragement. He loved all sports: lacrosse, soccer, field hockey, basketball. He especially liked sports that involved one-on-one competition and physical contact. Three times he was called before the headmaster.

"I hope I shan't have to tell you again, Mr. Lear, that you play too rough. Your aggressiveness on the playing fields is attracting unfavorable notice. The purpose of athletics is to build character as well as the body."

"I supposed the purpose of a game was to win it, sir," Jack said in his defense. "I play within the rules. I don't cheat."

"That is not the point. You play too rough. What if someone were hurt?"

"I risk being hurt, too, sir."

"Mr. Lear, I specifically order you to take it a bit easier when playing games."

"Even if Academy loses, Sir?"

"Even if Academy loses."

Five

CURT FREDERICK RETIRED. He was sixty-six, and Jack couldn't talk him out of it. He bought a home in Scottsdale, Arizona—a stuccoed house supposed to look like adobe, so oppressed by the blazing sun that the front yard was green gravel instead of grass, which wouldn't grow there. The air conditioning was industrial strength, and in the backyard lay a large walled-in pool surrounded by lush shrubbery kept alive by nightly drenchings of water.

The Fredericks had been gone from New York about

six months when a short story by Jason Maxwell appeared in *The New Yorker.* In part it read:

> Many years ago, George Blake, being then a man frustrated and alone, had entered tentatively into a gay relationship. That is, he took a lover nicknamed Zip, a younger man willing to play the female role to his male role. In time George grew bored, even repelled, by his situation and left Zip and took a wife.
>
> Zip was shattered. He felt he could not live without George's affection, without George's fatherly support, without even the discipline George had imposed on him—and George had imposed discipline on him, assiduously. Zip skidded downward in life, until he became a panhandler on the streets of New York.
>
> Zip might have blackmailed George. He never did. He loved him too much to do that. He did one day diffidently suggest that George might help him a bit. George's wife, Jane, was a woman of fine Christian instincts, which is to say she was sympathetic and charitable, perhaps to a fault, and she suggested that Zip come and live with her and George. He could earn his keep, she said, by being useful around the apartment.
>
> Thus was Zip turned into a domestic servant. He thrived in the role. George would no longer discipline him, but Jane would. Among the penances she imposed on him was requiring him to leave off his clothes for days at a time. Very close friends were allowed to see Zip. They were startled, to say the least, to be served cocktails by a stark-naked houseboy, and this in the home of a highly respected and eminently successful professional man.
>
> Such a situation could not continue to run a smooth course indefinitely. Jane was hugely annoyed that Zip did not at all mind what she had supposed would be painful humiliation. No. *Au contraire.* Nothing could have pleased him more.
>
> And so . . .

When Anne read the story she lied to Jack for the first time. Rather, she didn't actually lie to him; she just didn't tell him about the story Jason had written. Jack didn't read *The New Yorker* and didn't see the story. None of their friends said anything about it. The Fredericks said nothing about it. Maybe they hadn't seen it either.

But Anne was appalled. She knew that "George" was Curt, "Jane" was Betsy, and "Zip" was Willard Lloyd—Cocky.

She also knew how Jason had gotten the idea that Cocky ran around the Fredericks' apartment naked. Betsy had invited her to go to lunch one day. Anne had gone to the apartment to meet her. Betsy herself had answered the door. They had sat down for a drink before they went to the restaurant, and Betsy had served. Anne knew that Willard Lloyd, pleading abject poverty, had been allowed to join the Frederick household as a servant, and she had asked, casually, if it was the houseboy's day off. No, Betsy had said, Cocky was in the kitchen. Then Anne caught a glimpse of the houseboy and saw he was naked. With that, Betsy had laughed and called Cocky into the living room. "Our little secret," she'd said. "I've always known who the little bastard is, and when I agreed to take him in as a servant I demanded— Don't tell Jack."

Anne had not told Jack. But one day she had confided it to Jason, who apparently had found it too good a scene not to use.

She called him on it. "Jason, *for God's sake!* I trusted you!"

"And?" he asked, grinning. "Nobody's hurt. So far as I know, you're the only person who recognized the Fredericks. I've had no calls, no letters. But the story is *delicious!*"

Six

IN THE FALL, Kathleen Horan found herself enrolled at a women's college with the phrase "Sacred Heart" in its name. Until now she had been educated at Sacred Heart day schools, but she would board at the college. No longer could she escape overnight from the strictures of the nuns.

She had heard stories of how the Sacred Heart nuns engaged in self-flagellation. Here, at the college, girls in the dormitory had seen nuns whipping themselves, never each other, with what they called "disciplines." Under their habits some of them wore hair shirts that chafed them all day long. Small wonder that they were irritable and impatient.

They were capable of great kindness too, and no one could deny their devotion, but Kathleen quickly came to believe she had been placed in the custody of a gaggle of madwomen.

On the afternoon when she heard of the assassination of President Kennedy, she left the school without permission and went home. Her mother drove her back immediately, and Kathleen was campused for a month, meaning she could not leave her room after seven o'clock, except to go to the bathroom. Her mother approved, agreeing with the mother superior that Kathleen was becoming a bit willful.

Kathleen decided she hated everything about the school and everything about her life, including her pietistic mother. But there was no escape.

Seven 1964

ALTHOUGH JACK OWNED and ostensibly controlled Carlton House Productions, he left its day-to-day operations in the hands of skilled men and women who had been with the company for a long time. His brother Bob had essentially retired. He and Dorothy had built a home in New Mexico and spent most of their time lying in the sun and playing golf.

Carlton House owned a vast and valuable library of films. Jack had authorized the spending of money to buy up the libraries of studios that had ceased production. He enlisted CH in a program to preserve old films, transferring them from the brittle and flammable materials on which they had been shot to more durable materials. Opening old film cans often resulted in bitter disappointment—the film had dissolved and lay as dust under corroded reels.

Selected films were copied to videotape. This made

them available for television broadcasting. Dr. Loewenstein believed that a new business would develop: that of selling videotapes to home consumers, as video players came down in price for a consumer market. The tapes would be a lucrative business asset, he predicted.

The CH soundstages were now devoted almost exclusively to television production.

Sally Allen had quietly remarried Len, somehow managing to avoid publicity. They came to Jack and proposed to make a picture based on the lives of two married couples who were neighbors and shared the ups and downs of everyday life. Jack read Len's script. It had humor, but it was not a comedy. Sally would play a serious dramatic role. Jack consulted with people whose judgment he trusted and agreed to make the picture. They put it together fast, on a low budget, starring Sally and players from several successful but now canceled situation comedies.

To Jack's dismay, when Oscar time came, Sally Allen and Joni Lear both were nominees for Best Actress. Sally won.

Eight 1965

FOR THE FIRST TIME, Jack went to St. Croix without Anne. She had begun to feel chronically tired, and at the suggestion of her doctor she checked into Greenwich Hospital for a few days for a series of tests. Not wanting Jack to hang around the hospital wringing his hands, she virtually ordered him to fly to St. Croix for a few days in the sun.

The day before he was to leave, he ran into Jason Maxwell at lunch. He mentioned his trip and said sadly it was going to be a lonely few days because neither Anne nor any of his children could accompany him. Jason brightened and said he'd be glad to fly down and try to be amusing.

Jack accepted his offer and said he'd pay his fare. Jason wouldn't hear of it.

They arrived in St. Croix on Wednesday, February 17.

Jason was as diverting as he had promised he would be. During the whole visit he rarely wore anything but a pair of skimpy shorts—cutoff jeans with frayed bottoms—and a hat made of palm fronds, which he'd bought from a beach peddler.

Jason was just thirty-two, which reminded Jack that *he* had only a year to go before he turned sixty.

The hair was gone from the front of his head, leaving his forehead bald. The rest of his hair was thick but mostly gray. He combed it forward as best he could, but it still didn't cover his entire pate. He had developed jowls, and the flesh under his chin was loose. His eyes, which had always tended to droop, now had wrinkles at their corners. Nonetheless, his face was still lively and expressive, and he smiled readily.

His body did not show his age as much as his face did. Even without dieting or exercising in any systematic way, he remained nearly as trim as he had been as a man of forty. He had not slowed down.

On their third night in St. Croix, Jack encouraged Jason to dress so they could go out to dinner. After a couple of rum cocktails, they ate a seafood dinner accompanied by wine. It was a pleasant evening, largely because of Jason's all-but-obsessive effort to be entertaining. Over dinner he gossiped about a dozen celebrity-type men and women, not so much about sexual peccadilloes as about embarrassing situations into which they had fallen.

One story had to do with a Broadway actress who had wet her pants at 21. Another had to do with a United States Senator who had been wakened by the police in the stairwell leading to a cellar that housed a notorious Queens numbers drop.

Jack knew these were the kinds of stories Jason told Anne because they so much amused her. When the two men arrived back at the house, Jack poured brandy and sat down in the living room to hear more.

They drank, and Jason told two more stories. Then he fell moodily silent.

"Well," said Jack. "I suppose it's time to call it a day."

"Jack . . ." Jason murmured.

"Hmm?"

"Have you ever slept with a man?"

Jack shook his head.

"Did you ever want to? Did you ever think about it?"

Jack, who had been poised to stand, settled back in his chair. "I can't say I've never thought about it or wondered about it. Why?"

Jason lifted his eyebrows and smiled. "Well . . ."

"It's your thing, isn't it? What am I hearing, a proposition?"

"A suggestion. Respectfully offered. You won't hate me for asking, will you?"

Jack leaned back in his chair and for a moment closed his eyes. "No, Jason, I'm not going to do it, but I won't hate you for asking."

"You impress me as a man who wants to experience everything this world has to offer. I imagine there is not much that could happen between a man and woman that you haven't tried. That's why I thought you might want to complete your inventory of experiences."

Jack reached for the bottle and poured himself more brandy. He handed the bottle to Jason and said, "I won't deny that it's an intriguing idea. You're right when you suggest there is little I haven't experienced."

Jason curled his lips in a salacious smile. "Me too," he said. "I have a friend—I see him rarely, and you'll understand why—who beats me with a whip. He puts real *welts* on me, Jack! And—can you believe this?—it is *delicious!*"

Jack stared into his glass for a moment. "My first wife was like that: an utter masochist. Not at first. Later, when it took more and more to satisfy her. Jason . . . it killed her."

THIRTY-THREE

One 1965

DR. HAROLD MANNING sat in the chair beside Anne's hospital bed. He was a young internist, only three years out of his residency, but she knew he had already developed an excellent reputation at Greenwich Hospital. She liked him and had confidence in him. The only fault she could detect in him was his tendency to smile a little too much and a little too broadly.

"How are you feeling this morning, Mrs. Lear?"

"I suppose a little better," she said. "Bed rest . . ."

He nodded. His smile faded. "Yes. Rest is good. I'm afraid we're going to have to ask you to rest more."

"Oh? Why?"

"I've asked Dr. Philip DeCombe to join us for a conference. He has worked with me on your diagnosis. He'll be here in a moment."

"This sounds ominous," Anne said.

"Well, I'm afraid our findings are not the most encouraging," Dr. Manning conceeded. "Dr. DeCombe is a specialist."

"A specialist in what, Doctor?"

Dr. Manning drew a deep breath. "Cancer," he said quietly.

"What kind of cancer?"

"Mrs. Lear, before I tell you, let me say that people live for years with this particular disease. Not only that, they live normal, productive lives. It's only in the final stages that it becomes debilitating."

"Final stages . . ."

"Yes. We— Ah. Dr. DeCombe," he said looking up at the older man who had entered the room.

DeCombe had come directly from surgery and was wearing greens. He was tall, rail thin, and absolutely bald. He said good morning, making no effort to be cheery.

"I've begun to tell her," said Dr. Manning.

Dr. DeCombe nodded grimly. "You have leukemia, Mrs. Lear."

Two

WHEN JACK and Jason arrived at Kennedy Airport, Anne was waiting. She offered to drive Jason into the city, but he insisted on taking a cab.

Jack waited until they were in the car before he asked her what she had learned at the hospital.

"It seems I'm a little anemic," she said. "They prescribed some medicine for it. My blood count's up already, and I'm feeling better."

"What's the cause of it?"

"This particular anemia seems to have been caused by a virus. It's not serious. I may have to take the pills for some time, and I'm to go in and have a blood count taken periodically, but I'm not going to be an invalid."

"Jesus, Anne . . . I don't know what I'd do if—"

She laughed. "Don't think about it. Don't worry. I'm not, so there's no reason for you to."

Three

THE RITUALS of major quiz shows had always been the same. Contestants entered a soundproof booth, usually with lights shining up from below to make deep, dramatic shadows. They then frowned and pondered over the questions posed by a vacuous host or master of ceremonies.

For *You Bet!* the host was Art Merriman, the morning-show host whose shtick of capering up and down the studio aisles trying on women's hats had grown not only thin but also impossible as women stopped wearing hats.

The teenage baseball expert Glenda Bonham was an appealing contestant. A plump little blond who wore miniskirts, she chewed gum and giggled as she answered the questions. In her appearances on *You Bet!* she had attracted the highest rating any Lear Network show had ever received.

On her final night, the show clearly would have far outstripped every other show on television if Lear had had stronger outlets in some markets. Many viewers still did not receive UHF channels.

"Now, Glenda," Merriman intoned, "we have a two-part question. Here's the first part. The Baseball Writers Association began naming the Most Valuable Player of the Year, for each league, in 1931. Since 1931 a number of players have been named Most Valuable Player twice, but only a few have been named three times. Who were the players named three times?"

The lights outside the booth went down. The studio filled with recorded music. Glenda Bonham frowned, wrote one name on her pad, frowned some more, wrote another, and finally wrote a third.

"Glenda! Who were the players?"

She giggled. "Jimmie Foxx, Stan Musial, and Joe DiMaggio."

Merriman applauded wildly, as did the studio audience.

Then Merriman turned somber. "Now, Glenda, the toughest question of all. Are you ready?"

"I'm ready, Mr. Merriman."

Merriman nodded grimly. "The player who hits the greatest number of home runs in the National League and in the American League wins the home-run championship for that league. Only once in the history of modern baseball have those two championships been won by players who hit the *same number* of home runs in the National League and the American League. What year? Who? How many?"

Glenda Bonham grinned as she quickly wrote on her notepad. She stood relaxed and confident and smiling as the rigmarole of lights and music played out.

"Glenda?"

She giggled. "In 1923 Babe Ruth hit forty-one for New York, American, and Cy Williams hit forty-one for Philadelphia, National."

"You have just won . . . one . . . hundred . . . thousand . . . dollars!"

Four

DICK PAINTER hugged Cathy McCormack. "I told you the kid would be good!"

"How much could she have answered on her own?"

"Most Valuable Player—She knew the answer to that one flat out. Home runs—She knew it was Babe Ruth and Cy Williams, but she didn't know the year, and she wasn't sure who Williams played for. She had the basic stuff. We just had to help her fine-tune her answers a little bit."

"But she knew what she'd be asked?"

"Cathy! Don't be naive. *Of course* she knew what she'd be asked. If you believe in an unrigged quiz show you believe in the tooth fairy!"

Five

TWO WEEKS after Jack returned to New York from St. Croix, a messenger delivered a package to his office. He opened it to find a netsuke, a tiny Japanese ivory carving, maybe an inch and a half tall. It was valuable, a collectible. Like many of the genre, it was erotic and depicted two Japanese men fellating. It was a gift from Jason.

He could think of no way to explain to anyone why Jason Maxwell had sent him such a gift. He returned it to its velvet bag and little wooden box and put it in a desk drawer.

His telephone buzzed. "Mr. Lear, there is a Mrs. Horan on the line, calling from Boston."

He took the call.

"Jack, I've got to tell you something. Kathleen has disappeared! She ran away from her college, and we don't know where she's gone. I've never told you anything about her and never looked to you for any help with her. You've been very good about her. You've never interfered, as you promised not to do. But I—" Connie wept and couldn't go on.

"Did you ever tell her about me?"

"No. I brought her to Mrs. Wolcott's funeral so you could see her. But we didn't tell her who you were."

"Don't you have any idea where she's gone? A girl nineteen years old can't just disappear. Does she have a boyfriend?"

"No! She was in a convent school. She met boys, but she didn't date."

"Other friends, then."

"We've called everybody."

He was silent for a moment, then asked, "What can I do for you, Connie?"

"I don't know. Probably nothing. But I thought you should know. Maybe she's come down to New York."

"Connie, do you have anything with a set of Kathleen's fingerprints on it?"

"Fingerprints?"

"Yes. If anything horrible has happened, somebody will take fingerprints. Do you have—"

"Of course I have!" Connie wept.

"All right. A woman named Rebecca Murphy will be calling you. You give her whatever you have that has Kathleen's fingerprints on it. Also photographs."

"Who is she?"

"She's a private investigator who's done good work for me in the past. Missing-persons bureaus can't do much. They don't have the resources. But Miss Murphy will have, because I'll pay her. I'll call her as soon as I get off the phone."

Six

"IF YOU WERE a naive nineteen-year-old running away from home, where would you go?" asked Anne.

"New York?" Jack suggested.

"Maybe. But I'd rather think California. Los Angeles. Lotus Land."

Jack slammed his fist into the palm of his other hand. "The girl has no goddamned education! She's been made to live in a never-never land! The first man who figures her out will take advantage of her."

An hour later, when they were at the dinner table, the telephone rang. Because it was Rebecca Murphy calling, Jack went in the study and picked up the telephone.

"News," said Rebecca. "She boarded a bus in Concord."

"Going where?"

"Hard to say. She bought a ticket for Hartford. I'll drive over there and see what I can find out."

Back at the table, Jack shook his head and muttered, "Hartford."

Little Jack, who was now seventeen and no longer little, frowned and said, "May I know what's going on?"

Jack glanced back and forth between Little Jack and Liz, then at Linda and Nelly, and then at Anne.

"You might as well tell them," she said.

Jack nodded sadly. "A very beautiful nineteen-year-old girl has disappeared from a college just outside Boston. She's run away. Everybody is terribly worried."

"Why are *we* worried?" asked Liz.

Jack glanced around the table. "Because she's your half sister."

Seven

LITTLE JACK would graduate from Brunswick Academy in June. In the meantime there was the baseball season. During his first season, the manager had started him as a pitcher; but when he hit two home runs in one game and two more in the next, the coach switched him to first base. In the middle of his final season he was batting .408. He intimidated defensive players. Stretching singles into doubles, he slid into second base with his spikes up, daring the second baseman to tag him. He spiked two second basemen so badly they required treatment at a hospital. Coming into home, his tactic was to hit a waiting catcher so hard that the catcher would drop the ball. One schoolboy catcher was put out of baseball for the season with broken ribs after Jack Lear collided with him at the plate.

Late in April the headmasters of the preparatory schools that played in the league with Brunswick called a meeting. After no more than ten minutes discussion, they passed a resolution that Brunswick would forfeit any game in which Jack Lear was put forth as a member of the Brunswick team.

Little Jack's career as a secondary school athlete was over.

He pretended not to care. He told his father the preppy boys were sissies. He'd play ball in college. He had been rejected by Harvard and Yale, but had been admitted to Ohio State University in Columbus. Maybe Woody Hayes would want a hard-tackling guard.

Eight

REBECCA MURPHY showed photos of Kathleen Horan to the people who worked in the bus station in Hartford and learned that the girl had bought a ticket for Cleveland. Becky caught a flight, hoping to arrive at the Cleveland bus station before Kathleen. She was an hour late. And there the trail went cold. Rebecca had nothing to report except that Kathleen seemed to be heading west. She returned to Boston and persuaded the police to distribute the girl's picture and fingerprints on police wires.

Days passed, and nothing happened. Connie and Dan Horan were frantic. Jack was doing something, through Rebecca, but they themselves could do nothing. Dan flew to San Francisco and wandered the streets of Haight-Ashbury, a place where runaway youngsters were known to congregate. He showed Kathleen's picture to everyone: police officers, narcs, priests, street people. Some sympathized. Some didn't. He flew back to Boston, defeated.

Dan didn't say so to Connie, but his thought was that

the Lear in Kathleen was coming out—as maybe it had been bound to do.

Jack was in a state of suspension. He canceled a business trip, for fear of being where he couldn't be reached if word came. He drank too much. He didn't sleep well. Anne watched him closely. She did not like what she saw of how her husband handled a personal crisis.

Finally, several weeks after Kathleen disappeared, Jack flew to Houston for a meeting with Doug Humphrey. He couldn't put it off any longer. Lear Communications was planning a major offering of preferred stock, to raise half a billion dollars of capital, and the two bankers on the board of directors—Douglas Humphrey and Joseph Freeman—wanted to meet with the chief executive officer. Billy Bob Cotton and Ray l'Enfant would be there, too.

Jack arrived the evening before the meeting and had dinner with Doug, Billy Bob, and Ray—plus Mary Carson, who now often sat in on their meetings. In the morning the group sat down beside the pool as usual, spreading their papers out on a glass-topped table.

The meeting had only begun when a call came from Rebecca Murphy. Jack picked up the phone at the table.

"Bingo! I know where she is."

"Good news?" Jack asked hopefully.

"Not very. It could be worse. She's in jail in a town called Grant, Nebraska."

"In jail, for Christ's sake! *Why?*"

"Nothing terribly serious. It seems she walked out of a café without paying. She's serving out a fine at the rate of three dollars a day. I spoke with the sheriff. She's still got a bus ticket for Los Angeles and a few dollars in cash, which she won't apply to her fine. What's more, she refuses to tell them who she is or allow them to contact her family."

"What'll it take to get her out?"

"About eighty dollars, at this point. I can transfer funds to—"

"No. Then we lose her again. I'll fly up there and take care of it. I'll take her home. Don't call the Horans or anyone else."

Nine

JACK HAD FLOWN to Houston in a Beechcraft Super H18 that cruised at nearly three hundred miles per hour. He called the pilot before he left Humphrey's and told him to plan a flight to the airport nearest to Grant, Nebraska, and also to arrange for a rental car at the airport.

They took off at 10:30 A.M. and landed at Ogallala in midafternoon. From there it was a short drive to Grant, the county seat of an adjoining country.

Elmer Hastings, the sheriff, was tall, tanned, and raw-boned. He sat behind a scarred yellow-oak desk wearing a khaki uniform with badge and a straw hat.

Jack introduced himself. "I understand you've spoken with my private investigator, Miss Murphy."

"Yes. Quite a gal, that one. Piece of work to find out where Miss Horan is. You say you're her father, but Miss Murphy told me the girl's name is Horan. Yours is Lear."

"Long story," said Jack. "I can tell you the details if you want. What I'd like to do is pay off her fine and take her with me. I've got a company plane on the field at Ogallala. I hope to be able to get Kathleen to New York tonight."

"Well, let's see here. Her fine was a hundred dollars, plus court costs of $14.75. She's been here eleven days." The sheriff figured on a pad. "That's $114.75 less $33.00. Comes to $81.75. How you figure on payin'? Cash, I hope."

"Cash," Jack agreed.

"Jerry," the sheriff said to a deputy who seemed to be listening to this conversation with great interest, "you go back and tell Miss Horan to get her stuff together. Her daddy's here and bailin' her out."

Jack put four twenties, a one, and three quarters on the desk.

"May have a little problem here," said the sheriff.

"What's that?" Jack asked skeptically.

"She may not want to go. She's a stubborn girl. Before I write you a receipt, maybe you better talk to her and make sure she'll go. She's said she's goin' to California and not back east, no matter what. In eleven days she hasn't changed her mind, and she knows she's got twenty-seven more. Maybe—"

"I'd like to talk to her."

The women's jail was not a line of cells, just a cage some ten feet square with steel bars on three sides. It was furnished with two cots, a toilet, and a basin. Kathleen was the only prisoner, and she sat hunched forward on a cot, staring apprehensively through the bars. She wore a tartan skirt, white blouse, and dark-blue cardigan sweater. She was the mature, graceful blond he had seen on the stage at the convent school. But she was marred. Her face was hollow and thin and colorless. He looked at her for only a moment before he made a vow to himself.

Jack nodded and smiled at Kathleen. She rose and came to the bars. "Who are— Mr. *Lear?* They said *my father* was here."

"They said right, Kathleen. I *am* your father."

Her mouth dropped open. She gripped the bars with both hands as if to steady herself. Then she nodded and began to cry. "I *knew* something was wrong," she said. "I've always known they were lying to me. About something. I always knew there was something different about me." She drew a deep breath and stifled her sobs. *"You!* Why didn't you come to me years ago?"

"I couldn't. We have a lot to talk about. I have a private plane waiting. We'll be in the air for hours and can talk and talk."

"I'm not going back to Boston. I'm not going back to that school!"

"That's right. You're not going back to Boston, and you're not going back to that school."

Kathleen slipped her right hand higher on the bar. She dropped her left hand and let it lie on the crosspiece. "You and my mother?"

"That's right. She is your mother."

"They say you're a Jew. I mean . . . Connie and Dan say—"

"They would, wouldn't they? That's important to them."

Kathleen grinned. "If you're a Jew, then *I'm a Jew!* That's why they shoved their religion— Have I got a surprise for them!"

"Don't make any big decisions right now, Kathleen. You've got a lot of time to think. I love you, and I'm going to take you home, and we can work out something good for you."

THIRTY-FOUR

One 1965

CHRISTMAS WAS a strange but joyous holiday at the Lear house in Greenwich. Priscilla, who was still with the family, declared she had never seen anything so grand.

Jack and Anne presided happily over three separate parties and an expanded household.

In the spring, Linda would receive her Ph.D. in microbiology from Columbia. She had applied for faculty positions at several universities. She was dating and would not live with Jack and Anne after this academic year. Nelly was eight and had announced her goal in life: to play the cello.

Joni and David Breck came from Los Angeles. Joni had been nominated for an Academy Award again, this time for her role in *Dandelion.* She was four months pregnant. It did not show yet. She and David said they would marry before the baby was born, but they were uncertain as to when. Harry Klein had given David a strong supporting role in *Dandelion,* and he had a nomination for Supporting Actor. News of her pregnancy out of wedlock would kill enough votes to deny both of them an Oscar, so they were playing the situation very carefully.

The most interesting addition to the household was Kathleen. The Horans came to Greenwich, and the confrontation had been angry, almost violent.

"What in the world can you be thinking of?" Connie had shrieked. "You're a Christopher and a Child of Christ! Some of the sisters still think you have a vocation."

"Ignorant, dried-up old bitches," Kathleen had muttered.

"That will be enough of that kind of talk," Dan had declared darkly.

"I'm going to take instruction in Judaism and have a bat mitzvah," Kathleen had said.

Dan and Connie had glared at Jack, who had shrugged and said, "I told her I never had a bar mitzvah."

"What you are going to do, young lady, is come home and go back to school," Dan had said with an air of finality.

Kathleen had shaken her head with just as strong an air of finality.

"I'll *make* you come!"

Jack had pointed a finger at Dan. "No. That you *won't* do. Persuade her if you can."

They couldn't.

Later, when Kathleen went to see the rabbi at Temple Shalom, he gently advised her that the decision she proposed to make could not be made in anger and resentment. Even so, he agreed to let her begin instruction in Hebrew and in the Jewish faith. She saw a lawyer. She wanted her name legally changed to Sara Lehrer. He told her they could discuss it again after she'd given the matter more thought.

Kathleen, who asked now that they call her Sara, was a loving and helpful young woman around the house. In spite of her insistence that the convent schools had provided her with a poor education, she was able to help Liz with problems of calculus and to show Nelly what a close relationship existed between music and mathematics.

Two 1966

IN MARCH Jack was summoned to appear before a senatorial committee investigating misuse of television broadcasting franchises. He sat down at a table behind a bank of microphones, in the glare of television lights, and faced ten senators and their counsel.

The committee counsel was a young man with a mop

of unruly hair and chipmunklike teeth. His name was Roger Simmons, and he asked most of the questions.

"Mr. Lear, is it your opinion that you use the valuable television frequencies assigned to your company in the public interest?"

Jack had been thoroughly coached for this appearance. He wore a handsome dark-blue suit and sat respectfully but confidently at the witness table, his hands clasped in front of him. His lawyer sat to his left. Anne sat behind him. Joni sat behind the lawyer.

"Obviously, Mr. Simmons, a broadcaster would serve the public interest best by broadcasting nothing but educational shows, in the manner of the public television stations. Unfortunately, we can't make money that way, and we must make money if we are to remain in business. I am one of those who deplore the banality of a lot of what is broadcast by the networks, including the Lear Network. We do focus on quality in programming, and I think we do at least as well as any of our competitors."

"Mr. Lear, at the present time your network is the only one that continues to broadcast quiz shows with big prizes. Egregious cheating on such shows was exposed and all but killed them. How do you explain your network's reviving that format?"

Jack took a sip of water, then said, "I don't try to explain it. Generally speaking, I don't choose the shows that are broadcast on the Lear Network. That is done by others who are more attuned to the public taste than I am. My impression is that the public enjoys quiz shows and wants to see them."

"You broadcast a show called *You Bet!* Is that show honest?"

"I have no reason to believe otherwise."

"Then you are not prepared to testify to a certainty that it *is* honest?"

Jack smiled comfortably. "To tell you the truth, Mr. Simmons, I have never even *seen* it. I signed off on it—meaning that I told my people to go ahead and do it. They wanted to do it, and I said yes. That's the only contact I've had with it."

"Mr. Lear, if we show evidence that *You Bet!* is rigged, will you deny that it is?"

"I will neither affirm nor deny anything about it," said Jack smoothly. "I have nothing to do with *You Bet!* It makes money. That's why we broadcast it. Otherwise, I wouldn't put it on the air."

"Do you think it is banal?"

Jack nodded. "It is one of many shows on television, on my network and others, that are banal."

Three

JACK AND ANNE did not return to New York immediately. Later that day they sat in their suite in the Mayflower and watched the afternoon session of the Senate committee.

Dick Painter was the witness.

"Is *You Bet!* a rigged show, Mr. Painter?" Simmons asked.

"Absolutely not," said Painter, adopting an air of indignation. "We all went through that sort of thing a few years ago. We at Lear are not stupid enough to let it happen again."

Simmons opened a thick file. "A few days ago one of the contestants who won a great deal of money on *You Bet!* testified in executive session of this committee. We took the testimony in executive session to protect that person's identity. That person testified that the questions to be asked on the show were revealed in advance, so that he or she could learn the answers before airtime. That person testified that before each half-hour broadcast you personally, Mr. Painter, asked the questions and heard the answers, which were then repeated on the air. Is that true? Did you do that?"

Painter's lawyer grabbed his arm and pulled him away from the microphones. They conferred for a minute; then Painter faced the microphones and the committee again and said, "Since I don't know who your witness was, I can't possibly answer your question."

"Oh, I believe you can, Mr. Painter," said the committee chairman, Senator Donald Hooper, a Democrat from Kentucky. "Let me rephrase the question. Did you or did anyone else, to your knowledge, ever reveal the questions in advance to *any* contestant on *You Bet!*?"

Painter leaned over and conferred with his lawyer. Then he said, "I respectfully decline to answer the question on the ground that my answer might tend to incriminate me."

Jack sprang from the couch facing the television set and grabbed a telephone. He put through a call to Cap Durenberger in New York.

"You saw? You heard what Painter said? He's going on with it, taking the Fifth to every question! Cap, advise security that Painter is not to be allowed to enter the offices. Seal his office. Seal his files. I'm issuing a statement from here that we are sealing his office and files and will allow only authorized federal investigators to have access to them. Kill *You Bet!* Run any goddamned thing in its time slot tomorrow night. And . . . one more thing. Have security put Cathy McCormack out the front door. Right now! Advise her she's fired."

Four

ONCE MORE Joni failed to receive the Academy Award for best actress. David Breck, though, received an Oscar for Best Supporting Actor, for his work in her picture *Dandelion.*

Joni was bitter and decided to shoot a finger at Hollywood. She announced her pregnancy and announced at the same time that she was not going to marry the father of her baby.

David was in love with her. Even so, neither of them was enthusiastic about marriage. Both of them liked the flexibility of things the way they were. They continued to live together, and David said he would help her rear the child, as its acknowledged father.

In June the baby was born, a little girl they named Jacqueline Michelle. Jack and Anne flew to California in the new bizjet the company had acquired, ironically a Lear Jet. Joni assured them that she was very happy.

Five

ANNE ARRANGED TWO PARTIES for Jack's sixtieth birthday, one at home with the family and one at the Four Seasons restaurant in New York for an extended group of friends.

No one guessed that she was deliberately seizing every opportunity she could find to bring the family together. Her blood count was low, and her doctors had switched her to a different, stronger medication. She could feel her energy diminishing, but she forced herself to be active.

Despite her failing health, Anne telephoned and wrote all the invitations and made all the arrangements for the two parties.

Of all those Anne called to invite to the family party, only Joni sensed the anxiety in her stepmother's call. She and David suspended discussions with Harry Klein about a new picture and flew home.

Joni tried to find a time to take Anne aside and talk to her alone. Sitting by the pool one evening, she saw Anne coming out of the house and asked David to go inside and leave her to talk with Anne alone. Anne sat down beside her, but in a moment Liz and Nelly came out to swim, so Joni suggested to Anne that they walk down to the lake.

Anne preferred to swim in the lake anyway and slipped into the warm green water. Joni followed her, and for a few minutes they swam. They came out and sat down on the grassy bank in their wet bikinis.

Anne said nothing. She stared at the water and at the setting sun. Joni had noticed this tendency of Anne's to lapse into introspective silence.

"Will you forgive me if I intrude into something that is none of my business?" Joni asked.

Anne frowned. "I'll forgive you, but you won't forgive yourself. If I take you into my confidence, a heavy burden will fall on your shoulders. It might be just as well you let it go."

"Anne, something's wrong, isn't it? Something bad."

Anne nodded. "I need to talk to someone. How old are you, Joni? Thirty-one? If I talk to you, I need your absolute, unqualified promise you won't tell your father. Or anyone else."

"Is it a man?" Joni asked, suddenly alarmed and hoping that was all it was.

"No. Not a man. Will you promise?"

"I promise," Joni said emphatically. "What is it, Anne?"

"I'm dying, Joni."

Standing by the pool, watching Liz and Nelly swim, Jack saw Anne and Joni embrace and cling to each other. He smiled. His grown-up daughter had become a friend to his wife.

Six

JONI KEPT THE SECRET. The family weekend continued.

Little Jack, home from Ohio State University, proudly announced that he had tried out and been accepted for the football squad. He swaggered. His sister Liz despised him.

Linda, who had accepted a position as a microbiologist on the staff of Yale–New Haven Hospital, was engaged to a young man named Guy Webster, a senior associate in a New York City law firm.

When the young man was introduced to people at Jack's birthday party, he promptly informed them that he was a member of the John Birch Society. He impressed Jack as a rather stiff, self-important young man—in fact, a boring nincompoop—and Jack wondered what in the world Linda saw in him.

Joni, too, concluded that Guy Webster was a consummate ass. Seventeen-year-old Liz reached the same conclusion and shared it with Joni.

Jack was standing by the pool talking with Joni when Liz ran up to them laughing. "I heard Linda say something to him! You'll never guess! She said, 'If you tell one more person you're a member of the John Birch Society, I'm going to kick you in the balls. It's bad enough that you are, without my having to hear you brag about it.' "

Jack grinned and shrugged. "Maybe she knows what she's doing after all."

"I wish we dared to interfere," Joni said grimly.

Seven

IN AUGUST another short story by Jason Maxwell appeared in *The New Yorker.* Part of it read:

> Overheard at Lutèce:
>
> "You wouldn't think it to look at him, but he's the sexiest man alive."
>
> "Dear! I *did* it with Jack Kennedy."
>
> "Jack Kennedy! Really. That's not what I mean. You know nothing until you've spent a night with the master."
>
> Jefferson Le Maître was a man of catholic tastes when it came to the erotic life. His first wife had been a woman of universally recognized elegance who had smoothed his rough edges and made him the cultured, cosmopolitan gentleman he was. That first wife introduced him, however, to another sort of taste. Their most intimate friends, and their most intimate friends only, knew that elegant Madame Première was an obsessive masochist who loved to be bound and beaten. Le Maître was at first unwilling to accommodate her; but ultimately, to keep her happy and to keep their marriage intact, he consented and learned to flog her with abandon until she screamed for mercy.
>
> He was a man of Catholic tastes as well, and a fling with a gorgeous Catholic lass resulted in the termination of his first marriage.
>
> Wife One found another partner to play sadist to her masochist. They played rough games. Some times she hung from a rafter by handcuffs while he whipped her with a riding crop. One night while she hung, her arms spread by two pairs of handcuffs, he suffered a myocardial infarction and died before her horrified eyes. She could not escape. She hung there for agonizing hours, until at last she too died.
>
> Jefferson Le Maître deeply regrets the tragic way his first wife died. Even so he cannot resist say-

ing that, in a medical sense, she died almost exactly the same way Christ died—of circulatory failure caused by hanging with outspread arms.

Le Maître. The master, the teacher. *Der Lehrer.* The teacher. Johann Lehrer had been a teacher in Germany. Erich had changed the family name to Lear. The connection was obscure—but not to anyone who knew Jack's family history. The masochistic first wife. A few people knew about that. A very small number of cognoscenti would know who Jefferson Le Maître was.

Eight

"We don't dare even cut him," said Anne.

She lay on a sofa in the living room of the Manhattan apartment. The magazine lay on the coffee table. She had read the Jason Maxwell story this morning, and now Jack had read it.

"I'd like to kill him," Jack said.

"No. We invite him to join us for lunch at Lutèce. We must be seen with him in public, like great good friends who have nothing to quarrel about. That says to the world that it has never dawned on us that he could have been writing about us. About *you.* If we cut him, that says he *was* writing about you, and we know it."

"Are we to pretend that the story is amusing?"

"We might as well. There are not fifty people who know he was writing about you. If we do anything negative, a hundred times that many will guess."

Jack sighed loudly. "All right. I only wish I could find some way to stick a knife in *his* back."

Nine

Joni called her father from California. Her voice was cold. "Couldn't you have told me how she died?"

"I'd have had to tell John, too. I didn't think either of you needed to know. You were just twenty-two, Joni."

"I'm thirty-two now. You could have told me. Anyway, I warned you about Jason Maxwell. How many people are going to make the connection?"

"Anne and I are taking the little bastard to lunch. We want to make it look like we're all buddy-buddies, so he couldn't have been writing about me."

"Good luck. And, uh . . . Daddy . . . I always knew you were the sexiest man alive."

THIRTY-FIVE

One 1967

NO ONE SAID ANYTHING. It was plain, just the same, that more than a few people had made the connection between Jason Maxwell's Le Maître and the real-life Jack Lear.

Men who had nodded at Jack in the Harvard Club bar now nodded and smiled. At the harvest ball at the Greenwich Country Club, women asked him to dance and then whirled around the floor beaming at their friends, as they nestled in the embrace of "the sexiest man alive."

A writer for *Esquire* called and said she wanted to do a profile of him for the magazine. During the interviews with him and Anne, not a word was said about the Maxwell story, and no mention of it was made in the subsequent profile; but it was plain from the tone of the interview and the story that readers would want to know more about the real Le Maître—and that most of them would know that Jack Lear was Le Maître.

Worst of all, Jack and Anne had to appear in public with Jason Maxwell and pretend he was still their amusing friend. When the three of them lunched together at Lutèce, the meeting received notice in three gossip columns, one of which specifically identified Jack as the prototype for Le Maître. Photographers were not allowed inside Lutèce, but the *Post* published a picture of the three leaving the restaurant and walking, with conspicuous smiles, along the street.

Over lunch Jason said nothing of the story. Neither Jack

nor Anne mentioned it. Jason tried to amuse them with a story about how a month ago a janitor cleaning the Oval Office had found a pair of Jackie Kennedy's panties under a couch. "How'd he know they were Jackie's?" Anne asked. "She had her initials embroidered on all her underwear," Jason confided. Anne changed the subject. She congratulated Jason on the publication of his new novel, *Norma,* which had won gushing reviews everywhere and was already at the top of the best-seller list. "A bagatelle," said Jason.

Jack could see nothing to do but live with the new notoriety Jason had given him. He was angry but not devastated.

Two

HARRY KLEIN was a bigger producer than ever. Joni looked around his office, which she had first visited seven years ago. It was a lot more impressive now that Harry had two Best Picture Oscars displayed in it.

Harry had always kept autographed photographs of stars on his office walls, but now he had pictures of some of the biggest successes of the past seven years. Joni was pleased to see that her autographed photo was displayed among the others. Framed and prominently displayed also was an autographed picture of Harry shaking hands with a grinning President Kennedy.

Harry himself, almost fifty years old now, had changed little. If his hair was turning gray, he was having it colored. He still favored dark-blue polka-dot bow ties. He'd changed his style in only one respect: gone were the big horn-rimmed glasses he had made almost a trademark; in their place he wore contact lenses.

"I hear you're gonna be featured in *Esquire,"* he said.

"Yeah. As the often-a-bridesmaid-never-a-bride girl," Joni said acerbically. "The twice-nominated actress."

"Hey! What do you expect? Cary Grant's never had an Oscar. Tyrone Power never got one. Bob Hope's never had one. There's a lot of *respect* for you in this industry."

"I've done three pictures in seven years."

"You could have done five or six. Don't forget the scripts you've turned down."

"Harry, I want the role of Jason Maxwell's Norma."

"My God, Joni! That's penciled in for Ingrid Bergman!"

"She's too old."

"Audrey Hepburn's interested."

"She's not earthy enough. No audience is ever going to believe Liza Dolittle is Norma."

"Joni, I don't see how we can give you Norma."

"I *need* it, Harry. It will make a hell of a big difference."

"You put me in a hell of a position."

Joni smiled lazily. "Suppose I get into a hell of a position? Let's go back to square one, Harry. I'm asking you to do something for me, the same as I did seven years ago; and I'm willing to do what I did seven years ago, to persuade you."

"How can I say no to that?"

"Just remember, I'm good enough for the Norma part. You're not making any big-deal sacrifice. You're just going to do me a favor. And I'll do one for you."

"One?"

"Now and again. Whenever. Deal?"

He reached for her hand as though to shake it, but when he had his grip on her he jerked her into his arms and kissed her fervently. Neither of them undressed. On her knees, she pulled out his parts. She slavered over his cock and over as much of his balls as she could reach through his underpants. It was not the way it had been before. He came in a minute.

Three

JACK AND ANNE flew to Columbus, Ohio, to see Little Jack play football for Ohio State. Liz refused to go.

She missed a spectacle of grand dimensions. Their host, the manager of the local Lear television station, drove Jack and Anne from the airport to the stadium, detouring through some residential neighborhoods to show them a display of glorious gold and red maples and oaks. The stadium was an immense horseshoe, filled with some eighty thousand rabid fans who generated pandemonium. The university band —all men, no women—marched with military precision and played the same way. Its trademark formation was to spell out "Ohio" in script. The band marched through the letters until the word was complete. Then a bandsman capered dramatically into place and dotted the *i* with a big white sousaphone.

Coach Woody Hayes had decided Little Jack was not the big, heavy boy he thought he was—not big or heavy enough to play guard or tackle, as he had supposed he would. Instead, he played as a linebacker. He was heavy enough for that, and he was fast. For good work, Coach Hayes awarded players buckeyes—outlines of buckeye leaves painted on their helmets. In this, his second season, Little Jack had six buckeyes on his. He earned a seventh that afternoon by sacking the Wisconsin quarterback so hard he knocked the ball loose, which Ohio State recovered.

The kind of play that had been decried by his prep school was extolled in big-time college football. Little Jack loved to hit. There was nothing personal about it; he just loved to hit a ball carrier and knock him sprawling. College football players were in such superb physical condition that getting hit didn't hurt them. Little Jack was in such superb physical condition that he could take return hits, too.

His nickname, Little Jack, was known at the university, but it didn't seem quite appropriate, and the undergraduates gave him a new nickname: LJ. Twice during the game, when he'd made a spectacular hit, the crowd chanted, "LJ, LJ, LJ!"

Because Coach Hayes did a postgame show on the Lear television station, he made himself available to Jack and Anne for a short private visit. They met in a Spanish-style restaurant not far from the stadium. A little later they would join the crowd of supporters and parents in the main room, but the coach took his first drink with Jack, Anne, and Little Jack.

"I like your boy's spirit," said Coach Hayes. He was a big, square, expansive man with a wide and ready grin. "He's got the right kind of stuff to be successful on the football field or wherever he decides to go."

"Well, thank you," said Jack. "I don't know if he's told you, but he had a half brother who had the right kind of spirit, too. He was killed in a night carrier landing in the Pacific."

"LJ, you never mentioned that."

Little Jack grinned. "I didn't know if I should."

"You should have. Now, tell us, LJ," said the coach with sincere enthusiasm, "just what did we learn from today's game?" He turned to Jack and Anne. "The boys are expected to learn something from every game. We play to win, yes; but we play for the learning experience, too. What did we learn today, LJ?"

"I suppose it was the importance of practice, Coach."

"That's right, that's *exactly* right. Let me speak with your parents alone for just a minute." When LJ had stepped away, Coach Hayes said, "He's a *brainy* player. That boy reads the football field about as well as any boy I ever coached. When he got that quarterback this afternoon . . . *I* didn't guess where that kid was going, but LJ did and went right after him. You can be proud of him."

Four 1968

THE COURT granted the petition of Kathleen Horan to change her name to Sara Lehrer.

Even so, she did not pursue her studies with the rabbi far enough to make her bat mitzvah. She went to the temple sporadically, then stopped going.

In June she would graduate from Columbia, which she had entered with advanced standing and with Linda's help. She told Jack she didn't know what she wanted to do. She confided in Anne more than in Jack and told Anne she would give anything in the world do be able to do what Joni did, yet she had to be realistic. She knew she had neither the talent nor the looks to become a movie star. Anne suggested she go to Los Angeles and spend a few days with Joni, where she might learn something that would surprise her.

Joni gladly agreed to receive her, and shortly after graduation, Sara flew to Los Angeles.

Five

DOUGLAS HUMPHREY was eighty-two years old and decided to retire from active participation in business. He notified Jack that he meant to resign from the LCI board of directors and asked Jack to come to Houston to meet with him and discuss the question of who would succeed him.

Jack took the company jet from Westchester Airport and flew to Texas on a Monday in July. Humphrey liked to meet beside his pool. Jack unpacked in the guest room and went out wearing a pair of swim trunks. Humphrey sat under his big umbrella, as usual; and, as usual, Mary Carson was swimming.

Humphrey was cracking crab claws. He shoved the platter toward Jack.

"I've written a will," he said. "I leave as much as I can to Mary. She'll own most of my interest in everything. She's helped me a lot the last few years. She knows as much about things as I do, just about."

"She impresses me very positively," said Jack. "Always has."

"My son was killed in Normandy in 1944. I had supposed he would inherit from me and run the businesses, but — Mary is the child of my middle age. I was forty years old when she was born. She is divorced. She has given her recent years to me."

"You are fortunate to have her," said Jack.

"How would you react to Mary's replacing me on the LCI board of directors?"

Surprised by the question, Jack glanced at the husky, deeply tanned, bikini-clad woman who was swimming laps in the pool. "Doug, I can't think of a reason why not."

Humphrey smiled. "You'd give me a reason if you could think of one, right?"

"I suppose so, but I can't think of one."

"If I vote my stock and you vote yours, for Mary, it's settled."

"Okay. It's a deal."

"Mary! He agrees."

She climbed out of the pool and came to the table. She poured gin on the rocks for herself and raised her glass.

Six

WHILE JACK was in Texas, Anne went to the hospital and received her first X-ray therapy. It made her nauseous. She thought she'd throw up, but she didn't.

Dr. Manning gave her a shot to relieve the nausea. "Have you told your family yet?" he asked her.

"My stepdaughter knows," she said quietly.

"You're not going to be able to keep it a secret much longer," he said.

"I haven't got much time left."

"I wish I could tell you how much. Sometimes X-ray therapy arrests the disease for months, even years. But—"

"You said maybe five years. I've only had three and a half."

"Your children are grown, aren't they?"

"My son is a loutish hunk of a football player for Ohio State. My daughter graduated from high school this year and will go to Princeton in the fall. I've been spared long enough to see them out of the nest. It's my husband who is going to need emotional support."

"Who's supporting *you,* Mrs. Lear? Emotionally."

"It will be bad enough for Jack when it happens. I don't want him to have to suffer through it for months ahead of time."

Seven

HARRISON WOLCOTT died in June, aged eighty-seven. Jack and Anne flew to Boston for the funeral. The Horans, who had appeared for the funeral of Edith Wolcott, did not show up.

In July, Linda brought Nelly for a swim in the pool and

told Anne that her marriage to Guy Webster was not working out. She was taking the Pill to prevent getting pregnant by him, but he wanted to begin a family.

"I don't want to have a child by that man. I've never done anything so stupid!" she wailed.

"Don't have a child you don't want," Anne said softly.

Linda stared at Anne for a moment. She drew her lower lip in between her teeth for a moment, then said, "Anne, you're losing weight. Are you dieting?"

"No, I'm anemic. It's causing me to lose weight, and it saps my energy."

Linda frowned hard. "Anne . . . ?"

"Joni knows," Anne whispered. "Now I guess you do, too. It's our secret. It will come out soon enough. But not yet."

"Anne, I married bad. I came here today to ask how you and Jack would react if I walked away from Guy and came here to live for a while. That's what I want to do. You're going to need somebody here."

Anne covered her face with her hands and began to sob. "Only if you're sure you want to leave your husband for other reasons," she wept.

Eight

ANNE AND JACK were sitting at the dinner table with Linda and Nelly. "I think we— I think we—" Anne couldn't finish her sentence. Suddenly she pitched forward, and her face struck her plate.

"*Anne! Anne!* No!"

Jack hovered over her, patting her shoulders and back, trying to revive her.

Linda called the emergency squad.

On Wednesday, September 18, 1968, Anne's secret was revealed.

Jack spent the next ten days at the hospital, twenty-four hours a day, getting a little sleep in the chair in Anne's room. He watched her weaken. He watched the desperate efforts taken in the hope of effecting a remission. She turned more and more lethargic. Her hair fell out, leaving her completely bald. She did not seem to know it. Certainly she did not care.

She was weak and slept most of the time, but during her waking hours she was alert; she knew and understood everything.

"I kept it from you as long as I could," she told Jack. "You're suffering enough. There would have been no point in making you suffer all of the last three years."

"I would have shared your suffering with you, at whatever cost," he whispered.

"We've had twenty-two years together," she said. "I would have paid this price for those years even if I had *known* what was going to happen."

When she was asleep again, Jack sat in the vinyl-covered reclining chair and sobbed as quietly as he could.

After Anne's tenth day at the hospital, Dr. Manning asked Jack to sit down with him in the day room on the hospital floor. "She can go home now, Mr. Lear," he said.

"To die," Jack said numbly.

The young doctor ran his hands over his eyes and cheeks. "We've done all we can," he whispered.

Anne came home in an ambulance and was put to bed by two nurses. She would have round-the-clock nurses from then on.

Anne sat up in bed as much as she could. She asked Jack to play Scrabble with her, and as long as she remained alert she played well and seemed to enjoy it.

Jack called the children home. Liz came immediately. LJ said he had an important game Saturday but would try to get away and come home Sunday. Jack called Woody Hayes, who personally drove LJ to the university airport and put him aboard a Lear jet offered by an Ohio business corporation to fly the boy to Westchester Airport. He missed the game. The LCI jet brought Joni from Los Angeles. Sara came with her.

The family knew they were assembling to say good-bye to Anne.

She insisted on being brought down to the living room to see the family, even though she had to be carried. She sat in a wing chair to one side of the fireplace, wearing gray wool slacks that hid her emaciated legs and a dark green sweater that hid her emaciated arms. She did not cover her head. After drinking a Scotch and eating a bowl of soup, she urged the family to go in to dinner. She would not let them see Jack and the nurse support her on the stairs.

When she was asleep and Jack came back downstairs, he was weeping. He had not left the house except to go to the hospital since the day Anne had collapsed. *He* had collapsed as well. He could not function. Others were running the business. Mary Carson had flown up from Houston and assumed the chairmanship of an executive committee of the board of directors, to run the company until Jack returned. No one even tried to call him.

The next day Anne came downstairs again. She sat in the library and saw each of the children individually. She was calm. The truth was, she was resigned. She had resisted the idea of dying for as long as she could.

They were not to stay any longer, she said. She might die tomorrow; she might live through Christmas. Nothing could distress her more than watching them interrupt their lives to sit around and wait. Jack was doing that—she couldn't talk him out of it—and that was bad enough.

Except for Linda, who was living in the house because her marriage had failed, the family scattered again.

On Sunday, November 10, Anne died peacefully, early in the morning. The night nurse woke Jack to tell him, then left him to writhe in agonized sobs in his bed.

THIRTY-SIX

One 1969

ON MONDAY, January 6, Jack finally reappeared at his office. He was gaunt. For the first time that anyone could remember, he wore a suit that did not fit him perfectly. He was also deeply tanned, since he had been in St. Croix since Anne died in November. Linda had been there with him most of the time. Nelly had stayed at home in the care of Priscilla until mid-December but came as soon as her school closed for Christmas break.

LJ and Liz joined Jack in St. Croix for Christmas, as did Joni and David. Sara, who had found a job in Los Angeles, visited during the week before Christmas.

All of them had seen him cry. They would find him sitting on the beach, staring at the waves coming in, and sobbing.

By telephone from St. Croix he had called a meeting of LCI executives and ranking staff, to convene in the boardroom at ten o'clock on Monday, January 6.

Mary Carson was there, sitting at the foot of the big conference table. Also present were Mickey Sullivan, Cap Durenberger, Herb Morrill, Dr. Friedrich Loewenstein, and Raymond l'Enfant. Other executives sat in chairs around the walls, and still others stood.

Jack rose. "I want to thank all of you for relieving me from my responsibilities for more than three months. It has helped me tremendously to know that during a period when I was not able to do my job, competent and committed people were here doing it for me. I am sincerely grateful.

"I am going to ask you to do me one more service. I know that all of you want to offer your sympathy. I have received your cards and letters and will in time reply to every one of them. I do ask you, though, not to offer any further sympathy. When we sit down together privately, don't begin our conversation by telling me how sorry you are about my loss. I know you are. But each kind expression of sympathy just reminds me once again—"

His voice broke, and for a minute everyone stared at the table or the floor, not at him, while he struggled to regain his composure.

"Ladies and gentlemen, we have a company to run. When I called from St. Croix I suggested an agenda for a management meeting this morning. I would like to ask all those seated at the table to remain—also Dave and Margaret. The rest of you I thank again. I will be sitting down with each of you individually during the week to discuss what you are doing and what we need to do."

For a moment, before he flipped the pages of his notebook and introduced the first item on his agenda, he glanced around the table at his self-conscious officers, directors, and staff. There had been changes. There would be more. Painter was gone, of course. He would have to be replaced by a programming man. Cap Durenberger was seventy-nine and would retire soon. There were rumors that Ray l'Enfant might be offered a position in the Nixon administration. He was euphoric over Nixon's election and wore an enameled American-flag pin on his lapel. Mary Carson was no longer the bikini-clad young woman Jack had seen in the pool but a mature woman, with her hair cut shorter and wearing a pair of reading glasses.

Two

AT DINNER with Mary Carson, Jack learned that she wanted to be more of a hands-on director than her father had been.

Having listened to her ideas during the day, Jack said he would recommend that the board elect her a vice president.

It was nearly eleven o'clock when he arrived home. Mickey dropped him off, and Jack let himself into the house with his key. Linda was waiting for him in the library, where she was watching television and at the same time scanning a book.

She switched off the television set and put down her book. She stood. She was wearing a yellow baby-doll nightgown, not sheer but short enough to expose her legs and yellow panties. She stepped toward Jack and into his arms. They kissed.

He had called her, so she knew he'd had his dinner. "Let's go up," she whispered.

They didn't use the master bedroom suite where he had slept with Anne. He had moved into one of the guest rooms. The master bedroom suite had been left as it was the last night Jack and Anne slept together. Even Anne's nightgown was laid out, as it had been in September before she went to the hospital for the last time. The guest room would have been rather spare, but Linda had moved some things into it, including the erotic prints Anne had bought for Jack. His clothes hung in the closet. One drawer in the bureau was reserved for her lingerie.

While Jack undressed, Linda chose something to wear. She carried her selections into the bathroom and changed into them. When she came out, she was wearing a sheer black jacket, a black satin G-string, dark stockings held up by lacy black garters, and black patent-leather high-heeled shoes.

Jack, who himself had stripped to white slingshot underpants, had poured them two brandies, and they sat on a love seat—Linda in his arms. It was eleven o'clock, and he clicked on the television set. It was their habit to watch the news, then at least part of the Johnny Carson show each night.

He pulled down her G-string. She kept her crotch shaved, and she had the most prominent wattles he had ever seen, red and fleshy and visible. He fondled them, and Linda stiffened and moaned. She seized his penis.

As usual, the news was less interesting than what they were doing. They hurried to the bed and plunged into a round of lovemaking. They finished by the time the Carson show started and returned to the love seat, both naked now except that she still wore her stockings. They cuddled.

Linda had been his salvation. Providence seemed to have brought them together. Neither had planned it. For five weeks after Anne died, Jack and Linda had been alone on St. Croix. Linda had given him support and sympathy. Joni would have interrupted the shooting of *Norma* to be with him, but Linda had said she could take a leave of absence from Yale–New Haven Hospital to go to St. Croix with him. Jack was immensely grateful.

Linda knew how to hit the right notes with him, when to be solemn, when he was ready to be cheerful, when he wanted to brood alone on the beach, when he wanted her to walk with him into town to prowl the market. When he took her hand in the market one day, she squeezed his. Everything from that point on was settled.

"Jack," she said when Carson broke for commercials, "I'm going to have to move out of this house."

"My God, no!"

She kissed his neck. "We can't be what we are. We've got to stop it. I can't let Nelly find out I'm sleeping with her grand father. We can't let the rest of the family find out."

He ran both hands down over his face. "I know . . ." he whispered. He reached for her hands. "Linda, I might have killed myself if it hadn't been for you."

"No. You wouldn't have."

"I might have. I'd give anything in the world if—"

"People would hate us. My parents, to start with. I mean, they'd *hate* us, Jack."

He sighed and nodded in reluctant agreement.

"That's why I've got to find someplace else to live. I'm not going back to Guy, for damned sure. I—"

"Hold on a minute," he interrupted. "You don't need to find a place to live. You live here. *I'll* move out."

"You can't do that."

"I can. Think of the problems it solves. I'll live in the city. I don't want to live in Greenwich anyway. Not now. Still . . . this is the family home. I'm reluctant to sell it. When Joni or LJ or Liz comes home, this place should be here for them. And Kathleen, too—I mean Sara. This house is also home to Priscilla. She's been with us more than twenty years. I'll move into the brownstone. I'll take a few personal things, and—Linda! Do it! Make this your home, for you and Nelly. I'll come out from time to time. And we don't need to—"

"Yes, we do. And we will. Occasionally. But we need to find other people. Both of us do." She kissed him. "I love you, Jack," she whispered. "In all the ways it's possible to love someone."

"I love you, too, Linda—in all the good ways."

Three

AT JONI'S REQUEST, Mo Morris had tried to find film work for Sara. When he did not succeed, he offered her a job in his office. To everyone's surprise, including hers, she fit in well and learned the business rapidly. Six months after she joined his agency, Mo had new business cards printed:

THE MO MORRIS AGENCY

Mo Morris, ***President***

Samuel Friden Peter Dole Sara Lehrer

Offices in Los Angeles, New York, London

Mo was seventy-five years old and was beginning to let his junior partners take on more of the responsibilities of the agency. Friden should have inherited a big client like Joni Lear, but Mo knew she would want her half sister to represent her if possible. He kept his own hand on Joni's career, but he let Sara take on some of the nuts-and-bolts work.

Sara proved to have a fine eye for small clauses in contracts. Independent producers, including stars producing their own films, had a penchant for departing from standard contracts and writing contracts of their own, with unusual clauses that were often not to the actors' or directors' advantage. It was the agent's job to spot these things—and Sara did.

Though she liked her new name, she stopped pursuing her conversion to Judaism. She began to spend time with a young writer named Brent Creighton. She surrendered her virginity to him, and he introduced her to a commune, where she learned to smoke pot and socialize in the nude.

Four

Joni won her Academy Award at last, for her role as Norma in the film adaptation of Jason Maxwell's novel. In addition she won the New York Film Critics Award and the Golden Globe Award.

Jack made his first major public appearance since Anne's death at the Academy Awards ceremony. Joni had promised him he would escort a famous actress that night, and with the help of Mo Morris she arranged a date for him. Beaming, he emerged from his limousine, then extended his hand to help Ava Gardner out into the glare of camera lights. She accompanied him, too, to the triumphant supper where Joni clutched her Oscar and received the homage of two hundred guests.

Sara was there, with Brent Creighton. In a crowd where every woman was a spectacle, or meant to be, she attracted attention for her fresh beauty and for her dress: a simple sheath of thin red silk, under which she very clearly was wearing nothing at all. She wore only one piece of jewelry, a diamond-studded bracelet that had been Anne's.

Liz was also there. She had flown to Los Angeles with her father on a company jet. She was escorted by her brother. LJ had been chosen All-American and had signed a contract to play professional football for the Miami Dolphins. Liz detested him, but she had to admit it was glamorous to be escorted by a looming hulk of All-American football player. She was nineteen years old and did not pretend to compete for attention in the Academy Awards crowd. She wore a silver lamé dress that attracted admiring glances for its bold front and back décolletage.

Linda too had arrived on the LCI jet. In her form-fitting beaded black dress, with dark sheer stockings and black shoes, she was stunning.

After the supper, at two o'clock in the morning, Jack

assembled the family in his suite at the Beverly Hilton—just the family, none of the dates or escorts..

He raised a glass of champagne. "Joni . . ." he said quietly. "We are all proud of you. My children are achievers, all of them. If only—" He paused and bit his lower lip. "If only John and Anne could be here. . . . And, Joni— Even Kimberly. She'd be proud of you."

Five 1970

CURT FREDERICK was as bored in Arizona as Jack had predicted he would be. When Jack suggested he come back to New York and do a monthly interview show, Curt talked it over with Betsy, and they agreed. He would have to spend no more than a week or ten days in New York each month. Jack invited Curt and Betsy to stay in the Greenwich house whenever they came east.

Linda was glad to have the Fredericks in the house for a week or so each month. She put them in the master bedroom suite, knowing Jack would not object—and knowing *he* would not use it. He came out two or three nights whenever they were visiting.

Each hour-long show featured two live interviews. A variety of people were happy to be interviewed by Curt Frederick. He still had a worldwide reputation as a giant of broadcast journalism. President Nixon not only agreed to be interviewed, but came to New York for the purpose. Former Texas governor John Connally appeared and talked about being in the car with President Kennedy on November 22, 1963. Israeli defense minister Moshe Dayan came to the studio and answered Curt's questions. Among other showbiz personalities, Dinah Shore, Ingrid Bergman, and Marlene Dietrich sat before the cameras and chatted with Curt Frederick.

One evening in Greenwich, Jack offered Curt a suggestion. Curt leaped at it.

On the evening of Wednesday, April 22, the two guests on his show were Averell Harriman and Jason Maxwell.

Harriman was, of course, smooth, suave, and statesmanlike. Everyone expected that Jason, in the second half hour, would offer a dramatic contrast.

Jack sat down in the greenroom where guests waited to go on. Jason had been made up—that is, he had been slightly dusted with powder—and was ready for the cameras, but he was tense with nervous energy.

"I'm gonna have a Scotch, Jason. Join me?"

"Well, maybe one."

"One Scotch. You got it."

Jason sat staring at the ceiling, nervously rubbing his hands together as Jack poured their drinks. He did not notice that Jack took a small glass vial from his jacket pocket, shook it, then poured it into a glass. He poured a generous shot of Scotch over it and added ice.

"Here y' go," he said to Jason as he handed him the glass. He returned to the little bar and poured Scotch over ice for himself. "Cheers!"

Jack tipped back his glass and took his drink all at once. Jason frowned but did the same.

"Well. We *could* have one more," Jack said. "Two little drinks before you go on—"

Jason nodded. "The problem, you know, is that authors on talk shows usually don't have anything much to say. We pour all we have out on the page."

"You used to keep Anne and me in stitches with your stories."

"But I can't tell those stories on television." He glanced up at the monitor, where Averell Harriman was solemnly answering some question put to him by Curt.

"Tell about your new book. What's it gonna be called?"

"Haven't figured that out yet," Jason said as he downed his second Scotch. "Tha's th' hardest part about writing a book: thinkin' up a . . . *title.*"

"You want one more? A little one?" Jack asked.

"Jus' a li'l one."

Jack was less generous with the third one. He didn't want Jason to pass out before he went before the cameras.

A young woman knocked on the door and said, "Three minutes, Mr. Maxwell!"

Jason straightened his tie and ran a brush over his hair. The director came for him, and they went out into the studio.

Jack picked up Jason's glass with a handkerchief. He took it in the bathroom and rinsed it out. He returned it to the room and poured a tablespoonful of Scotch over two ice cubes. Back in the bathroom he took the little vial from his pocket, put in on his handkerchief, and stepped on it. He flushed the shards of glass down the toilet, together with the tiny plastic cap.

Jason did not stagger into the broadcast studio. He walked to the chair assigned to him and sat down. He wriggled as though it tickled when the sound technician clipped a microphone on his lapel and ran the wire under his jacket and out the back.

"Our second guest this evening is Pulitzer Prize–winning novelist Jason Maxwell. His credits include the novel *Norma*. Joni Lear, playing the title role, won an Academy Award for best actress. Mr. Maxwell, Miss Lear has personally asked me to thank you for the wonderful role you wrote for her."

Jason grinned and nodded. "An' I never even slept with her," he said and then laughed.

"You *have* met her, though?"

"You bet! An' lemme tell ya. Till you've seen tits like hers, you haven' seen tits."

Curt changed the subject. "It is said of you, Mr. Maxwell, that your novels are romans à clef, which is to say that your characters are based on real people. I suppose everyone has guessed who Norma was. But do you want to say?"

Jason pursed his lips and nodded. "Sure. Nnnnorma Jean. Mara-muh. Maremem *Mum-ROE!*"

"Does your character Norma accurately reflect the real Marilyn Monroe?"

"Why not? Idn't it?"

"Mr. Maxwell, it has been suggested that you don't write your novels and stories, that they are in fact written by your cousin Gladys Maxwell. Is there any truth to that?"

"Gladys cou'nt write a letter!"

"Then who wrote *her* novel? It's been well received. Did *you* write it?"

Jason shook his head. "I never even *slept* with Glad—Glad-uss."

"I suppose not, since she's your cousin."

Jason began to nod rhythmically. His mouth hung open. "Well . . . Pull th' curtain of *decentness!* De—"

"Mr. Maxwell, don't you feel well?"

The camera was not able to turn away fast enough to avoid sending out over the whole network the image of Jason Maxwell vomiting.

"We'll take a commercial break," Curt said loftily.

THIRTY-SEVEN

One 1970

AFTER TWENTY-ONE SEASONS *The Sally Allen Show* went off the air. The American public seemed to have lost its taste for variety shows. Sally was not upset. She was fifty years old, and a little long in the tooth, she thought, for dancing in tights and singing. Even so, Jack was not about to lose her as a talent. He offered to star her in a picture to be made by Carlton House Productions. Since the soundstages were all committed to television production, Jack told Len, who would write the script, to set the entire film on location. He did. He wrote a touching comedy set in a beach house at Malibu. It needed some doctoring, though, and Sara suggested Brent Creighton. The resulting script was a masterpiece. It was a love story about two couples, and Mo Morris offered Joni for the second female lead.

Dick Painter, with all his faults and ambition, had been a first-class programmer. In the three seasons since his departure, the network had lost market share. Mary Carson suggested bringing him back. Jack adamantly refused. He did, though, acknowledge the necessity of finding another programmer attuned to what he insisted was the deteriorating taste of the American public. Mary raided CBS and brought over one of their vice presidents, Ted Wellman. A believer in what Jack called small-minded shows—sitcoms and cop sagas—Wellman soon had LCI's ratings climbing. Jack shook his head and kept his peace. He *still* didn't think Jack Benny was funny.

Two

IN ONE SENSE Jack was a lonely man. In another sense he wasn't.

Though he stopped sleeping regularly with Linda, she never ceased to welcome him. He brought Rebecca Murphy down from Boston to spend occasional weekends with him in Manhattan. These women—his thirty-five-year-old daughter-in-law and the fifty-year-old investigator—gave him their sympathy and affection, but it was plain that neither of them would become the third Mrs. Lear, if indeed there was going to be a third Mrs. Lear. Gossip columns suggested there would be, but Jack had no intention of marrying again.

In the summer of 1970 he began to see a woman the columnists immediately fastened on as the successor to Kimberly and Anne.

Valerie Latham Field was heir to a quarter of the Latham fortune and half of the estate left by her late husband Ralph Wiggams Field, which made her a multimillionaire. In the stuffy tradition of the more conservative society pages she was called Mrs. Latham Field. Otherwise she was known as Val.

Every summer a charity match was played on a polo field in Greenwich. The sponsors served a champagne luncheon under a tent, and the wealthiest and most notable people in the town gathered.

Jack and Anne had attended for many years. In 1969 he hadn't gone. In 1970 Linda urged him to. So, on a Sunny Sunday afternoon he appeared under the big tent, with Linda on his arm.

Val was selling raffle tickets and so was circulating through the crowd. They had met before, several times. "Jack," she said, "I'm glad to see you."

"Val, this is my daughter-in-law, Linda."

"Oh, yes," said Val. "Make Jack buy you lots of tickets. This necklace is one of the prizes."

Val was wearing a spectacular emerald-and-diamond necklace. At fifty-six, she had a few small wrinkles at her throat, which the necklace covered nicely. She also wore diamond earrings and a diamond-studded bracelet. Her blond hair stood out in a bouffant style. Her face was long and thin. Her mouth was wide. She was a handsome woman, and she was dressed handsomely in an off-white linen jacket and a burnt-orange skirt, not quite mini but well above her knees. She was obviously a woman who was content with herself and who didn't look to anyone else for approval.

Jack bought a dozen raffle tickets at fifty dollars apiece. He gave them to Linda, and during the drawing she won the necklace.

Beaming, Val took off the necklace and fastened it around Linda's neck, as everyone applauded.

Val sat down beside Jack. They began to chat and laugh. That was all it took for the rumors to start. Before the afternoon was over, there was talk under the tent that Valerie Latham Field and Jack Lear were a pair.

He didn't know. But Val was sensitive to these things and guessed what was being said. It amused her. When he asked her to dinner, she promptly agreed. They left the tent, Linda on one arm Val, on the other.

Three

THEY SAW EACH OTHER five times in August, usually for dinner, though once he took her to a baseball game at Yankee Stadium. He decided to fly to Los Angeles in September, to see how things were going on the location at Malibu, and he asked Val to come with him.

It was aboard a company jet forty thousand feet above the Mississippi River that Jack kissed Val for the first time. He'd been under no compulsion to press her—after all, he could sleep with Linda or Rebecca whenever he wanted to—and had allowed the relationship to develop slowly. She was a woman of presence and dignity, he felt, and to have pawed at her would have driven her away, for sure. They had discovered they shared certain interests. He admired her and enjoyed her company but was not certain he felt romantically inclined toward her.

Then on the plane he was driven by a sudden impulse to draw her into his arms and kiss her.

She put her arms around him and participated in the kiss. "I hope we won't be sorry about that," she said quietly.

They sat close together, and Jack kept his arm around her, but they did not kiss again during the flight.

He asked her if she would mind sharing his two-bedroom suite. She smiled and shrugged.

They went on the set and watched a shoot. Early in the evening they went to dinner with Joni, David, Sara, and Brent. At the end of a pleasant day they retired to their suite.

As Val opened the door to her bedroom, Jack kissed her again. She returned his kiss by gently nibbling on his lips. She relaxed in his arms.

"Jack . . . this is kind of silly, isn't it?" she whispered, pointing at the doors to the two bedrooms. She pushed her own door wide open. "Come on in."

Val was unique. At least she was in *his* experience. She undressed. She lay back on the bed and waited for him. She welcomed him into her. With her eyes wide open, studying his face, showing no particular expression on her own, she thrust upward to meet his downward thrusts. She grunted a few times, and her breathing became heavier; otherwise she stared into his eyes and smiled faintly until she felt him come, when her smile broadened and she used her arms to draw him down on her. He was reluctant to let all his weight settle on her, but she pulled him down and seemed to luxuriate in being pinned beneath him.

She reached up and tousled his hair. "So far, so good," she said. "Monsieur Le Maître, you live up to your billing."

"Oh no, Val! I'm not Le Maître."

"Of course you are. How'd you manage to get that slimy little creep so drunk before he went on the air? Nembutal?"

Four 1971

WHEN THE FAMILY GATHERED on St. Croix between Christmas and New Year's, Val was there. She was the only one in the party who could water-ski. Jack tried but consistently went over on his face.

When the rest of the group left the island, Jack and Val flew to New Hampshire, where she owned a ski lodge. Jack did not ski, but she did and enjoyed it exuberantly. She skated, too.

Back in Greenwich in the spring, she introduced him to horseback riding. That he could do, but he could not conceal from her the fact that he did not enjoy it. When she took a fence, Jack would not even try it. Then came sailing. Val had friends who owned a sloop, and she was a skilled crewman. Jack tried. He pulled on the ropes as they told him to do, but he didn't understand what he was doing or why and was not a quick study. What was more, he didn't play golf.

Val placed a great deal of emphasis on outdoor sports. But she didn't play bridge. Jack had not played much in recent years, but he was still a formidable bridge player. People in Val's circle knew of his prowess at the table. Aboard the sloop, while Val and her closest friends were on deck working the sails, Jack and three others would sit at a table in the cabin and contentedly play bridge. That annoyed Val.

Their sex was good. She was adventuresome and let him introduce her to tricks she insisted she'd never tried before. But by the time they had been seeing each other for a year, they had to accept the fact that they were not compatible enough to commit themselves to each other. He continued to take her to dinner from time to time, and she slept with him in Manhattan every now and then. But the occasions occurred less and less frequently.

Five

CAP DURENBERGER retired when he turned eighty-one. The banker Joseph Freeman also retired. To replace them, the stockholders elected Billy Bob Cotton and Ted Wellman. Dr. Friedrich Loewenstein had earlier been elected to replace Painter.

In the hallway late one afternoon Jack spotted Cathy McCormack. He walked up to her. "Didn't I fire you?"

"Yes, sir," she said. "Five years ago."

"And . . . ?"

"Mrs. Carson was kind enough to bring me back."

"Come in my office."

Cathy sat down in Jack's office. She still wore the uniform Dick Painter had required of her: white blouse, black skirt. Jack tried to remember how old she was—approaching sixty, he imagined.

"I fired you because Dick Painter was a liar, a cheat, and a thief. And you were his woman, in every way."

She nodded. "Yes. I was. I haven't seen him since the day you locked him out of the building. He had a few things in my apartment. He didn't even come for them."

"So Mrs. Carson—"

"Took pity on me, Mr. Lear. I was out of work again. Too old."

"Too old?"

"Yes, sir."

"Where's your loyalty now, Miss McCormack?"

"My loyalty has always been to the person I worked for. When I worked for Dick Painter—"

"But you didn't just work for him."

She lowered her eyes. "No."

"He abandoned you."

"Probably he didn't have any choice. He thought he might go to jail."

"You had another job, and they let you go because they said you were too old?"

"As God is my witness, sir, there was no other reason."

Jack stared at her. "I didn't mean to put you on the street, Cathy. You impressed me as a hell of a competent secretary, and I thought you'd find another job easily enough."

She shook her head. "It *wasn't* easy."

"What are you doing here?"

She lowered her eyes again. "I'm in the secretarial pool."

"Jesus . . ." He glanced at his watch. "Well, you were probably leaving. Would you like to have a drink somewhere?"

Cathy nodded. "Yes, sir."

She was happy to have the drink in his apartment. He took her to dinner at the Quilted Giraffe. She spent the night with him.

Six weeks later his secretary of ten years took the early retirement she had long ago been offered, and he gave the job to Cathy McCormack.

Six 1972

He took Cathy with him to St. Croix after Christmas. She had not been at the Greenwich house at Christmas, and the family was more than a little surprised by her. She could have hardly been more different from Valerie Latham Field, who had accompanied Jack the year before. Still daring to wear a bikini—actually wearing one because Jack had urged her to—Cathy was conspicuously mature. She was intelligent and soft-spoken, but she was his secretary, and it was all too obvious why she was traveling with him.

The only member of the Jack's family who did not join him in St. Croix was LJ. The Miami Dolphins were in the American Conference playoffs. He had flown home for a short visit at Christmas, and had brought with him a Miami cheerleader named Gloria, a vapid teenager with a sumptuous figure. Liz called her "the chippy."

LJ had not been able to resist swaggering around his family. The Dolphins were having a highly successful season, and Howard Cosell had called him one of the finest tight ends in football.

Liz continued to despise her brother. She would graduate from Princeton in the spring and had been admitted to Harvard Law. She was happy with the challenge and looked forward to practicing law or perhaps teaching it. She slept regularly with a young man from Richmond but had not met his family or brought him to meet hers. When she did decide to bring her friend home, she hoped her hulking jock brother would not be there.

Joni's daughter, Michelle, was six. She knew David was her father and called him Daddy. She was not yet old enough to suffer any embarrassment from the fact that her father and mother were not married. Jack urged them to marry, for Michelle's sake.

During that week on St. Croix, Joni observed that her father was reasonably content. He had not gotten over the death of Anne; she knew he never would, but at least he had found life again. Joni learned something surprising about him: that at this stage of his life he cherished contentment. He would be sixty-six this year. Business would offer him challenges enough. He didn't need any others in his personal life. Joni understood that the problem with Val had been that she was a challenge to him. Cathy, little as Joni might esteem her, made her father happy because she offered no challenge. Well, if that was what he wanted . . . Still, Joni couldn't help thinking that he was too young to stagnate. Anne would never have allowed it.

Seven

IN APRIL, Douglas Humphrey died at the age of eighty-five. Mary Carson inherited the bulk of his estate, including, of course, his stock in Lear Communications, Incorporated. Shortly after her father's death she invited Jack to join her for dinner in her Manhattan apartment. They ought to discuss the company, she said—the two of them, alone.

Whether to make an unusual statement or because it reflected her taste, Mary Carson had decorated her Manhattan apartment in Southwestern style, with wool rugs woven by Indians, tall cacti in tubs, and couch and chairs covered in tan leather. Jack recognized a large painting on her living room wall as a Georgia O'Keeffe.

Mary was dressed as she had been in the office that afternoon: in a rose-colored mini-dress accented with silver buttons. She pointed to a chair.

"Scotch?" Mary asked.

"Please."

Mary went to the kitchen to pour the drinks. She returned with their glasses and a silver tray of hors d'oeuvres.

"You didn't know my father very well," she said to Jack. "He was an infantry captain in the First World War. He was wounded and also decorated. As soon as he got home he married, then fathered my brother Doug. Doug's mother died in 1924. Dad married *my* mother in 1926, and I came along in 1927. Doug, too, was an infantry captain. He died on Omaha Beach. Dad was shattered. Then my mother died shortly before you met him. My father made millions, but his life was filled with tragedy and disappointment."

"I told him he was lucky he had you."

Jack took a swallow of Scotch and reached for an hors d'oeuvre.

"Before we go to dinner, let's talk business and have it out of the way," said Mary Carson crisply. "You're sixty-six years old. You're like my father; you don't have an heir. Oh, you have wonderful children, but you don't have one who's going to succeed you as head of LCI. Am I right?"

"Well, I suppose you're right. My children aren't likely to *want* to succeed me in the company."

Mary put a hand on his left hand. "Well, *I do,*" she said bluntly. "Not until you're ready. Not until you *want* to retire. But I'm twenty-one years younger than you are. I'd like to work closely with you, Jack, so that when the time comes we can achieve an efficient transition."

He nodded. "I haven't thought much about retiring."

"Of course not. We're not talking about soon. But eventually . . . What do you say?"

"I can't think of any reason to say no."

"I want to be executive vice president, clearly understood to be your Number Two. Number *Two.* For sure. Okay?"

"Again, I can't think of a reason to say no."

"Well, I'm going to give you a reason, Jack," she said quietly. She lowered her eyes and seemed to be struggling for self-control. "I'm going to tell you something in confidence. Complete confidence. Okay?"

"Sure."

"You remember my daughter, Emily, She was nine, I think, when you first met her. She was in my father's pool." Mary smiled faintly. "She was nude."

"And not embarrassed," said Jack.

Mary nodded. "Well . . . that little girl is grown up now. And she's in prison. She's serving a five- to ten-year sentence in the federal reformatory for women at Alderson, West Virginia. Once a month I fly to White Sulphur and visit her."

"My God! Why?"

"Because I'm a bad mother, probably. I kept her under terribly tight rein. So she ran away. She got hooked on heroin. She became a revolutionary, a member of the Weather Underground. So there's a horrible skeleton in the closet of your would-be executive vice president."

Jack shook his head. "You never told me, Mary. I never heard about it." He assured her. "Of course, if it ever comes up, I'll say I knew all about it and appointed you anyway."

"Thank you, Jack."

THIRTY-EIGHT

One 1972

On the evening of Friday, November 10, 1972, Jack suffered a heart attack over dinner with Mary Carson at Lutèce. He collapsed and was taken to Columbia Presbyterian Hospital.

For the first twenty-four hours the doctors could assure no one that he would survive. Mary Carson sent an LCI jet to Los Angeles to pick up Joni and Sara and a Beech twin to Boston for Liz. The Dolphins were in the middle of an undefeated season, and LJ sent word that he would fly to New York after Sunday's game.

For two days Jack lay flat on his back, colorless, sedated, breathing oxygen from tubes in his nostrils. Only on Sunday did he recognize Joni and squeeze her hand.

On Monday, December 11, he was transported by ambulance to his home in Greenwich, where he would be attended by round-the-clock nurses. Except for LJ, whose undefeated season was continuing, the family came and filled the house.

The faithful Priscilla put up two Christmas trees, a cut one in the living room and a live one by the swimming pool. She saw to it that the temperature was raised in the pool, because Jack's cardiologist recommended that he float in a life jacket and do a little gentle exercise.

Jack sat in the greenhouse much of the time, happy to watch Joni's little Michelle paddle in the water. Linda's daughter, Nelly, was fifteen, and she brought her cello out to the greenhouse and played Christmas carols for her grandfather.

Jack had lost twenty pounds and looked gaunt. His skin was pale. But Dr. Philip Hagan, his New York cardiologist, insisted he was recovering well. The week before Christmas, Dr. Hagan took him to Greenwich Hospital for a more complete examination by local cardiologists, and they concurred that he had suffered relatively little permanent damage.

Mary Carson knelt by Jack's chaise longue beside the pool and kissed the palm of his hand. "Not yet, for Christ's sake!" she whispered. "I want your job, but not fuckin' *yet!*"

Jack nodded. "No. Not fuckin' yet. Bet on it!"

LJ came for three days at Christmas. He brought Gloria again. Liz sneered, but Jack shook his head and quietly told her he was glad to have Gloria in the swimming pool—the chippy in her iridescent green thong bikini. "She gives me an erection," he whispered, "and I'm damned glad to know I *can* have one."

Dr. Hagan vetoed the annual visit to St. Croix. He didn't want Jack flying yet, and he wasn't confident of the hospitals there. He suggested that Jack travel by train to a beach town in Florida.

Newly retired Mickey Sullivan knew of a waterfront house in Deerfield Beach that could be leased. It was big enough so that the also-retired Cap Durenberger and his wife, Naomi, could move in and be alert companions during Jack's stay. What was more, the house had a pool and a room for Joni or Sara.

Jack agreed. He left on an Amtrak train on January 10. Linda rode with him. Her father, now Admiral Hogan, met her in Fort Lauderdale, and she went with him to Pensacola for a few days. Mickey and Cap drove Jack to Deerfield Beach.

He sat on the beach as he had sat on the beach on St. Croix after Anne died, staring out to sea, no longer mourning but wondering what he had left of life. Hemingway had written that when a man loses his optimism it is time to go.

A man came to him there on the beach who took away more of his optimism—or maybe, as he thought about it, gave him new optimism.

Junius Grotius, as he introduced himself, was a wizened man of more than seventy years, wearing an odd flowered sport shirt, slacks, and a straw hat. He sat down in the sand and spoke to Jack in a strange, melodious accent.

He came quickly to his point. "I will not take much of your time. You may have heard my name—"

"I have heard your name, Mr. Grotius."

"Then you know I am president of Wyncherly-DeVere, Limited."

Jack did know. WDV was a multinational communications conglomerate, owner of television and radio facilities, newspapers, magazines, two wire services, and other assets.

"I hope I am not being ghoulish to come to you when you have just been ill," said Grotius . "But at such times a man necessarily thinks about changes, perhaps about lightening his load of responsibilities and moving a little aside so as to enjoy more fully what he has earned."

"I am not quite ready to sell, Mr. Grotius ."

Grotius nodded. "I didn't expect you would be. But let us resolve to keep in touch. We may wish to explore many alternatives. We may find one that will be attractive to you."

Jack smiled. "Yes. Let's do keep in touch. But I am not quite ready to think of retiring. I haven't lost *all* my optimism yet."

Two 1973

JACK LEAR was not the only one who had lost his optimism in the winter of 1973. Richard Nixon had just been handily reelected President of the United States. To many Americans, Nixon and his administration represented a newly developing mean-spiritedness that was poisoning America. Many Beltway insiders left Washington for a while because they could not face the rites that would attend the second inauguration.

One of those who had fled the capital was New Jersey Congresswoman Diane Hechler. She represented the Sixteenth District, which comprised a number of suburban counties west of metropolitan New Jersey. Although she was a Republican, she despised Richard Nixon. She excused herself from everything associated with the inauguration by pleading that she was suffering persistent bronchitis and had been told to spend some time in the sun.

She was spending the month in the beach house of a family from her district. It was a hundred yards or so south of the house Jack had leased. She walked past him on the beach half a dozen times, then one morning stopped and said hello.

"You're Jack Lear, aren't you? Lear Communications?"

He stood. "Yes, and I understand you are Representative Diane Hechler."

"Oh, sit back down," she said. "Relax. That's why we're in this ghastly place, isn't it? So we can relax."

He laughed. " 'Ghastly.' Thank God I'm not the only one who thinks so."

She sat down beside him. The waves running up the sand reached their toes. Jack had been thinking of moving back, but he guessed this woman would let the water run up around her. Even before she had stopped to speak to him, he had seen in her a defiant, adventuresome spirit. It was in the way she walked with her shoulders set, in the way she set her pace on the sand.

She was forty-seven years old, tall and thin, though her breasts filled the top of her swimsuit. He guessed her hair was coiffed and frosted by a professional. Her red bikini showed little skin south of her navel and nothing of her butt.

"I read about your cardiac and know why you're here," she said. "I'm sorry, but I know more about you than you could possibly know about me."

"Well, let me see," said Jack. "I know that you're serving your umpteenth term in the House—"

"Fourth."

"Fourth. Well, I knew it was not your first. And I believe you're a Republican."

"An *independent* Republican."

"The very best kind. And . . . And I guess I do run out of information right about there."

"I'm in my forties," she said. "I have never been married and have no children. I am a lawyer as well as a politician, and I like baseball and football. I love to visit art galleries but can't stand sitting quietly and fidgeting through a concert. I don't mind walking on the beach for an hour or so, but I'm looking forward to a nap, followed by a civilized cocktail hour and a nice dinner."

Three

THEY SAT AT A TABLE facing a broad window that overlooked the angry surf pounding hard on the sand of a Fort Lauderdale beach, sending water up to the pilings that supported the restaurant.

Diane drank a dry Beefeater martini, and Jack drank Scotch.

They talked about the politics of the 1970s. Jack was surprised by some of her opinions and was forced to acknowledge he had never given enough attention to some of the issues she raised. She spoke of the Dolphins' undefeated season and said she'd seen LJ on television. Jack told her LJ would be coming to Deerfield Beach to visit, after the Super Bowl, and Diane expressed regret that she wouldn't get to meet him because she would be back in Washington by then.

She swallowed the last of her martini and signaled the waiter. She was wearing a simple white off-the-shoulder dress that showed off her cleavage. The matching jacket was on the back of the chair. "Jack," she said. "I'd like to go out fishing. Want to go?"

"How?"

"Oh, we charter a boat with a captain and a deckhand and head out to the Gulf Stream to see what we can hook. I've never done it, and it would relieve the boredom of ten days in Florida."

Jack sighed. "I'm not sure how my cardiologist would like it."

"Fuck your cardiologist," she said with a big smile. "Look, Jack, life is to be cherished, for sure. But life is to be enjoyed, too. It's not to be hoarded like a miser's money. What you want to do? Stop living so you can keep on living?"

Jack nodded. "My wife Anne knew for almost three

years that she was dying. She kept it from us and lived her life as if it wasn't happening, until almost the last."

His lips and chin stiffened, and he stopped, holding back tears. Diane touched his hand.

"When can we get this boat?" he whispered.

Four

THE BOAT RUMBLED out of the inlet at eight-thirty the next morning. Diane had chosen it: a rugged, unglamorous little boat with a sixty-year-old captain and a teenage deckhand. It was painted white with light-blue trim, and the deck was not varnished but painted. One icebox was filled with bait, another with beer and sandwiches. They wore what they had been told to wear: knit shirts with long sleeves to protect their arms from the sun, and hats with wide brims to protect their foreheads and necks.

The captain gave Jack and Diane brief instructions on how to handle a fish if they got a strike. The boy baited their hooks and cast them overboard.

For an hour they trolled without a strike. Then Jack got the first strike. He reeled in a bonito about thirty inches long—not an exciting catch. The boy sliced off fillets for bait and threw the rest overboard.

Diane got a strike and pulled aboard a mackerel, another lackluster catch. The boy put it in the bait box. It was edible and would wind up on his family's table or on the captain's.

Diane and Jack popped beers. The captain changed course, chasing something he thought he saw in the water that would lead to fish. By now the coastline was out of sight.

Jack tossed his beer can overboard. A minute later he got a hard strike. The captain grabbed his pole and gave it a jerk to set the hook.

"Good'n," he said. "Y' got work to do. Ma'am, reel in so's the fish don't tangle lines with you."

It was more strenuous work than Jack had imagined. The fish broached, and he saw a big sailfish that was determined to fight the hook that was painfully lodged in its mouth. The boy took the wheel, and the captain stood anxiously beside Jack, instructing him on how to play the fish. It was arduous. Jack had to haul up on the pole, dragging the fish a few feet closer, then reel in line. Again and again. He began to sweat.

Diane unstrapped herself from her chair and came to stand behind Jack. She wiped the sweat from his forehead on the sleeve of her shirt.

He began to gasp for breath.

"Jack, maybe you ought to let the captain cut it loose."

He glanced up at her. His eyes were wide. "No way," he grunted. "This sumbitch's not gonna beat *me.*"

He fought the sailfish for half an hour. And defeated it. But it defeated him, too. Once it was aboard, he struggled out of the chair and dropped to his back on the deck, lying parallel to the fish. The captain screamed at the boy to head for home, throttles open.

"No," Jack muttered. "Just a little short of breath. It's okay. Be okay in two minutes. Diane hasn't caught hers yet."

She knelt over him and kissed him.

In the two minutes he had specified, Jack rose and sat in his chair. "Turn around," he said, pointing out to sea. "What's the matter? Never see an old man get tired before?"

The captain looked at Diane. She nodded. The captain told the boy to turn again. Diane took sandwiches and beers from the cooler and sat down on the deck beside Jack's chair. The captain measured the sailfish and announced it was six feet eleven inches long, by no means a record fish but a very respectable one for sure.

Jack did not put out a line again. He sat in his chair and watched Diane. She caught another bonito, then a five-foot barracuda that gave her a long struggle and was another very respectable catch.

In the middle of the afternoon they turned toward shore. The captain suggested that Jack and Diane get in out of the sun. They went inside the Spartan cabin and sat on a bunk where, seized by impulse, Jack threw his arms around Diane and kissed her hard. She had been seized by the same impulse and hugged him and returned his kiss.

"Oh, Jesus, lady," he muttered in her ear. "You know what? You've brought me back something I'd lost and needed bad."

"What's that?" she whispered.

"My optimism," he said. "You're a flowing spring of it. I can't tell you how much I appreciate it . . . appreciate *you.*"

Diane felt she could not stay in Florida beyond the end of January. Jack was supposed to stay through February. He summoned a corporate jet to the airport at Fort Lauderdale. On Thursday, February 1, it took off for Washington, carrying him and Diane. Before she left the plane at Washington, they kissed, and he promised her he would be back in Washington within two weeks.

Five

MARY CARSON called a meeting at the Petroleum Club in Houston. On an evening in March she sat down with Billy Bob Cotton and Raymond l'Enfant.

When they'd had drinks and had chatted socially for a few minutes, she asked a question: "Has either of you seen Jack Lear lately?"

"No, not since the heart attack," said Ray.

Billy Bob shook his head.

"Well, he was away from the office, away from the business, for three months. When his wife died, he was away longer than that. To be brutally honest, I think Jack has lost it. He's going to be sixty-seven this year, he's had a big heart attack, and he's looking over his shoulder for the Grim Reaper."

"I wish you wouldn't say that," said Billy Bob. "I'm gonna be sixty-five shortly myself."

"But you haven't had a major heart attack," Mary retorted. "What's more to the point, he's lost interest. If you want to face the truth, gentlemen, Jack Lear has never been wholly devoted to LCI. The fact is, he has always devoted too much of himself to outside interests."

"Carlton House," said Ray.

"Well, that and his personal life," said Mary. "Jason Maxwell didn't call him Le Maître for nothing. You know who he's sleeping with now? Cathy McCormack, Dick Painter's former secretary. Christ, she's sixty-two years old! I'm surprised he hasn't tried to hit on *me!*"

"Disappointed?" Ray asked with an amused smile.

"Sort of," she said, smiling as broadly as he was. "But he's away from the office a lot now for another reason. He's got a girlfriend. I mean, it looks like something serious. She's a congresswoman from New Jersey named Hechler. He flies a company plane to Washington twice a week."

"Why are we sitting here talking about this, Mary?" Billy Bob asked impatiently. "You asked us to come. You must have something in mind."

"I do. I think we had better start thinking of alternatives to Jack as CEO."

Billy Bob shook his head and frowned. "You mean, take the company away from him?"

"Keep him as chairman of the board. Let him have his office and perks. Give someone else day-to-day operational control."

" 'Someone else,' " said Ray. "Meaning you."

"A company cannot be run by someone who has less than complete devotion to it. A chief executive officer works fourteen hours a day. Jack Lear never has—not since I've known anything about LCI."

"Well, you'd have to outvote him in a stockholders' meeting."

"Each of you gentlemen owns 5 percent of the stock," she said. "My father left me 5 percent, and I've bought another 13 percent on the q.t. Those shares are not in my name, but I control them. I can vote 18 percent. You can vote 10 percent. Dick Painter still has the 1 percent he was given when he came to the company, and he'll be with us. That makes 29 percent, enough to control most companies—except a closely held one, which LCI is not."

"Don't forget that Jack has his own allies. Harrison Wolcott had 6 percent, which he left to Joni and Linda. Joni has bought 2 percent more. Frederick, Durenberger, Morrill, and Sullivan got stock bonuses way back when and still hold their shares—1 percent apiece, making another 4 percent likely to vote with Jack. Sally Allen owns 2 percent, and she probably figures she owes Jack something. Of course, he has 10 percent of his own. Have you added all that up?"

"Okay, 24 percent—which ain't as good as 29 percent. Besides which, we can pick up some proxies."

"So can he, and he's got a hell of a big name," Ray reminded her.

"Let me throw something else into the equation," said Mary. "I don't think Jack gives a damn, and I don't think he'll fight. All we have to do is toss him a bone so he'll save face, and he'll shrug and walk away. You can count on it."

Billy Bob shook his head. "I *wouldn't* count on it, Mary," he said. "Jack Lear's not the kind of man you can toss a bone to. He *built* the company. He built it from nothin'. He's not going to give it up."

Ray l'Enfant sighed audibly. "It'd be the end of an era," he said sadly.

"Everything comes to an end," said Mary. "Good things. Bad things."

THIRTY-NINE

One 1973

Joni held David's penis in her hand. "You know what I like about your cock?" she asked him.

"Not its size, I should imagine," he said. "It's nothing extraordinary."

She sucked his foreskin between her lips and ran her tongue over it. His shoulders stiffened, and he drew a loud, deep breath.

"I'm going to make a confession to you," she said. "Only two living people know this. This is how much I trust you. I like this cock because it's so much like the first one I ever saw, ever touched. You want to know whose that was?"

David raised an eyebrow skeptically. "Do I want to know?"

She lowered her head and ran her tongue over his scrotum. "I'm going to tell you. It was my brother's. He was like you. I like cocks that haven't been surgically mutilated—circumcised."

"*Your brother?*"

"My brother who was killed. I used to suck his cock all the time. You want to know why I sucked it? Because he got me pregnant doing it the other way. I had to have an abortion when I was fourteen years old."

"My God!"

"I loved him. He loved me. I mean, we loved each other *that* way, besides loving each other as brother and sister. But

I learned to suck cock at a very early age." Joni smiled. "Not a bad thing to learn. I may be the last big star who—"

"Don't kid yourself. I know it's not supposed to happen anymore. But the money and fame and glamour involved—"

"It's a matter of *power,* isn't it?" Joni suggested. "It happens everywhere, anywhere and everywhere." She shrugged. "I can't get hysterical about it. I wasn't *forced*. I was never forced or raped. It wasn't an ordeal for me."

"Humiliating," he suggested. "Debasing."

"The first time, yes."

"You've done it more than once?"

"Be realistic, David."

"Recently?"

"Not recently. Uh, change the subject. I'm going east for a few days. I hope you can come with me."

"Going anywhere with you is like going to heaven."

"We're going to a wedding. My father is getting married again."

"That's rather sudden, isn't it?"

"He says at his age you don't have time to diddle around."

Two

DIANE HECHLER was a surprise to everyone.

Kimberly and Anne had been exquisite beauties. Diane was an attractive woman but not one who would turn heads on the street. Her face was long and thin. Her eyes, under sleepy lids, were gray. Her mouth was wide, her lips narrow.

She was tall and tended to hold her chin so high that many people, on first meeting her, judged her haughty and formidable. A few minutes with her was enough to dispel that impression. She never lost an iota of her dignity, but she tempered it with a quick and earthy sense of humor.

The weekend before the wedding, most of the Lear family trekked to a New Jersey country club, where a hundred politicians and lawyers gathered at the cocktail hour to gape at the broadcasting tycoon who was marrying their representative to Congress.

"A hundred of us would have liked to do what you're doing," one politician told Jack. "She's jus' the greatest ol' gal in the world!"

Diane's parents greeted Jack with enthusiasm. William Hechler was an active trial lawyer, with the characteristic flamboyance of a successful trial lawyer. Diane had practiced in his firm until she went to Congress. Diane resembled her mother, a tall slender woman.

Diane's sister, Nelle Davidson, looked nothing like her mother. She was three years older than Diane, and now that her children were grown, she was chiefly a country-club drinker.

"Should have been here twenty years ago," the same politician said to Jack with a big grin. "Nelle was on the fourteenth tee. She had on these skimpy shorts and a halter. She took one hell of a swing, and her tits popped out! She didn't know it. She just watched her ball and watched her ball. Not one of the guys around the fourteenth tee had any idea where her ball went, I can promise you!"

Nelle's son, George, it turned out, was casually acquainted with Liz Lear. They had seen each other in the library at Harvard Law. He was a year ahead of her. He attached himself to her as though it had been arranged in advance that he would be her date for the evening.

The wedding presents from New Jersey were on display in a room adjacent to the dining room. Diane's parents' gift was a silver-gray Mercedes-Benz sedan that was parked outside. The Republican Party of her district gave a set of sterling silver. President and Mrs. Nixon sent a sterling creamer and sugar engraved with the Great Seal of the United States.

The Lear family attracted reporters and cameramen to the country club. Reporters read the cards and made notes.

Joni was swarmed by reporters, one of whom had the temerity to ask who pretty, seven-year-old Michelle was. She answered, "None of your fuckin' business."

Joni and even her father were eclipsed by the big football star, LJ Lear, who still toted around the cheerleader named Gloria. LJ had a keen instinct for public relations, and Gloria carried a portfolio of glossy photographs that LJ would sign at the least suggestion.

Liz still despised him. She was pleased to see that George made no effort to meet him.

After the cocktail reception the families gathered in a private dining room. Diane had forbidden speeches, even toasts, and had put place cards on the table in order to mix the two groups. Observant, she had slipped into the dining room just before dinner and moved George's card to a place beside Liz.

Just before midnight George knocked discreetly on Liz's door at the motel where the Lears were staying. She let him in. He left at six the next morning.

Three

THE WEDDING was at eleven-thirty on Thursday morning, April 12, in the living room of the house in Greenwich. The minister of the Diamond Hill Methodist Church conducted the ceremony. Diane wore a knee-length white silk brocade dress and carried a tiny bouquet of white flowers. After the brief ceremony, the families and a few friends and neighbors shared a champagne brunch. Not long after one that afternoon Jack and Diane were driven to Westchester Airport where a company jet took off for San Francisco. They would spend their wedding night at the Fairmont Hotel and in the morning catch their flight to Tokyo. Their wedding trip would include Tokyo, Hong Kong, Bangkok, Tahiti, Hawaii, and a return visit to San Francisco.

They had a light dinner delivered to their suite. As they ate and drank a little wine, they exchanged caresses and knowing smiles—thinking of the bed that awaited them.

Diane had told him she was a virgin. At forty-seven, she had never been to bed with a man. They had talked about it over dinners and while traveling. She had been unwilling, she'd explained, to do it casually and had never met an unattached man she wanted to commit herself to. She had never made any determination not to have sex, but occasions for it had slipped by year after year.

Jack had never done more than hold her and kiss her. He had never undressed her. He had never touched her breasts or her legs. He wondered how she would react when he did.

When they had finished their dinner she asked him to stay in the living room while she went to the bedroom to change. "My sister helped me pick out a nightgown. I hope it's—"

While she was in the bedroom, Jack wheeled the dinner cart out into the hall, keeping only the ice bucket and some champagne.

Diane opened the bedroom door. A white silk lace-trimmed bra lifted her breasts. A lustrous white silk gown attached to the bra fell smoothly to her ankles—but only to either side, because a long wedge of sheer material, beginning at the center of the bra and widening below, displayed all of her from her breasts to her ankles.

She paused in the doorway and smiled at him. It was the first time he had ever seen Diane short on confidence. He realized that in a sense he had married the equivalent of a teenage girl. She had never shown herself to a man before and was not sure how he would like her. What was more, she was apprehensive about what was going to happen next.

"You are gorgeous," he said quietly. "The nightgown is beautiful. Perfect." He stood and stepped toward her. "I'm the most fortunate man in the world, and I hope you have some idea of how much I love you."

When she saw his penis she said it was the first one she had ever seen. She'd looked at pictures, of course, but had been unable to gain a sense of how big her husband's organ would be.

"Oooh!" she whispered. "That goes inside me? All of it?"

Jack grinned. "When it's all in, you'll frown and say, 'Is that all there is?' "

She managed a nervous little laugh.

After they had hugged and kissed a few minutes more, he helped her out of her nightgown. As he stared at her naked body, Diane actually blushed.

She was painfully self-conscious about her breasts, which were big and soft. Freed from the confines of a brassiere, they hung like two soft grapefruits almost to her lowest ribs. Jack bent forward and kissed each nipple, then lifted and squeezed each breast. He murmured appreciatively.

He put a hand between her legs and rubbed her pubes.

She grunted and closed her eyes. She was quite dry, and when they lay down together on the bed he continued to stroke her gently there, inserting a finger just a little, until her fluids came and made her slippery

He encouraged her to lie on her back and spread her legs. He used his penis as he had used his finger, to stroke and stimulate her. When he judged she was ready he paused and smiled at her, as if to let her say no if she was not ready. She didn't, and he pressed himself into her. She stiffened. She sighed then and relaxed, and he gently pushed in until their bellies touched.

At first she lay passive with her eyes closed, accepting him, learning; but a little later she began to squirm and to spread her legs wider and welcome him in deeper. He had not been certain this woman would enjoy the carnal pleasures, but plainly she did, which gladdened him immensely.

"Am I a good woman, husband?" she whispered when they lay side by side.

"You are a delight."

Four

DIANE WAS AWARE that Jack's first two wives had been rare beauties and that Anne had been repeatedly named one of America's ten best-dressed women. He told her again and again that she was not competing with anyone, or with anyone's memory, but she was determined to make herself as cherished as any woman in his life had ever been. One way to do it, she seemed to imagine, was to be more adventuresome in their intimate life than any other woman had ever been.

In shops on the Ginza she bought daring lingerie. "Back home, if I were even seen in a shop like this, the scandal would probably cost me dear. So let's buy what we can while we can."

In a shop in Bangkok they saw and bought something that neither of them had ever seen before and had not known existed: nipple clips. They were exactly like small battery clips, except that the springs were not nearly as strong and the tips were coated with rubber. A little knurled screw adjusted them for size and tightness. They came in pairs with a chain between them.

That night in their hotel room, Jack rolled Diane's nipples between his fingers until they hardened, and then he pinched the handles and let the clips close on her wrinkled buds. One fell off, and Diane herself tightened the adjusting screws. After that, she could walk around the room with the chain swinging between her nipples.

Jack admitted that the sight of the clips on her breasts aroused him. She said they weren't painful; to the contrary, they aroused her. She laughed as she moved her breasts and swung the chain.

The shop had also offered labial clips. Since the nipple clips had proved painless and stimulating, Diane and Jack returned and bought a pair. These were much larger and heavier. The clips were as broad as index fingers and were made of cold stainless steel, without rubber. They were not adjustable but simply squeezed tight on her fleshy lips. They too were connected by a short length of chain, that hung between her legs. The weight of the clips and chain stretched her visibly. She admitted that they hurt a little, but she insisted she would wear them for a while. As it turned out, Diane wore them until they left for dinner and asked Jack to put them on her again as soon as they returned.

Except when she tightened the adjusting screws on the nipple clips the first time she wore them, Diane would not touch the clips. She wanted Jack to put them on her, and she wanted Jack to take them off. They were novelties that she wore every night for the rest of their trip.

Five

THE MANHATTAN PLACE was perhaps the place that most reflected the late Anne Lear's tastes and background and interests. Diane sensed that but had made no effort to change it.

The fragment of Grünewald altarpiece was still there, as was Dürer's sketch of himself nude. The plump teenage nude by Boucher, gift of the Tenth Earl of Weldon, was there —though Jack had advised the Earl that it would be returned when he died. The Calder mobile still hung from the ceiling, and the erotic pre-Columbian jug still stood on the Empire writing table.

Diane knew she was not the exquisite woman her predecessor had been, and she did not try to compete. Jack could not help but compare the two women occasionally. When he did, it pained him to be reminded of what Anne had been, but it also distressed him to think that Diane could even imagine she might be expected to replace his deceased wife. He didn't expect that of Diane; he didn't want her to try to be Anne. She was Diane, and she was more than he could possibly have asked of her.

Now Billy Bob Cotton settled comfortably on the couch and accepted a Jack Daniel's on the rocks. He still wore the snakeskin boots Jack had learned to recognize as his trademark, and he had put aside in the foyer a champagne-colored Stetson. For a minute or two he was just sociable, and then he said, "Y'understand, nobody knows I've come to see you."

Jack glanced at Diane. "That's ominous," he said. "Isn't it?"

"Well, I've got something to tell you about business. Uh . . . maybe I shouldn't bring it up in front of Mrs. Lear."

"Think of her as my counsel," Jack said. "She's an experienced and highly skilled lawyer."

Billy Bob nodded at Diane. "Ma'am," he said. "Well, Jack, we've been friends for many years. I sometimes think about the time we went out to Oklahoma and watched the tornado working its way south. We've done pretty well together, too, haven't we?"

"Very well, Billy Bob."

"That's why I'm going to tell you what some folks figure I won't tell you. Jack, there's a plot afoot to kick you upstairs and make you chairman of the board and to put all the operating authority of the corporation in the hands of Mary Carson."

"I'm not entirely surprised," Jack said grimly. "She's been using her father's money to buy up stock. She's the largest stockholder now."

"You have to make a decision," said Billy Bob. "You going to fight or not? Ray and I want to know."

"You're damned right I'm going to fight. Does that cunt think I'd let her take my company away from me?"

"You're sixty-seven years old. She figures you—"

"When I'm *eighty*-seven I'll—"

Billy Bob grinned. "I figure you will."

"For right now," said Diane, "let's go to dinner. We've got a big surprise for Mrs. Carson. Mrs. Lear will fight beside her husband—and Mrs. Lear fights *dirty!*"

Billy Bob's grin widened. "Figured you would, ma'am. I'd heard your name before Jack met you, and I never had no doubt about you."

Six

DIANE SAID NOTHING about what Billy Bob had told them, until they were undressed and had made love.

Diane rolled out of bed and went down to the living room to get a bottle of Scotch. "Let's start doing a little figuring," she said. "How are we going to fuck that bitch?"

"I don't know for sure, babe," said Jack unhappily. "The numbers don't look good. And a lot of people are going to be persuaded that at the age of sixty-seven and having had a heart attack, I should let somebody younger take over day-to-day operating responsibility."

"Mary Carson is betting you'll give up. I'm betting you won't."

The conversation drifted off, and before long they went to sleep.

When Jack awoke it was about three in the morning. He heard Diane's even breathing and knew she was asleep. He closed his eyes but couldn't fall back to sleep. He opened them again and stared at the ceiling.

"You'll never be comfortable watching someone else running the business you built."

That was what Anne had said when he came back from Texas in 1949—twenty-four years ago—and told her he'd sold most of his stock in Lear Broadcasting to a group of investors headed by Douglas Humphrey.

She had spoken those words here, in this room, though not in this bed, since he could not bear to sleep with another woman in the bed he had shared with Anne and had long ago replaced it.

Twenty-four years ago. He heard her words as clearly as if she had just spoken them, as if she were the woman sleeping beside him.

"You'll never be comfortable watching someone else running the business you built."

FORTY-One

1973

DIANE'S WASHINGTON APARTMENT was comfortable, but it had the atmosphere of a hotel suite she did not expect to occupy permanently. Only the bedroom furniture and a couple of chairs she'd brought down from New Jersey were hers. The rest of the furnishings had been there when she leased the apartment.

She had also brought her collection of framed Spy prints clipped from the old London *Vanity Fair.*

Jack and Diane sat on her couch late in the afternoon. He had taken off his jacket and tie and was comfortable. For the sake of comfort, too, Diane had taken off all her clothes but a half-slip, which she wore pulled up under her armpits, making a sort of teddy. They were sipping sparingly from drinks—his a Scotch, hers a Beefeater martini—because they were going out to dinner that evening at Le Lion d'Or with Cap Durenberger and his wife.

Jack had left his office at about two that afternoon and been driven to the Manhattan town house. Lately he'd had all his personal mail delivered there. He had stuffed it into his briefcase and carried it with him to Teterboro, where he boarded a company jet for Washington. During the flight he had glanced over the mail, and now he was showing it to Diane.

"Your daughter is a jewel," Diane murmured as she read a long letter from Joni. "I'm afraid her tour is not going to make a significant difference, but it's wonderful that she's doing it."

Joni had telephoned from the Coast and offered to set aside everything else she was doing in order to help Jack win stockholder votes. He had asked her to visit every stockholder who owned more than five thousand shares; there were about thirty of them. She had visited fourteen so far and had lined up the votes of all but one, who said he'd have to think about it. Having a big movie star visit them, maybe even take them to dinner, was flattering enough to persuade a lot of them. Jack had counted on that.

"I've already seen the letter Sally Allen sent out," Diane said. "How many did she send? A thousand? Whose idea was it to have her say she was signing every letter personally? And did she?"

"She sent fifteen hundred, and, yes, she signed every one of them personally. What she was saying was 'Here. Here's a personal autograph from a big star. Now vote for my friend Jack Lear.' That was Sara's idea. Mo Morris suggested we send an autographed photo, but I vetoed that. God knows how many votes those fifteen hundred letters will get us."

"Sara's idea . . . You've got a wonderful family. Liz would have dropped out of school for a semester, if you'd let her. She was ready to address envelopes— Anything."

"*Your* family—which has nothing much at stake, really—has been more than kind. George has been tremendously supportive of Liz."

"Because he's in love with her."

Jack smiled and nodded. "Either one of them could have done a lot worse." His eyes narrowed, and his mien darkened. "The hunk is, of course, too deeply involved in football to give any attention—"

"He's got the possibility of another Super Bowl ring," said Diane.

"Super Bowl . . ." Jack muttered. "*Super Bowl!* Name me something more banal. Of all my kids, he—"

"Don't say something you'll later wish you hadn't said."

"I . . . Oh, baby! It's all coming to shit, isn't it?"

Diane moved toward him and clasped him in her arms. "No way, my lover. No way, my husband. No matter what happens now, your place in history is made."

"Maybe Lincoln was lucky," Jack whispered. "Maybe Kennedy was. The fuckin' *endgame!*"

Two

THEY MEANT TO HAVE a short nap before going out, but the buzzer sounded, and Cap Durenberger announced he was downstairs. Diane dressed as he came up.

"Naomi's relaxing and putting on her face. She'll meet us at the restaurant," Cap said. "Can you spare a man a drink that she won't know I've had. Vodka, so she won't smell it."

At eighty-three, Cap was frail and a little hunched but he had lost nothing of his zest for life. If he'd found the opportunity, he would still have been the scrounger he had been thirty years ago. Because Naomi thought he should not fly, they had come up from Florida on a train, which had taken most of two days.

"You know how long it takes to get from Miami to Houston by train? Goddamn!"

"What were you doing in Houston, Cap?" Jack asked, surprised.

"Looking around, boss. Looking around. I never did trust Doug Humphrey, as you will remember. Well, I never trusted Mary Carson, either. So I went to get the skinny on her. People trust an old fart like me. My God! how they trust me."

Diane handed him a short vodka on the rocks. "What'd you find out, Cap?"

"Let's start with this: how did Mary Carson come to get divorced from her husband? Out on the west side of Houston, people remember. Nude swimming parties in the Carsons' pool. And key parties. Know what those are?"

Diane nodded. "People toss their house keys in a bag and—"

"And draw," said Cap. "Man draws a key and goes home with the woman whose key it is. They fuck their heads off all night, and in the morning everybody meets someplace for breakfast so husbands and wives can be sorted out and put together again. I was born too soon."

"So?" asked Jack.

"Carson got another woman pregnant. Besides that,

they're not sure Mary's daughter, Emily, is Carson's daughter. Doug Humphrey went into orbit about it. He arranged the divorce. Maybe Mary and Carson didn't want it, but when Doug said they were going to get divorced, they got divorced. He was of the old school, a paterfamilias, and took no guff. When he wanted something done, it was done. Anyway, it was all accomplished very neatly. Except for one little thing. It left the horny Mary single and a threat to every marriage in Bayou Oaks. But Doug clamped down on her. He made her live with him, and he cut her off from every dime but the little allowance he gave her. She learned to hate the old buzzard."

"What's this got to do with our problem?" Jack asked curtly.

"You ain't heard it all yet," said Durenberger. "You know where Mary's daughter, Emily, is?"

Jack frowned.

"Doug Humphrey had a talent for keeping stuff out of the newspapers, off television. But his granddaughter"—Cap stopped to grin—"is in the fourth year of a five- to ten-year sentence in a federal slammer. Oh, it's a long story. It has to do with Emily escaping her mother and grandfather, getting hooked on heroin, and turning tricks to get the money to buy fixes." He lowered his voice and shook his head. "I mean it, guys. That's what I was told in Houston: that Emily went on the street and hustled."

"Jesus Christ, Cap!" Diane cried.

"She was rescued," Cap went on. "By guess who? The Weathermen. They dried her out—as you might say, forced her to go through withdrawal cold turkey—and then recruited her. She became a bomb chemist. It was just luck that none of her bombs ever killed anybody. But she did get nailed eventually, and she's doing five to ten in the federal women's prison out in the boonies in West Virginia. There's a clackety skeleton in Mary Carson's closet."

Jack pressed his hands together and ran them down his nose, over his mouth, and down his chin. "Cap . . . *So what?"*

Cap grinned a little hesitantly, sensing that Jack did not like what he had said and was not going to like the rest of it. "Okay. We've got stockholders with Southern Baptist morals who aren't going to like the Bayou Oaks parties even a little bit. We've got stockholders who believe in law and order who are going to shudder at the word 'Weatherman'—not to mention the news that their proposed new CEO has a daughter who did hard drugs and now is doing hard time. You don't want to use this?"

Jack shook his head. "I already knew all that," he said. "Give the lady her due; she told me herself."

"No, Cap," Jack said in a quiet but dead firm voice. "No. If we lose, we lose, but I promised not to use that."

FORTY-ONE

One 1973

On Monday evening, November 19, the night before the stockholders meeting, Jack and Diane held a dinner in their suite in the New York Hilton. Joni and David were there. So were Liz and her boyfriend George, Diane's nephew. Little Jack was there, as was Sara. The cheerleader Gloria and Brent Creighton, Sara's friend, were having dinner downstairs, since Jack and Diane had decided they didn't want to talk business in front of them. Similarly, the wives of Herb Morrill, Mickey Sullivan, and Cap Durenberger were dining downstairs, not because they were not trusted to hear the discussion but because they would probably be bored by business talk. Curt and Betsy Frederick had come from Arizona. Sally Allen had come from Los Angeles.

Sitting in the living room of the suite after dinner, the group reviewed the situation and found it gloomy.

From shares owned by himself, his family, and his friends, plus shares he could vote through proxies, Jack could count on 275,000 votes—27.5 percent of the outstanding common stock of LCI. If Billy Bob Cotton and Ray l'Enfant voted with him, he would have 37.5 percent.

"I want to read some names on a few of the proxies," said Diane, unfolding a list. "Taken together, they don't change the total much, but they're evidence of some cherished friendships. We have a proxy, fifty shares, from Constance Horan. We have proxies for a hundred shares apiece from Harry Klein and

Benjamin Lang, Joni's producer and director on several films. Thank you, Joni. I suspect they bought the shares just so they could vote on this. We have a proxy, one hundred shares, from Mo Morris, Joni's agent and Sara's partner. We have a proxy for five shares from Edward Martin, a farmer in Okmulgee, Oklahoma, who sent along a good-luck letter with his proxy. Rebecca Murphy, a private investigator in Boston, ten shares. Arthur, Earl of Weldon, two hundred shares. Finally"—Diane grinned at Jack—"we have a proxy from Valerie Latham Field, who apparently bought a hundred shares not long ago, for reasons on which we need not speculate."

That was the last light moment of the evening, Everyone knew perfectly well that 27.5 percent or 37.5 percent was not going to save control of the company.

Diane was livelier and more active than Jack was that evening, moving among the guests, saying a word here, a word there. She wore tight powder-blue stirrup pants and a loose white cable-knit sweater.

Jack sat rather heavily in an armchair in a corner of the living room, wearing one of his signature dark-blue suits, with a white breast-pocket handkerchief folded precisely in two sharp points. He knew people were glancing at him, appraising him, and—God forbid!—pitying him. He knew they were looking at him more closely than they had ever looked at him before, taking special note of the liver spots on his head and hands, his droopy eyes, and his loose jowls. He smiled at each one he caught looking at him, showing them he was preserving his sense of humor.

Suddenly the room was silent, as though everyone had simultaneously run out of things to say. Instinctively, they turned toward him.

"Wouldn't it be funny," he asked quietly, "if all our worry and anxiety turned out to be for nothing? Remember how in 1948 when H. V. Kaltenborn insisted all night you couldn't really tell how the election was coming out until the farm vote was counted? Well, the farm vote and the shrimp-boat vote haven't been counted. If Billy Bob Cotton and Ray l'Enfant weigh in with us, we'll have 37.5 percent, which makes it a whole lot closer."

He didn't raise the spirits of the others.

In a corner of the room, Curt Frederick talked with Cap Durenberger. "I think about the years . . . the things. It's going to be an end of an era. Goddamn, we have to be glad we've retired! I wouldn't want to be at LCI anymore."

Sara and Liz stood apart from the group. "I wish I'd known him longer and better," Sara said.

He's a great man," Liz said simply. "I don't know if *he* will, but I'm going to drop a letter to your mother, thanking her for buying some stock and giving us her proxy. That's a real vote of confidence, Sara."

"Maybe I should do that, too."

Little Jack talked with Diane. "You have any idea how it was with my father and me? He was never around."

Diane sneered. "Another little boy who resents his father because the old man was out working his ass off to make a living. That's a cliché, LJ—and a pretty wretched one, too."

"Okay. He gave me the best of everything."

"Another cliché, but never mind, LJ, your father *built* Lear Communications, Incorporated. Apart from the three major networks, LCI is the biggest communications enterprise in the United States. *He built it,* LJ. And tomorrow he's going to lose it. Do you so much as give a damn?"

"Does *he* really give a damn about what *I've* done?"

"What *have* you done?" Diane asked with an almost Gallic shrug. "You never grew up. You've played a juvenile game all your life. Oh yeah, you've made money at it and won some temporary glory; but when you retire you'll be forgotten very quickly. Your father won't be."

"Is this what he thinks of me?"

"Ask him, LJ. Your father speaks for himself."

Mickey Sullivan talked with Herb Morrill. "Jack's old man would be proud of him. In spite of the fact that they clashed hard, Erich thought the world of him."

"Don't make this sound like a funeral, for Chrissake!" Herb whispered shrilly.

Joni talked quietly with Diane. "I could throttle Mary Carson," she said. "I love my father *so* much, and to think of her— Diane, this could kill him."

Diane shook her head. "No, it won't. If anything could have killed him, it would have been Anne's death."

The buzzer sounded, and Diane went to the door. Billy Bob Cotton was there.

The crowd knew his arrival was a significant development. They stood apart as Jack and Diane led Billy Bob into the suite's master bedroom and closed the door.

"Bourbon?" Jack asked as Billy Bob settled into a chair.

Billy Bob shook his head. "After," he said.

"You're not here with good news," said Diane.

"No. Jack . . . Diane . . . You'll probably have my votes in the morning. But not Ray's."

Jack stiffened. "Not Ray's? I thought—"

"So did I. But then . . . something happened."

"What?" Diane asked.

"Ray's got something in his craw."

"Which is?"

"Emily."

"What about Emily?"

Billy Bob crossed his legs and, as he sometimes did when he was nervous, rubbed his snakeskin boots with the fingers of his right hand. "You know about a stockbroker named Elsie Sennett?"

Jack shook his head. "The name's on the list. She inherited— I think it's five thousand shares. That's all I know."

Billy Bob sighed. "She lives in Baton Rouge. Two weeks ago she got a telephone call from Cap Durenberger, whom she'd met some years ago. He asked her to give you her proxy. She was kind of wavering, so Cap said something like 'Well, you ought to know about Emily Carson' and went on to tell a really wretched story about Mary's daughter."

"I know about that," Jack said. "Mary told me, a long time ago."

Billy Bob went on. "Well—Elsie Sennett called Ray, who's a friend of hers, to report what she supposed was an awful lie about Mary and her daughter. Ray knew all about Emily. He was a much closer friend of Doug Humphrey than I ever was. In fact, he tried to help Doug get the charges reduced. Anyway, Ray called Mary to tell her the story was being used against her. Because it came from Cap Durenberger, both Ray and Mary supposed it came from you. Mary is furious. She says she spoke to you in confidence about Emily, and—"

"I did not betray her confidence!" Jack said vehemently. I told Cap nothing about it. He found out for himself. He came to us with the story, and both Diane and I told him not to use it. From the day Mary told me about Emily to the day Cap came to us in Washington with the story, Diane was the only one who heard it from me."

Billy Bob frowned. "I'll take that bourbon now," he muttered. "And of course I accept your word and will vote my stock for you."

"Where *is* Ray?" Diane asked.

"He's got a room at the Plaza," said Billy Bob.

Jack stood at the bar, pouring three drinks. "We're not calling him, Diane. I won't beg for his vote. When he heard the story, he should have called and checked with me. He accepted the idea that I'd betrayed a confidence and didn't even have the decency to talk to me about it. To hell with him!"

"You could say to hell with me, too, I guess," said Billy Bob.

"Why? You're here. You faced me with the story, I told you the truth, and you accepted my word." Jack stomped across the room. "Mary, too. She could have had the goddamned decency to *ask* me if I—"

"The worst thing for Mary is that she figures that any publicity that gets loose about Emily will make it more difficult for Emily to get her parole. She's been in four years, and there's some hope she might get a parole before Christmas."

"What fuckin' publicity? Why should there be any publicity?"

"Cap—"

Jack strode to the door and jerked it open. "Cap! Come here!" He lowered his voice so only Cap could hear. He jabbed Cap's shoulder with his finger. "Not another fuckin' word to anybody about Emily Carson! *You understand me?* Another word and I'll find a way to cut off your fuckin' pension!"

Leaving Cap Durenberger flushed and gaping, Jack slammed the door in his face.

"I'll talk to Ray," said Billy Bob. "Also to Mary."

"Please do," said Jack. Now— If you will excuse me, I've got a call to make."

Billy Bob left the room. Jack faced Diane.

"Grotius ?" she asked softly.

Jack shrugged. "Grotius. Why not? Our fallback position."

"Not exactly."

"I like it better than the other way."

Diane's smile was soft and wistful. "He who tries to screw you had better cover all points of the compass," she said.

Two

THE STOCKHOLDERS MEETING was held in a ballroom at the New York Hilton at ten o'clock the following morning.

Jack and Diane were standing in the corridor outside the ballroom with Joni and LJ shortly after eight. Joni wore a pink mini-dress and looked every inch the glamorous movie star. LJ wore a gold-buttoned blue blazer and gray slacks, also his Super Bowl ring. The tycoon, the congresswoman, the screen star, the football star—they made a formidable team. Each of them was asked for autographs.

Mary Carson appeared only as the meeting opened. She sat beside Jack at the head table. "I apologize for doubting your word," she said softlty. "I apologize for not calling you."

"Cap did a rotten thing," Jack said in a firm, controlled voice. "But it was rotten of people who have been my friends for many years to distrust me the way they did."

Jack opened the meeting. He presided and delivered a ten-minute speech, reporting to the stockholders on the condition of the company but referring them to the printed annual report for most of the information.

"The next order of business," said Jack, "is the election of a board of directors. Nominations are now open."

Billy Bob Cotton rose and nominated a slate of directors—people who would support Jack as CEO. A Dallas lawyer nominated a different slate. Jack was on the ballot for both slates and would remain a director of the company no matter which slate won. But the majority of the nominees for the Dallas slate would cast their votes for Mary as new CEO.

"If there are no other nominations," Jack said, "we will designate the slate nominated by Mr. Cotton as Slate A and the slate nominated by Attorney Lovell as Slate B. Voting is by paper ballot, and you may vote for either slate simply by writing *A* or *B* on your ballot."

While the tellers were collecting the ballots, Billy Bob Cotton came to the table. He spoke to Jack, but Mary could hear what he said. "Ray has gone home," he said. "He gave me his proxy with instructions to vote for you."

The tellers were ready. Jack stood at the lectern and rapped the gavel.

The chief teller read the results: "Present or voting by proxy, 777,255 shares. Votes for Slate A—379,412. Votes for Slate B—397,843."

The room was silent. No one applauded. Everyone—even those who had won—were stunned.

Mary put her hand on Jack's arm. "I want you to keep your office exactly where it is. Your salary will remain the same. Your access to company planes, cars, and so on will stay the same."

"Well, I'm afraid it isn't going to be quite that simple, Mary. I'm going to say a few words to the stockholders, and then there's a man here I want you to meet."

Jack rose and stepped to the microphone.

"Ladies and gentlemen, before this meeting of stockholders adjourns, I would like to make an announcement. You have been kind enough to elect me a director of Lear Communications, Incorporated. I thank you, but I decline to accept. What is more, I resign all offices I hold in the corporation.

"Julius Caesar once said he would rather be first in a small Spanish village than second in Rome. So would I. Either I run this company or I want nothing to do with it.

"Those who have engineered this . . . coup—I think that is what it must be called—have a surprise coming. I have asked Mr. Junius Grotius to come forward. That is he, there.

"Mr. Grotius is president of Wyncherly-DeVere, Limited, the British and Dutch communications conglomerate. For some time Mr. Grotius has had outstanding with me and others an offer to buy our shares in Lear Communications.

Very recently I signed an option, allowing Wyncherly-DeVere to buy my shares in the event I should lose control of the company. Members of my family and friends and associates have signed similar options. What is more, Mr. Grotius has obtained options from two banks that hold substantial blocks of stock. Today Wyncherly-DeVere will exercise those options and others. After today, Wyncherly-DeVere will be the biggest stockholder in Lear Communications.

"As I said, if I can't run the company I want nothing to do with it. It will pass now—rather quickly, I imagine—into the control of a communications conglomerate with the capital and know-how to make it a bigger player in the field than it has ever been before—bigger than I dreamed of making it. And the stockholders of this company will benefit hugely."

Jack stepped back from the microphone. He pointed and nodded at Junius Grotius. The crowd applauded tentatively.

Jack bent down over Mary Carson. "Let's see you screw *them,* my dear," he said quietly.

Diane and Joni pushed their way forward through the crowd of stockholders. They embraced Jack as he came down from the platform and moved to shake hands with Junius Grotius. Suddenly the crowd burst into loud and sustained applause. Jack and the two women he loved moved slowly through a crush of people who wanted to shake their hands, even to kiss them as they worked their way toward the door.